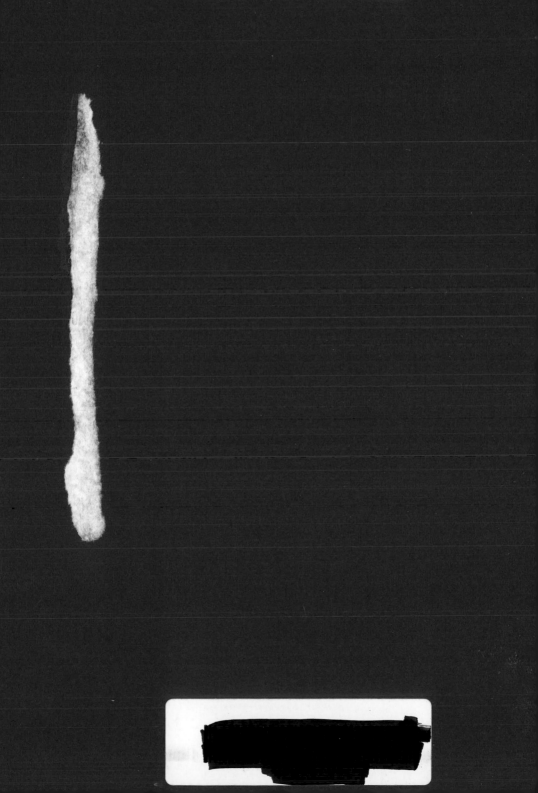

Mark Billingham has twice won the Theakston's Old Peculier Award for Crime Novel of the Year, and has also won a Sherlock Award for the Best Detective created by a British writer. Each of the novels featuring Detective Inspector Tom Thorne has been a *Sunday Times* bestseller. *Sleepyhead* and *Scaredy Cat* were made into a hit TV series on Sky 1 starring David Morrissey as Thorne, and a series based on the novels *In the Dark* and *Time of Death* was broadcast on BBC1. Mark lives in north London with his wife and two children.

MARK BILLINGHAM

Their Little Secret

Little, Brown

LITTLE, BROWN

First published in Great Britain in 2019 by Little, Brown

13 5 7 9 10 8 6 4 2

A CIP catalogue record for this book
is available from the British Library.

Hardback ISBN 978-0-7515-6697-0
Trade Paperback ISBN 978-0-7515-6698-7

Typeset in Plantin by M Rules
Printed and bound in Great Britain by
Clays Ltd, Elcograf S.p.A.

Papers used by Little, Brown are from well-managed forests
and other responsible sources.

Little, Brown
An imprint of
Little, Brown Book Group
Carmelite House
50 Victoria Embankment
London EC4Y 0DZ

An Hachette UK Company
www.hachette.co.uk

www.littlebrown.co.uk

For Michael. Onwards and upwards . . .

It is my belief that the problems arising
from love – infatuation, jealousy,
heartbreak, trauma, inappropriate
attraction and addiction, to name but
a few – merit serious consideration and
that the line which separates normal
from abnormal love is frequently blurred.
The merest spark of sexual attraction
can cause a fire that has the potential to
consume us . . .

Dr Frank Tallis,
The Incurable Romantic

I want you,
The truth can't hurt you, it's just like the dark,
It scares you witless,
But in time you see things clear and stark,
I want you,
Go on and hurt me, then we'll let it drop,
I want you,
I'm afraid I won't know where to stop . . .

Elvis Costello,
'I Want You'

PART ONE

The Bed and the Beach

ONE

Tom Thorne watched as the bag containing the woman's body was lifted, as gently as was possible, from the tracks. He saw the telltale sag in the middle before it was laid down on the platform, where those pieces that were unattached had slid together. Where liquid had pooled inside the plastic.

What was *left* of the woman's body . . .

He watched as DS Dipak Chall finished his conversation with an officer from the British Transport Police and walked back along the platform towards him. Now, Chall was carrying a plastic bag of his own; small and clear, stained by its contents. He held it up, somewhat gingerly, so that Thorne could see what was inside.

A brown leather handbag, some keys, a mobile phone.

'We've got a name,' Chall said.

It was Thorne's turn on the Homicide Assessment Team, a mobile unit dispatched to the location of any sudden death to determine if circumstances were suspicious and further investigation warranted. Once the on-call HAT car had been alerted by uniform, it was down to Thorne and Chall to attend and report whenever a body was discovered; to examine those scenes where even an intellectually challenged cadet could see that a murder had taken place, but also to check the state of any premises where an apparently natural death had occurred. To look for signs of violence or forced entry. To take note of any drugs – prescription or otherwise – at the property, before passing the case on to the necessary team and waiting for the next one. Their first call that morning had been to a flat in Wood Green, where they had quickly been able to establish that the old man slumped in a chair in front of *The Jeremy Kyle Show* had died of natural causes. The request to attend an incident at Highgate underground station had promised, initially at least, to be every bit as straightforward.

'They've looked at the CCTV,' Chall had said after his first conversation with the officers already at the scene. 'She was standing on her own at the near end of the platform.' He'd pointed. 'Where the train comes in. Started running towards it just before it came out of the tunnel.'

Thorne had said little, watching those still working on the tracks; gathering up what was left after flesh and bone had met a train travelling at forty miles per hour and then fallen beneath it.

'Seems pretty cut and dried,' Chall said now.

Thorne stared at the bag, the keys, the phone. A gobbet of something smeared against the plastic. 'I suppose,' he said.

'Don't know how people can do it.'

'Kill themselves?'

'Like that, I mean.'

'It usually gets the job done,' Thorne said. Not always, though, he knew that. The woman in the bag had been lucky, in that the outcome for her had presumably been the one intended. There were many, whose timing was not quite as good, who simply ended up losing multiple limbs.

'It's the driver I feel sorry for,' Chall said. 'He's got to live with it, hasn't he?'

'Yeah, true enough.' Thorne had glimpsed the train driver in the station office on the way in. Pale, shaven-headed and cradling a mug of something as he was spoken to by someone from the London Underground Emergency Response Team. Nodding as a tattooed arm was laid gently around his shoulder. Thorne knew that the man would be offered trauma counselling, had read somewhere that any driver unlucky enough to get 'one under' three times was immediately offered fully paid retirement.

It was probably an urban myth, Thorne decided. Like the secret station at Buckingham Palace or the community of cannibalistic savages haunting the tunnels.

He had seen some of the passengers as well, gathered in clusters outside the entrance to the station, having been ushered off the train. They too would be offered as much support as was needed. Thorne couldn't help wondering if the woman whose actions had triggered all this activity was ever offered any kind of support. If they would be here if she had.

'Don't know how you get over something like that. You know, if you're not used to it.' Chall stepped to the edge of the platform. On the tracks below him, men and women in high-vis jackets were moving with rather more urgency now that the body had been removed, eager to get the power switched back on, the trains moving again.

The DS turned to look at Thorne. 'You OK, boss?'

'Just a bit warm down here, that's all.'

Chall nodded, humming something. Without thinking, he began to gently swing the plastic bag, a rivulet of blood running back and forth along the bottom. He checked himself and stopped.

The weather outside was as unforgiving as one would expect in the last week of January, and the breath of the passengers outside had plumed in the air as they had stood chatting nervously or smoking. Nevertheless, Thorne felt clammy and uncomfortable, headachy. He unzipped his leather jacket, took a deep breath when Chall looked the other way.

Suicide had never agreed with him.

His first body had been a hanging and he had never forgotten it. For good or ill, Thorne remembered most of the bodies he had encountered over the course of his career. He certainly remembered all the murder victims and, try as he might, he could never forget those who had been responsible for them.

It had been a teenage girl, that first one. A slip of a thing dangling from the branch of an oak tree in Victoria Park. A ripped blue dress and legs like sticks and the muddy heels of her trainers kissing.

He remembered himself and a colleague and a rickety stepladder.

That skinny body so much heavier than it looked.

'So, what do you reckon, then?' Chall asked.

In many ways, he found murder simpler to process and deal with, because the questions were always the same. Who had done it, why and, most importantly of all, how was he going to find them? The questions thrown up by a suicide were often the ones that bothered Thorne the most, because, nine times out of ten, he was never going to find out the answers.

'Sorry?'

'Should we leave this lot to it?' The DS nodded up towards the station entrance. 'Move on . . . ?'

'Do we know anything else about her?'

Chall opened his mouth, closed it again. 'No, but if you want to find out, it shouldn't take too long.' He raised the plastic bag again. 'We know who she is.'

Now, Thorne could see a few credit cards scattered at the bottom of the bag. An Oyster and a driving licence spotted with blood. He leaned closer to look at the picture and thought he could see the hint of a smile on the face of the woman to whom it had belonged. 'OK, well, it might be worth asking a few questions.'

'Really?' It was clear from the look on Chall's face that he believed their job at the station was done. The death, though certainly sudden, was not suspicious, so surely there was no more reason to look any further into the life of the woman in the bag than there had been to follow up on the old man in the armchair in Wood Green. He stepped closer. 'Any reason to think there's an issue?'

Thorne shook his head.

'Have I missed something?'

A few feet away, two men clambered up on to the platform, then reached down to help colleagues from the tracks. For the umpteenth time since they'd arrived, a woman's voice, distorted by a tannoy, announced that the station would remain closed until further notice.

'I mean, the CCTV was pretty clear cut.' Chall looked towards the camera mounted high at the end of the platform. 'There was nobody even close to her.'

'I might just . . . poke around a bit later on, that's all.'

'Up to you, boss.'

Thorne walked away towards the station office to see if he could grab a few words with the train driver. While he was there he could try to scrounge a couple of aspirin. He stepped aside to let two men pushing a gurney go past, thinking about something Chall had just said.

Nobody close to her . . .

TWO

Sitting at the kitchen table she had waxed and polished an hour earlier, Sarah watches the woman opposite tucking into a slice of carrot cake as though she hasn't eaten for a month. The woman – Karen, with the first syllable pronounced like *car* – hums with pleasure and dabs at her mouth with one of the napkins that Sarah had carefully ironed after the table had been polished.

'Oh. My. God.' The woman flaps her hands as if the sublime taste has temporarily robbed her of control of her limbs.

'Glad you like it.'

The woman swallows. 'Did you make this yourself?'

Some things are just not worth fibbing about. 'Sainsbury's, I'm afraid. I wish I had the time to cook.'

'Tell me about it.' The woman glances across at the pile of Lego bricks pushed into one corner, the scattering of DVD cases – *Dino Man* and *Curious George* – on the countertop above it. 'Not enough hours in the day, right?'

Sarah smiles and shakes her head, but she had caught the flash of something like disapproval on the woman's face. A grimace, barely held in check. The suggestion that, however busy things get, there is simply no excuse for being slovenly.

Especially when you have visitors.

'It's ridiculous, isn't it?' The woman pushes her hair back then begins to pick at the crumbs left on her plate. 'You drop the kids off, then straight back to deal with the carnage at home, a bit of lunch if you're lucky and, before you know what you're doing, it's time to pick the little sods up again.'

'Hard enough when you've only got the one little sod.'

'Well, of course it is.' The woman licks her fingers. 'Not to mention trying to find time to walk the dog, rain or shine . . .'

Sarah nods, sips at her coffee.

It's how the two of them had met, a fortnight or so before, in the park at the end of the road. Sarah dragging her dim old mutt around the lake and Karen fussing over a yappy little Cockapoo. The dogs sniffing at each other's backsides while the two women greeted one another in a rather more civilised fashion.

Yes, it is nice, isn't it? I wish they'd do something about the litter, though, and the boys smoking weed by the benches. The smell of it, you know? Oh, bloody hell, Monty's chasing the ducks again, better dash . . .

A bit more chat on the following day, a couple of walks together and here they were.

Coffee and cake, nice as you like.

'I think my two are a bit older than yours, aren't they?'

'Yeah, he's only six.'

'Well, sorry to tell you that it just gets harder. Muddy football kit all over the place and homework and what have you. You've got all that to look forward to.'

Sarah laughs and rolls her eyes because it's the appropriate thing to do. 'So, where do yours go?'

'St Mary's. It's very good, I think. You should get your boy's name down nice and early.'

Karen's children are not at the same school as Jamie. It might have been a little awkward had they been, but Sarah would have coped. She has found herself in a similar situation a few times before but has always managed. She has become very good at thinking on her feet.

The woman has picked up her phone and is busy scrolling. Without taking her eyes from the screen, she reaches down to pick up her bag and says, 'God, it'll be pick-up time in an hour, I need to shoot.' She raises her head up and smiles. 'This was *so* lovely, Sarah.'

'I'm really pleased you could come.'

'My place next time, yes?'

'Fantastic.' Sarah laughs. 'And don't worry, I won't be expecting a freshly baked cake.'

The woman laughs in return, a grating bark. 'Good, because you won't be getting one.' She stands up, looking pleased with herself as though she's just had a truly wonderful idea. 'Actually, why don't you come over for dinner, instead? You know, you and your . . . ?'

'There isn't a my *anything*,' Sarah says.

'Oh, right.'

'Divorced.' Sarah takes the woman's empty plate and places it on top of her own. 'Looking.'

'Well, I hope you took your ex for every penny.' The woman looks around. 'I'm guessing that you did.'

'I did my best,' Sarah says.

'Well, anyway.' Karen picks up her coat and steps towards the doorway. 'Just having coffee's nice, too. Happy with that, if you are.'

Sarah smiles.

Of course, she thinks, *you can't possibly be inviting a lonely single woman for dinner, can you? That's best avoided. It's awkward and embarrassing for all concerned.*

'I'll see you in the park, then.'

'You certainly will,' Sarah says.

'I'll be the one chasing an unruly Cockapoo and picking up dog-mess.'

Sarah moves towards her, but the woman waves a hand graciously, then leans to lay it on her hostess's arm. 'Don't be silly, I can find my own way out. I'll leave you to carry on clearing up.'

She could probably do the school run in her sleep. Left on to the main road, the cut-through down to the tube station, then straight on past the posh houses; the 'village' green and the over-priced gastropub, crawling through traffic which thickens with oversized 4 × 4s every half a mile or so.

It makes her feel slightly ashamed of her own little car.

Parking, when she gets to Brooklands Hill, is the usual circle of hell. The angry gestures and the leaning on horns as the battalion of shiny black Chelsea tractors jostle for a spot as near to the school as possible. Sarah isn't bothered. Once in a while, someone with no idea what indicators are for will pull out of the ideal space just as she's arriving, but she always drives past, letting the car behind her nab it. She much prefers somewhere on one of the roads a little further away.

She parks and walks the few minutes back, waving at one or two parents who have already collected, until she reaches the school gates. A woman called Savita immediately beckons her over.

'Bloody nits again.'

'Oh, God. Arjun?' Sarah is very good at remembering the other children's names.

'Well, not yet, but it's only a matter of time. Going around apparently. Be a good idea to check Jamie.'

'Yeah, I will.'

'Makes me feel scuzzy just thinking about it.'

'It might just be in one class.'

'No chance. Spreads like the bloody plague . . . '

Now, Heather – definitely one of the nicer mums – has arrived, and David, a single dad, is right behind her. They all greet one another. Air-kisses, like actors mingling outside a premiere.

'I was just telling Sarah there's nits going round,' Savita says.

David barely has time to react before his daughter comes charging through the gates, followed quickly by Savita's son, Arjun.

Sarah looks beyond them towards the school and shakes her head. 'Jamie's taking his time as usual,' she says.

She and Heather say goodbye to David and Savita as they usher the children towards their cars, but no sooner have they gone than a woman named Caroline bowls up, dressed to the nines, as always. If there's time, Sarah tries to make an effort on the school run, but she draws the line at full make-up and Ugg boots. Caroline begins talking before anyone has had so much as a chance to say hello.

'Stupid meeting overran again. It makes me so angry, because they know I need to get away.'

'Don't panic,' Sarah says. 'Jacob hasn't come out yet.'

'Plus, I've got a mountain of paperwork to do when I get home.'

The woman is a little full of herself, forever banging on about her high-powered job as a PA to someone or other and how she *just* manages to juggle career and motherhood. From the little Sarah has seen of her son, Jacob – who is only marginally less fond of trumpeting his achievements than his mother – the apple hasn't fallen too far from the tree.

Heather catches Sarah's eye and winks. 'That's what comes with having it all, Caroline,' she says.

Sarah smiles at Heather. 'Living the dream,' she says.

For a few minutes, she listens to Heather and Caroline talk about some school quiz-night they've let themselves get roped into. There's a microphone to organise, and catering, and a raffle. Sarah's happy enough to stand back, because she's never really been the type to get involved with fetes and fund-raising, committees and what have you.

It's fair enough, because some people aren't, are they?

Though she's rarely the one driving the conversations, Sarah's content to spend this time here every day, hanging out at the gates and chewing the fat with an interesting bunch of fellow parents. She's grown fond of Heather and Savita. There's a dishy dad called Alex who she flirts with a bit sometimes, and a woman called Sue with whom she's been having a fascinating debate about the stringency of DBS checks.

There's all sorts.

Most are pleasant and made her welcome when Jamie first started, and even if one or two – she glances at Caroline – can sometimes be a little . . . poisonous, she always enjoys the banter, the intrigue and the silly chit-chat, while she waits for her son.

Eventually, once quiz-night duties have been allocated, Sarah steps forward and, after another hopeful look towards the exit, says, 'I suppose I'm going to have to go in and look for him. Again!'

'Don't worry, mine's the same,' Heather says.

'Send Jacob out if you see him,' Caroline says, busy with her phone.

They continue to make sympathetic noises behind her as she moves through the gates and heads across the playground. She smiles at the children, bundled up in hats and coats on their way out, exchanges nods with several of the teachers, then pushes open the doors to the school and steps inside.

Sarah closes her eyes for a few moments.

The warmth and the smell.

It's where she feels safest, where she feels as though she's *part* of something.

THREE

Mary Fulton lived in a small house in a side-street off Shoot-Up Hill, close to Kilburn station. Waiting on a freezing doorstep for his knock to be answered, Thorne was thankful that the death message had already been delivered; that the woman he had come to see had been told about her sister's suicide the previous afternoon by two of the officers who had been first on the scene.

The shitty end of the stick for uniform, same as usual.

When the door was finally answered, Thorne presented his warrant card and introduced himself. He said, 'I'm very sorry for your loss,' hoping that his surprise at seeing a woman so much older than he had been expecting was not obvious. As usual, his face had failed miserably to disguise what he was thinking.

'Pip was twenty years younger than me,' Mary said. She shook her head and manufactured a thin, sad smile. 'She always called herself "The Accident".' The woman was probably in her late sixties, her grey hair cut fashionably short. She wore a long tartan skirt and dark cardigan and, as the smile evaporated, she reached to toy with a silver chain that hung at the neck of a white blouse. 'Sounds horrible now, doesn't it?'

14

'Well . . .'

'Not that it was an accident, of course.'

'No.'

'The exact opposite, if anything.'

Looking over her shoulder into the house, Thorne caught sight of a younger woman emerging from a side room. She glanced towards him before turning away down the hall. 'I'm quite keen to take a look inside your sister's flat,' he said.

'Oh.' The older woman looked nonplussed. 'Do you need my permission?'

'To be honest, I'm not really sure,' Thorne said. Had Philippa Goodwin been the victim of a murder, then by now her home would have been swarming with police and Crime Scene Investigators, but there was no clear protocol when it came to those who had taken their own lives. 'I'd like it, though.'

'Well, yes, I suppose so.'

'Thank you.'

'I'll have to go over myself at some point, of course.' She turned briefly away, as though distracted by something. 'Sort things out.'

Thorne reached into his pocket for the bunch of keys that had, as per health and safety requirements regarding personal effects contaminated by blood, been thoroughly disinfected. 'I've got these.'

'Oh.' Mary tentatively reached out a hand and Thorne laid down the keys on her palm. The woman's fist closed slowly around them.

'Actually, I was hoping you might come with me,' he said.

'Really?'

'Only if you feel up to it, obviously.' He watched as the woman uncurled her fist and stared down at her dead sister's keys. She rubbed the worn leather fob between her fingers. 'I'd quite like to talk to you about Philippa on the way. Again, only if you want to.'

'Can my daughter come too?' She turned as the younger woman appeared in the hallway behind her once again. 'She's been here ever since we got the news.'

'Of course.' Thorne waited as the two women looked at one another. The younger one seemed a trifle reluctant, but eventually shrugged her assent.

Mary Fulton said, 'Just give us five minutes.'

The older woman said little, hunched in the front seat of Thorne's BMW as they drove east towards Tufnell Park. The younger woman in the back seat was considerably more talkative, though she spoke as if for the sake of it, her tone colourless. Looking at the woman in his rear-view, her eyes puffy and red-rimmed as she stared out of the window, Thorne guessed that talking was preferable to weeping.

'This is a nice car,' she said.

'I used to have a vintage one. Much nicer.'

'Policemen must get paid a lot more than I thought.'

'This was second-hand.' Thorne slowed for lights, took another glance at her. 'Very second-hand.'

'Don't get me wrong. I'm not saying they *shouldn't* be well paid. I mean, it's a horrible job, isn't it? Horrible. Seeing people at their very worst, seeing terrible things, dealing with the . . . fallout, whatever. It's hard to imagine all that wouldn't change someone, day in day out, do something strange to them . . . and I *really* can't imagine anyone actually enjoying it.' She lengthened the seat-belt and leaned forward. 'Do *you* enjoy it?'

Thorne eased away from the lights as Mary Fulton turned to look at her daughter.

'I'm not really sure that's—'

'I'm only asking.'

'It's fine,' Thorne said.

'Ella's got no filter at the best of times,' Mary said.

'That's not fair.'

'So, now ...' Mary tightened her grip on the black handbag clutched in her lap. 'You know, being so upset.'

Thorne made eye contact with Ella in the rear-view. 'Were you close to your aunt?'

Ella sat back hard and shook her head. 'What kind of question is that?'

'Sorry,' Thorne said.

'Jesus ...'

'It was a stupid question.'

'They were very close,' Mary said.

Half a minute crawled past, somewhat awkwardly, then Ella sighed and spoke as if she were talking to herself. 'She was more like my best friend than my aunt. She was only a few years older than me ...'

They drove on in silence to Chalk Farm, then Thorne took a series of cut-throughs he knew well and turned on to Kentish Town Road, no more than two minutes from where his own flat was. It had begun to rain, which did little to improve their progress in traffic heavy enough to grace rush-hour almost anywhere else in the country.

Thorne said, 'I hope you don't mind me asking, but do you have any idea what might have made Philippa want to take her own life?'

The silence returned with a vengeance and Thorne sensed the tension immediately. He looked in the mirror and saw Ella Fulton turn her blank gaze back towards the shops crawling past her and the grim-faced pedestrians scuttling through the rain. Next to him, Mary Fulton flinched when a driver ahead leaned on his horn.

'Are you going to tell him?' Mary asked her daughter. 'Or shall I?'

Ella said nothing.

'What?' Thorne waited.

Behind him, the younger woman shook her head. 'I'm not sure—'

'Oh, come on.' Mary turned to look at Ella. 'We've been tiptoeing around the subject ever since we found out what happened. You know what Pip had been going through as well as I do.' She smacked her hand against the top of her seat. 'Ella . . . ?'

Ella puffed out her cheeks and leaned towards Thorne. 'There was a man she'd been seeing.'

'I can think of a few other words for him,' Mary snapped.

'It didn't end well.'

'Was she dumped?' Thorne asked.

Mary grunted. 'That's one way of putting it.'

'Pip was extremely unhappy,' Ella said. 'The whole thing obviously hit her very hard.'

Mary Fulton turned in her seat until she was staring at Thorne. She said, 'So, not only can I tell you *why* my sister jumped in front of that train, I can tell you the name of the man who was responsible for it.'

FOUR

Mary Fulton muttered, 'Right then,' and used the keys Thorne had given her to open the front door to Philippa Goodwin's flat. The rain had petered out. Ella moved forward to slip her arm through her mother's and the two of them stepped inside.

'Why did she walk all the way to Highgate?' Mary seemed unduly bothered by the question. She turned and pointed. 'There's a station just round the corner.'

'I don't suppose we'll ever know,' Thorne said.

Giving herself enough time to change her mind, he thought. Or to pluck up the courage. Once mother and daughter had gathered up the mail from the tiled floor, he followed them into the hallway.

A selection of brightly coloured hats and scarves had been hung in a row above a large mirror. Beneath it, a shiny black bicycle was leaning against the wall, its lock neatly coiled inside the basket. Thorne watched Mary touch the saddle as she walked past.

It was warm inside and what sounded like folk music drifted down from the property upstairs. Thorne thought he could smell caramel, or vanilla. He looked and saw one of those glass infuser things with sticks sitting on a low table.

'It's all junk,' Ella said, dropping the mail on to the table next to it.

Thorne was no expert on London house prices, beyond knowing that they were stupid, but he could not help but wonder how a university lecturer had been able to afford a flat which took up the entire ground floor of a large terraced house in Tufnell Park. Mary Fulton clocked his expression as they walked into the sitting room and, once again, it became apparent that the question had registered on his face.

'Our parents were pretty well off,' she said. 'Big house in Hampstead, all that. When they died there was enough for me to pay off the mortgage and for Pip to get this place.' She nodded towards her daughter. 'For Ella to get somewhere, too.'

'Must have been a hell of a big house,' Thorne said.

'Not really.' Ella crossed to one of the windows and raised a blind, revealing a decent-sized rear garden.

'Actually, there was still plenty left over,' Mary said. 'Enough for all of us to have something tucked away for a rainy day.'

Thorne nodded. It sounded as if the Goodwin family money could buy any number of gold-plated umbrellas.

Ella sank, sighing, into an old-fashioned armchair; one of several items of artfully mismatched furniture. Talk of her inheritance had changed her grief-stricken expression into one that seemed rather more sullen. 'My place isn't quite as nice as this, by the way. I mean it's a bit bigger, but it's not in a very nice area.'

Thorne said nothing, asking himself why it was that so many people with money – especially those into whose laps it had conveniently fallen – seemed embarrassed by it, or even ashamed, taking time to let you know it actually meant nothing; that material worth did not define them.

That it hadn't spoiled them as human beings.

He began to mooch around, casting an eye towards Ella Fulton every so often and wondering if he should perhaps volunteer to make things a little easier for her. He was here to help, after all. He could ask if she fancied bunging the odd ten grand his way, seeing as having a few quid in the bank was clearly such a burden to her.

'What is it you're looking for?' Mary asked.

'I honestly don't know,' Thorne said.

The stripped wooden floor had been all but covered with a selection of faded rugs and the walls were randomly decorated with framed prints: pencil sketches; Mediterranean landscapes; posters for exhibitions and film festivals. There were magazines strewn across almost every available surface, textbooks lying open on a desk next to a dusty computer and many more stacked in a floor-to-ceiling bookcase near the window. He stepped closer to take a look. There were a few authors whose names he recognised, but none he had ever read. There seemed no apparent method to the way the titles had been arranged – fiction next to non-fiction, hardback next to paperback – and he could not help but think how outraged at least one person he knew would be by such haphazard filing; by the chaos.

'He's looking for a note,' Ella said.

Mary said, 'Oh,' and sat down on an old leather sofa, opposite her daughter. 'Yes, I suppose she'll have left a note. They usually do, don't they?'

Thorne would have been very happy to have discovered that Philippa Goodwin had left a note – something which might provide some of those answers he did not usually get – but he wasn't holding out much hope. He said, 'No, actually they don't.' The truth was that most people who took their own lives did so without leaving written notification of intent or convenient explanation. That they did was one of the many myths. Thorne knew very well that most suicides did not, in fact, take place around Christmas or between three and four o'clock in the morning

21

and that even though more men than women killed themselves annually, women made more attempts.

He knew, he thought, rather too much.

Thorne walked into the next room and saw that the somewhat disordered state of the sitting room was in direct proportion to the neatness of the small kitchen. Either Philippa hadn't eaten at home in the days before her death or simply believed that order and cleanliness mattered in some places more than others. A quick look in the bathroom confirmed the latter theory.

Standing in the doorway to the sitting room, he said, 'Tell me a bit more about Patrick Jennings.'

The man Mary and Ella had mentioned in the car.

'She met him about three months ago, I think,' Ella said.

'More like four.' Mary sat forward. 'In the pub after some university thing.'

'You thought he was nice,' Ella said.

Mary shook her head.

'To begin with, at any rate.'

'So, you met him a few times?' Thorne asked.

'Yes, Pip was keen to show him off,' Mary said. 'She'd been on her own for quite a long time.'

'He was certainly charming.' Ella looked at her mother. 'You have to admit that much. I mean, I can see what Pip saw in him. A bit of a silver fox, she said.'

Mary curled her lip. 'Yes, he was ... elegantly greying.' She spoke the words with evident distaste, as if she was actually saying *morbidly obese with the breath of a syphilitic dog.*

'I don't suppose either of you have got a picture?'

Ella said that she didn't.

'I don't think Patrick was very fond of having his picture taken,' Mary said. 'I was going to take one when he and Pip came over for dinner and I remember that he wasn't keen.'

Ella nodded. 'Well, some people aren't, are they?'

Thorne felt a prickle on the back of his neck; something

disturbing the fine hairs at the nape, just for a moment or two.

'I'm sure there are some pictures of him on Pip's phone, though. Do you still have it?'

Thorne nodded, remembering the mobile in Chall's plastic bag, the smear of blood on the screen. He wasn't sure if it was even working, but if it was, it was almost certainly locked. He thought that he might ask one of the team in the phone-tech unit to sort that out for him, just to satisfy his curiosity.

'So, why do you think he dumped her?'

'He didn't dump her,' Ella said. 'He ghosted her.'

Thorne had heard the term before, but Mary looked confused.

'He just disappeared one day and cut her off.' Ella leaned towards her mother. 'Not returning calls or messages, like he'd never existed. Like a *ghost*, Mum.'

The older woman nodded. 'Oh, I see. Well, whatever the right word is, it was certainly a shock. One minute he and Pip are all lovey-dovey and talking about setting up some sort of business and the next thing she's crying down the phone.'

Thorne felt that tickle again. 'What sort of business?'

'Some computer thing, I think.' Ella looked at her mother. 'Videos?'

'An educational resource,' Mary said. 'Putting lectures online so students could access them. Pip thought it was a great idea.'

'Well, it is a great idea,' Ella said. 'Just a shame they split up before they could get it going.'

'Yes, a shame.' Mary waited until Ella had turned away, then looked at Thorne and widened her eyes. As though silently articulating a suspicion her daughter was refusing to entertain. 'I suppose we should start thinking about what to do with everything.' Mary was looking around, a film of tears appearing suddenly as she clutched at her handbag. 'Pip had such a lot of stuff . . .'

Thorne told them that he was, of course, happy to drive them home, that he would wait in the car and give them a few minutes alone.

23

'That's very kind,' Mary said.

He closed the front door behind him and walked quickly towards the car, sensing that the rain was ready to return, dialling Nicola Tanner's number as he went.

'Can you do me a favour?'

'Tell me what it is first,' Tanner said.

'Can you take a quick look at Philippa Goodwin's finances for me? Bank statements, building society, whatever.'

'The suicide?' Tanner's tone was much the same as Chall's had been the day before. An enquiry as to why Thorne was following up on a death that was not, strictly speaking, his to investigate.

'It won't take you five minutes,' Thorne said.

'I know how long it'll take me,' Tanner said. 'But that's not really the point, is it?'

'I'm at her house, that's all, and—'

'Is there a problem, Tom?'

'Well, only with the way she arranged her bookshelves.' Thorne keyed the fob to unlock the BMW. 'You'd have a breakdown . . .'

FIVE

It's not as if there's any shortage of coffee shops within spitting distance of Brooklands Hill, but it had been clear – from the moment Sarah had become one of their number – which establishment had been chosen by the movers and shakers of the morning drop-off brigade. There are two of the well-known chains represented, the same as on almost any major high street, as well as a bakery that docs a decent latte, but *HazBeanz* was always going to be the preferred option. The coffee's good, *obviously*, the food gets rave reviews, and the décor is predictably ... quirky. Mismatched metal tables and exposed brickwork. It's friendly, with a nice, funky vibe, but most important of all, it's an independent, which can't hclp but reflect well on its customers.

It tells the world that *they* are independent, that they look beyond brands and are eager to do their bit in supporting local businesses. It says that they make informed choices. Above all, it trumpets the simple fact that they can afford to pay a little bit more, each morning, for their hand-ground espressos and fancy pastries.

None of it makes any real difference to Sarah, who would be

perfectly content to get her coffee from the local garage or, better yet, free from the supermarket, because she's got a loyalty card. She prefers builders' tea anyway and is far happier with a bacon sandwich than a cranberry and macadamia muffin. It's all a lot of flummery and fuss, she reckons. It's style over content, same as with a lot of things, but that's not really the point.

She needs to be where they are.

Sometimes, she has to kill a few minutes mooching around the shops, because she doesn't like to be the first one there, but today she's pleased to see that Savita, Heather and Caroline are already inside.

Their usual table in the window.

Coffees and cakes.

Chit-chat . . .

She waves as she passes the steamy window, then summons up the correct expression before she pushes open the door and steps inside. Happy to see them, but suitably harassed, as they all are, of course. Because the drop-off really is a nightmare, isn't it? It's no wonder they all need their overpriced coffees afterwards, a sugary treat and the chance to kick back and relax a little.

'The truth is, I'm completely exhausted after getting Jacob ready every day,' Caroline had told her once. 'Absolutely wiped out. I need that jolt of bloody caffeine after I've got him to school, because I've still got a full day's work ahead of me.'

'Yeah, I know what you mean.' Sarah had nodded sympathetically, then exchanged a knowing look with Heather. 'Sometimes I go home and get straight back into bed.'

Caroline had looked as if she wanted to punch her.

As soon as Sarah has ordered – a skinny latte and a cinnamon bagel – she sits down at a table for one just across from the others. Sometimes she joins them if she's feeling brave, but most of the time she prefers a bit of space and some time alone. Heather beckons her over, because she's nice and she probably needs a break from Caroline, but Sarah shakes her head and holds up the laptop case she's brought with her. Heather nods her understanding and Sarah mouths a *sorry*. There's work she needs to be pushing on with, they always understand that, and if any one of them walks past or comes across for a chat, she'll close the laptop before they can get a look at what she's actually doing.

It doesn't matter very much if they see her close it, because they all know why she keeps what she's doing private.

'So, what is it you do?' Heather had asked her a couple of weeks earlier.

'I'm a ... writer.'

'Really? That's amazing.'

'Not a very successful one or anything. Just a few short stories, you know.'

'I'd love to read one. I'm in a book group actually, so maybe—'

'No chance.' Sarah had laughed. 'I never let anyone I know read my stuff. It's hard enough showing it to the people who pay me for it, to be honest. Not that there's many of them. And I write under a pseudonym, so there's no point looking for anything.'

'I've always thought maybe I could write something,' Heather had said.

'So, why don't you?'

'Well, I'm sure it's a lot harder than people think.'

'It's just making things up, really.' Sarah had stepped away, keen to bring an end to it. 'I've always been good at that.'

Now, she opens her laptop and stares at the familiar screen-saver, then looks up from the screen as single father David comes through the door. He smiles automatically as he crosses to the counter to order. She smiles back, but actually she's a little disappointed that Alex hasn't shown up. He's not a regular, but he comes in a couple of mornings a week and, had he done so today, she would certainly have been happy to join the larger group towards which he usually gravitates. There's no future in it, she knows that. He's a happily married stay-at-home dad,

27

but still, she reckons there's definitely a spark and a little flirting doesn't hurt.

A little . . . imagining.

She watches David go to join the three women by the window, and it's only then that she sees the man sitting at the table next to her. Or at least, becomes aware that he's looking at her.

Was he there when she came in? She can't be sure.

He leans towards her and says, 'Now, you're either writing a hard-hitting literary novel, or . . . '

'Sorry?'

'I mean, *definitely* not chick-lit.'

She looks at him.

'Or you're just messing about on Twitter or something.'

She shrugs, trying to keep the panic in check.

He smiles and takes a sip of coffee. 'I'm trying to decide, that's all.'

He's definitely not a Brooklands Hill parent, she's sure of that because she knows them all by sight. Always makes a point of it. So, he can't possibly know the things she's told them about herself. But she's equally certain that she doesn't know him from anywhere else, so how could he know anything at all?

She feels the blood rising to her face.

She doesn't like the feeling, never has.

'Let me know when you've reached a decision,' she says, turning back to her screen.

'OK, I'll do that,' he says.

He's somewhere in his mid-forties, she decides, a few years older than she is. He's got a suit on, a thick pinstripe, but he has an open-neck floral shirt and a baggy flat cap. Smart but casual; trendy, she supposes. A look he's certainly taken some time over. He's got a silvery goatee beard and a small stud in one ear. He's wearing glasses with thick brown frames and, behind them, his eyes are very green.

'I'm struggling, to be honest,' he says after a minute or so.

'Shame,' she says.

'To be sure, I'd really need you to answer a few questions.'

Glancing over at the table in the window, she notices that Caroline is watching. It makes her happy. She slowly lowers the lid of her laptop and says, 'You can have three.'

'Three?'

'It's a one-time offer.'

He nods and sits back, like he's thinking about it. 'What's your name?'

It takes her a few seconds. 'Sarah.'

'Do you live locally?'

'I'm not far away.' She bites into her bagel and chews. 'One question left ...'

'I'd better make it a good one then.'

'Yes, you better had.'

He leans towards her again and lowers his voice just a little. 'Do you ever give your phone number to strange men?'

She feels herself start to redden again, but it's for a different reason this time and she doesn't mind it. 'Are you strange?'

'Definitely,' he says.

'You give me yours.'

He reels off a number and she keys it into her phone. She dials, and a few seconds later his phone starts to ring. He glances at the screen, nods, and turns the call off.

'Well, strange but honest,' she says.

'Is that good?'

'It's OK,' she says.

They fall silent after that, as if they have both decided that enough has been said. She looks across and sees that now, Heather, Savita and Caroline are all watching her. It's a nice result. She likes the fact that, for once, she's the one setting the agenda for later on, that she's giving them something to talk about at pick-up.

She smiles.

Is *this* a pick-up?

Well, yes, it certainly feels like one and she's surprised at how happy she is about that. It's been a while.

When the man stands to leave, he ties a scarf at his neck and says, 'My name's Conrad by the way. Oh, and my money's definitely on something literary.'

She watches him leave, then opens her laptop again, knowing she has no need to check that she's still being observed by the trio of mothers in the window. Her screensaver appears again, and she doesn't bother trying to hide the grin.

A dark-haired boy in a Chelsea shirt. Gap-toothed and goofy, thumbs held aloft. Squinting against the sun, with the unbroken blues of sea and cloudless sky behind him.

Jamie . . .

SIX

The look on the face of DCI Russell Brigstocke was, give or take a frown or two, the one Thorne had been expecting, but that didn't make it any less formidable. He had seen the same confusion in Chall's expression two days earlier on that platform at Highgate tube. He had heard it in Tanner's voice when he'd called her from the dead woman's flat. Coming from his senior officer, though, it was a different thing entirely, especially now that the initial bewilderment was playing second fiddle to serious irritation.

'I'm sure I've got a dictionary in here somewhere,' Brigstocke said. He began to open and close the drawers on his desk, shaking his head in mock-annoyance.

'Sir?' When it came to showing due deference to rank in matters of address, Thorne had a small, emergency supply which he could draw on in situations like these. It was not a word which had ever tripped easily off his tongue, besides which, he was sure that Brigstocke could smell the sucking up a mile away.

A final drawer was slammed shut. 'It's probably me being a bit dim, but you know . . . I just wanted to check I knew exactly what *homicide* meant.' Brigstocke peered beyond them, towards the incident room. 'That *is* what it says on the door, isn't it?'

'Homicide and serious crime—'

'I know what it says, Tom.'

Thorne said, 'Right.' He had been very well aware when he walked into Brigstocke's office that, in every sense, he would need to make a case. It was why he fought to keep his own irritation in check and to make everything he said, however baseless it might sound, seem as reasonable as possible.

And it was why he had brought Nicola Tanner with him.

He mumbled another 'Sir' for good measure, and Tanner did the same.

'And suicide hasn't actually been a crime, serious or otherwise, for a long time.'

'It was decriminalised in 1961,' Tanner said.

'Thank you.' Brigstocke stared at her, thin-lipped and decidedly ungrateful.

'Come on, Russell.' Thorne took half a step towards Brigstocke's desk. 'It's not the suicide we're talking about. It's this shyster, Patrick Jennings.'

'Oh, I know that, too, because, surprising as it might sound, I've actually been listening. Same as I know that it's *sir* when you want to kiss my arse and *Russell* when you're asking me a favour.' The DCI took off his glasses and rubbed his eyes. 'Christ almighty . . .'

Thorne said nothing; a decision, based on hard-earned experience, that it would be wise to wait out this minor storm. He had certainly come through worse. Yes, he and his boss had clashed countless times before, but Thorne knew the DCI to be a decent and humane copper who wrestled constantly with the demands of seniority. The Bullshit Bingo engaged in daily by those senior to *him*. Outside the grim, grey walls of Becke House, he and Thorne were still friends.

More or less.

He waited until Brigstocke had replaced his glasses before glancing at Nicola Tanner.

You're up . . .

Tanner moved forward to Thorne's side and opened her notebook. 'Three weeks before she killed herself, Philippa Goodwin transferred seventy-five thousand pounds from her savings account to an account in the name of LectureCom Ltd.'

'Jennings,' Thorne said.

Brigstocke remained impassive.

'That account was emptied and closed two days after the transfer was made,' Tanner said. 'We're looking at the details used to open the account in the first place, but we can be fairly sure it was all done with fake ID documents, so it's not going to get us very far. It's one of these online banks that doesn't even bother with credit checks. A couple of dodgy utility bills as proof of address and a few hundred pounds deposited to get it up and running. You can do it in minutes.'

Tanner put her notebook away. Thorne's turn.

'So . . . Jennings, or whatever his real name is, forms a relationship with Philippa Goodwin, gains her confidence and persuades her to invest all her savings in this non-existent company.'

'I get it,' Brigstocke said.

'I mean, he's probably shelled out for a few bits and pieces, just so everything looks kosher. You know, a nice-looking logo, some fancy presentation stuff, but the rest of it's smoke and mirrors.'

Brigstocke shook his head to call a halt and sat back. 'Look, I don't need my dictionary to tell me that you're describing a simple fraud, and any numpty with a warrant card could tell you there's a huge team in a nice shiny office that deals with this stuff every day of the week. Because. That's. Their. Job. One phone call to ActionFraud and you've done yours.' He looked from Thorne to Tanner and back again. 'Do you want me to give you the number?'

The question hung, unanswered. Tanner looked at her feet, the awkward silence cut short by the conversation of colleagues

33

walking past the door, laughter fading as they moved away down the corridor.

'She killed herself, Russell.' Thorne said it as though Brigstocke did not already know, as though it might change everything, when he was almost sure that it would not. He did not have a lot else left.

'Yeah, it's horrible.' Brigstocke leaned across the desk. 'But aside from the fraud—'

'Because of *him*. Because of what he did and how that made her feel. He took everything she had; he *humiliated* her.' Thorne glanced at Tanner. She was nodding, casting her own doubts aside to provide the support she'd promised. 'He as good as pushed her under that train.'

'I think that's stretching it a bit.'

'I don't agree.'

'Actually, it's stretching it a *lot*, and "as good as" doesn't cut much ice in court.'

Thorne wheeled around, took a few seconds to swallow down some seriously industrial language, then turned slowly back to the DCI. 'They prosecuted a case in Birmingham a few months back. Another one up north at the end of last year.'

'Newcastle,' Tanner said.

'Right. Two morons from these suicide chat rooms, and both got sent down for encouraging others who went on to kill themselves. Goading them, telling them which were the most efficient methods or whatever, daring them to do it.'

'Right,' Brigstocke said. 'But as far as we know, this man wasn't doing any of those things.'

'I talked to a woman I know in the CPS.'

'Oh, did you?'

Thorne raised a hand to ward off the dressing-down he could rightly sense coming. 'It was just over a drink, all right? Nothing official. Anyway, she reckons that if we can catch him, there might be a case for looking at what Patrick Jennings did in a different way. She says we'd need to prove premeditation, but that shouldn't be too difficult.'

'Different how?'

'So, not just as a fraud, but as a campaign of carefully planned out and systematic psychological abuse. We get a couple of friendly experts in court to testify that the abuse played a significant role in Philippa Goodwin's decision to kill herself and . . . we're in with a chance.'

'A chance of what? Whatever the CPS conjure up, it won't be murder.'

'No. Manslaughter, maybe? I don't know . . . ' Thorne turned to Tanner again, but did not like the look on her face, so turned away. 'This woman I was talking to was getting pretty fired up about it, though.'

Now Brigstocke was wearing another expression Thorne knew very well. Annoyance, exhaustion and something – happily – like resignation. He sighed and said, 'What is it you're after?'

'For now, just a forensic team to go over Philippa Goodwin's flat, that's all. Jennings will have been pretty good at making himself invisible, wiping away all the official traces, but there's not a fat lot he'll have been able to do about prints and DNA. We'll see if that takes us anywhere.'

'And if it doesn't?'

'No harm done. Like you said, we give the fraud team everything we've got and let them get on with it.' Thorne waited. 'Look, we've not got too much on the books at the moment—'

'At the moment.'

' . . . and it goes without saying, if we catch something big, that takes priority.'

'Which we will,' Brigstocke said. 'Or maybe you're too busy hobnobbing with our friends from the Crown Prosecution Service to read the murder figures.'

'I prefer something with a happy ending,' Thorne said. 'A nice romance or what have you.' There were more voices, right outside the office door. 'So, what about this forensic team, then?'

The DCI made no effort whatsoever to disguise his own pithy but industrial language; muttered, but still audible above the conversation outside.

Thorne knew Brigstocke well enough to take it as a yes.

Back in the incident room, Tanner said, 'So, who's this woman from the CPS?'

'Didn't I mention her?'

'No.'

'Probably because I made her up,' Thorne said.

'For God's sake.'

'I was thinking on my feet. Well, actually, I thought about it in bed last night, but you know what I mean.'

'Right.' Tanner folded her arms. 'So, if, by some miracle, this actually comes to anything, what happens when Brigstocke asks you to liaise with your imaginary lady friend from the CPS?'

'I'll tell him she was fired or retired. Or dead.' Thorne shrugged. 'I'll think of something.' He was smiling, but it quickly became clear that Tanner was not impressed. 'Come on, Nic, it'll be fine.'

Tanner turned and walked away and Thorne took a few half-hearted steps after her, before giving up. From a desk nearby, Dipak Chall caught his eye, having witnessed the exchange. Thorne shook his head.

Move along, nothing to see.

He would catch up with her later.

When Thorne had first met DI Nicola Tanner, she had been just about as Job-pissed as any officer he'd ever encountered. It felt as if she'd written the book she set such store in working by and would no more have dreamed about pulling the wool over a senior officer's eyes than she would of taking a bribe or having sex with someone in possession of a penis.

Now though, they had been working together for the best part of a year, and things were a little different. Sometimes, Thorne liked to believe that Tanner's rather more laissez-faire attitude when it came to procedure was down to him; that he had been a bad influence for the better. On occasion she would even suggest it herself, but both of them knew it was simply a convenient explanation.

More palatable than the truth.

The killing of Tanner's partner, Susan, had changed her in ways Thorne had only fully come to understand at the climax of a case seven months before. A gore-spattered crime scene and an incident rarely spoken about since, but one which had bound them together for good or ill.

Lies and illegality, *blood*, which charged every moment between them and which had made Nicola Tanner a little more willing than she might otherwise have been to do Tom Thorne favours.

Thorne had sensed her doubts about this particular favour back in Brigstocke's office, even as she was doing as he'd asked and playing her part to perfection. The sensible one, the officer the bosses could have faith in. The truth was that Thorne *had* been thinking on his feet and was no more convinced than Tanner that they could ever put Patrick Jennings away for anything other than his financial misdemeanours.

He knew that he wanted to catch him, though.

He walked back towards his office, thinking about that body-bag, sagging as it was lifted from the tracks, and Mary Fulton plucking nervously at the chain around her neck.

Not that it was an accident, of course . . .

Yes, catching him would be enough.

He wanted to be there when Patrick Jennings, or whoever he really was, got sent down. To watch, then wave goodbye as the man he truly believed to be responsible for Philippa Goodwin's death was escorted from the dock, to disappear from view for as long as possible.

Now, *that* was Thorne's idea of ghosting.

SEVEN

Margate

*It isn't a seaside town she's been to before and Michelle's first thought
is that, even if it smells every bit as fishy, it's nothing like the places
she remembers visiting as a kid. A fancy art gallery and a tarted-up
amusement park. A decent smattering of trendy types. You don't have
to look too hard though, for the grubby arcades, the burger joints and
the shops stuffed with cheap and tacky souvenirs, and it doesn't take
long to find a crowded bar knocking out jugs of Sex On The Beach
or Porn Star Martinis for less than a tenner a pop.*

She doesn't think that any of it will take long.

*She's smoking on the pavement, her head bobbing to the awful
music from inside, when the boy pushes out through the crowd in the
doorway and lights a cigarette of his own. They exchange a nod as he
swigs from a bottle of Smirnoff Ice. She tosses her butt into the gutter,
waits half a minute, then steps across.*

'You got another one of those?'

*'You've just put one out,' the boy says. He leans from foot to foot.
He's seventeen or thereabouts, cute enough in a denim jacket, a Fred
Perry buttoned to the neck.*

Not that cute has anything to do with it.

Michelle shrugs, says, 'Yeah, you're right,' then smiles, watching as it dawns on him. The realisation that she doesn't want a cigarette at all, that it had just been an excuse to start a conversation.

A glamorous woman, old enough to be his mother.

A MILF . . .

A living, breathing female who doesn't use WhatsApp or own a selfie stick and probably knows exactly what she's doing in the bedroom.

The colour rising in his face when the penny drops. A sniff and a deep drag on his cigarette to cover it. A half-turn away and another swig, like something more interesting might come along.

'You here with your mates, then?'

He nods rather more times than he needs to. 'Yeah. Friday night, you know?' He has a nice smile, she has to give him that. 'You?'

'Girls' night out,' she says. 'Boring, though.'

'Yeah?'

She mimes an exaggerated yawn. 'Talking about their husbands and their kids, making one glass of wine last an hour.'

'You not talking about your *husband, then?'*

Michelle looks at the boy as if she's impressed at his cheek, as if she hasn't already clocked him checking out her left hand. She says, 'Well, he's not here, is he?'

They both look up at the roar of a souped-up something-or-other as it drives past. A bass-beat that must surely be deafening anyone inside pumping from the open windows, and a neon strip beneath the chassis, as though its driver is casually cruising along the seafront in Miami or Rio.

'Look at that twat,' the boy says. 'What a—'

'Do you fancy going for a walk?'

EIGHT

Their cars are in different areas of the huge car park, so they linger for a minute or two outside the multiplex, neither one appearing keen to move as they button up coats against the cold and reach into pockets for keys.

He asks Sarah what she thought of the film.

It was a decent enough thriller, scary even, once or twice, but she thinks the ending was completely ridiculous and tells him so. He says they usually are, that endings are tricky things to get right. Twists that come from nowhere, all that. It doesn't have to get quite that stupid though, she says, and he laughs, like he agrees with her.

'A quick drink?'

Sarah knows that it's still early, but she looks at her watch anyway.

'Super quick?'

'Just one,' she says. 'Childcare ...'

The place he's talking about isn't far away, they can actually see it, but walking would mean trying to cross six lanes of busy traffic on Southbury Road. They take her car, because it's nearest, and within five minutes they're sitting with drinks at a corner table in a busy bar/restaurant that's serving cheap and cheerful Thai food.

He raises his pint glass and she touches her bottle to it.

'Making me hungry.' Sarah nods towards the plates of satay and spare ribs on an adjacent table, at a waitress passing with something sizzling.

'We could eat something, if you fancy it. Wouldn't take long.'

'Like I said.'

'Right.' He sits back. 'Babysitting's pricey, I know.'

She looks at him. 'You got kids, then?'

'No.' He says it like he's relieved and lifts the glass to his mouth. 'I mean, it just *is*, though, isn't it?'

She nods. 'Eight quid an hour I pay this girl. *And* I've got to get her an Uber home afterwards.'

'Bloody hell, *I'd* do it for that,' he says.

They look around at the other customers, at each other. She'd noticed when he arrived at the cinema that he was wearing the same baggy cap that she'd seen in the coffee shop and been pleased to see, when he'd taken it off inside, that he had a decent head of hair. Silver, cut very short, but certainly not thin. He's wearing jeans that she guesses are pricey – maybe those stupidly expensive Japanese ones she's read about – and a long-sleeved polo shirt she thinks looks ... soft. She likes his shoes, too; gleaming brown brogues.

Not that Sarah hasn't made an effort herself. She likes to dress up and she knows how good she is at doing it when she gets the chance, at tailoring her outfit to any given situation. To the people she's likely to be spending time with. It had been a little harder than usual, deciding what to wear for this evening, because she wasn't altogether certain how much of herself she was ready to put on show.

She still isn't.

It's exciting though. The dance. This feeling each other out.

'So, you live in Enfield, too?' She waits. Where Brooklands Hill is, and *HazBeanz*. The Cineworld he'd suggested when he'd called.

'Well, *home* home is actually in the Midlands.'

'Oh.'

He pulls a face, as though revealing a dirty secret. 'I'm only down here on business really and I had a few meetings in Enfield the other day, just round the corner from that coffee shop.'

'Right.'

'Lucky for me I happened to fancy a coffee.'

She tries to hold his stare but can only manage a few seconds. 'I mean, probably not that lucky for you ...'

He smiles, and she notices again what great teeth he has. Like in a toothpaste advert. She wonders, just for a few moments, if they might even be false, then dismisses the idea. 'What kind of meetings?'

He waves her question away. 'Oh ... just with investors.'

She nods, to make it clear she's impressed.

'No, just ... trying to raise some more money for this thing I'm putting together. Massively tedious as it happens. No, seriously. I mean, like "wanting-to-scoop-your-own-eyeballs-out-with-a-spoon" tedious.'

She laughs, takes a swig of beer.

'I mean, actually *you* might find it mildly interesting, but trust me, I've had it for days, so I'd much rather talk about something else. About *anything* else.'

'Like ... ?'

'Like, *you*?'

She laughs again, enjoying herself. 'I'm good with that.'

A waitress stops at their table and asks if they've had a chance to look at the menus. He tells her that everything sounds great but that they're not stopping, so she quickly moves on.

'So ... what *were* you writing the other day? In the coffee shop.'

She takes a few seconds, decides that it's way too early to let her guard down, not even a little. 'Well, put it this way, I don't think you'd guess.'

'No?'

'Not a chance.' She likes to throw a nugget of truth in there sometimes, to give her little lie ... substance.

'You *are* some sort of writer, though, yeah?' He cocks his head and moves fingers across silvery stubble. 'I know a lot of people sit in places like that with laptops, making out like they're working on some masterpiece when they're actually doing bugger all, and yeah, I know I was taking the mickey a bit the other day ... but I looked at you and I swear I thought you were probably a proper writer.'

'I'm ... trying to be,' she says.

'OK. So, does it pay the bills?' He shakes his head and stares down into his glass. 'Sorry, that's way too pushy for a first date.'

Sarah studies what little remains in her bottle. She's thinking it would probably be a good idea to leave soon. She's thinking that he's got that look about him, that if she let him shag her, she'd probably stay shagged.

She says, 'Well, I probably make less than my babysitter, so it's a good job I'm not relying on it.'

'Other strings to your bow.'

'Something like that.'

'You enjoy it, though?'

'Oh, yeah.'

He raises his glass again. 'Main thing, right?' He sees her glance at her watch and quickly downs what's left of his drink. 'OK, best let you get home.'

She pushes her chair back, but in truth she's not really in any hurry to leave. Then, she thinks about Jamie; snuggled up in bed at home, knees pulled up to his skinny chest and his thumb in his mouth like he's still a baby. 'I better had ...'

'Do this again though, right?'

'If you ever need a break from your boring meetings.'

43

'Always,' he says.

'Well, you've got my number.' She reaches across the table to briefly touch his hand. 'And I've got yours.'

They stand up to gather bags and jackets. They check their phones. A man with a drink in his hand is waiting to pounce on their table, but they're in no great hurry.

'I'll drive you back to your car,' she says.

'There's no need.'

'You'll kill yourself trying to get across that road.'

'I'll be fine, honestly.' Conrad ties his scarf, carefully. It's silk, Sarah thinks, watching the material glide through his fingers. 'It's good to take a few risks now and again,' he says. 'Don't you reckon?'

NINE

Tom Thorne and Phil Hendricks stepped out of the Bengal Lancer and began walking south down Kentish Town Road. It was cold but, thankfully, dry. Thorne was humming some tune that had been stuck in his head all day and carefully carrying a brown paper bag containing the remains of the Dhaba Lamb he hadn't been able to finish.

'God, I've missed that place.'

Hendricks belched Kingfisher and grinned. 'Well, you don't have to miss it, do you, mate?' He punched Thorne on the shoulder. 'Not now you're living back up here.'

'For now.'

'Really?' Hendricks's Mancunian drawl stretched the word out, the sarcasm screamingly obvious.

'I told you, it's just a trial thing.'

'Course it is.'

'We're seeing how it goes.'

'Right. So, how's it going, then? What's it been . . . six weeks?'

Thorne said nothing.

It had been almost two months, in fact, since his partner

Helen – if he could still call her that – had dropped the bomb-shell and announced that she needed some space, that perhaps they would both be happier if they tried living apart for a while. It was hard wasn't it, she'd said, two coppers together? Harder than normal. There were extra . . . stresses.

A break might do us both some good, and it feels like I need to spend some time on my own with Alfie . . .

Thorne had not bothered to argue, knowing Helen as he did and seeing straight away that there would be little point. Hendricks had been the first person he'd told and, knowing *him* as well as he did, he had not been expecting anything as conventional as sympathy.

Which was fortunate.

'Yeah, well, I can't say I'm surprised,' Hendricks had told him. 'I mean, don't get me wrong, I love Helen to bits, but I always wondered how long she'd put up with you.'

'Great, cheers, Phil. So, how did that stint with the Samaritans work out for you?'

'You ask me, deep down you always knew this was going to happen.'

'Go on, then.'

'Hanging on to your old flat, just in case. A lifeboat, kind of thing.'

'That's bollocks. The rent came in seriously bloody handy. Besides, this was Helen's idea, not mine.'

'She dumped you?'

'No. Like I told you—'

'So, what happened?'

In truth, Thorne was still far from sure. He had certainly been happy enough and had believed that the same went for Helen. There had been some tension a few months before the split, but certainly nothing he saw as terminal and largely down to what Thorne had seen as interference from her younger sister, Jenny. It was ironic, in retrospect, that Helen's need for 'space' had manifested itself only a short time after he and Jenny had cleared the air, when she had confessed that *she* was the one trapped in a miserable relationship and had, in actual fact, been jealous of his and Helen's.

Had she been lying?

Had she continued to undermine him, thinking he would no longer suspect?

Or had she simply not known her sister as well as she thought she did?

It was all academic anyway, because Helen had made her decision and there was no shifting her. In time he thought he might come to understand why and, despite his best friend's cynicism, he still wanted to believe there was a chance she might decide to try again. He loved Helen, he remained fairly confident that she still loved him, they had been through so bloody much together.

And yet . . .

He knew that a good deal of the pain he had felt, *still* felt, was down to nothing more than a bruised ego. He'd known how that went since his first girlfriend had chucked him for some knob in the school rugby team. He knew that it didn't last. The truth was that, for all the misery that was part and parcel of his re-acquaintance with a – theoretically – single life, he was slowly getting used to it.

He was even starting to enjoy himself just a little.

His flat, his favourite restaurant, his local pub. It was good to be based somewhere close to Hendricks again. Thorne had never quite made peace with living at Helen's place in Tulse Hill and that had not just been because of a more difficult journey to work every day.

He was happier, always had been, on this side of the river.

He felt more like himself.

They slowed, then stopped at the corner of Prince Of Wales Road. From here, Thorne would be heading right, just five minutes' walk from his flat, while Hendricks would continue on to Camden, to his own.

'I really miss Alfie,' Thorne said. Helen's five-year-old. Thorne had packed up and left when the boy was at school and had only seen him a few times since.

'Meaning you don't miss Helen?'

'No, you daft twat. Course I do.'

'Helen doesn't mind you seeing him, does she?'

Thorne shrugged. 'She's fine about it. I had dinner round there last week, matter of fact.'

'So . . . ?'

'So . . . nothing. Just saying, that's all.'

Hendricks was about to say something when a man coming in the opposite direction gave him a long, hard stare. Hendricks stared right back, turning to carry on staring when the man had walked past. 'Bang up for it, he was.'

'What would Liam say?'

'Liam's well aware how irresistible I am. He knows I'm going to get checked out.'

Thorne pointed at the man who was now disappearing. 'That, mate, was astonishment, pure and simple.'

'Too right it was.'

'Not in the way you're thinking. It's not everyone who's used to coming across someone with quite that much metal in their face. Not even round here. You need to stop thinking that look of horror . . . ' Thorne opened his mouth and widened his eyes to demonstrate, 'is the same as someone fancying you.'

Hendricks laughed, then belched again. 'What you were saying, about Alfie.'

'Nothing.' Thorne sniffed and adjusted his grip on the precious brown bag. 'Just . . . '

'Come here.' Hendricks stepped forward and pulled Thorne into a fierce and only partially drunken hug. Thorne was happy enough to be drawn in and to hold on. 'I know you better than anyone, remember? You don't need to prove to me that you're as soft as shite.'

When they had separated, Hendricks straightened his leather jacket, rubbed a palm across his shaved head. He said, 'Anyway, I hope you get this conman business sorted, so you can get back to nicking killers. It's not like they've all taken a holiday, is it? There's no shortage of bodies on my slab, mate.'

'He *is* a killer,' Thorne said. 'As good as.'

'Come on, I'm not sure you really believe that.'

'Either way.'

Thorne had told Hendricks about the case while they'd eaten: the suicide; the man who had destroyed the life of an innocent woman; the small window of opportunity granted them by Brigstocke. A window that would only stay open while there was a chance that the forensic sweep of Philippa Goodwin's flat yielded significant results.

'There was sod all on her phone,' Thorne said.

'You told me.'

'This bloke managed to erase every picture, every text, whatever, before he scarpered.'

'Right.'

'Covered his tracks very nicely, and I'm betting he's done it plenty of times before. So we'd better hope we get lucky with the DNA.'

Hendricks was already moving away, shaking his head and saying, 'You told me,' again. Without turning round, he shouted, 'Now, you hurry up and get home, mate. And keep cheerful, for God's sake. I hear there's a lot to be said for wanking into a tear-stained pillow . . . '

When Thorne got back to his flat, he put the leftover curry in the fridge, stuck the kettle on and mooched around. He turned on the TV and changed channels for ten minutes. He drifted off to sleep, but woke again soon afterwards, his neck aching.

Then he called Helen.

He said, 'It's me,' then realised he was talking to her voicemail.

He swore quietly and said, 'Sorry, I'm guessing you're in bed. Course you are . . . just calling to see how you're doing, really. Anyway, hope you're OK and give the boy a cuddle from me. That's it . . . '

The second he hung up, he began to wish he hadn't called. He was feeling maudlin, there was no more to it than that, and the two pints in the Lancer hadn't helped. Or the two in the Grafton Arms before that. A garbled, late-night message wouldn't change Helen's mind, after all, and he couldn't swear that he wanted her to change it.

He stood up and walked towards the bedroom.

Not too much he *was* sure about.

Curry always tasted better the next day.

George Jones had a better voice than Frank Sinatra.

And manipulative, sociopathic arseholes weren't actually killers just because he wanted them to be.

TEN

Of late, Thorne had grown used to waking up feeling a little out of sorts, but today was different, because he had dreamed about his mother.

It did not happen often and always left him feeling . . . bruised and somewhat discombobulated. He did not feel comforted, as anyone dreaming about a dead parent might have expected, and there was never anything pleasant to dwell upon after these dreams about a woman he missed as much as he did.

It was not as if they were ever extraordinary. There was nothing to mull over or pour out to a therapist, had he been the sort to waste his time doing that. This, like the others when they came, was simple enough. Memories of things that probably never happened.

Mundane . . . .

Her voice and her smell; Camay and Parma violets. Watching her in the garden from his bedroom window. Her hair tied up in a red scarf.

All the same, he woke fidgety and irritable.

It was guilt, he felt, hard as it had been to name and to accept.

Guilt that was completely irrational, he knew, but no less painful for it, because he did not dream about his mother as much as perhaps he should.

Nothing like as much.

It was only natural, he guessed, that he should dream about his father more. Thorne had been there throughout a terrible decline that had dragged out over a number of years; watching as the Alzheimer's had slowly drawn the old man into the darkness, then locked a door to which Thorne had no key. When he dreamed of him, his father was almost always as sharp and quick-witted as he had been when Thorne was a boy. He was the parent again and Thorne the child, the way it was supposed to be. When these dreams of his father came, they made Thorne feel good. He woke, miserable at their brevity, their transience, at being unable to hang on to them for longer; angry at being torn away.

No. The guilt was not because he dreamed about his father more than his mother. It was because he dreamed of her so very rarely, while dreaming far too often about others.

He dreamed about a man called Stuart Nicklin more than he dreamed of his mother. About men named Francis Calvert and Arkan Zarif. He dreamed about killers and rapists the way other people dreamed about flying or falling or sleeping with a celebrity. About men who hated and hurt because they were breathing and for whom life only sang when others were in pain.

Monsters, if you believed in that sort of thing.

While the woman he had worshipped and who had loved him more than any other person on the planet was given no more than a walk-on role.

'All good, Tom?'

Thorne looked up from behind his desk to see Tanner settling into a chair on the other side. He grunted and let his gaze drop once again to the same piece of paperwork he had been staring at for the previous fifteen minutes.

He tried to focus.

He said, 'Ticking along.'

'To be honest, I've seen you look happier,' Tanner said. 'Actually, I've seen corpses look happier.'

Thorne did his best to match that, at least. 'I'm fine. Just ... any news on the Goodwin thing, yet?'

The thing. Not a *case*, not yet.

'Should be today sometime.'

Thorne looked at his watch. It wasn't even eleven o'clock.

'To be honest, I'd thought you'd be a bit more cheerful about it. I mean it's all going in the right direction so far. We know they got plenty of prints and some decent samples, right?'

A historic blood trace in the bathroom, where Patrick Jennings might have cut himself shaving. Hair with follicles and roots intact and flakes of dried skin. It had been easy enough to obtain DNA from the body of Philippa Goodwin, so separating the two profiles before running Jennings's sample against the national database would not be an issue. Same with the fingerprints.

'Even so,' Tanner said, 'I can't see much point in holding your breath.'

'I thought you were with me on this.'

'I am.' Tanner leaned forward to straighten the in-tray on Thorne's desk, nudging it one way, then the other, until she was satisfied. She sat back. 'Up to a point.'

'Which is?'

'When you stop being realistic.'

The forensic team had been dispatched to Philippa Goodwin's flat in Tufnell Park almost forty-eight hours earlier, as soon as they had got the grudging go-ahead from Russell Brigstocke. Thorne knew he was being overly optimistic at best and knew equally well that his impatience for a result was misplaced. In some cases – rape being the prime example – DNA could be analysed and samples compared within a matter of hours, so as to shorten the ordeal of victims. When a life was deemed to be at stake or a clock was ticking down to the release of a suspected killer, stops would obviously be pulled out, but that certainly didn't apply in this case.

Not for a suicide.

This was nobody's idea of a rush job.

'And anyway, whatever we said to Russell the other day, it's not like we've got any shortage of stuff to be getting on with. Well, *I'm* certainly not sitting around twiddling my thumbs.'

Tanner was right, of course, and Thorne was well aware that he had plenty on his plate already. He needed to prepare evidence for a trial the following week. A man charged with strangling his girlfriend to death, who persisted in claiming that he acted in self-defence; his legal team cocky as hell thanks to the superficial stab wounds on his arms, until it was pointed out that their client's fingerprints were the only ones found on the knife. A suspicious death at a hospital in Edmonton had come in overnight and there were still the three gang-related stabbings in Tottenham that he had been tasked with reviewing.

Nothing making his blood jump quite the way this was, though.

Patrick Jennings . . .

He could not have told anyone why.

Thorne wasn't holding his breath, not exactly. He knew as well as Tanner that they would need to get seriously lucky, that a man as smooth, as careful as Jennings would not have taken too many risks when it came to masking his identity. It was how he lived, after all, how he *earned*. Still, a slim chance was better than none. Perhaps he had been done for punching a copper when he was a student or nicked for drink driving. Either way, his prints would almost certainly have been taken and potentially a DNA swab.

He would be in the system.

Plenty on his plate, but because that chance was slim – more or less *anorexic*, Hendricks had said – Thorne would need to think of other ways forward. A strategy that did not rely on knowing who this individual was and would not drop him in it too much with his DCI.

He was already thinking, but so far had produced precisely nothing.

When Thorne looked up to see Tanner still sitting there, he said, 'This what you call not twiddling your thumbs?'

She stood up. 'I only popped in to see if you fancied coming round for dinner tomorrow night.'

'*Your* place?'

'Why not?'

'Well . . . '

She scowled. 'I'm getting better. I mean it'll only be pasta. Presuming you're free . . . you know, Saturday night, I'm sure you're beating them off with a shitty stick.'

'I'll need to look at my diary, obviously.'

'You're still . . . ?'

Thorne only just stopped himself saying *wanking into a tear-stained pillow*. 'On my own, in my flat, yeah.' Tanner knew what had happened between him and Helen and had been rather more sympathetic than Phil Hendricks. To his relief, she hadn't asked too many questions since he'd told her. Though perhaps, Thorne thought, that was what the dinner invitation was all about.

Pasta and a spot of casual interrogation.

'About half-seven, then,' Tanner said.

'I'll make sure I eat before I come.'

'And there's no point looking at your watch every five minutes, because it won't make the results come any faster. "Wait and see pudding". What my mother used to say . . . '

And Thorne remembered his dream.

And the bubble of guilt rose up hard into his throat, sudden and sour.

It was a good job that Tanner had already turned away and was walking towards the door, because Thorne's expression would have made a corpse look positively gleeful.

ELEVEN

They're sitting in Pizza Express on Silver Street, across the road from Enfield Town overground station. They're sharing a large bottle of Peroni, small plates of garlic bread and olives. They've been talking almost constantly since the moment she arrived and joined him at the table, and now they're laughing about how much time – or rather how little time – he had let go by before calling her again.

'OK, but it wasn't like I was suggesting we get together the next day, was it?'

'Fair enough,' Sarah says.

'That would have seemed too keen, I reckon.'

'Yeah, a bit needy.'

'Anyway, I wanted to give you a day to get your childcare sorted.'

'Very thoughtful.' She pops an olive into her mouth. 'I admire the planning.'

'It pays to think ahead,' he says.

A waiter arrives and lays down the pizzas. She smiles and shakes her head as she unfolds the napkin into her lap. 'Why do blokes always go for the meatiest thing on the menu?' She points and laughs as he drizzles chilli oil over his pizza. 'And then make it as spicy as they can? Do you think it makes you seem more ... manly, like there's testosterone pouring out of your ears? You know ...' She growls. '*Meat!* Like it makes us go all daft and floppy, like it makes us think you're probably animals in bed.'

He glances up, already tucking in. 'You're absolutely right.'

'About?'

'All of it.'

They carry on chatting while they eat, though it's as if both have taken the decision to avoid anything ... weighty. So they talk about the extortionate prices of almost everything in London and the chocolate bars they liked as kids. His pathological dislike of being late and her somewhat bizarre addiction to darts on TV.

'How have your meetings been going?' she asks. 'These investors or whatever.'

'Still as boring as they were two days ago.'

'Well, I hope you're splashing out on a nice hotel, at least.'

He nods. 'Oh God, yes.'

'Chocolate on the pillow?'

'Of course. And plenty of nice smellies to pinch out of the bathroom.'

'Take back to the Midlands.'

'Right. I've got a cupboard full.'

When the plates have been cleared and the table wiped, he orders another bottle of beer and says, 'So, tell me about Jamie's dad then.'

It's a very smooth move, Sarah thinks. Showing her that he's sensitive and not remotely threatened by the previous men in her life. Or trying to appear that way. Either way she's happy enough, because it's a nice easy one.

'He's called Peter, and thankfully he lives a long way away, and marrying him was the biggest mistake I ever made. Or anyone's ever made, come to that. Seriously, it's right up there with the Millennium Dome, or buying a ticket on the *Titanic*.'

'A short-sighted Dalek trying to shag a dustbin?'

Sarah laughs. 'Basically, it was a really stupid thing to do. I mean I got Jamie out of it, so not *all* bad. Just mostly bad.'

'What happened?'

'He was just awful to live with. Horrible. He had a foul temper which only got worse, because I didn't like him trying to turn me into someone I wasn't. Oh, and there were a couple of affairs, mustn't forget those, which I stupidly thought I'd be able to handle. He ground me down, basically.' She picks up her glass. She sits back and grins. 'Until I just woke up one day and told him where to go.'

'Nice,' he says.

'Yeah, eventually. I got the house, all paid off and worth a damn sight more than it was when I threw him out, and there's a nice fat cheque for child support which pops through the letterbox four times a year, so I'm sorted.'

'Certainly sounds like it.'

'I make enough from the writing to buy food and pay the bills. For the phone, the car, all that stuff . . . and I can treat me and Jamie to a few trips away.' She shakes her head, brushes a loose strand of hair from her face. 'If I'm honest, I lie awake at night sometimes, wondering if that was really me, you know? Putting up with all that. It's like it happened to someone else.'

He nods, thoughtful, sympathetic. 'Does Jamie still see him?'

'A couple of times a year, that's all, because that's what we agreed, but it's starting to upset him.'

He looks confused.

'Jamie, I mean. Peter's just this bloke who takes him on holiday twice a year and buys him toys he doesn't play with. Jamie doesn't know him, never really even talks about him. That's not being a dad, is it?'

For a second or two before he looks down at the table, she sees something dark wash across his face. 'No,' he says. 'It isn't.'

'So, go on, then. What about you?'

When he looks up, the smile is back on full beam. 'Well, there've been a few mistakes, I suppose. Nothing as bad as *that* . . . not *Titanic* level, but, you know, plenty of false starts.'

'Such as?'

'Oh, just usual relationship stuff. People getting jealous or feeling pressured or whatever. Work getting in the way. Probably my fault as much as theirs, a lot of them.'

Sarah raises her eyebrows as she pours what's left of the bottle into her glass. 'So, there've been a lot of them?'

'About average, I reckon.'

He asks her if she fancies pudding. She rubs her stomach and shakes her head. She watches him signal for the bill and says, 'In the end, it's all about timing, isn't it? Meeting the right person at the right time.'

'Absolutely.'

'In the right coffee shop.'

He leans towards her. 'Sometimes, it's just blind luck.'

'Luck or not, it's about learning from your mistakes and trying not to repeat them.'

'Oh, I'm not going to make *any* more mistakes,' he says.

She lets him drop her off, though she only lives five minutes away. It's a big deal, she knows that, letting him see where she lives. It's cold anyway and, in truth, she didn't much fancy the walk, but she'd guessed that he would offer and had decided in advance that it was a step she was prepared to take.

They undo their seat-belts and sit in his car – a high-end Mercedes – with the engine running. The car is immaculate, which Sarah takes as a very good sign, and there's some kind of air-freshener, which would normally make her feel a bit sick, but doesn't. She thinks it makes the car smell almost as nice as he does.

As fresh and ready to spoil.

'Asking you to come in for a coffee or whatever would be

pushing it a bit, wouldn't it?' She turns to look at him. 'Be a bit slutty.'

'Hugely,' he says.

'Long as we agree.' But she very much wants him to. Something else she's been thinking about all day. Three days since she met him, but she'd happily take him inside to show him just how slutty she can be.

Or shy, yet willing.

Or helpless . . .

Whatever he wanted.

Music had begun playing as soon as he'd started the car. Something laid back and jazzy, but with a tune, which she likes. She watches him reach to turn it down. He's got perfect fingernails.

He says, 'Thanks for a nice evening. Another one.'

'I aim to please.'

'Oh, you do . . . ' He leans across to kiss her. She parts her lips, but he angles his head at the last moment to kiss her cheek.

She leans away, breathing faster and harder than she can remember in a while. 'OK,' she says.

'Don't want to seem too *needy*.'

'I think I can see how needy you are.' She nods towards his lap, his excitement clearly visible, even beneath the thick denim.

He grins, wolfish, and lowers a hand to cover himself. 'Don't worry, I can sort myself out when I get back to the hotel.'

A line comes into her head and she feels blood rising to her face. She almost says, *Well, call me if you need a hand*, but decides he already knows exactly what she's thinking.

Sarah opens the car door.

'The best things come to those who wait.' Conrad pushes a button and the car purrs into life. 'The best.'

TWELVE

Thorne held up a bottle of wine when Tanner opened the door. 'The finest in the Oddbins reasonably-priced-and-not-too-disgusting range.' He handed his offering across.

Tanner examined the label. 'Excellent. And I've got a few cheap cans of beer in the fridge for you. Let's drown our sorrows.'

'My sorrows, you mean,' Thorne said. 'You've got nothing much to be sorry about, because you weren't expecting it to go anywhere.'

The results of the forensic tests Thorne had been waiting for had come in just before knocking-off time the previous day. The fingerprints belonging to the man who had conned Philippa Goodwin were not on record and his DNA was not on file in the national database.

'OK,' Tanner said. 'So let's not bother naming it and just get hammered.'

She moved back to let Thorne in and stood to one side. Thorne stepped forward, taking care to look straight ahead as he entered, to keep his eyes from the floor while trying not to be too obvious about it. The carpet in Tanner's hallway was no longer brand new, but he remembered the state of the one it had replaced well enough.

The bloodstains and the white spatter where the bleach had spilled.

This was the spot on which Tanner's partner, Susan, had been stabbed to death almost a year and a half earlier.

'Go through and sit down,' Tanner said. 'I'll grab you a beer.'

Thorne did not need to ask if Tanner had tidied up because she was expecting company. The woman simply did not do *un*tidy. If anything, the TV listings magazine lying open on the coffee table and the slippers, side by side next to the couch, made the place appear positively messy in comparison to its normal state of show-home perfection.

'Getting a bit sloppy in your old age,' he said, when she brought his beer in.

'Piss off,' she said. Then, 'What?'

Thorne pointed and Tanner moved quickly to fold and file the magazine beneath the table and gather up the offending footwear. 'Dinner's only going to be five minutes,' she said. 'I just need to heat it up, basically.'

'M and S pasta, is it?'

Tanner raised a finger and turned away, shouting back as she walked towards the kitchen. 'I told you, I'm getting better.'

A running joke, with a dark heart.

While Tanner had always been the organised half of the partnership – the bill-payer, the book-balancer – Susan had most definitely been the one who had done the cooking. Unfortunately, she had also been a little too fond of drinking wine with her meals, breakfast included, and the tensions her addiction had caused between herself and Tanner remained – sadly – unresolved at the time of her death.

Thorne winced at a sudden clattering in the kitchen. He sat down and put away half the beer in his can.

He knew he was not the only one dealing with guilt.

Looking around, the place seemed almost back to the way it had been before an arson attack which had almost cost Tanner her life. Uncluttered, obviously, but still cosy enough. There were now a lot more books lined up on the shelves either side of the fireplace, and he was happy to see that Tanner's colour-coding system was back in evidence once again.

When Tanner's cat, Mrs Slocombe, padded in and dutifully ignored him, Thorne leaned back happily and drank a little more. He could feel himself starting to relax.

'Here you go.'

Tanner came in and laid down a tray on the coffee table. A dish of something that looked appetising enough, some paper serviettes, salt and pepper. She hurried back to the kitchen to fetch her own tray, this one bearing an added roll of kitchen towel, just to be on the safe side.

'Carbonara,' she said. 'Get stuck in.'

'Great . . . '

Thorne lifted the tray on to his lap. He had barely managed a forkful when Tanner said, 'So, what's happening with you and Helen?'

He swallowed fast. 'I thought so.'

Tanner feigned innocence.

'Bloody hell, you haven't even read me my rights yet.'

'No point pissing about,' she said.

As they ate, Thorne told her what there was to tell since the last time, which wasn't much. He and Helen were still 'seeing how things went', they were getting on well enough, he was all right being back in his flat.

'You're missing Alfie though, right?'

Thorne looked at her.

'Well, I mean, course you are. I've seen the two of you together, don't forget.' She laid down her fork. 'Look, I don't know how you want this to turn out and, for all I know, you don't either . . .

but whatever happens, happens. And in the end, it'll probably be the best thing for both of you.'

'That it?'

She nodded and picked up her fork again.

'I tell you this,' Thorne said. 'When the Job goes tits-up, there's an agony column with your name on it.'

The food was good enough for Thorne to ask a beaming Tanner for a second helping. Once that was finished and they'd carried everything through to the kitchen, scraped the few left-overs into the bin and loaded the dishwasher, they moved back into the sitting room. Tanner opened a cupboard housing a mini stereo system and put a CD on. Some bloke with a guitar and a whiny voice, singing a whiny song about whining, but Thorne didn't think it sounded too horrendous.

That was enough to tell him just how relaxed he was.

'Just noise, that's what you said once. Remember? You told me that music was just noise.'

She shrugged. 'Some noises are better than others.'

They sat and listened for half a minute, then Thorne low-ered his voice and said, 'Are you trying to seduce me, Mrs Robinson?'

Tanner stared. 'Mrs *who*?'

Thorne laughed and waved it away. 'Doesn't matter.'

'So, where do you go from here with the Goodwin business? Finding Patrick Jennings.'

'What do you mean, where do I go? I mean, that's the end of it, right?'

'Well, it should be,' Tanner said. 'I know you better than that, though.'

'So, what would *you* do?' Thorne sat forward. 'I know you wouldn't do anything, but ... hypothetically.'

'Why not talk to the ActionFraud team? Find out what their next move's going to be and see if you can get in ahead of them.'

'Right, because that sounds nice and easy.'

'Or you could just let them get on with it. Sit back and wait for them to catch him. Either way, I've sent them all the information we've got.'

'Bloody hell, you don't mess about, do you?'

'I try not to.' An edge was creeping into Tanner's voice.

'Might have been nice if you'd told me, that's all.'

'Russell didn't really give me a lot of choice. Plus, it's the right thing to do.'

'Yeah, if giving up is the right thing to do.'

'Listen to yourself, Tom.'

The look on Tanner's face was enough to bring an end to it. Thorne closed his eyes for a few seconds and leaned back. 'I try not to,' he said. 'I don't half get on my nerves, sometimes.'

The whiny singer gave way to something instrumental – light and Latin-ish – while the beer gave way to a couple more, fuelling an exchange of the latest incident room gossip. A DS whose boy-friend had just been caught with indecent images on his laptop; a CSI who 'ruined' a crime scene thanks to some dodgy prawns the night before; a male DI on another team who now wished to self-identify as a female one.

When Thorne announced that it was time he made a move, Tanner pointed to the empty cans on the coffee table.

'Only if you came on the Tube,' she said.

'Come on, Nic . . .'

'You want to get pulled over, lose your job?'

'What, are you going to make a call?'

Tanner let her breath out slowly. 'The spare room's made up.'

'Thinking ahead,' Thorne said.

'It's always made up.'

Thorne sighed and got slowly to his feet. 'There'd better be a full English waiting for me in the morning.'

'I can do you toast.'

He trudged out into the hallway and began to climb the stairs.

Suddenly, he was tired. He turned on the landing to see Tanner below him, already double locking the front door.

'So, what would you have done if I'd got in my car then? Would you have done anything?'

She looked up at him. 'I would have been ... conflicted.'

Thorne leaned against the banister. Thinking: *You weren't too conflicted seven months ago, when both of us were bleeding. In that flat, with a poker in your hand ...*

He said, 'So, any more thoughts? About this place?'

'Yeah,' Tanner said. 'I think I'll stay put for the time being.'

Thorne nodded. 'Whatever makes you happy.' An insurance policy had paid off the mortgage after Susan's death and Tanner now owned the two-storey house in Hammersmith outright, but it was too big for her. Felt too big. Seven months before, she had been looking to move, had been viewing suitable flats.

Until she had walked into the wrong one.

Until life – death – had got in the way.

Thorne said goodnight and opened the door to Tanner's spare room. A towel had been laid out at the foot of the bed, from where the cat sat staring at him, stock-still and daring him to shift her.

'Don't *you* fucking start,' Thorne said.

THIRTEEN

Margate

'Sorry . . . ?'

It sounds to her like the boy's voice, reedy enough to begin with, has gone up an octave or something.

'I said, do you want to go for a walk?'

Michelle takes a pace back to allow a small group coming out of the bar to move between them. Then she steps back towards the boy. He isn't going to say no, she's sure of that much, but still, it annoys her that she's having to wait.

'Bloody hell,' he says.

'What?'

'I mean—'

'It's not a big deal.'

'No.' He flicks what's left of his cigarette towards the gutter, but it doesn't quite make it. 'Course not.'

'It's not like my evening's ruined if you don't.'

She can already see how much of a big deal it is to him. She wonders how many men – of any age – she would need to proposition before she found one who would turn her offer down. A good many, *she's certain of that, and, not for the first time, she asks herself why most men are so ... pathetic.*

'I should probably let my mates know,' he says.

'Seriously?'

'Well, I don't have *to.' The boy takes another quick swig of his alco-pop. 'I don't suppose it really matters.'*

Perhaps pathetic *is too strong a word, she decides. The truth is that she doesn't believe women are necessarily any choosier than men, just that they like to pretend they are. It's simply that, if a woman wants sex badly enough, she pretty much just has to go out and ask. OK, so maybe she'll weigh up the available options a little more carefully than her male counterpart, but in the end it's there for the taking, if she fancies it. Men seem rather more ... indiscriminate, because they're made to work that much harder and get used to being knocked back, so they're hardly likely to turn down an offer when it falls into their laps.*

Way of the world, isn't it?

Same way a dog will eat whatever's put in front of him, just in case it's the last meal he's going to get.

'How long d'you think we're going to be?'

She's aware, of course, that there is still time to walk away. To find a different bar and just raise a glass or two instead. It's a good plan, she knows that, a plan that will work, so maybe getting to this point is all that she needs.

She says, 'Well ... '

She knows that for some people, just to get this close, to know that they could have done it if they'd wanted to, would be enough.

Not for her, though. Not now.

Michelle says, 'We'll have to see how it goes, won't we?'

FOURTEEN

Sarah retrieves the small metal box from behind assorted pots of paint and dusty bottles of drain cleaner and windscreen wash. She takes out one of the pre-rolled joints, lowers herself into a ripped and ratty deckchair and lights up. The fan heater hasn't really kicked in yet, so it's seriously cold in the garage, but she has to come out here to smoke.

She can't have the smell in the house.

She doesn't want the dog-walking woman or the window-cleaner or whoever else catching a whiff and calling Social Services. They'd be doing the right thing, she knows that, and she would probably do the same. A house stinking of weed is definitely not the ideal environment in which a single mother should raise a six-year-old, but no official knock at the door is ever going to work out well for her.

It's decent stuff, bought from one of the older kids in the park near Brooklands Hill before pick-up, and she feels it start to kick in after the second hit. The drift and then the lightness moving through her.

She lays her head back and thinks about him, about what she'd said in the restaurant and the way he'd reacted. What was in his eyes and what was coming off him. She thinks about the side of him he seemed so keen for her to see and those other things he couldn't hide.

About every awful thing she'd wanted, sitting there just an hour before in his big, shiny car.

She reaches for her phone and sends him a text: **have u sorted yourself out yet?** She stares at the screen, waiting for a reply.

She tries to remember the last time she'd felt remotely like this about anyone, then gives up, because she's sure that she never has. Desire, yes, because everyone needed that lovely itch scratching once in a while, but this sort of connection is not one she recognises. She starts to wonder if it's him and not the weed that's making her feel so light-headed and couldn't-give-a-monkey's reckless. So ready to abandon herself. She laughs out loud.

He terrifies her too, of course.

Not *him*, not who he is or what he wants, but the power he so obviously has to transform her, whether he knows it yet or not. To create a very different kind of desire; one that's taken hold so quickly it's ridiculous and feels so much more overpowering than anything physical.

Yes, *way* stronger than that, even as she pictures him lying in bed.

Conrad, or whatever his real name is.

Because what really frightens her, what sucks the breath from her when she so much as thinks about it, is that she wants, more than anything, to tell him the truth.

There's certainly no chocolate on his pillow and nothing in the bathroom anyone would fancy taking home. A sliver of soap in plastic and a few miniature bottles of shampoo from the market. It's a turn-up for the books that there's even a remote for the TV and that the sheets have been cleaned, considering how cheap the place is.

He could have afforded to splash out a little, of course, considering his recent windfall, but he's always been thrifty, never seen the point in throwing money around for the sake of it.

Maybe next time, he thinks. After this one has paid out.

He sits at the semicircle of MDF attached to the wall that passes for a desk and opens his notebook. It's still a little early to make a viable plan, obviously – he needs to get to know the mark first – but it doesn't hurt to be prepared. Sometimes the perfect opportunity to make his pitch comes well before he'd thought it would, because, in an ideal world, *they're* the ones who dictate the pace. That last one was hugely keen, almost caught him with his pants down. From the first moment he'd mentioned that lecture business, she was practically begging to throw her money at him.

Candy, baby, whatever.

The alert sounds on his phone. He picks it up and reads her text. It doesn't look as though this one will take very long either.

He starts to make notes. A few areas of interest to think about, the kind of thing that might tickle her up a bit. She's arty, stands to reason, so that's where he needs to start. Some kind of publishing thing would be an obvious one, maybe a company that specialises in undiscovered talent. That might be the thing, but he knows less than nothing about it, so he'll need to do more than his usual amount of homework.

He's not sure where to start . . .

He looks at her message once more. It makes him want to climb straight back on to that skinny hard bed and sort himself out all over again.

He should probably go online and get the basics about a few books as well, make out like he's keen on reading. Some proper novels, he decides, not just airport thrillers or whatever. He needs to sound passionate, because that's what always gees them up, gets their purses open.

He fires off a reply: **Yeah and guess who I was thinking about?**

Still thinking about, is the truth. The shape and the smell of her, something dirty when she laughs and the way she'd opened her mouth when he leaned across in the car.

He tears out the page, the few scribbled notes, and screws it up. There was nothing much to get excited about, he knows that, but still he's shocked, because the truth is, his heart isn't in it. He can't do the work. Because that's not the way he's thinking about her, hasn't been since she sat down next to him in that cinema.

He's kidding himself, because he felt something happening the first time she looked at him in the coffee shop.

An instinct he ignored and a voice he didn't listen to, telling him to run.

Christ, he thinks, there's a first for everything, and how's this going to pan out, and he doesn't really care, and his phone is still in his hand while he sits like a horny sixteen-year-old and waits for her to send him a message in response.

His mind on nothing but Sarah; what she's thinking, feeling, what she wants. Not how much she might be worth and not how much he can take her for.

For the first time since he was old enough to pull, not that.

FIFTEEN

By the time Thorne slipped quietly into the back of the crematorium, the funeral had already begun. He closed the door as carefully as he could and took his seat. He picked up an order of service from the empty chair next to him and stared down at the picture of the young woman on the front; one taken during her student days, it looked like. The cliché came unbidden and impossible to ignore.

Her whole life in front of her.

Thorne turned the page and glanced through the contents.

It was a humanist ceremony and Thorne saw that he'd missed the officiant's opening remarks and the singing of 'Amazing Grace', a tribute from friends after the plain wooden coffin had been carried in to the strains of 'Everybody Hurts' by REM.

He wondered about that. Hadn't the song been written for someone contemplating suicide? Perhaps the dead woman had simply liked the song and picked it well before she'd made that decision. Maybe others had made the choice, unaware of its connotations and without listening very carefully to the lyrics. Or perhaps those closest to Philippa Goodwin had seen no reason to shy away from the truth and known exactly what the song was about, which was precisely why they'd chosen it.

Either way, it was a nice song and it could easily have been worse.

They hadn't plumped for 'Going Underground' by The Jam.

While the minister – a smiley, middle-aged woman – gave the address, Thorne looked around. Aside from a couple of rows at the back, the place was full, a hundred people, maybe. It was usually the way, he thought, after a premature or unexpected death. The crowds began to thin out the longer friends and relatives clung on. Craning his head, he saw Mary and Ella Fulton on the front row next to a man he presumed was Mary's husband, and an elderly couple; an uncle and aunt, perhaps.

The celebrant spoke over a litany of sobs and sniffles.

Once she had finished giving her thoughts on life and death – with no mention made of a life taken by choice – Mary Fulton stepped forward to pay tribute to her sister. She fingered the delicate silver chain around her neck as she described a woman who had been generous and full of life, who had always tried to see the best in people. She paused briefly at that point and Thorne had a good idea what was going through her mind. *Who.* Then it was Ella's turn to stand up and read a poem, which she struggled to reach the end of.

Better by far you should forget and smile,
Than that you should remember and be sad . . .

The committal came after a minute or so of silent reflection and then the room slowly began to empty, the sobs and scraping of chairs just audible above a piece of classical music by Elgar, which Thorne was surprised to recognise. Perhaps he'd heard it on some advert, he thought.

Outside, he joined the mourners gathering to look at the floral tributes lined up near the doors, inching along and stooping to read what had been written. It was at this point, he thought – in films or crime novels – that one message in particular might catch the detective's eye. Something cryptic, scribbled by person or persons unknown, that might give a clue as to why any of them were there at all.

Of course, there was nothing of the sort.

Gone too soon.

Miss you, Pip.

Sleep well, my darling.

Thorne turned to see Ella Fulton walking towards him and, without being altogether sure why, he stepped away from the others and across to her, so that they would not be overheard.

'It's really nice of you to be here,' she said.

'It's no problem.'

'Is it . . . I mean, is that normal?'

Thorne could not give her any good reason why he was there. Having taken the decision to dig out his black suit, he had toyed with the possibility that Patrick Jennings himself might decide to turn up. He had certainly known sociopaths, such as Jennings probably was, to do the same thing in the past. Almost immediately, of course, he had seen how ridiculous the notion was. A man like that would have been away on his toes as quickly as possible, would in all likelihood have already moved on to his next victim.

On top of which, unless he showed up in disguise, he would have been recognised by Ella Fulton and her mother.

'I wanted to come,' Thorne said.

'Well, it's lovely that you did.'

They turned together to watch the mourners, several now moving away towards the car park. Others were lining up to make donations to the Humanist Society or shake hands with the minister. Mary Fulton and her husband were hugging each other in the doorway.

'Do you mind if I ask you about the song?' Thorne said.

She looked at him.

'The REM . . .'

'I chose it,' Ella said.

'Right. I was wondering, that's all.'

'Pip would have thought it was funny, I know she would. Besides, she hated bullshit.' She looked down for a few seconds, nosed the toe of her shiny black shoe through the gravel. 'Makes it all the more ridiculous that she fell for it. Fell for *him*. You know?'

'He must have been very convincing,' Thorne said.

'He would have had to be.'

'Well, I think we can be pretty sure he's done it before.'

She nodded and lowered her voice. 'So, did you find out anything?'

Thorne saw that Mary Fulton was hovering, clearly keen to speak to her daughter about something. She nodded and smiled at Thorne. He raised a hand.

'I'm not really sure this is the place . . . '

'Can we talk on the phone then? I'd like to know what's happening.'

'Of course.'

'Or perhaps you could come over, if you're not too busy. For tea, or whatever. Have you got my address?' She unzipped a handbag and began to dig around.

'I'm sure I can find it,' Thorne said.

'Right.' Ella closed her bag, smiling as she stepped backwards. 'You're trained for that sort of thing, aren't you?'

Thorne turned and walked away, exchanging a nod with the driver of a hearse that was already pulling up, bearing the next customer in line. He had taken off the black tie by the time he reached his car.

SIXTEEN

Today, Sarah's even happier than usual to join them in the coffee shop after drop-off, to sit with Savita, Heather, Caroline and soppy David. Savita had beckoned her over to the top table the moment she'd come through the door in fact and Caroline had shuffled her seat across to make room. What a welcome! There's no sign of dishy Alex this morning, but that doesn't matter because she's not thinking about him any more and there's certainly no need to bring the laptop out, to look as if she's 'writing', because she's far too busy on her phone.

She and Conrad have been texting since she woke up.

Once the drinks and the cakes are delivered, Savita and the others are keen to make conversation. Leaning towards her, conspiratorially, desperate to know what's going on. The big secret she's so obviously itching to share with them. The smile she can't keep from her face. The mystery man she'd been talking to in here the week before.

It's so rare and thrilling to be the centre of attention and she's determined to milk it for all she's worth. To be fair, she can hardly blame them for wanting to know. They can clearly sense what's happening to her, the magnitude of it, so it's only natural they should want her to toss a morsel or two their way.

Another message arrives.

OK. Done film done dinner so what next?

Sarah holds the phone close to her face so that they can't see the screen, but she can feel their eyes on her as she replies.

what do u think?

'Somebody looks happy,' Savita says.

She nods and smiles. 'Well, this cake is seriously gorgeous.'

'Yeah, right.' Savita rolls her eyes at Heather. 'The cake.'

The message alert pings again. She could have turned the sound off, of course, but she wants them to hear. Every time.

Theatre?

She says, 'So, I'm in a good mood, so what?' as she's typing her reply.

ecch!

'It's a man,' Caroline says. 'It's so obviously a man. Should have seen her mooning around yesterday at pick-up.'

'I wasn't *mooning*,' she laughs. 'I was probably just looking bored waiting for my bloody son, as usual.'

'Why does it have to be a man?' Heather asks. 'Maybe it's a work thing.'

They wait, but she's not going to make things easy for them.

'Is it a work thing?' Heather asks.

Sarah says nothing.

A gallery or something?

'Told you,' Caroline says. 'Of *course* it's a man. Look at her.'

double ecchh!!!

'So anyway ... how's Jamie doing?' Bloody David, the one least interested in the gossip. The one who's always banging on about Ofsted or pastoral care or something equally dull.

'He's good,' she says.

'Great.'

'Driving me mental, obviously, and he's never where he's supposed to be.' David seems keen to continue the pointless conversation, but she's saved by the arrival of another message and focuses on her phone for half a minute.

Help me out here.

i'm sure u can think of something.

I can think of LOTS of things . . .

She hesitates. She's thinking about just replying with a smiley face to match her own, but she's not a child.

'Is it that bloke who was in here?' Caroline asks. 'Wednesday, was it?'

'I don't know who you're talking about,' David says.

'You remember . . . wearing a cap. They were talking. I think I've seen him in here once or twice before, actually.'

'Really?' Heather shakes her head. 'I can't say I do.'

Caroline turns to look at Heather. 'Actually, I'd got it into my head he was a friend of *yours*.'

Sarah glances up from her phone.

Heather seems amazed. She says, 'Well, I don't know where you got that from. I'd never clapped eyes on the bloke until the other day.'

'My mistake,' Caroline says.

'Either way, he looked nice,' Savita says. 'Fit.'

Caroline sips her coffee. 'Yes, I suppose you'd have to admit that much. You know, if you were looking.'

Sarah stabs at the keyboard, thinking: *You could look all you bloody well like and it wouldn't do you any good, because he was looking at me.*

i bet you can

'Good for you,' Savita says. 'I mean, I didn't know you *were* looking, but as long as you're happy.'

Sarah lays down her phone, just for a few seconds, to fork in a mouthful of cake. Happy? She feels mad with it, and bound up by it, by him. She feels like she's on the edge of something and, even though she knows that it's dangerous, that she might even be out of her depth, she's never known a rush that comes close. She's buzzing, *boiling* with it.

She feels utterly invincible.

I could come to your place.

'Bloody hell,' Savita says, when the alert sounds again. 'I hope you've got plenty of battery on that.'

Another message arrives almost immediately: **Well?**

Heather can barely control herself. She leans in close and wriggles like she might wet herself with excitement. 'So, come on then.' She actually claps her hands. 'Details, woman, details.'

Sarah grins while she's considering how much to let slip. It would be churlish not to give them something, and besides, she desperately wants them to know. She shrugs and says, 'It's . . . early days,' as she's sending a reply.

i wondered when you'd get round to that!

Heather says, 'Yes,' and pumps her fist like she's scored a goal or something, while Savita sits nodding happily. Caroline, though, is half turned away, saying something to David and pretending that she's already lost interest. Like none of this is particularly important, like *Sarah* is not important.

Sarah wants to lean across and pour hot coffee into the woman's lap.

Savita raises her own coffee cup like it's a champagne glass. '*You*, Sarah, are such a dark horse.'

SEVENTEEN

Ella Fulton lived midway between Archway and Highbury Corner, on a narrow side street off the Holloway Road; the top floor of a drab, three-storey block. Climbing up the noisy metal stairs after being buzzed in, Thorne guessed that the place had once been an office building of some sort; council, maybe.

Utilitarian, re-branded as edgy, and doubtless horribly expensive.

'Used to be the local dole office, apparently.' Ella had been waiting for him at the top of the stairs, and Thorne had asked the question as she'd shown him in to her flat. 'Still has some of that intimidating charm.'

'Blimey,' Thorne said, looking around a space that clearly occupied the entire floor of the building. He was breathing a little more heavily than he would have liked.

There were photographs everywhere. Poster-sized and hung in frames, leaning against the bare brick walls or stacked in trays on either side of a huge computer screen on the desk. Thorne could see immediately that many of the images featured local landmarks. He recognised the listed exterior of Holloway Road tube station behind the young Rasta gurning at the camera, his mouth filled with gold teeth. An old couple kissed on the canalside next to the Islington Tunnel and a homeless woman lay sprawled among bags in the doorway of Argos at Nag's Head. Other shots were non-figurative: blasted trees and rusting metal; the sky reflected in dirty puddles or rainbow-slicks of petrol.

'Flat-cum-studio,' Ella said.

She was wearing jeans and a comfy-looking cardigan that came down to her knees. Crocs and socks. Her hair, which had been curling around her shoulders the first time they'd met, was tied up rather more loosely than it had been at the funeral two days before. Thorne nodded towards one of the photographs. The camera equipment he could see lying around was enough of a clue, even for a detective having a bad day, but he asked anyway. 'So, did you . . . ?'

'Yeah, but sadly, these aren't what pay the mortgage.'

'OK.'

'I make videos, as well. You know . . . arty, black and white shit without a plot, but nobody wants to pay me for that, either.'

'So . . . ?'

'I take pictures of food.'

'Really?'

'Really. If you can eat it, I've shot it.'

'What, like in magazines?'

'Sometimes, but that's not the bread and butter stuff.'

'You take pictures of bread and butter?'

'Oh, I have done,' Ella said. 'I do stuff for menus, mostly.'

'Classy,' Thorne said.

She laughed. 'Well, it depends where you're eating, doesn't it? I've done some swanky places, but I've also done those pictures above the counter in kebab shops. So . . . '

'Doesn't matter where it is,' Thorne said. 'The food never tastes as good as it looks in the photo.'

'Yeah, well there's a good reason for that.'

As he continued to move slowly around, looking at Ella's photographs, she followed, talking him through a few of the food-stylist's secrets; the tricks of her trade. Ice cream was more often than not mashed potatoes and food colouring, she told him. Cakes were decorated with paint, while grapes were made to look dusty and delicious using talcum powder.

'So, what about kebabs, then?' Thorne asked. 'I know that people have usually had a few when they're buying one, but they always look so tasty and . . . shiny.'

'Motor oil,' she said.

Thorne saw that there were books about photography piled up on several tables and a collection of vintage cameras displayed along the wooden bench that ran beneath a grimy, full-length window.

'I know, I'm basically a hoarder.' Ella walked across to pick up one of the old cameras. She wiped something off the lens and gently set it down again. 'It's all a bit chaotic, to be honest.'

'Same as your aunt,' Thorne said.

'Absolutely.' Ella smiled. 'She reckoned it was all about being creative.'

'Her kitchen was spotless, though.'

'Yeah, well at least I don't have to worry about that, because I haven't got one.'

'There's no kitchen?'

'Bed and shower up there . . . ' She pointed to the spiral staircase in one corner, a smaller mezzanine level above. 'And the rest of the place is for work. So, do you want tea, or something?'

'I thought you said—'

'I do have . . . facilities.'

She walked across to the desk, which was when Thorne spotted the small fridge next to it, a plastic kettle and a box of tea bags sitting on top. She flicked the kettle on and took a carton of milk from the fridge, then reached up to the bookshelf above for two mugs.

'I eat out a lot,' she said.

When the tea was ready, Ella carried the mugs across to where Thorne was staring at some photos that he'd missed, on the wall by the door. A flock of umbrellas on Waterloo Bridge. A street performer shot from behind, the awestruck expression of a toddler, watching. 'These are great,' he said. He looked at her, wanting her to know that he meant it.

'Thanks,' she said.

Art of any sort always unnerved Thorne a little, made him feel as though he was out of his depth, but he'd always preferred photographs to paintings. They seemed more honest, *touched* him – he supposed that was the word – though he knew how much the likes of Phil Hendricks would take the mickey if he ever said as much out loud.

'They're not shiny kebabs, but you know . . . '

He turned to see a series of photographs arranged on the opposite wall. A row of abandoned and derelict underground trains. The washed-out carriages were twisted and covered in graffiti, while the pictures taken inside showed seats that were torn and sodden, littered with fragments of glass smashed from the windows. It looked like a graveyard.

'I should probably take those down,' Ella said.

They sat on a worn leather Chesterfield, a multicoloured throw tossed across the back. Elsewhere in the building, laughter was echoing from a stairwell and they heard a siren grow loud outside, then fade as an emergency vehicle raced south.

Thorne said, 'I wish I could tell you that we got anywhere, or that I've got any ideas about where to go next.'

'Patrick Jennings . . . '

'We managed to get his prints and a DNA profile, but he isn't in the system.'

'Right.'

'I mean there's always a chance he'll do something stupid at some point in the future. If he's arrested for *anything*, we've got him.'

84

'He never struck me as particularly stupid,' Ella said.

'No.'

'So, that's it?'

'Well, ActionFraud are obviously going to be looking at it. We've passed all the information on.'

'They're good, are they?'

'There's nobody better equipped.' Thorne looked away briefly. Wasn't that exactly what Brigstocke had told him, before Thorne had chosen to take matters into his own hands? Before he had decided to proceed as though he was chasing a murderer? 'Something we've sent them might tie in with intelligence they already have, you never know. I'm sure Pip wasn't the first woman he's fooled. Oh, and that doesn't mean she was . . . '

'I know she wasn't stupid.'

'What your mum said in church, remember? Men like Patrick Jennings prey on people who aren't cynical.'

'She was lonely,' Ella said. 'She couldn't afford to be cynical.'

Thorne downed what was left of his tea and sat forward. He was wondering how cynical, or otherwise, Ella Fulton might be. 'Obviously, if I hear anything I'll let you know.'

Ella stood up and took Thorne's empty mug from him. 'Thanks again for coming the other day. It meant a lot to my mum.'

'So, are you going to tell her?' Thorne got to his feet. 'That we're no closer to finding Jennings than we were?'

'I'm not sure there's much point,' Ella said. 'Whatever she thought about him, I think she's still finding it very hard to handle the idea that Pip was tricked like that, you know? How that must have made her feel. That she was driven to it. However obvious it looks, my mother can't really cope with that. She hasn't talked about it much since that time we were at Pip's flat, to be honest. Like it's easier for her to believe that Pip was just . . . ill.'

'Everyone deals with this stuff differently.' Thorne looked at her, waited.

'Oh, I just go out and take pictures,' she said. 'And imagine taking Patrick Jennings's balls off with a hacksaw.'

Back at Becke House, Thorne found Tanner at her desk. He pulled a chair across and kept his voice down.

'Not sure this is something that ever comes up in the exams, but I was just wondering . . . '

She turned to look at him.

'What's the protocol . . . I mean, are there any guidelines as such when it comes to getting involved to any . . . extent with someone who's related to a suicide victim?'

He had Tanner's attention. 'Romantically involved?'

'Yeah, as an example.'

'This would be Philippa Goodwin's niece?'

'I popped over there,' Thorne said. 'To let her know what was happening. What *wasn't* happening.'

'Because you couldn't do it over the phone?'

Thorne inched his chair a little closer. 'Look, I've probably read it all wrong, what do I know? But she was definitely a bit . . . it felt *flirty*.'

'How old is she?'

'I don't know, mid-forties?' Younger than he was, but older than Helen, which was something. The age gap was one of the things Helen's sister had taken issue with, if she had actually been taking issue with anything, of course. Thorne could no longer be sure.

Tanner nodded as though she was considering the question.

'Nothing's happened or anything. I was just thinking, that's all, and I wanted to run it past you.'

'Seriously?' The look on Tanner's face did not bode well.

'Just out of interest.'

'OK, so let's say we get lucky and we, or another team, do manage to catch Patrick Jennings.' She looked at him. 'You see where I'm going with this? There's a trial, for fraud or maybe even manslaughter, because that's what you want, yes? And this woman who you've been getting *flirty* with is going to be a witness, isn't she? A very important witness, probably. I can't swear to it, but I think there are plenty of guidelines when it comes to officers getting involved with witnesses in their own cases.'

Thorne watched as Tanner turned back to whatever she'd been doing before. 'I knew I should have asked somebody else,' he said.

'Come on, you knew the answer before you asked me.'

Thorne grunted.

'No need to feel bad about it,' Tanner said. 'What with this strange situation between you and Helen, now you're living apart. You're just testing yourself.'

'Am I?'

'Seems like that to me. And you passed.'

'Something, I suppose,' Thorne said, eventually. 'I'm not usually that good at passing tests.'

EIGHTEEN

They have a quick drink first, in the less-than-lovely pub at the bottom of her road, but it's not as if they need it. It's something to do beforehand, that's all. A small pretence, which each of them is happy to play along with, because they both know exactly what's going to happen.

Because good things come to those who wait, even if it's only for a little while longer.

They hardly speak at all. Sarah likes the fact that he looks ready for it, that he's trying hard not to seem nervous. Her own heart is like something with wings, trapped inside a house and smashing itself against the window, and she's grateful for every mouthful of wine, as her mouth dries up within seconds of swallowing.

It's like waiting to step off a cliff.

'I'm done,' he says, when his drink is finished.

She says, 'I seriously hope not.'

They walk along her road in silence, not touching, like they're just two friends out for an early-evening stroll. Sarah thinks how perfect it would be if she was to bump into one of the mums from school – Caroline, in an ideal world – but she sees nobody she knows. Not even a neighbour. She looks hopefully at each house as they pass, but there is not so much as a twitching curtain.

It doesn't matter, but it might have been a nice bonus.

He steps through her front door and bends to make a fuss of her dog when it scampers to meet her. She claps her hands and ushers the dog into the kitchen, quickly unlocks the back door and lets it out into the garden. When she comes back to him, he is still standing in the hall, looking around. 'Very nice,' he says.

'I earned it,' she says, taking off her scarf.

'You've got good taste, I mean. I really like it.' He nods approvingly and walks through to the kitchen, like he owns the place.

She's made an effort to tidy up, of course. Jamie's toys and games have been gathered from the floor and piled into a plastic box in the corner. Every surface is gleaming, and she made sure to spray something nice around before she left the house. There are candles burning. In the bathroom and the bedroom, too.

Everything is clean and fresh and smells wonderful.

Sarah had remembered how it was in his car, so guessed that he wouldn't want it any other way.

For the first time, she thinks, he appears a little awkward, and she loves it that he's finally showing a hint of nervousness. She wants to be the one in control, to begin with anyway. Later on, he can make the running, if that's the way he prefers it. She steps across and holds out a hand to take his jacket, the thin leather one she really likes. He takes it off and adjusts the collar of his shirt. He's wearing the cufflinks she'd spotted that first time in the coffee shop.

Hard to believe it was just over a week ago.

She leans back against the worktop and says, 'We could have coffee.'

'Yeah, we could.'

'We could do all sorts of things.'

'All sorts of things sounds good to me.'

It's hard to be sure which one of them makes the first move, leans in slightly or angles their body just enough, but in the end they come together hard, and by now the smiles have gone, because this is serious business; the grabbing and moaning.

Tongues and teeth.

She grunts and tugs at his shirt trying to free it from the waistband of his jeans, while his hands are already busy below her own. They grind, and pull, and lick. She starts on his belt, as he brings his hands up fast, her blouse coming with them, like he's trying to pull it over her head . . .

'Stop.'

Sarah steps away and turns, unbuttoning, then walks towards the bedroom expecting him to follow.

The first time is quick and urgent, but both get what they want. Sarah has condoms in the small cupboard next to the bed, but neither of them brings the subject up and it's fine, because even though she's happy to take the risk, such as it is, he doesn't come inside her.

They barely take a breath.

They slow things up and take the time to explore, mouths and fingers, until both of them are desperate for it. They change positions and move each other around on the bed, they tell each other what they want. This time, when he tries to pull out, she holds him inside her, rising to him; shakes her head when he looks at her to find out if she's sure.

At that moment, she is certain, because something has . . . shifted.

Afterwards, they laugh and move slowly apart, rearranging the tangle of sheets until they are still and their breath has returned.

'Like I said, good things are worth waiting for.'

'Great things,' she says, and moves her leg until it's touching his.

'Oh, God, yeah . . . '

They lie in silence for a minute, two, then she turns her head. 'I know your name's not Conrad.'

He turns his.

'And I'm pretty sure these investors of yours don't really exist, not in the way most people would think, anyway. That there isn't actually anything to invest in.' Her hand reaches quickly for his and squeezes. 'And it's fine, it's absolutely fine. Just, you don't need to carry on spinning it out with me, that's all.'

'You think you know what I do?'

His voice is so calm suddenly that it frightens her, but the fear is exciting and she dares herself to nod.

'You think you *know*?'

'I can guess,' Sarah says. 'And it doesn't matter. I swear, right this minute, I can't think of anything I care about less.'

He turns away and closes his eyes for a while. 'So, should I carry on calling you *Sarah*?'

'Why wouldn't you?'

'Well, there doesn't seem much point, not now we're getting things out in the open. If we're really being straight with each other.' His voice sounds different, coarser somehow, but she likes the way it sounds. 'That's what we're doing, right?'

She moves closer to him. 'How can we not?'

'So ... I'll call you Sarah if it makes you happy, I'll call you anything you want. Long as you're not kidding yourself, because I know damn well it's not what you're called.'

'It's just a name,' she says.

He opens his eyes and turns his head again and their faces are almost touching. They breathe into each other's mouths. He says, 'Same as I know that nobody plays with those toys out there in the kitchen.'

NINETEEN

She stands naked and perfectly still in the semi-dark, the fridge cool against her back. The dog is barking outside and scratching at the kitchen door to be let in, but Sarah ignores it. In truth, she barely registers the noise.

She is remembering a morning many years before.

The excitement, and what the excitement became.

The girl she had been back then and the man her father showed himself to be . . .

He is already grinning when she charges down the stairs as soon as the sun is up, a grin almost as wide as hers, as any good girl would have on a special morning like this. The card he produces with a flourish says MY BIRTHDAY GIRL *and she tries to look pleased when she opens it and reads the funny poem inside, but they both know that she's only really thinking about one thing.*

The special present he promised her.

He smiles, like he's made her wait long enough, then nods towards the back door. She throws it open and tears out into the garden where she knows her new bike will be waiting, and she sees it straight away.

It takes a moment for her to fully understand, because it looks so . . . stupid, and she turns round to see her father watching from the doorway. She looks back, but it still doesn't make any sense. The only part of her new bike that is visible are the handlebars.

Just the handlebars, sticking up from the ground, because the rest of the bike has been buried.

Sarah wraps her arms around herself. She is starting to get cold.

Nobody plays with those toys . . .

Lying there next to Conrad, she had felt herself freeze when he had said what he had, but it had been no more than momentary. A version of something she lives in terror of hearing, daily; the knowing remark, the veiled suggestion from this busybody or that concerned parent. Sarah has rehearsed any number of different responses.

Shock, anger, outrage . . .

A few minutes before, her skin hot against his, she had been able to do no more than whisper, 'How did you know?'

And he had blinked and said, 'How did *you*?'

She had slipped quickly from the bed after that and walked from the room, feeling his eyes on her at every step as she struggled to stay upright, to keep it together.

She had needed time alone – just a few minutes, no more – to process and settle, to wait until her guts had stopped jumping and the scream inside her head had died away. Until that panic button had been reset.

She stands, still not quite able to believe it, as the hum of the fridge moves through her.

It's impossible, she thinks, a million to one.

A week before it was only her and her story, him in a different place with a story of his own. Neither of them aware that each was moving slowly towards the other, that however outrageous the odds, every single thing was about to change.

That any of this was coming.

Sarah turns and opens the fridge, takes out a bottle of water and a plate of cold, leftover chicken which she carries back into the bedroom. She climbs back into bed and they eat with their hands, wiping their greasy fingers on the sheets and on each other. She can't remember the last time she enjoyed food – *any-thing* – as much, as if every taste and touch has been intensified. She can feel the air moving across her skin, the thread in the cotton sheets and the places where they're sticky. She watches him chew and swallow, the muscles working in his neck and jaw and she feels dizzy with it, almost weightless; a thrill that vibrates in every bone and sings in her blood, because he knows her.

Truly.

Because he has *seen* her.

When the food is finished, they fuck again. There's something almost vicious about it this time, but it's nothing that they aren't both eager for. They demand and comply, all gentleness forgotten, and they don't stop until they're exhausted and slick with sweat.

The moment they're done, Sarah straddles him and pushes herself up. She says, 'This means something, doesn't it?'

'It means I won't be able to piss straight for a week.'

'Seriously.'

He reaches for her hands and squeezes. 'It means *everything*.'

'I need to know I can count on you,' she says. 'To be sure that you're not going to let me down.'

'Why would—?'

'Too many other men have promised not to hurt me.'

'I'm not other men.'

'No,' Sarah says. 'You're not.'

He shifts slightly beneath her. 'So . . .'

She sits up higher on him and claps her hands like an over-excited child. 'We should celebrate,' she says. 'We should celebrate *this* . . .'

'If you like.'

Sarah smacks him on the arm and laughs when he winces.

'Of *course* we should.' She pushes damp strands of hair from her face and stares, unblinking at the padded headboard, serious suddenly. 'Because this is special, don't you think?'

'Definitely.'

'So, we should do . . . something we're always going to remember.' She leans towards him, her hands pressing down on to his chest. 'Something together. We need to *mark* this.'

He thinks for a few seconds, then says, 'What about a trip to the seaside?'

'I love the seaside.'

'There you go, then. Seaside it is.'

Sarah's smile flashes just for a second, then creeps back to stay. She says, 'Perfect,' and lowers herself slowly until her head is resting just below his collarbone, and her lips move against his neck as she speaks. '*You* are perfect.'

TWENTY

It had been a while since he and Hendricks had been to a north London derby together and it was only a shame, Thorne decided, that it hadn't been a better match. Or even a half-decent one. It was their custom, despite the fierce split in allegiances, to sit together among the home fans at whatever ground the fixture was taking place, so a Monday night game at the Emirates meant Thorne had been forced to endure the cheers and chants of the Arsenal fans surrounding him in the Clock End. Though his fellow Tottenham fans had not been far away, he had been able to do no more than hunker down amidst the banks of red and white; keeping any partisan critique well under his breath and wondering how he would combat the urge to celebrate when Spurs scored.

He needn't have worried.

The rivals had ground out a largely tedious nil-nil draw, only marginally redeemed by a sending-off five minutes from time.

'Now that,' Hendricks said as they pushed towards the exit, 'was a *famine* of football.'

Notwithstanding the lacklustre display from both teams, Hendricks had certainly enjoyed himself. He had known many of those sitting around him and, when he hadn't been joining in with the community whingeing or tuneless bellowing, he'd enjoyed nodding towards Thorne and pointing out that they had the enemy in their midst. It had all been good-natured enough, though Hendricks did have the decency to look uncomfortable when a few of those nearby had cottoned on and begun to chant 'Yiddo.'

Thorne had always believed that, provided you weren't paying very close attention, his friend looked rather more like a stereotypical football fan than he did. The shaved head, tattoos, whatever. The piercings that were visible marked him out though, of course, and on closer inspection the tats were a little more ... artistic than some of those on show around him. The Union Jacks rippling on necks or bellies. The badly inked cannons and, more disturbingly, the shields and crosses of the Football Lads Alliance or the English Defence League.

Thorne had seen rather more of those around since the result of the Brexit referendum.

They walked beneath the railway arch, a choir of cheerful Gooners singing nearby as they negotiated the horse-shit. Headed to their regular post-match haunt, they carried on past the Che Guevara, where many fans gathered before the games, to listen to South American music or more likely ogle the under-dressed Latina bar staff. The journey always reminded Thorne of others he'd taken a long time ago; the walk home from White Hart Lane with his father. Things had been very different then, and not just because of the rattles and scarves, the pies and Bovril at half time.

His old man talking ten to the dozen, singing and full of it.

Crossing the Seven Sisters Road, they spotted the white Maserati which had been illegally parked in the same spot after every match for as long as Thorne could remember.

'I'm going to find a traffic warden one of these days.' He was still sulking at the temporary hiatus in gloating rights. 'Grass that twat up.'

'Or you could just key it.'

Thorne had heard worse ideas.

'Tell you what, why don't you do it next time your boys beat us? The way they played tonight, I reckon he'll be all right for a couple of seasons . . . '

Despite the speed with which they'd left the stadium, plenty had beaten them to it and The Swimmer was already packed with fans. Thorne pushed his way towards the bar, waving at the barman above the heads of the small crowd gathered around a curly-haired comedian he recognised.

They carried their drinks outside.

Hendricks sat at a damp wooden table and hunched his shoulders against the cold. 'Just the one, yeah?'

It suited Thorne. 'I've got plenty on tomorrow.'

Brigstocke had been bang on of course, three weeks before, back when Thorne was wheedling to get the go-ahead to look into the Philippa Goodwin suicide. Almost as soon as that particular misadventure had hit its brick wall, there was a sharp increase in the murder rate. A spike, or an anomaly, depending on your point of view, on whether you were a copper or a politician. Three violent deaths in one weekend, and though the killers had all been identified quickly enough – one only to be killed himself before he could be arrested – there was still plenty to do before anybody was brought to court.

Thorne was certainly busy enough.

'Yeah, me an' all,' Hendricks said. 'People do have this annoying habit of snuffing it all the time.'

'Thoughtless, if you ask me.'

'Right . . . '

For ten minutes, Thorne's friend regaled him with a few of the more recent and choicest tales from the pathology lab.

As ever they were dark as all hell, but a damn sight funnier, and a woman nearby stared as Thorne all but spat out his Guinness. Hendricks had always been the same, quick to leaven the horror with a smart remark. These days, however, the jokes came a little faster and more often than usual and were not there simply to balance out the grim nature of the work he did.

It was easier, Thorne knew, than acknowledging the only professionally dishonest thing Phil Hendricks had ever done. The post-mortem results from seven months before, a crucial element falsified to match one particular version of events and save Nicola Tanner's career. Thorne's, too, almost certainly.

Not much to it, no more than a few millimetres, the relative thickness of a dead man's skull. The lie told to save his friends, a few more to back it up, and now the three of them carried a bagful around.

'Any more news on the Helen front?' Hendricks asked.

Thorne swallowed and shook his head. He had spoken to her several times since the night he'd left a semi-drunken message, but they hadn't seen one another and nothing very much appeared to have changed.

'Up to her, isn't it?'

'Don't you have any say in the matter?'

'Probably,' Thorne said.

'There you go, then.'

'Only, I don't really know what I want to say—' He sighed, reaching for his mobile, which had begun to ring on the table in front of him. He answered and said his name.

'You're a hard man to get hold of.'

Having clearly overheard, Hendricks piped up, just loud enough for the caller to hear. 'I don't think *anyone's* been getting hold of him recently.'

Thorne got up and moved a few steps away. 'Sorry, who's this?'

The man identified himself as DI Colin Hatter from Kent

Serious Crime and asked Thorne if he had a few minutes to talk. 'I think you might be able to help me out,' he said. 'Well, we might be able to help each other out.'

'I'm listening.' Thorne watched Hendricks downing what was left of his pint and pretending not to eavesdrop.

'We caught a murder ten days ago, in Margate,' Hatter said. 'Young man got his head caved in at the beach. We got some workable DNA at the scene, OK? A few spots of blood from the murder weapon. Killer must have cut himself on the rock he was using to batter the lad.'

'Who said you couldn't get blood from a stone?'

'Better yet, we got a hit.'

'Nice one,' Thorne said.

Hatter sniffed. 'So, here's the thing. It matched with a sample you uploaded to the database a week or so before that. Your sample doesn't have the name of a suspect attached, but we're assuming that's because you don't have one.'

'Come again?'

The DI began to reel off a reference number, but Thorne did not need to hear it. It was the sample extracted during the forensic sweep of Philippa Goodwin's flat.

Patrick Jennings.

Thorne said, 'There must be some screw-up somewhere.'

'I don't think so.'

'It doesn't make sense.'

'We ran it more than once to be sure.'

'The suspect you're talking about is a con artist, that's all.' Now Thorne could see that Hendricks had stopped pretending not to listen and was mouthing something at him. 'Everything on that individual got passed over to the Fraud team.'

'Well, I reckon it might be getting passed back,' Hatter said. 'So we should probably talk about the next step, don't you think? Put our heads together, at least.'

Thorne paced aimlessly to the kerb, then turned and walked

back again, trying and failing to process what he had been told. 'Listen, Colin, this bloke's just a chancer. He's a poxy scam-merchant who makes his money conning women.' He moved towards the table and what little was left of his own drink.

Inside the pub, someone had begun to sing.

'Maybe he was,' Hatter said. 'But the evidence suggests he's moved up in the world.'

TWENTY-ONE

Margate

The boy turns back towards the doorway of the bar and peers above the heads, as though checking to see where his mates are. Perhaps he's concerned that they might be worried about him if he goes with this strange woman, but more likely he's just looking for someone he can tell.

'You coming or not?' she says.

'Yeah.' The boy nods again, quickly. 'Where—?'

Michelle has already begun moving away, glancing back to see the boy quickly finish what's left of his drink and come after her. 'Don't make it obvious,' she says, when he has caught her up. She leans towards him and whispers, fingers brushing his jacket 'Stay, I don't know . . . twenty feet back? Just follow me.'

They walk along the seafront, past the bars and the pizza palaces, then cross Marine Drive before cutting down on to the beach. She takes off her shoes. The sand is cold and clammy. He stays a decent distance behind her, like a good boy, the two of them drifting slowly and surely away from the noise and the lights. Away from any cameras.

'Here,' she says, eventually. A spot that is dark and deserted, shielded from view by a high wall and a concrete overhang. A spot she might easily have picked at random.

It's as quick and desperate as she'd expected, every bit as fumbly, until she makes it perfectly clear what she wants. She has no interest in the preamble, in his tongue or his pudgy, scrabbling fingers. It's fine though, because it just sounds as though she can't wait, as though she wants him.

He does his best.

She pulls him close and makes the necessary noises, his mouth wet against her ear, grunting with every tragic thrust, until the moment when the boy feels strong hands pulling him off and away, spinning him over and pressing him into the cold sand.

Then he just tries to cover himself and says, 'What?'

There are seagulls screaming overhead, and there's music, just audible from somewhere above and behind them. No more than a beat, like an insect buzzing against a window.

She sits up, because she wants to watch, because there would be little point otherwise, but still she flinches a little when the hand that is holding the rock comes down the first time. The sound, like someone stamping on a bag of nuts. She crawls closer as it comes down a second time, and a third, until the boy has stopped making any noise and, to be honest, there isn't much of that face left at all. Not even enough for a mother to recognise.

She will remember it, though; they both will, for a while at least.

'Are you OK?'

She nods, buttoning her shirt. She stretches to retrieve her underwear, then crawls across the sand to him, her arms reaching out as he rises to his knees, breathing fast and hard, worn out with it. Her hands are on him as he tosses the rock away and wipes a hand across his mouth.

'I'm fine,' she says. 'What about you?'

The memory will probably fade in time, Michelle knows that. That look on the boy's face. She doubts, though, that she will ever forget the taste of his blood on her lover's lips.

103

PART TWO

Above and Beyond

TWENTY-TWO

There were a couple of different blouses laid out on the bed and she was struggling to choose. She liked both of them, but there was no question that one would reveal a little more than the other, might perhaps raise an expensively threaded eyebrow or two. No bad thing usually, but those sorts of games didn't seem to matter quite as much any more, didn't get her excited in the way they used to. She'd tried both of the tops on already, of course, and had now been staring down at them for five minutes but was still no closer to making a decision.

She walked to the open bedroom door, leaned out and called downstairs to him.

'I need your help. Conrad . . . ?'

He shouted something back, but she couldn't make it out.

'Conrad . . . '

She still got a thrill from saying his name; the taste of it in her mouth almost – but not quite – as good as the taste of him. She said it a lot, more, she knew, than was strictly normal when the person himself was right in front of her, but she couldn't help herself. She loved the fact that he did the same thing.

She called him Conrad and he called her Sarah.

That first night together, when they'd told each other so much, he'd confessed that *Conrad* was, in fact, the name on his birth certificate. Even if it was one he hadn't used for as long as he could remember. Even though nobody, save for schoolfriends or close relatives – of which luckily there were very few – would ever think to call him that.

'I don't know why I told you,' he'd said. 'That very first day in the coffee shop.'

'I'm glad you did.'

'Even back then,' he'd stroked her arm, 'I think I must have known you were more than just another mark.'

She'd told him her real name too, of course, but he'd been about as fond of it as she was. So, they'd decided to stick with Sarah. He dug out old 'Sarah' songs by Bob Dylan and Thin Lizzy, another one by Hall and Oates that they both loved and which she would sometimes catch him singing when he thought he could not be overheard. He sang the name she had chosen for herself, while she scribbled his in her diary or on random scraps of paper, like a teenager inking a boyfriend's initials on a pencil case.

S 4 C 4 EVER . . .

'What?'

She turned from the bed to see him standing in the doorway and sucked in a fast breath. He was wearing old jeans and a T-shirt, a ratty pair of slippers she'd laughed at when he'd dug them out from his suitcase, and even so, the punch of pleasure staggered her. As if she hadn't seen him for days.

His being there changed the way the air moved in the room; *charged* it.

'I need you to help me choose a top,' she said. 'For the school pick-up.'

'Really?' He stepped across to the bed and looked down. 'I don't know ... they're both nice.'

She leaned into him, playful. 'Come on.'

'You don't need me to choose.'

'I do,' she said. 'Always.'

'Really?' He grinned, like a little boy praised for being a good one.

'Even if I'm somewhere and you're not there, it feels better that I'm wearing something I know you like ...'

It's the way it had been since that night, from the first moment she'd felt him inside her. She thought about him all the time, obviously, thought about little else, but she wanted him *there*, part of him at least, wherever she was and whatever she was doing. She needed that sense of Conrad always being with her, because anything else felt like grief.

Mad, they'd both said. Ridiculous. They were still saying it ...

Falling, that's how something like this was always described – she *fell* for him, they *fell* for each other – and if there was a better word, she couldn't think of it. Certainly, not for them, the incredible speed of it. However long someone was falling for and whatever waited for them when the fall was over, it was always fast.

Two weeks, more or less, that's all it had been. A glance at the next table in that coffee shop and all of a sudden here he was, sharing her bed, sharing everything. The decisions had been made quickly and easily, in bed or afterwards, laughing and giddy with it. Yes, of course he should move in, because there was no point wasting money on hotels, however cheap they actually were. As far his ... *occupation* went, there was no good reason why he shouldn't carry on, if that's what he wanted. They would need the money it would bring in, and in any case, they both thought it was important that two people, however much they were a *couple*, maintained their own interests, held on to their own ... individuality.

She would never deny him that.

'You know what it's going to mean?' he had asked her.

'Of course I do.'

'And you're OK with that?'

'Why wouldn't I be?'

'With me seeing other women?'

'*Seeing* them, yes.' Her hands on him in the early hours, whispering. 'Look, I know there are things you'll have to do. I know there are certain things you'll need to say to them if everything's going to pan out the way you want ... the way *we* want. I know that you'll have to take them out somewhere nice and spend time with them, and obviously I know you'll have to sleep with them and pretend that you're enjoying it, because it's part of the job. But trust me, love, I'm more than OK with that. I'm always going to know exactly what you're doing and, while you're busy doing it, I'll be lying here in bed all on my own, thinking about it. Where your fingers are, where your mouth is ... '

He'd nodded. 'A job, Sarah, that's all.'

'A man needs a job, my love. Needs something to feel good about when he gets home. Anyway, I'll have my hands full with Jamie, won't I?'

'Right.'

'I mean, being a mum's a full-time job.'

'I'm not arguing.'

They had taken a few rather more sensible decisions, too. These days, in bed, they were getting through those condoms in the drawer. Yes, they had both got a little carried away that first time, but Conrad didn't think they should be taking unnecessary risks quite this soon.

'Whatever you think,' she'd said. 'Anyway, I'm really not sure how Jamie would react to a baby brother or sister.'

'Yeah, that can be tricky,' he'd said.

There were so many reasons to love him already, so many

reasons why she knew, with absolute certainty, how very much he loved her. Top of the list though, if she had to pick one, was the simple fact that he had never asked her about Jamie, had never questioned it.

Not once.

If what Conrad had done for her on that beach had not been enough to prove it beyond a doubt – which of course it was – she knew that he loved her, that he was *hers*, because of that.

Now, Sarah pushed the two blouses to one side and sat down on the bed.

'Tell me about some of them,' she said. 'The women.'

Conrad stared at her. 'Why?'

'Because I want to know everything about you, what you've done.'

So, he sat down next to her and told her all about the fifty-two-year-old woman in Leicester who had believed he was a doctor and had given him twenty-five thousand pounds to fight a malicious malpractice suit. The young widow in Bolton who had handed over her life savings to fund a film he was never going to make. The woman in Glasgow who couldn't wait to pay for the operation his dying daughter needed.

'You make it sound so easy,' she said.

'You just need the right stuff, that's all,' he said. 'Documents that look convincing. A couple of pictures in your wallet of a little girl with cancer, letters from lawyers, whatever. That film one was a piece of cake. I just printed out some screenplay I found online and mocked up a couple of letters from agents and actors. I even showed her one from Benedict Cumberbatch, agreeing to play the lead.'

She shook her head, impressed. 'So, what devious schemes had you got lined up for me?'

'There weren't any.'

'You must have had some idea.'

'I thought about it for like, five minutes,' he said. 'But I told you, it wasn't what I wanted. I couldn't think of you as . . . that. The same way I saw them, you know?'

She felt him stiffen a little next to her and, seeing his expression darken suddenly, she reached to take his hand. 'What?'

'Nothing. The last one was a bit . . . weird, that's all. The one I was seeing before I met you. This woman in Tufnell Park.'

'Blimey, that's not a million miles away.' She smiled. 'Might be a bit awkward if we ever bump into her.'

'Not much chance of that. She killed herself after I left.'

Sarah said nothing for several seconds, then began to laugh. She saw him turn to stare at her and the laughter became uncontrollable. Towards the end, she put her hand across her mouth and giggled into it.

'Jesus,' he said, when she'd finished.

'Sorry . . . it was the look on your face, that's all.'

He stood up and leaned back against the bedroom wall. She stared at him but he was looking away and those few moments when she was unable to tell what he was thinking were almost unbearable.

She said his name.

He looked at her.

'Right . . . are you concentrating, because I'm going to be late for pick-up, so we really need to decide.' She gathered up the two blouses and held them towards him. 'I'm going to try both of these on one more time, and you have to choose.' She set the tops down again and slowly began to unbutton the blouse she was wearing.

Three buttons down, she raised her dark eyes to him, and suddenly everything was fine again, because now it was perfectly obvious what he was thinking.

'I don't want to be late . . . '

He stepped towards her. Said, 'Take *everything* off.'

112

TWENTY-THREE

Thorne caught an early train from St Pancras, and by ten o'clock he was standing on a damp and dull stretch of beach, his face screwed up against the wind as he stared down at the spot where a seventeen-year-old boy had been battered to death almost a fortnight earlier.

Colin Hatter took a few steps away and pointed back towards the promenade. 'Can't be seen from up there,' he said. 'Perfect, if you're after somewhere to sneak off for a quick shag.'

'Or if you're looking for a place to murder someone,' Thorne said.

'Yeah, that too.' The Kent DI was older than he'd sounded on the phone, late forties probably, but he clearly took steps to keep himself fit and a nicely tailored suit emphasised the results.

Thorne shoved his hands deep into the pockets of a brown leather jacket that had seen better days. 'So, it was probably planned.'

'Whatever *it* was,' Hatter said. 'Got as much physical evidence as we're likely to get and we're still none the wiser as to what actually happened.'

Thorne knew that, at the same time of day nearly two weeks before, much of Margate beach would have been cordoned off. Onlookers with nothing better to do would have huddled together behind the tape like extras in a crime drama, mobile phones held aloft, while emergency vehicles were pulling up on the promenade and a forensic tent was erected over the spot on which he and Hatter were now standing.

It was a somewhat less populated scene this morning.

A couple of dog walkers had drifted past them in opposite directions, while an old man with a metal detector was sweeping the sand twenty yards or so away. A somewhat shorter distance offshore, only the red cap and flailing arms of a swimmer were visible, as he or she ploughed through rough water that was the colour of stewed tea and just about as inviting. Shivering a little at the sight of them, Thorne decided that, man or woman, they were almost certainly certifiable.

'Time of death was somewhere between eleven and twelve on the Friday night,' Hatter said. 'Poor bugger was lying here until the beach cleaners came on first thing the next morning. Whoever killed him had covered the body with sand, but it wasn't really like they were trying to hide it.'

'They wanted it to be found.'

'Well, they weren't that bothered, put it that way.' Hatter bent to free one of several jagged rocks that were embedded in the sand nearby. Having decided that it was not quite the right size, he chose another one and weighed it in his hand. 'A bit smaller than this,' he said. 'The one that was used.' He pointed. 'Just lobbed away over there, afterwards.'

'Tell me about this woman,' Thorne said.

'Not much to tell.' Hatter lobbed his own rock away.

'Yeah, you said.'

114

Hatter wiped the sand from his palm and clapped him on the shoulder; colleagues now, *mates*. 'Don't worry, I can show you when we get back to the station. The CCTV . . . '

The old man with the metal detector was a lot closer now and, as they passed him on their way back towards Hatter's car, he took off his headphones and said, 'Lad was killed over there, couple of weeks back.'

Hatter reached for the lanyard around his neck, his ID flapping in the wind. 'We know.'

The old man nodded and tapped his nose, as though their identities were a secret he was agreeing to keep. 'Got it.'

'Any joy?' Thorne asked.

'Usual rubbish,' the man said. 'Bottle tops and old ring-pulls. You never give up though, do you?' He put his headphones back on and spoke a little too loudly as he began sweeping again. 'We just turn up every day hoping we get lucky.'

Trudging up the concrete ramp to the promenade, Hatter said, 'Silly bastards.'

'Them or us?' Thorne said.

Folkestone, where the Major Crime team was based and the incident room had been established, was thirty miles or so down the coast. It should have been no more than an hour's drive, but even out of season the traffic in Margate was barely moving and, ten minutes after getting into the shiny new Astra, they were still crawling through the centre of town.

'You been here before?' Hatter asked.

'A couple of times when I was a kid,' Thorne said. 'Wasn't quite as flashy, back then.'

'Oh, it's all changed round here, mate.'

'You local then?'

'No, but I've seen it happen, last couple of years. Dreamland, the new art gallery, all that . . . and loads of Londoners coming down here and buying up the houses while they're still cheap.

You know what they call this place now?' Hatter didn't wait for an answer. 'Shoreditch-on-Sea.'

'Really?' The East-End hipster enclave was not a part of London Thorne was particularly fond of. It was all a little ... full of itself for his liking. 'Dirty' burgers, whatever they were, and shops knocking out overpriced vintage tat that was probably meant to be ironic. A few too many gastropubs serving parsnip dust or garlic foam and more artisan bakeries than you could shake a shiitake mushroom at. 'God help you.'

'That artist woman lives here as well. The one who did the bed.'

Thorne looked at him.

'*You* know, the one who won all those prizes for her bed. Jizzy sheets and johnnies all over the floor.'

Thorne nodded because he knew what the man was talking about, though he couldn't remember the artist's name. What he *could* remember was how he'd felt a few weeks before, standing in that studio in Holloway, looking at Ella Fulton's photographs. Flailing around, like that swimmer. Art, generally, was not something he was ever comfortable giving an opinion about, but it was definitely the modern stuff – beds and bricks and pickled sharks – that left him most confused. 'Yeah, right,' he said.

The traffic eased as they were finally able to turn away from the sea and head inland. Hatter put his foot down, the first chance he got.

'So, you reckon this bloke's a conman, then?'

'I don't *reckon* anything,' Thorne said. 'I know he is. I told you on the phone. He did a number on a woman called Philippa Goodwin, got seventy-five grand out of her.'

Hatter pulled out to overtake a lorry. 'So, how come you were looking at him? Fraud isn't really an MIT job, is it?'

'She killed herself afterwards,' Thorne said.

Hatter was getting rather too close to the car in front of the lorry. 'OK, but even so ...'

If the DNA match about which Hatter was so excited turned out to be genuine, Thorne guessed that this would probably be the last time he would be asked to explain himself. To justify his interest in Patrick Jennings. He thought about what the old man on the beach had said, and about how, so often in Thorne's line of work, getting lucky meant a body turning up.

'God knows,' he said. 'Maybe I'm psychic.'

TWENTY-FOUR

In an incident room somewhat brighter and cleaner than the one he was used to, Thorne was escorted to a desk and Hatter dragged a spare chair across. He logged in to his computer and called up the necessary file with a few practised clicks.

He said, 'Here we go . . . '

Thorne leaned in to study the grainy black and white footage; a doorway, brightened by a streetlamp and a pavement which appeared oddly shiny, perhaps because of the light or simply because it was wet. The time-code on the bottom of the screen read 04/02, 22.41 and a figure was moving at the edge of the frame. Smoking, a head covered by a baseball cap and nodding, Thorne assumed, in time to the music coming from inside the bar.

'That's the woman,' Hatter said. 'Hard to be sure from this angle, but you get a better look in a minute.'

Thorne kept watching.

People moved in and out of frame as they left the bar or entered it, their eyes blazing white just for an instant, as they glanced in the direction of the camera.

'Here he comes . . . '

A boy stepped out from the bar. He took a swig from the bottle he was carrying, then leaned against the wall and lit a cigarette.

'That's Kevin Deane,' Hatter said. 'Poor bastard's last fag.'

22.44. The figure in the baseball cap walked across to Deane and now, viewed side-on, Thorne could see that it was a woman. Slight enough to have been a boy perhaps, but not moving like one. She and Deane talked for a couple of minutes, certainly appearing to get on well enough, before she turned, her face remaining hidden from the camera, and walked away. The boy stayed where he was for half a minute, peered briefly back into the bar, then hurried out of shot in the same direction.

Hatter leaned in and called up another file. 'Right, we pick them up again a few minutes later, just briefly . . . here.'

Another camera, this one a good deal further away. Cars moved, blurry through the shot, a group of lads with bags of chips or burgers. The woman in the cap crossed the main road heading towards the beach, Kevin Deane a few seconds behind her, before both left the frame.

'That's the lot.' Hatter shut the file down.

Thorne sat back. 'So, Kevin Deane and our mystery woman go down to the beach . . . '

'Right, and we know they have sex,' Hatter said. 'We got her DNA from Kevin Deane's body.'

'No match on that though?'

Hatter shook his head. 'Just the DNA we got from the blood on the rock. The DNA that matches the sample you uploaded to the database. We've got casts of footprints, too. The most likely ones, anyway. There'd been people walking around there all day. Like I said, we can't be sure exactly what happened *after* they had sex, but it looks very much like Deane followed this woman down to the beach—'

'Looked to me like she picked him up,' Thorne said.

'Well . . . maybe.'

119

'Followed her because she asked him to.'

'Either way, they get down there, he shags her and then . . . I don't know, her boyfriend turns up?'

'What, her boyfriend just happens to be wandering along the beach minding his own business and comes across somebody else shagging his girlfriend?'

'Maybe they'd had a row or whatever, and she was doing it to get back at him.'

'Having told him exactly where she'd be when she was doing it?'

The DI smiled as though conceding that Thorne had made a fair point, but it was a little icy. 'It's one explanation, that's all. Could be that it was just random, and whoever killed Kevin Deane was nothing to do with either of them.'

Thorne nodded, acknowledging the possibility, but he was still thinking about the man he knew only as Patrick Jennings. Asking himself how a run-of-the-mill con-artist could possibly be the same man who had used a rock to bludgeon a seventeen-year-old boy to death.

The evidence suggests he's moved up in the world . . .

'You know, just some mental case who was mooching around looking for someone to kill, and Kevin and this woman were just in the wrong place at the wrong time.'

'So, why just kill Kevin? And if that's how it played out, what happened to the woman? Why hasn't she come forward?'

Hatter nodded. 'Yeah, that's what's bothering me, too. Like I said, as of now, we've got no way of knowing what really went on.'

It was easy, of course, to look at a piece of CCTV footage and see what suited you, the interpretation that fitted your theory. Thorne had done as much himself, many times. Watching the last known footage of their victim, though, it had seemed clear enough to Thorne that for those few minutes outside the bar, it had been the woman setting the pace. That she had been the one making the arrangements.

'You considered the possibility that the woman was in on it?' He turned to look at Hatter. 'Her and the killer together?'

The DI leaned back in his chair. 'Yeah, *considered* it.'

'There are couples who get off on all sorts of weird shit.'

Hatter considered it again. 'OK, swapping and threesomes and whatever, maybe. Men who get turned on watching their partners with someone else, and women who like it when their other half watches them with someone else. I know stuff like that goes on, because, well . . . I've seen some of the films.' He flashed a theatrically lascivious grin, then held up a hand. 'So, look, it's a fair enough suggestion, but not when it comes to something like . . . *this*.'

'Like murder.'

'Yeah, like murder. I mean, who in their right mind . . . ?'

Thorne had to admit that the twisted scenario that had suddenly begun to take shape in *his* mind was rather more disturbing than even he was accustomed to. Rather more frightening too, because whatever it was that people got off on tended to be something they would want to do more than once.

'You're probably right,' he said.

Smiling, Hatter got to his feet. 'I can certainly think of easier ways to spice up your relationship, put it that way.'

With another click or two, the DI opened up the Kevin Deane case file and told Thorne that, although all the information would obviously be shared digitally with the Met, he was welcome to take a look through it while he was there. 'I'll leave you to it for a bit,' he said.

Once Hatter had disappeared, Thorne went in search of the tea he had not been offered. Perhaps Hatter had simply been keen to crack on with things, but Thorne could not help but wonder if the DI's lack of hospitality was really about making a point. That this was a Kent inquiry, that Thorne's involvement was strictly down to the coincidence of the DNA match, that he was only there as a favour.

If that was the case, Thorne was happy enough to go toe to toe.

After all, there wouldn't *be* a DNA match if he hadn't decided to go after Patrick Jennings.

Either way, he wanted tea.

He eventually located a fancy drinks machine in a corridor and, while he was waiting for his *premium-quality hot beverage* to brew, he fell into conversation with a DC who had just stepped out of the Ladies, tucking something into her handbag.

She saw Thorne clock it. Said, 'Sneaky vape.'

'I won't tell anyone.'

'Cheers.'

'So . . . what do you reckon to the Kevin Deane murder, then?'

The woman snuck a second look at the ID around Thorne's neck. 'God knows,' she said. 'All just guesswork at the minute, deciding on one likely explanation today, changing our minds tomorrow. I think the guvnor's leaning towards the jealous boyfriend, but I know he's not really convinced.'

'You think the woman knew the killer?'

She nodded. 'Doesn't make sense, otherwise. I mean, none of it makes *sense*, but . . . '

'How old do you think she is?'

The DC thought about it. 'Older than Kevin Deane, definitely. Quite a bit older, I reckon.'

'What makes you say that?'

'I don't know . . . hard to be certain, baggy clothes and the cap and whatever. Just a feeling I got the minute I saw it. She seemed . . . confident, you know?'

Taking what you thought you'd seen in a piece of CCTV footage and tying it conveniently to a prevailing theory was rarely a wise move, but Thorne believed that often snap judgements made without overthinking things could turn out to be the right ones. He'd read something about it once, the unconscious drawing on past experience to make the right decision almost immediately.

Something like that . . .

Back at the desk, he read though the witness statements: the woman who'd found Kevin Deane's body on the beach; the friends he had been with that night in the bar; a man who remembered seeing Deane following a woman down from the promenade. He saw the text that Deane had sent to one of his friends as he was walking away from the bar.

pulled mate!! laterz ☺ ☺ ☺ ☺ ☺

He studied printouts of the CCTV footage he had just watched, then, last of all, he looked at the crime scene photographs.

The boy lay twisted, one arm thrown back above his head and the other across his chest. His shirt was crusted with blood and his trousers and underpants were down around his ankles. A shot of his face showed no more than raw pulp and teeth, like the close-up of a half-eaten peach tossed away and covered in sand.

Thorne's tea did not taste quite so premium-quality any more; did not taste of anything.

Hard though it still was to believe that the person responsible for this was the same one who had skilfully charmed then fleeced Philippa Goodwin, the DNA suggested Thorne was mistaken. It was the only real evidence of any sort they had, and it was probably time for him to stop arguing with it.

However much it went against the grain.

If he was sure about one thing, though, it was that the man he and the Fultons knew only as Patrick Jennings took great care to stay elusive and keep his real identity hidden. If Thorne was going to catch him, he might well be better served by looking for whoever he was with.

He would need to find the woman first.

When Thorne was ready to leave, he went in search of Colin Hatter and eventually found him at a meeting in one of the offices; sleeves rolled up, all business.

'What do I do about a lift to the station?'

Hatter held his arms out in a gesture of helplessness and looked at the others around the table. 'I would, mate, but I'm a bit tied up now. I could try and find someone who's not doing anything . . .'

Thorne waited.

'Actually, it's only a fifteen-minute walk. If you're feeling fit.'

'I'm not,' Thorne said.

TWENTY-FIVE

Before now, Sarah would have been hard pressed to say whether she had actually *enjoyed* the pick-ups and the drop-offs. Certainly, they had never been easy. She had done it so often that they weren't shit-herself scary any more, but that didn't mean there weren't jitters every single time, and countless trips to the bathroom, before she steeled herself to leave the house and drive to Brooklands Hill. It didn't mean that when she got home she wouldn't still be shaking just a little, or that she wouldn't need to reach for a bottle before collapsing on to her sofa, drained by the effort and aching with relief.

No, *enjoyed* would not have been the obvious word for it.

Now, though, aside from the time she spent with Conrad, these were the high points of her day. She woke thinking about the journey to school and her hands were no longer tight around the wheel as she sat in traffic singing along with the radio. If Conrad wasn't there, the thought of pick-up in only a few hours . . . one hour . . . twenty minutes . . . would be what got her through the empty afternoon. When he *was* at home, and those were red-letter days obviously, he could

125

see it too; watching from the hallway as she ran upstairs to get changed.

'No need to ask what you're so happy about, is there?'

She thought she'd been doing a pretty good job up to now, had been starting to fit in with the group and find a place for herself. Yeah, she'd been bowling along quite nicely BC (Before Conrad), making decent progress, but now they were all over her like a rash. Heather, Savita and the others. Even Caroline, the Queen Bee herself, was keen to get in on the act, nice as pie all of a sudden and twice as sickly.

If she'd been made to choose, Sarah would have said that pick-ups were probably the best, that they just edged it. When it came to the coffee shop after drop-off, there was always the issue of where you'd end up sitting, who you'd be next to. Milling around outside the gates every afternoon, though, she could move around as she chose and pick her moments.

She could wander over and chat to Savita if she felt like it or drift across and pull Heather away for a quiet word and a giggle. Caroline, maybe, or Eve or that simpering idiot David . . .

Any of them, whenever *she* wanted to.

It was her choice and, best of all, every one of them was desperate to talk to her.

They were all there when she wandered up, waiting for the gates to open and their precious little darlings to come charging out. She saw them glance towards her as she approached. Just a nod from Caroline – trying to look cool like always – and a smile from a couple of the others, like they weren't stupidly excited to see her and gagging to hear the latest.

She raised a hand and casually said 'Hi' when she joined the group. The tail-end of a tedious conversation about sports day. Caroline yammering about how unfair it was that Jacob wasn't allowed to enter some race or other, because for heaven's sake he was *actually the fastest* and it was all part of this ridiculous 'everyone needs to win something' attitude that so got on her nerves.

'Because that's not how life is, is it?' She looked to Savita, who could usually be relied upon to back her up.

'I suppose not,' Savita said.

'Of course it isn't. No harm in kids learning that lesson, is there?'

'They're just trying to spread it around a bit,' Heather said. 'That's all.'

David nodded. 'Losing can be tough on them at this age.'

'Well, it's pretty tough on Jacob, too,' Caroline said. 'On any child who's quicker or stronger or brighter than some of the others. Teaches them that trying to be the best doesn't mean anything.'

'I get what you're saying,' Savita said.

Heather turned to Sarah, evidently unable to wait any longer. 'So, come on then ... how's *Conrad*?'

Sarah blinked. She could not remember actually telling Heather Conrad's name. Then she realised that, obviously, Heather must have heard it from one of the others she *had* told. It was a little pathetic, she thought, just how much time and energy these people expended on gossip and rumour, how empty their lives would otherwise be.

Pathetic and fabulous.

'Conrad is fine, thank you very much.'

Savita nudged Heather. 'You know he's moved in with her, right?'

'Wow,' Heather said. 'Really?'

'Already?' Caroline pretended to look shocked.

Sarah smiled. Like the woman wasn't green with envy.

'Don't you think that's a bit previous?' Heather laughed, nervously. 'I mean it's none of my business, but ... blimey.'

'We were ready for it.' Sarah shrugged. 'It just felt right.'

'But you barely know him.' Heather glanced around and reddened, aware that everyone was looking at her. 'Like I said, none of my business.'

127

'What can I say?'

Heather shrugged. 'OK. Well . . . if it feels like the right thing to do, I'm happy for you.'

Sarah laid a hand on Heather's arm and mouthed a 'thank you', though she didn't think the woman looked particularly happy.

'How does Jamie feel about all this?' David asked.

'Oh, he's chuffed to bits.' Sarah fought the urge to step over and slap the studied expression of concern off the man's face. As if she wouldn't have considered her son's feelings, as if that wouldn't have been her primary concern. 'Jamie thinks Conrad's fantastic. Well, we both do, obviously.'

'Young love, eh?' Savita said.

Sarah laughed. 'I don't know about young.'

'I *thought* you were looking a bit knackered.' Savita laughed, dirty. 'I bet you hardly leave the house, do you?'

'Oh, please,' Caroline said.

'Only if we absolutely have to,' Sarah said.

It wasn't too much of an exaggeration, because unless Conrad needed to go out, and she understood that sometimes he did, Sarah was happiest keeping him all to herself. She thought a lot about that annoying woman she'd met in the park, the one who'd seemed so mortified at the idea of inviting a single woman for dinner. Now, even though she wasn't single any more and was tempted to show that fact off – to show *him* off – she could not think of anything she would rather do less. Annoyingly, she had not seen the woman since, so had not yet seized the chance to tell her where she could stick her invitation.

Conrad's work aside, she didn't want to share him with anyone.

At the sound of the bell, the gaggle of parents shuffled forward, craned their necks as the children began to emerge.

Sarah watched Heather's son, Ollie, come out, closely followed by the obnoxious Jacob. Heather, who still looked as though something was worrying her, mumbled a goodbye as she led her child away. Caroline left without bothering. David waved at the sight of his daughter, as if he hadn't seen her in months.

'God, I just remembered.' Sarah turned to Savita, sighed and shook her head. 'Jamie needs to bring a ton of painting stuff home with him today. I said I'd help him . . .' She pushed through the gates and began walking across the playground.

Savita shouted after her. '*HazBeanz* in the morning?'

Sarah raised a thumb without turning round and kept on walking.

If I can be bothered . . .

Stepping through the main doors to the school, she saw one of the teachers walking towards her. Short blonde hair, dark trousers and a nice, bright cardigan; one of the younger ones. Sarah smiled, heading towards the toilets, where she knew she could linger for ten minutes or so, but the teacher stopped in front of her.

'Can I have a quick word?'

'Sorry, but I'm in a bit of a rush.' Sarah felt her chest tighten as she looked at her watch.

The teacher leaned across to open a classroom door. 'In here . . . ?'

Sarah stepped into the room and heard the door close behind her. Her mind was racing as she looked quickly around: the map of the world on a rug; the colourful drawings pinned to the back wall; the open window she could climb through if things went really pear-shaped.

She felt a small shiver of relief at not seeing a police officer standing in the corner or the word LIAR scrawled on the whiteboard.

She tried to damp down the panic.

The teacher pulled two plastic chairs from behind the nearest of the low round tables. She lowered herself on to one and pointed towards the other. Sarah sat, desperately looking for something, anything in the woman's face that might allow her to relax a little.

Instead, she watched the woman take a deep breath, and when she eventually opened her tight little mouth, it was as though the speech was something she'd thought about for a while; that she'd rehearsed.

'I know exactly what you're doing here every day and even if I haven't got the first idea why, I'm afraid that it needs to stop. You don't have a child at this school, you don't have *any* connection with this school, so the fact is you simply can't be here. Do you understand?'

Sarah stared at the floor for a while, breathing in that smell that she'd loved so very much until this moment. She looked up, slowly. 'Are you going to call the police?'

'I should,' the woman said. 'But I've been thinking about all the reasons anyone might do something like this and . . . look, as long as you stop coming to the school, there's probably no need to take this any further.'

'Have you ever lost a child?' Sarah asked.

The woman shook her head. 'No, I haven't.'

'I've lost *three* of them, all right? One after the other.' Sarah's voice cracked and she clutched at the edges of the chair. 'Every time it seems like it's going to be fine, but something always goes wrong inside . . . ' The tears came nice and easily; pricking, brimming then starting to fall.

The young teacher looked embarrassed and she reached quickly into the pocket of her cardigan for a used tissue. Sarah shook her head and waved it away. She pressed a sleeve across her eyes.

'I'm so sorry,' the teacher said.

'There's no need to be. It's not your fault.'

'I'd wondered if it might be something like that.'

'It's stupid, I know,' Sarah said. Her voice caught again, and she lowered her head. '*So* stupid, but . . . I just can't stop thinking about what should have happened, that this is what I was sup-posed to be doing every day.'

130

'I can't imagine what it's like.'

Sarah looked up and tried to smile. She said, 'I wouldn't even wish *that* on you.' From the corner of her eye, she watched fifteen seconds tick past on the large plastic clock above the whiteboard and listened to the gabble of children in the corridor outside.

The teacher cleared her throat, then stood up and carefully replaced her chair behind the table. 'OK, well, then . . . '

Sarah got slowly to her feet, making use of her sleeve again.

'What you've been through sounds truly horrible, and like I said, I can't . . . but my main concern has to be the welfare of the children I teach, so I'm sure you can understand why I needed to say something.'

Sarah nodded and stepped towards the door.

'So, you know . . . as long as you promise to stop, I hope we can leave it there.'

'Thank you,' Sarah whispered. 'I'm really sorry . . . '

Marching back across the playground, children pointing and stepping aside for her, she knew it was possible that Savita or David or one of the others could still be there at the gates. That there might be questions to answer, that they would be confused as to why there wasn't a child clinging to her hand – her fist – but she knew she would come up with something, because she always did.

Thinking that perhaps Jamie had an after-school club he'd neglected to tell her about, or that he'd already gone to play at a friend's house, or that there was something he needed which she had stupidly forgotten to bring in and would now have to nip home and fetch.

Thinking that it didn't much matter any more, thinking that the story about the miscarriages worked like a charm every time.

Thinking, *bitch, bitch, bitch, bitch* . . . .

TWENTY-SIX

By the time Thorne had got off the train at St Pancras, there was little more than an hour of his shift left and by far the most sensible thing he could have done would have been to head straight home. The idea was seriously tempting. From King's Cross, it was only two stops on the Northern line to Kentish Town and, after all, he could easily do what he needed to by phone or email, but instead he took the other branch all the way to Colindale.

He finally walked into Becke House barely fifteen minutes before close of play, but he felt sure the effort would be worth it.

He'd wanted to get there before Russell Brigstocke left for the day.

'Come to gloat?' The DCI didn't bother looking up from his desk.

'Don't be soft, Russell. I just wanted to fill you in on my meeting with the team from Kent. You'll obviously be liaising with your opposite number down there, so I thought you'd want to know exactly what the lie of the land was.'

'Course you did.'

'Gloating would be childish,' Thorne said.

'Yes, it would.'

'A more insecure officer than yourself might even say it was insubordinate . . . but as I'm here, I might as well remind you that the individual you thought it was a waste of time looking at has now popped up as the prime suspect in a murder.'

Now, Brigstocke looked at him, his expression making it fairly clear that he wished he'd knocked off a little early. 'I'm well aware of that.' He reached for a sheaf of papers and waved it at Thorne, as though it were a lethal weapon. 'I've already started liaising.'

'Well, great,' Thorne said. 'All on the same page, then.'

'Anything else?'

'Not off the top of my head.'

'Sod off then, Tom.'

As Brigstocke had already gone back to whatever he was doing before being interrupted, Thorne allowed himself a smirk. The opportunity didn't come along very often and he could ill afford to waste it.

He said, 'Will do, sir . . .'

In the incident room, Tanner was still hard at work and did not look as though she would be ready to hand over her desk to her opposite number on the late team any time soon. It was tempting to believe that this was because she now had rather less to go home to than some of the others, but Thorne knew she'd been like this before.

'So, how was the seaside?'

'Oh, bollocks,' Thorne said. 'I meant to get some candyfloss.' He waited, but Tanner was clearly too busy for idle chat. 'Yeah, it was all right.'

'They OK with you?'

'Well, they caught the case, so I wasn't expecting a red carpet.'

Tanner grunted, continued to type.

'A bit of pissing about with tea and travel arrangements, but no worse than we would have been.'

'Than *you* would have been, maybe.'

Thorne leaned against the edge of Tanner's desk, as others were being vacated around him. He checked his phone for messages while he waited for Tanner to finish, then sent one to Phil Hendricks reminding him of their teams' relative positions in the league. He nodded a goodbye to those heading home, or to somewhere better equipped to take the day's rough edges off, then mumbled a greeting to a few familiar faces as the room began to fill with those settling in for the late turn.

When he finally had Tanner's full attention, he told her what had happened in Margate. The crime scene and the CCTV. What he'd seen and what he'd begun to suspect.

'You think it was a couple?'

'Only thing that fits,' Thorne said.

'Just because there's no sign of the woman?'

'What do you mean *just* because? I think it's fairly bloody significant, don't you? Yeah, it's always possible that this bloke killed Kevin Deane *and* the woman, then slung her body over his shoulder and wandered away into the night with it, without a single person seeing anything. I think it's unlikely though.'

'Could have put her in the sea.'

'*What?*'

'Bodies don't come back as often as people think.'

'He didn't kill her,' Thorne said. 'She was part of it.'

Tanner thought about it. She picked her handbag up from the floor next to her chair and laid it on the desk, as though finishing for the day had begun to look like a possibility. 'Hard to fathom,' she said, quietly. 'But it's not like we haven't seen it before.'

Thorne hadn't, not up close, anyway, but he knew what, and who, Tanner was talking about. A man and a woman whose union created something far more terrible than either would have become separately. A couple for whom hunting and killing was as much a part of their relationship, as crucial to it, as laughing together or good conversation was for others.

There was, of course, one infamous example. Before their

134

time and both halves of the couple now dead, but their names remained, for many, a simple definition of evil. If such a thing existed.

Thorne was grateful that his ringing phone spared him too much further thought about it, and, when he saw who was calling, he walked away from Tanner's desk without saying any more and carried the phone out into the corridor.

'Are you at work?'

'Yeah, but I'm done for the day,' Thorne said.

'I was just wondering if you fancied coming over tonight, that's all.'

'Oh, right.'

'Look, I know it's late notice, so it's really not a problem if you can't. I just thought it might be a nice idea . . . '

Five minutes later, when Thorne walked back into the incident room, Tanner was standing near the door with her coat on. She waited for him to say something and, when he didn't, she said, 'I was thinking we could grab a quick drink in the Oak.'

Thorne smiled, shaking his head. 'This must be how people feel when they win the lottery.'

'What?'

'Popular, all of a sudden.'

TWENTY-SEVEN

Sarah had a good deal on her mind – most notably the oh-so-earnest, *pitying* expression on the face of that teacher – so, when the call came, she was more than happy to be distracted for a few minutes. The voice at the other end of the phone was almost as solemn as the teacher's had been, to begin with anyway, but it was always nice to hear from one of her fellow parents.

Sarah thought it was sweet, if a little ironic, all things considered. She thought it was funny.

'I wanted to apologise,' Heather said. 'For earlier, outside school.'

'Don't be daft.'

'It was none of my business, like I said. You and Conrad. But, we're friends, so . . . '

'You were concerned,' Sarah said. 'I get that.'

'I should have kept my big mouth shut.'

'You still are, right? Concerned.'

Heather laughed. Sarah laughed, too. 'Well, a bit, I suppose. I *have* been thinking about it. I mean, it's just so *quick*.'

'Three weeks,' Sarah said.

'Bloody hell.'

'Bloody hell is right. I'm pretty gobsmacked myself.'

'I mean, yeah . . . he's clearly great and everything . . . it's just the moving in thing that worries me.'

'He hasn't stolen the cutlery as yet.'

Another giggle. 'Well, that's good. All the same, I wonder how well you can really know anyone after such a short space of time.'

'I know enough,' Sarah said. 'Everything I *need* to know.'

'It's . . . a mistake I've made myself,' Heather said. 'More than once. Not that I'm saying you've made a mistake—'

'Don't worry.'

'My big mouth again.'

'It's fine, honestly.'

'Anyway, I wanted to say sorry, that's all, for sticking my nose in.'

'Like you said, we're friends. I'm sure I'd be exactly the same.'

'Is he . . . ?'

'What?'

'God, I'm being an idiot. I was going to say is he nice to you. But he's obviously nice to you or you wouldn't be with him, would you? You wouldn't want him living there . . . with you and Jamie.'

'He's everything I want,' Sarah said.

'There you go, then.'

'There you go.'

'Time for me to shut up.'

'Thanks, though.' Sarah walked across to the living-room window, stared out in the hope of seeing Conrad's car pull up. 'I do appreciate it.'

'Right, I'll leave you in peace,' Heather said. 'I'm sure you've got stuff to do.'

'I've got loads to do,' Sarah said.

TWENTY-EIGHT

It seemed a little odd to be ringing the bell when he still had a set of keys, but it felt like the appropriate thing to do. Thorne was still wondering what the appropriate thing to *say* might be when the door was opened and, after a second or two of staring at one another, Helen beckoned him in and together they moved into a somewhat tentative embrace.

She stepped away and said, 'All right?'

'Yeah, not bad.' Thorne looked around as though taking in somewhere he'd never been before. 'Alfie in bed?'

'He's at Jenny's,' Helen said.

'Oh, right.'

'When I knew you were coming, I called and asked if she'd take him for a couple of hours.'

Thorne tried not to look too disappointed. By the time he'd got home, changed and showered then driven down to Tulse Hill, he'd known there was little chance of seeing Helen's son before bedtime, but had hoped he might at least be able to put his head round the bedroom door.

'Gives us more opportunity to talk.'

While Thorne walked across to the sofa, Helen went to the fridge. 'I've got some beers if you want one. I know you're driving, but ...'

Thorne still had no real idea why he was there. He wondered if Helen had asked him over to tell him that she was being stupid, that she'd changed her mind about everything and it didn't really matter how many beers he drank because he wouldn't be going back to Kentish Town tonight anyway.

Was that what he wanted to happen?

'Yeah, I can have one.'

He also found himself wondering if she'd gone out to fetch the beers because she knew he was coming or if they'd been sitting in the fridge already. And, if so, who had they been for?

Helen got a glass of wine for herself and joined him on the sofa. 'All good at work?'

He told her about his trip to Margate, said much the same as he'd said to Tanner a few hours before.

'Doesn't seem like that much of a stretch to me,' Helen said. 'Not when you've seen what some couples can do to their kids.' She told him about the case her own Child Abuse Investigation Team was currently working on; details that made them both glad they had drinks in their hands.

She said, 'Nothing much surprises me any more.'

Work had not usually been something they'd talked about in any depth at home. A good story maybe, when there was one, but rarely the nuts and bolts. Both had decided that the Job was something best left at the door with bags and coats, even if sometimes that proved to be impossible.

This was a conversation to be endured because it put off another that might be rather more difficult. To dispel some of the awkwardness that had bloomed between them almost overnight, like a clutch of stinging nettles.

Murder and child abuse, to break the ice.

'Alfie's missing you,' she said.

'Why would you tell me that?'

She looked at him.

'I mean, yeah, that's nice to hear and obviously I miss seeing him too. But at the end of the day, it's just . . . one more reason to feel shit about everything. Don't you think?'

'I don't feel great about it either,' Helen said. 'He asks where you are and I just feel guilty, like it's all my fault.'

'It *was* your idea.'

The speed with which Helen opened her mouth to speak suggested that her response might not have been one Thorne wanted to hear, but she stopped herself. Took a breath. 'I didn't ask you to come over so we could argue, Tom.'

'So, why did you ask me?'

'I wanted to see how you were, that's all, how you were getting on. Back in the flat and everything.'

'I'm fine.' Thorne shrugged and took a swig of beer. 'It's just . . . my flat.'

'That's good. Easier for work as well, right?'

'Oh, yeah.'

'Another half an hour in bed every morning.'

'Every cloud, right?'

She angled her body towards him. 'So, anyway . . . I was wondering whether you might fancy taking some of the stuff you've still got here back with you.'

Thorne stared at her. 'Suddenly pushed for space, are you?'

'No. I thought you might need it, that's all.'

'This how a trial separation usually works, is it?'

'I know there's still some CDs lying around you must be missing. Come on, it's not like there's a ton of it, is there? Probably get the whole lot in one suitcase.'

'So, what? You got a few beers in and went out and bought a nice new suitcase at the same time, get it all out of the way?'

'I'm not trying to get anything out of the way,' Helen said.

'Yeah, makes sense, seeing as I'm here. Might as well get me to clear all my shit out. I mean, that way I don't ever have to come back, do I?'

'You're being stupid.'

'Do you want the keys back?' Thorne began rummaging in his jacket pockets. 'Save messing about later.'

'That's not what's going on.'

'Right, well, I wish you'd tell me what *is* going on. Because I'm ... clueless.'

Helen sat back and closed her eyes for a few seconds. She said, 'Were you happy with how everything was? Properly happy?'

Thorne had thought he was; content, certainly. Yes, there had been occasions in the months leading up to this when his eyes had wandered a little and he had ... considered possibilities. That was only natural though, wasn't it? No harm in it, because thinking wasn't doing.

'I was happy enough,' he said.

'*Enough?*'

'You know what I mean.'

Helen drank.

'So, what about you?'

She stared at her glass, leaned forward. 'The same, I suppose.'

'So ... ?' He waited, but Helen had no answer for him, no easy one, at least. 'Look, I know this is probably going to piss you off, but ... is all this about anyone else?'

'What?'

'You know, just *tell* me—'

'Oh, for God's sake.' She stood up fast, stomped across to the chair opposite and dropped into it. It was another half a minute before she looked across at him, her smile a little wobbly. 'Fair enough question, I suppose. I mean, it's not like I haven't got form, is it?'

The affair just before the death of her former partner. The uncertainty as to exactly who Alfie's father was.

Thorne said nothing. It might have been Helen who had

141

brought the subject up, alluded to it at any rate, but he knew better than to dig in.

'The honest truth is, I really don't know what was going on,' she said. 'It felt like you were a bit distant, that's all. Last six months or so.'

'OK.' Thorne felt a worm of guilt, of *shame*, as it woke suddenly in his guts and began to stretch out.

'Maybe I was imagining it . . . '

She was a month or so out, and though Thorne couldn't really deny it, there was no way he would ever be able to explain. To confess. How could he tell her what had happened in that flat with Nicola Tanner, ask her to live with the lies he and Phil had told?

Sometimes, keeping a secret meant building a wall.

'I didn't mean to be.' It was the best he could do.

'I just started to feel . . . like I didn't know where I was. Like, this was it and everything was sorted, you and me and Alfie into the sunset. Or . . . it wasn't. I was waking up every day with no idea which one it was, and eventually it felt like I had to decide one way or the other.'

'But you still haven't?'

'I'm trying to work things out, that's all.'

'Fair enough,' Thorne said.

These days, he was doing much the same thing.

He looked at his bottle, saw that he had half his beer left. He decided that maybe it wouldn't hurt to stick a few CDs in a plastic bag as he'd come all this way. There was some George Jones it would be nice to have back at the flat and at least one Hank Williams album knocking around the place somewhere he *knew* would help. While Helen was working things out.

What had Tanner said the other week?

Wait and see pudding.

TWENTY-NINE

They stripped, threw a few towels down and had sex on the bathroom floor. Then they showered together, dried one another off and walked back to the bedroom in the fluffy white 'his and hers' dressing gowns Sarah had bought the week before.

She'd bought all sorts of things.

New sets of underwear for herself and an outfit or two for each of them to wear or enjoy removing.

Toys . . .

She sat at her dressing table and plugged in the hairdryer. 'That's nearly every room.'

'What?' Conrad was stretched out on the bed with a magazine.

'We've done it in the two sitting rooms, all the bedrooms, the kitchen and now the bathroom. Just the downstairs toilet and that's the full set.' She turned the hairdryer on.

Conrad spoke, but she couldn't hear what he was saying. She saw him waving at her in the mirror and turned the dryer off.

'I think that might be pushing it,' he said. 'I'm not a bloody contortionist.'

'You sit down on the lid and I straddle you,' she said. 'Easy.'

'OK.'

'We've got to do *every* room in the house, Conrad, no exceptions. We need to mark them all.' She grinned at him in the mirror. 'Then we should start doing it outside. In the park, whatever.'

She switched the hairdryer back on, and a few seconds later saw that he was waving at her again and switched it off.

'All about the danger, right?'

'What is?'

'Al fresco shagging.' He sat up. 'The possibility of getting caught.'

Sarah turned slowly round. 'We're never going to get caught,' she said.

When she had finished drying her hair, she walked across to the bed and sat down gently on the edge. She tightened the belt on her dressing gown and stared at the carpet until, after a minute or so, Conrad looked up. He laid down his magazine and said, 'What's the matter?'

'We've been honest with each other, haven't we?' she said.

Conrad took a second or two. 'Yeah . . .'

It seemed as though each had already told the other all there was to tell, that they had shared everything important. There were some details which would probably come out later, of course – childhood memories, travel stories, whatever – but there would be plenty of time for that, and what mattered were those things they needed to know about each other *now*. So that they could move forward. Sarah knew exactly how Conrad made his living and Conrad knew that Sarah, however good she was at making up stories, was no kind of writer. The house was hers, she'd told him, courtesy of her ex-husband, but the money she needed to buy food and clothes, to pay the necessary bills, had been earned doing market research from home, online or over the phone.

Asking people what they thought about shampoo, pet food, UKIP, for eight pounds fifty an hour.

144

'I want to tell you exactly what happened when I split up with Peter,' she said. 'That was his real name, by the way.'

'Always good to sprinkle a few facts in,' Conrad said.

'Seriously. You need to know how it was and why it happened, because then you'll understand how much I need Jamie.'

'I *do* understand.'

'Maybe you think you do.'

'Sarah—'

She shook her head and, when she finally began to tell him, quietly and with her eyes fixed on her bare feet, she did not have to exaggerate the pain or affect hesitation. She had no need to dissemble, because it was the first time she had told her story to anybody.

She needed Conrad, more than anyone, to know her.

'It's not like it hasn't happened to loads of women,' she said. 'It's such a cliché really, that whole mid-life crisis thing ... but there's nothing normal about how it made me *feel*.' She looked up, just for a moment. 'He ran off with a twenty-six-year-old. That's it in a nutshell. Same old story, right? Bought himself a whole new wardrobe of clothes, got a stupid haircut, started going to a gym, all of it. Can't be a flabby old bugger when you've got a fit young hottie to keep up with, can you? Mind you, when you're turning yourself into a new man, a *desirable* man, there are some things you have to say goodbye to, aren't there? Apart from your wife, I mean. So, obviously the poor bloke couldn't take all those Second World War books with him, could he? The ones he used to sit and read for hours on the toilet. Oh no, he left them behind ... because I don't think a twenty-six-year-old with nice perky tits and a thing for Disney princesses is going to be too impressed with any of that.

'Hitler books, while you're shitting ...

'And he knew I wanted kids, that was the worst thing. Knew how much I wanted them, always have. Never even gave us the time to find out whose fault it was we couldn't have them, did

145

he? Well, my fault, clearly, because he managed to knock his girlfriend up. Now, him and this girl, who can't even remember the Falklands or Princess Di, are playing happy families, with a toddler running about. A little boy. I saw him once.

'He told me I could keep the house, paid off the mortgage . . . as much out of guilt as anything, and that was about it. I saw him a couple of times after he'd gone, while we were still sorting everything out, and he told me he felt like a . . . fighter pilot. Can you believe that? Like he didn't know what was going to happen to him, that it might all end badly, but that he'd never felt so alive. I just stared at him. If I'd had a knife in my hand I would have been happy to put a stop to that right there and then.

'I could have sold the house, I suppose, got myself a little flat, but that wasn't how I wanted to live. That wasn't how I saw myself and it certainly wasn't how I wanted others to see me. Appearances are important, aren't they? Appearances are everything. For the little girl from a housing estate in south London who managed to lose her accent. The girl whose mum was the clever one but never got a look-in because she was married to an alcoholic waster. For the girl who landed herself a rich husband then got thrown away like a bag of rubbish, but found a way to keep on living . . .

'I couldn't do it on my own though, could I? My Jamie came along just when I needed him and saved my life, pretty much.' She looked up again. 'I can *see* him, you know? What he's wearing, whether he's happy or if something's bothering him. I can tell that just by the sound of his voice . . . just if his smile's a bit off or whatever that day. I can tell you exactly what he smells like.'

She raised her hand, moved her fingers. 'Just here, where it's soft at the back of his neck. It smells like toffees . . . '

Conrad waited until he was sure she had finished. Then he said, 'You've got me too, now.'

She nodded.

'You know that, don't you? You know I'll protect you. There's two of us ... *three* of us now, and I won't ever let anything get in the way of that.'

'Do you promise?'

'You really have to ask me?'

'I know, my love. I'm sorry.'

'Isn't it obvious?' Conrad asked. 'I mean, the beach ...'

'I just needed to hear you say it, to be sure.'

'You don't have to worry.'

'That's good,' she said. 'But what we did on the beach was just for us, a commitment we made to each other. Like a blood oath. Now, we need to honour it, because there might be a problem.'

'What problem?'

Sarah opened her dressing gown and began crawling up the bed towards him. 'Someone who's threatening us.'

THIRTY

Two days after his trip to Margate and his evening with Helen, Thorne's journey to work was not one he spent relishing the hours ahead. Most of the previous shift had been taken up with pre-trial work on the Tottenham stabbings, but the further he got into liaison with the CPS and the integrity of evidence chains, the more extra work seemed to present itself, as if from nowhere. It felt like one of those scenes in a film where someone has been locked up for being mad and, just as they stumble towards the end of a long corridor, about to escape to freedom, the door begins moving further away.

Well, it would have felt like that, except Thorne couldn't even see the door.

He got to his desk and readied himself to get stuck in again. He logged on to the computer system. He fetched a large coffee and, once he'd had the necessary jolt of caffeine, he arranged the jumble of paperwork into manageable piles.

Then he pushed them to one side and called Colin Hatter.

'You don't think I'd've let you know?' Hatter said. 'If we had anything new.'

'Maybe something just came in and you were about to pick up the phone yourself.'

'Yeah, right.'

'So, I thought I'd save you the trouble.'

'I wish it had, mate.' The line was muffled for a few seconds; Hatter covering the mouthpiece to speak to someone else. When he came back to Thorne, he said, 'This is turning into one of those, you know?'

Thorne knew all too well. One of those cases that appeared to defy any amount of bog-standard procedure, that would rely on evidence presenting itself that those investigating had been unable to find on their own. A key witness coming forward out of the blue to change the game. A tip-off or an unsought confession. Something that had been missed, perhaps, which would only surface way down the line when the case was re-investigated; months, or even years, after it had been shunted reluctantly on to the back burner before eventually going cold.

'I was wondering if we could get that CCTV footage enhanced.'

'Nothing worth enhancing, mate. Come on, you've seen it. We never get a look at her face.'

'OK, so what about trying to knock up a decent e-fit? Have you talked to the people working in the bar that night?'

'No point, is there?' Hatter was making a good job of sounding breezy while remaining stubbornly negative. 'What exactly is it we're supposed to ask? I mean, how many women between, say, eighteen and forty do you reckon were in that bar on a Friday night, and how many of them do you think the bar staff are likely to remember? No . . . the appeal was definitely our best bet.'

'Nothing from that, then?' Before he'd left Margate, Thorne had been told that local media would be used in an urgent appeal for information from anyone who might have been in the centre of town that Friday night. A statement from Kevin Deane's devastated family alongside stills from the CCTV footage. A standard attempt to jog memories or prick consciences when all else had failed.

'Nothing to get too excited about,' Hatter said. 'A few more sightings, that's all. Kevin Deane and the woman walking towards the beach. A man, who for obvious reasons *isn't* Kevin Deane, walking away from the beach with a woman, just before eleven-thirty.'

'The same woman?'

'Sounds like it. Baseball cap . . . '

'Leaving the scene with the killer.' Thorne waited for Hatter to respond, but there was just silence. 'That's hardly nothing,' he said.

'Well, it's nothing that really gets us anywhere, is it?'

'They're a couple. I told you.'

'Yeah, I suppose it adds a bit more weight to your theory about them being in it together.'

'Doesn't sound like a theory any more,' Thorne said. 'Sounds pretty bloody cut and dried and it's what we need to base enquiries on moving forward.'

'Fair enough.' The line was briefly muffled again. Hatter sounded as though he'd already lost interest in the conversation. 'Any thoughts as to how we actually do that, mate, I'm all ears.'

Thorne had little to offer, but he was buggered if he was going to let the DI from Kent go without making it perfectly clear what he thought about him, and other coppers like him. The sort who couldn't get worked up if a result didn't fall into their laps straight away and only felt they were doing their jobs properly when they were slapping handcuffs on.

Glory-hunters.

Thorne had been called one himself more than once, and back then those making the accusations had probably done so with good reason. Of course, there were some cases that got pulses racing more than others, there were times when frustration could lead you to do something stupid, but nine times out of ten it was all about putting the time in. Wanting it. Sometimes, getting that right result would mean long hours of admin and office work, but if that was what it took, it had to be done.

He glanced across at the heap of folders and files that he had yet to tackle.

He said, 'You can't always have it on a fucking plate, *mate*.'

An hour or so later Russell Brigstocke walked past the door of his office and Thorne called him back.

'You doing . . . paperwork?' The DCI reached into an inside pocket for his phone. 'I need to get a picture of this.'

Thorne flashed a fixed, ha-bloody-ha grin. Said, 'Look at me, I'm pissing myself.' Then: 'Where's Nicola this morning, anyway?'

'Caught a nasty one first thing,' Brigstocke said. 'Still over there with Dipak.'

'What's the story?'

'You can ask her yourself when she comes back.' Brigstocke's phone began to ring in his hand. It was clearly a call he needed to take, so he stepped away. 'Have a look at what's already on the CADS. You know . . . ' he nodded towards Thorne's desk, 'if you can bear to drag yourself away from that lot.'

Thorne logged straight on to the Computer Aided Dispatch System and read through the reports that had begun to come in just before seven o'clock that morning.

A HAT team dispatched urgently to an address in Walthamstow.

No obvious signs of forced entry.

The body of a young woman discovered by her boyfriend half an hour earlier and displaying clear evidence of foul play.

Thorne looked at his watch and saw that he had been at work for less than two hours. Despite having made a decent crack at it, there was still a good-sized stack of witness statements, evidence logs and CPS correspondence to get through. It was the kind of thing Nicola Tanner would have breezed through by now, would have *enjoyed*, for pity's sake.

Instead, she'd been the one to catch a fresh murder case.

That was how it went, sometimes.

He took a folder from the pile and opened it roughly enough to tear the cover sheet. He began to read, knowing how little he was taking in. Thinking about the kind of copper he'd had Hatter marked down as and telling himself that whatever his own short-comings might be, he could at least put his hand up if he had to and admit that sometimes he was a full-on, solid-gold hypocrite.

Thorne sat there and hated himself for feeling jealous.

When Tanner returned to Becke House just before lunch, Thorne all but dragged her into his office.

'What's happening in Walthamstow, then?'

'Can I take my coat off first?'

Thorne smiled, like it was really no big deal, and sat waiting impatiently until Tanner had settled into the chair opposite.

'Gemma Maxwell,' Tanner said. 'Twenty-six. Discovered at home by her boyfriend just after six-thirty.' She let out a long breath, as though it was one she'd been holding since leaving the crime scene. She looked wrung out, but there was something fierce, unmissable, around her eyes and, as she let her head fall back, there was an air of what seemed like disbelief at what she'd seen. Incredulity *still*, at what people were capable of, despite the fact that she'd attended many such scenes before.

She looked, Thorne thought, the way any half-decent copper ought to look afterwards.

He only gave her a few seconds, because he knew she would not need any more. 'How was she killed?'

'No sign of a murder weapon,' Tanner said. 'But it looks like blunt force trauma. Significant trauma, too: there was a *lot* of blood. So, something the killer brought along to do the job or picked up in the house and took away with him.'

'No forced entry?'

Tanner shook her head.

'What about this boyfriend?'

She shook it again. 'Junior doctor on a night shift, so any number of people can vouch for his whereabouts. The doctor at the crime scene obviously wouldn't give us anything definitive, but she'd already been dead at least eight hours by the time the boyfriend got in from work.'

'Where's the hospital?'

'Whipps Cross, about a twenty-minute drive away. Look, I know what—'

'He couldn't have left work without anyone knowing?'

'He's a doctor in A and E. I think he might have been missed.'

'Nipped home for an hour?'

'It's not the boyfriend,' Tanner said. 'I've been with him for the best part of four hours. He's in bits.'

'They're always in bits.'

'I know that, but these days I can recognise the real thing when I see it.'

Thorne watched her try to smile, but saw the pain spasm behind it, just for a moment. He said, 'So, what now?'

'The victim was a teacher at a school over in Enfield, so I thought I'd probably start there.'

'Sounds like a plan.' Tanner's partner Susan had been a teacher; a murdered teacher. Thorne looked at her, but whatever he'd seen in her face a few seconds earlier had passed.

Tanner got to her feet. 'Talk to a few of her colleagues tomorrow, after the post-mortem.'

'Want some company?' Thorne saw the question on her face. 'Russell won't mind – well, certainly not if we forget to tell him, and the Margate thing's going nowhere, so . . .'

'I should really take Dipak,' she said. 'He's on this already.'

'I'm sure you can find him something useful to do—' He stopped when he saw that Tanner was eyeing the paperwork that was still taking up most of the space on his desktop. 'Yeah, talking of which, I don't suppose you've got half an hour to spare, have you?'

It wasn't as if she spat it at him, it was spoken rather more matter-of-factly than that, but still, it was a word Thorne couldn't remember hearing Tanner use before. He watched her turn and march out towards the incident room.

He put his head round the door and shouted after her.

'I was *joking* . . . '

THIRTY-ONE

More than once driving over there, Conrad thought how easy it would be just to turn round and head back to Sarah's, to pretend his life before her had never happened. The way things were now, the man she'd made of him, it might just as well not have happened, after all.

Wouldn't it be easier, just to forget certain people from his past, to sever contact completely?

Easier for him, no question about that.

He couldn't, though, because the woman he was on his way to see wouldn't allow it. The texts had made that pretty obvious, but then, she'd always been needy. He could have changed his phone of course, let her send her increasingly fraught messages into the ether and kept his head down, but the fact that he hadn't done so told him something. He'd been needy too once upon a time and she'd been there, and he could never deny that he owed her something; that he owed her plenty. She'd been important to him then and there was no way she was going to be fobbed off with a phone call or ghosted like one of his marks.

He needed to deal with the problem face to face.

He needed to deal with *her*.

It was hard to read her expression when she opened the door, as though she hadn't been altogether sure what she would feel when she saw him. How she was going to react. It might have been the fury she'd been saving up, or a perverse delight in spite of herself, but in that moment they cancelled one another out, leaving only a blank.

As if he wasn't there at all.

She said, 'Hello stranger,' and turned to walk back inside.

Conrad stepped in quickly and shut the door behind him. He said, 'Sorry,' because he was. For the weeks of silence, of absence, for what he'd come here to do and how she was going to feel afterwards.

She told him sorry was a start, but that he still had a long way to go.

She told him to sit down . . .

Half an hour later, fighting the urge to lash out at the first thing within range, inanimate or otherwise, Conrad climbed back into his car, slammed the door and sat staring at the building he had just left. Wondering what the woman inside was thinking. He was hot, so he turned the cold air on, but it just made him feel clammy as the sweat began to dry on his neck and chest.

He thought about what had just happened, going over the conversation as best he could remember it, in the hope that, just perhaps, things might not have gone quite as badly as he felt they had.

Inside her flat, he had done as he was told and sat down next to her.

He hadn't taken his jacket off.

He'd been hoping it wouldn't take very long.

She'd begun ranting almost immediately, berating him for daring to think that he could just cut her off. As if nothing had happened between them, as if she'd just imagined it. She had

156

shaken her head and sniggered at the idiocy of such an idea. Asked him if he seriously believed she was the same as those desperate women he seduced, then took for all they had.

'Of course I don't,' he'd said. 'You're being stupid.'

She'd shrugged and told him that being stupid was something she was getting used to. That she had been profoundly stupid for expecting a call or a message from him, stupid for thinking he might be in hospital or under arrest or dead.

'I understand why you're upset.' He'd looked around the room he'd been in so often before; that he could never return to again. 'That's why I thought it would be better to do this in person.'

She told him how very thoughtful he was.

'Look, there's no need—'

He'd stopped when she leaned quickly towards him. Asked exactly what he wanted to do in person.

'I can't see you any more.'

'*Can't?*'

He'd guessed this was going to be difficult, because he knew her. He already had a feeling that she knew what was coming, had known very well before he got there, but she clearly had no intention of helping things along. She wanted to see him suffer on the hook a while before he was allowed to wriggle off it.

He thought it was probably what he deserved.

'I don't *want* to see you any more.'

She'd looked at him for a few seconds, *studied* him. Her face had stayed immobile, but her fingers gathered up the material of her skirt and balled it into her fists. She was waiting for him to say it, daring him.

'There's somebody else.' He'd almost winced, as though he were the one on the receiving end of it. 'Look, I'm not saying this to hurt you ...'

She blinked and sat back. She looked crushed, as if the sarcasm and bitterness had been no more than bravado. 'Oh,' she said.

'I'm just trying to be honest.'

157

After half a minute or so, she had begun talking quietly, as if there was nobody listening. She said that, if she was being honest, she wasn't enormously surprised. She'd always expected something like this to happen, because men like him were so hugely, *sadly* predictable. It had only been a matter of time, she said. It was always on the cards.

'I didn't go looking for it,' he said.

She'd smiled, thin and sour, told him *that* made it all right then.

'At the start I thought she was going to be like the others.'

She'd nodded, like she was impressed; happy for him. Happy that this other woman was not simply one of the herd. That he hadn't got her to open her legs just so she'd open her purse later on. That this one was different.

He'd said nothing.

She'd told him that the funny thing, the *really* funny thing, was ... she'd thought *she* was different. Surely he remembered telling her that.

'She's ... special,' Conrad said. 'She's a remarkable woman and I know that can't be nice to hear, but I thought you deserved to be told the truth and not just left hanging on or whatever.' He stood up and took a few steps towards the door. 'So, that's it ... I'm sorry. What else can I say?'

She had waved his concern away. Nodded and assured him that he had no need to worry. That they could talk about it some more next time.

He'd turned back to her. '*What?*'

That was when she'd told him that it wasn't the way these things worked. She spoke softly, as though to a child who through no fault of their own had failed to grasp a very simple rule. That it wasn't the way *she* worked.

'Look, I told you, it's finished.'

She knew exactly what he'd told her, she said. She was not hard of hearing or understanding. But that only meant things were finished according to him.

'I'm with someone else, now,' Conrad said.

She smiled and reminded him gently how long they had known one another, how he should know very well by now that she *always* had a say.

He had hoped things might pan out a little better than this, but he had suspected that would be asking a lot. It had been a comforting fantasy, that was all. Whatever he and this woman had once meant to one another, he had always been . . . wary of her.

'What are you . . . going to do?' he asked.

She had sat back in her chair then, done with him for the time being. She told him that she would need to think about it, to mull things over for a while.

It was a lot to take in, after all.

Now Conrad had plenty to take in, too. An all-consuming new relationship and an old one that refused to die, thanks to a woman who was stubbornly refusing to let it. He had no idea what her next move would be, or his for that matter, but he knew where he needed to go.

He started the car, pulled out hard into traffic and put his foot down, desperate to get back to Sarah. To somewhere which, despite everything, felt suddenly like a place of safety.

THIRTY-TWO

'Claw-hammer,' Hendricks said, when they were done. 'So much easier to be sure when they've used the actual claw bit.'

The pathologist used two fingers to illustrate, but Tanner didn't need any help. She was not squeamish, never one of those who stood off to one side and waited for the headlines. She had watched it all, from Hendricks's first incision to the moment, two hours later, when an assistant had come in to replace the organs and stitch the body back together.

She had seen the wounds to Gemma Maxwell's skull.

'Thanks, Phil.'

'Oh, and she was pregnant.'

'Jesus.'

'Only just. She might not even have known herself.' Hendricks kicked open the door. 'Full report by the end of the day, bit of luck.'

They dropped scrub-suits, gowns, masks, boots and gloves into the clinical-waste bins in the dress-out room. In silence, they slipped their own jackets and shoes back on. Each took a healthy squirt from the hand-sanitizer before they stepped out into the corridor and began walking towards Hendricks's office in the basement of Hornsey Mortuary.

A perfectly grim and perfectly ordinary start to the day.

'Be very nice if you got a result on this one,' Hendricks said.

'Always nice.'

'Yeah, course.'

'I know what you mean, though.'

'A fucking claw-hammer . . .'

'Let's hope what you found under her fingernails does us a favour.' Tanner looked at her watch. The sample had already been dispatched and she was hopeful of a result within a few hours.

Hendricks nodded. 'Scratched him when she saw what was coming. Must have done, because she certainly wouldn't have been able to do a fat lot after he'd started. First blow was enough to kill her.'

Once again, Tanner had seen the evidence.

The cracks and fissures, the ragged holes in the pale skull.

The first of many blows.

When they reached the office, Hendricks sat down and said, 'Tom not on this one, then?'

'He's trying to muscle his way in.' Tanner lingered in the doorway. There was no reason she needed to be there, but she had some time to kill before she was due at the school. Some of Hendricks's lewder pronouncements could still annoy her, but she had been starting to enjoy his company a lot more recently. 'I think he's bored.'

'You know he saw Helen the other night?'

'He didn't say anything to me.'

'Me, neither.' Hendricks moved files across his desk to give himself access to his keyboard. He typed a word or two, then slid his chair across to check something on the *Arsenal Legends* calendar pinned to a corkboard. 'Helen told me.'

'Oh yeah, I always forget you two are matey,' Tanner said.

'Come on, Helen's *way* nicer than he is.' He grinned. 'If ever a woman was going to turn me ... well, apart from your good self, obviously ... '

'So, how did it go?'

'Well, I don't think anything got sorted out, but it sounds like it was friendly enough. Cleared the air a bit, I think.'

'That's good.'

'Yeah. She told him he'd been a bit distant or something.' Hendricks glanced up. 'Keeping stuff from her.'

They didn't look at each other at all after that; didn't say anything else about it, because they didn't need to.

Tanner took a step out into the corridor. 'So, end of the day then, the report?'

'Fingers crossed.' Hendricks was already typing again. 'Mind you, you'll be lucky if you get your reports inside a month, the rate people keep killing each other round here. Pulling out knives at the drop of a designer baseball cap. Forget "worse than New York", mate, it's getting like South Africa or Columbia, whatever.'

Tanner had already gone.

Rachel Peake, the headmistress of Brooklands Hill, was somewhat younger than Thorne had expected. Perhaps it was simply the word itself that conjured fearsome images involving tweed and severity, or it might simply have been that teachers looked a lot more youthful the older you got, like coppers. Like everyone.

'We're obviously all stunned,' she said. 'Just ... numb, really.'

'Of course,' Tanner said.

As she and Thorne sat down, the headmistress took her own seat behind a glass and blond-wood desk and stared at them. Though she was dressed like a no-nonsense businesswoman, Thorne could sense a warmth and fragility in the woman, though it was impossible to know how much of that was down to the current situation. He looked around. If there was any tweed hidden away in her large, comfortable office, he certainly couldn't spot it.

'Just thinking about what we should do. You know, what we should tell the children. I need to talk to the governors, but I think we should probably shut the school for a couple of days.'

'It might be an idea,' Tanner said.

Thorne remembered the memorial service that had been held at Susan's school after her death, an event he'd attended as Tanner's 'beard'. The packed assembly hall. A Pete Seeger song and tributes from weeping children.

'I've started trying to write a letter to send out to parents, but ... what do you *say*?'

'It's not easy.' Thorne immediately began to wonder what he would say in similar circumstances. The pat phrases. *The sad loss of a much-loved teacher ... taken from us in tragic circumstances.* He would probably leave out the pregnancy and the part about the claw-hammer.

There was a knock at the door and the headmistress's secretary stepped in with tea things which she set down on the desk. She was rather more what Thorne had been expecting. The curt manner and air of self-importance he had thought was unique to GPs' receptionists. He watched the woman noisily wrangle cups and saucers, wondering what qualifications were specified on the application form for her job.

Good computer skills.

Administrative experience preferred.

Face like a smacked arse.

The Head nodded towards the door when the secretary had closed it quietly behind her. 'Janet hasn't stopped crying since she found out.'

Thorne shifted slightly in his seat, thinking that grief could take many forms. Thinking that he might usefully add 'insensitive arsehole' to his own job description.

163

While Peake poured milk and handed cups across, there was another knock on the door. 'I asked a couple of Gemma's colleagues to join us,' she said quickly. 'They knew her a little better than I did. I mean, obviously I *knew* her, but . . . I thought it might be useful.'

'Thanks. I'm sure it will be,' Tanner said.

'I should tell you that they don't know about Gemma yet. I wanted to let members of staff know individually, but . . . '

'It's not a problem,' Thorne said. *What do you* say? Easier to leave it to people who had become used to saying it.

The two teachers who came in looked even younger than the headmistress and if Thorne hadn't known that they had yet to hear the news, their expressions would have made it obvious enough. Curious, but more than a little apprehensive. Clearly, being summoned to the Head's office, even one as welcoming as this, was only marginally less scary for staff than it was for pupils.

Rachel made the introductions. Karl Sturridge was mixed-race and stocky with his hair in cornrows, and when Tanner calmly explained why she and Thorne were at the school his eyes widened, then began to blink fast behind designer glasses. Alice Thomason was a few inches taller than her workmate, mousey-haired and skinny in soft, woollen dungarees worn over a bright yellow top. She said, 'Jesus,' then 'Fuck,' and looked across at her boss, embarrassed.

The Head told the teacher not to worry, that she had said much the same when she had been told, then suggested that they all move across to a rather more informal seating area on the other side of the office.

'Who the hell would want to hurt Gemma?' Alice settled on to a low red sofa. She looked to Thorne and Tanner, to Karl. 'Oh God, poor Andy.'

Thorne glanced at Tanner. The boyfriend.

'I should call him.' Karl looked at Thorne. 'We used to play five-a-side together.'

164

'Maybe you should give it a day or two,' Tanner said.

'Oh, yeah, course . . .'

'Was everything OK between Gemma and Andy?' Thorne asked.

Alice stared at him and her mouth opened slowly.

Tanner stared at Thorne, too, then quickly sat forward. 'I know this is a huge shock and you're still struggling to take it in, and it's a natural reaction to say what you just said. To ask who could possibly do something like this to a friend of yours, why anyone might want to hurt her, but it's our job to ask you exactly that.' She looked at them both. 'So, you'd really be helping us if you could think very carefully about that, OK?'

Karl and Alice nodded, like children in one of their classes.

'What about a jealous ex?' Thorne asked. 'Anyone you can think of from her past?'

'She used to go out with a guy called Rob,' Alice said. 'But they're still good mates and he lives in France now, I think.'

'Any family problems? Siblings . . . ?'

'Just a sister,' Karl said. 'An . . . *elder* sister?' He looked at Alice.

She nodded. 'They're really close.'

'That's right,' Rachel said. 'Gemma talked about her sister a lot.'

'Did she ever say anything about anyone scaring her?' Tanner had her notebook open but had yet to write anything. 'Threatening her?'

'Not to me,' Karl said.

'Had she noticed anyone hanging around outside her house?' Thorne asked. 'Outside the school?'

'Well, if she did, she never said anything.'

Rachel Peake shook her head.

'Hang on.' Alice waved a hand, then a finger. 'She did tell me about this woman she was going to be having words with. It sounds a bit . . . weird actually, but there was some woman who was a parent and Gemma was convinced that she *wasn't* actually a parent . . . that for whatever reason she was just hanging around, pretending to have a child at the school. Gemma said she was going to confront her about it.'

'When was this?' Tanner asked.

'Back end of last week, I think. Friday, maybe?'

'What woman?' Thorne asked.

'Why did she never say anything about this to me?' Rachel sounded as though she had half a mind to tell the dead woman off.

'She was trying to avoid making it official, that's all,' Alice said. 'She wanted to try and sort it out herself first.' She looked at Karl. 'I mean, this woman obviously had . . . problems, you know? I think Gemma felt quite sorry for her, actually.'

'Yeah, that sounds like Gemma,' Karl said.

Now Tanner was writing. 'Did Gemma mention the woman's name?'

'I don't think she even knew it. But if you talk to some of the other parents, I'm sure they know exactly who she is. Gemma said she was always hanging around with the same group.' She turned to Karl. 'You know, the Year One mums.'

'Yeah, I think I know who she means,' Karl said.

Alice looked at Rachel. 'Jacob's mum is one of them . . . and Arjun's mum.'

The Head nodded at Tanner. 'I can give you those people's names.' She looked at her watch. 'Actually, the parents usually start to gather at the gates in about an hour and I'm sure they'll be there if you want to talk to them.'

Tanner closed her notebook. 'Thank you,' she said. 'We do.'

While Thorne was using the Gents, Tanner stood just inside the main door to the school, looking at the pictures tacked to the wall. Golden suns with radiating sunbeams and houses that all had four windows, a smoking chimney, and a perfect square of garden at the front, even though the majority of the kids who had drawn them did not live in places remotely like that.

'Why would someone pretend to have a child?' she asked.

Thorne had emerged and moved to stand beside her. He wiped wet hands off on the front of his jeans. 'I haven't got the foggiest.' He was thinking that these were the kinds of pictures Alfie drew, when he could be bothered to tear himself away from the screen of his iPad.

'Not really much point going anywhere,' Tanner said.

'Right.' Thorne was looking at another picture and, for no reason he could fathom, he was suddenly thinking about his mother. Another dream from a few nights earlier.

'Why don't we grab a coffee round the corner?'

'Yeah.' Thorne wasn't really listening.

'Come back at pick-up time . . .'

THIRTY-THREE

Sarah had always rather enjoyed spending time alone at home. There was usually something interesting to listen to on the radio or watch on TV in the hours between drop-off and pick-up and a big house to keep clean and tidy, so she was rarely short of something to do. Even if she was feeling lazy, there was plenty to sit and think about and there was the metal box out in the garage if she was in that kind of mood.

These days, though, the time she spent on her own dragged horribly, every hour and minute counted down until Conrad was with her again. Not knowing how soon that would be was excruciating and, right now, she was clueless about it, because he had gone out by the time she'd returned home, and she had no idea where he was.

What he was doing.

She'd left the house early herself. Woken Conrad with a kiss before going, getting nothing in return but a bad-tempered moan before he'd turned over and gone back to sleep. Often, she woke him in rather more exciting ways, but there had been no time for that this morning.

She'd had to think that bit more carefully about how she should dress. There were big decisions about exactly what to do with make-up and hair that had, of course, been dyed and re-styled the day after her confrontation with the teacher at Brooklands Hill.

She'd needed to get all that spot on.

It was a big day, because there were new schools to check out.

She'd looked at three in the end, another two that were local and one out in Woodford. The longer journeys every day wouldn't be much fun, but it couldn't be helped, so she'd already decided that she'd pick somewhere further afield if she had to. It made sense of course to do exactly that. She didn't want to move Jamie to a school just up the road from Brooklands Hill and run the risk of bumping into any of those parents. The likes of David and Caroline clucking at her, asking where on earth she'd been and what had happened.

No, this was all about finding a brand-new group, starting again.

She'd had to do it several times before, because Jamie rarely stayed too long at any school. She wasn't stupid and knew that any more than a few months was probably pushing her luck, so she'd become well used to moving on. She preferred to choose when that would be, but once or twice the decision had been made for her, thanks to a nosy parent who couldn't resist blabbing, or a teacher like that nosy little cow at Brooklands Hill, who paid a little too much attention to the adults, when really it was their job to be taking care of children.

Sticking their beaks in where they weren't wanted.

Well, now she had Conrad to help her, people like that would get what was coming to them.

She never went into the schools, of course, when she was visiting. There was no need to meet the head teacher or be given a tour of the facilities. It was more about what went on outside: the atmosphere at the gates; the parking situation; the local gathering

169

places. It was a shame, because she'd miss those mornings in the coffee shop. She'd actually grown to really like Heather and a couple of the others, but in the end she had to do what was best for her son.

After all, they'd do exactly the same, wouldn't they?

As it happened, she'd already taken quite a liking to the big school in Woodford. Bigger was always better and she'd spoken to one or two of the parents, who seemed very nice. She'd trotted out the same story, of course, as it usually did the trick.

Just moved to the area, so looking for somewhere that's going to make Jamie feel welcome. Hard on him, of course, moving around all the time, but kids are very adaptable, aren't they? Jamie has always been great at making new friends. Yes, he's a fairly shy boy, but once he's got the lie of the land he's happy to muck in, and he usually gets on with people.

She checked the kitchen clock again. It was impossible to know how long Conrad had been gone for. She'd already rung his mobile several times but couldn't get hold of him. Bad reception, probably, wherever he was. She thought about nipping out to the garage for a smoke but didn't want to run the risk of Conrad's coming back and catching her. They hadn't really talked about drugs, so she wasn't sure how he felt about it. It would be OK, she was pretty sure about that, because he'd want her to do whatever made her happy; course he would. He always did.

When she heard the key in the door, it was hard to control the urge to spring from the sofa, to rush and meet him. She waited until he came into the front room and stood up to kiss him. Like she was pleased he was back, that was all, not like she wasn't wearing any underwear.

It was the best part of her day.

'I've been calling you,' she said.

'I had my phone turned off.'

'Where were you?'

He didn't say anything.

She grinned, getting it. 'Have you found a new one?'

'Just looking,' he said. 'Feel like I should, you know?'

'Of course you should.' She pressed her hands against his chest. When he stepped away and walked towards the kitchen, she followed him. 'Anyone you fancy?'

'Not really.' He opened the fridge, took out a bottle of water and filled a glass. 'Thought I'd found a couple of likely candidates, but it didn't go anywhere.'

'Where?'

'Usual places, you know. I tried a couple of supermarkets, coffee shops . . .'

'I was thinking,' she said. 'Why don't you find them online? There's loads of those sites, dating apps or whatever.'

'I don't trust them,' he said. 'Never have.'

'Why not?'

'You'll laugh.' He looked and saw that she was waiting. 'Everyone's lying on those dating sites, aren't they?'

She smiled, in spite of everything.

'I can get a much better read off someone face to face. I can smell if there's money to be made, you know? Besides, when I'm with a woman, I want to be sure that at least one of us is telling the truth.'

Sarah nodded, seeing the sense of it. 'So, whereabouts have you been looking?'

He put his glass down. 'Why are you so interested?'

'I'm interested in everything you do.' She was trying not to look hurt, to sound weak. That was for bedtime. 'We're partners, aren't we?'

'Yeah, but this is *my* thing, isn't it? You said you wanted me to have my own life, remember? This is my work. Obviously, I'll tell you when things are happening, but this part's always tricky, you know? I don't really want to get into it until I've definitely got something on the go. It's like it might jinx it, or something.'

Sarah watched him empty the glass, avoiding her stare. Of

course, she understood what he was saying, and she respected his need to keep something for himself. Close as they were, closer than she thought it was possible to be, nobody wanted to feel suffocated, did they?

She knew he was lying, though.

She told herself that it was nothing to worry about, that he was just naturally nervous about starting a new job. It was a shame, because she was sure she could help him with it, maybe even help him find someone to work on, but that was up to him. So, she wouldn't push it.

'It was in the papers today,' he said. 'The teacher.'

'Oh yeah?'

'I saw it.'

Sarah didn't much care for the look on Conrad's face. Obviously she hated to see him worried, but really, there was no need to bring stuff like that into the house with him, was there? They'd had a problem and it had been dealt with and that was good news, surely.

'I think we should move,' he said.

'Move?'

'Yeah, get away. The police are going to be talking to people at the school, so they'll know about you.'

'Know what, exactly?' She laughed. 'There's nothing to know.'

'I just think we should be sensible—'

'This is my *home* ... *our* home, now. Why should we have to leave?' She studied his expression, searching for something positive. Why wasn't he happier? As happy as she was? 'Actually, I went to see some new schools,' she said.

'Any joy?'

'Maybe,' she said. 'One that definitely looks interesting.'

'That's great.'

He moved past her into the hallway. Sarah took a few steps after him, then stopped and watched him turn to go upstairs. 'I probably won't decide until I've seen a few more.'

She thought about asking him if he fancied going with her, had broached the subject in a roundabout way once already, but he hadn't seemed very keen. He'd been ... ambivalent, at best.

It was fair enough, Sarah decided.

Perhaps it was still a little too soon for all that, to be asking Conrad how he felt about being Jamie's dad.

THIRTY-FOUR

'*HazBeanz*?' Thorne stared down at the smiley face stencilled into his froth. 'God help us.'

'Coffee's good though,' Tanner said.

'I should bloody well hope so at these prices.' He raised the heavy earthenware mug. 'This expenses claim is probably going to mean three less coppers on the beat next month.' He looked around and wondered what all these people were doing there in the middle of the afternoon. What *he* was doing there, when there was a perfectly good café across the road.

'Why did you ask those teachers about Gemma's boyfriend?'

Thorne looked up. Tanner had her telling-off face on. He said, 'Well . . .'

'I told you yesterday it was nothing to do with him.'

'Because he looked upset?'

'He isn't involved.'

'Hardly solid evidence though, is it?'

'No, it isn't,' Tanner said. 'Which is why, just to be on the safe side, I sent Dipak to the hospital last night to speak to a few of his colleagues.'

'See? I said you could find something useful for him to do.'

'He was definitely there for the whole of his shift.' She waited, to be sure Thorne understood. 'So, you can forget about the boyfriend.'

'What boyfriend?'

'Good boy,' Tanner said. She sipped at her coffee and, the next time she looked at him, she had a face on with which Thorne was altogether less familiar. 'Listen ... what did you make of that teacher?'

'Karl? Even less likely than the boyfriend, I reckon. But if you want to check him out, you know, just to be on the safe side—'

'Alice.'

'What did I *make* of her?'

Tanner leaned towards him and lowered her voice. She was starting to redden a little. 'Did you think she might be gay?'

'What, just because she was wearing dungarees?'

'Shut up.'

Thorne shook his head in mock disapproval. 'That's *such* an offensive stereotype.'

Tanner waited, not a flicker of a smile.

'How the hell should I know?'

'OK ... look ... it doesn't matter.'

'So, what, the old Gaydar tweaking a bit, was it?'

'Sometimes I wonder whether I've even got one,' Tanner said. 'Always been rubbish at that. I just thought she was ... nice, that's all.'

Thorne sat back and folded his arms, keen to enjoy the moment. 'Can I just remind you about the lecture I got a few weeks back, when I asked you about Ella Fulton?'

'Not the same thing.'

'No?'

Tanner began to look uncomfortable.

'One rule for you and a different one for everyone else, is that what you're telling me, DI Tanner?'

'Just forget it.'

Thorne watched her turn away and immediately felt bad about making light of the situation. He could not recall a single occasion since Susan had been killed on which Tanner had expressed the remotest interest in another woman. Had even hinted that she might be considering the idea.

Maybe, he thought, she just had a thing for teachers . . .

'Call her,' Thorne said.

'What?'

'OK, well if you think that's a bit up front . . . look, there's any number of reasons we might need to talk to her again, isn't there? Bring her in to do this e-fit, whatever. A few follow-up questions.' Thorne held his arms out; job done. 'Then, just have a cup of tea and a chat with her afterwards, see how it goes. Or an expensive coffee.'

'I don't think so.' Tanner looked as though she was seriously regretting bringing the subject up.

'Why not?'

'You were right,' she said. 'It would be seriously unprofessional.'

'I was only kidding.'

'It's not a good idea.'

'Look, I get it,' Thorne said. 'You're a bit shy, but you shouldn't—'

'I'm not shy,' Tanner said. 'It's not about being shy.'

'So . . . ?'

'It's been eighteen months, Tom.' She looked down at the table. 'A year and a half.'

Thorne nodded, getting it. 'Yeah. It's a long time.'

'No, you don't understand.' Tanner wrapped her hands around her mug, held it against her cheek. 'I'm worried that it's not long enough.'

They decided that it might be counter-productive to wade straight into the gathering of parents waiting outside the gates, so having conferred with Rachel Peake, the Headmistress selected the group Alice Thomason had mentioned and invited them inside. She led the one man and three women into an empty classroom, where Thorne and Tanner were waiting. She had deliberately avoided the classroom where Gemma Maxwell had taught, outside which someone had already laid a bunch of flowers.

'I'll leave you to it,' she said.

One of the women said, 'Sorry, what's this about?'

The Head opened the door to let herself out. 'The officers will explain, Caroline ...'

Tanner introduced herself and Thorne, then asked each person for their name and noted them down.

Heather Turnbull.

David Herbert.

Savita Kohli.

Caroline Wood-Wilson.

'We're hoping you might be able to help us,' Thorne said. 'That's all. It's just a few questions—'

'Oh, God, is this about that murder?' Caroline again. She looked at her friends. 'It was in the *Standard*. I picked one up at the garage on the way here. A primary school in Enfield, it said.'

'*What?*' David stood up a little straighter.

Thorne looked at Tanner.

'It didn't *say* it was this school, but ... it is, isn't it?' Caroline leaned close to Heather. She could not help looking a little pleased with herself, at her powers of deduction or perhaps just the opportunity to share such dramatic news. 'One of the teachers.'

'You're kidding,' Heather said.

Tanner held up a hand. Said, 'Please ...'

As was usually the case, they had been hoping that the story might stay out of the press a little while longer, so had not issued any statements as yet, but with a major murder inquiry a leak of some kind was almost unavoidable. It was impossible to keep a crime scene as busy as this one had been secret from the victim's neighbours, and, though they would all have been spoken to by the officers in attendance, they could not realistically be sworn to silence. Equally, a SOCO may have let something slip in the pub, or it might have been someone from the hospital where the victim's partner worked. There had certainly been nothing in that morning's papers, but if a story – however vague – was being run in the early edition of the *Standard* it would be online already, on the news that evening and all over the nationals by tomorrow.

It didn't much matter now.

'I'm sorry,' Tanner said. 'But we can't divulge any information about our enquiries at this point.'

'Which teacher is it?' Caroline asked.

'As I said—'

Thorne stepped forward and tried to pick up where he'd left off, before he'd been interrupted by the Wood-Wilson woman. 'As of now, we just need to ask you a few questions about one of the other parents, that's all. A woman we've been led to believe you were friendly with. I'm afraid we don't have a name or a description.'

'If it's any help,' Tanner said, 'you probably won't have seen her for a few days.'

They all looked at one another.

'*Sarah*.' David nodded. 'Well, I certainly haven't seen her. I mean, she could be unwell, I suppose.'

'I've not seen her either.' Heather looked at Thorne. 'She hasn't been at drop-off or pick-up, so maybe it's Jamie that's not well.'

'Jamie's the name of her son, right?' Thorne said. 'That's what she told you?'

Heather looked at him.

'Sarah . . . if that's the woman we're all talking about . . . didn't actually have a child at this school. We're not sure why yet, but for some reason she was just pretending she did.'

178

'I knew there was something strange about her.' Caroline turned to Savita, who had yet to say anything at all. 'I said that to you, didn't I? Yes, there was definitely something ... off about her.'

Savita appeared a little uncomfortable to see that everyone was now looking at her. She said, 'Why would she do that? Why would you want to pretend?'

'I never ever saw Jamie.' David nodded, as if he finally understood. 'Not once. Did anyone else?'

Heather and Savita shook their heads.

'Well, of course you didn't,' Caroline said, as though she had worked everything out months before.

'Do you know Sarah's second name?' Tanner asked. 'Or have any idea where she lives?'

There was more head-shaking. 'Sorry, it just ... never came up,' Heather said. 'You chat at the gates, you have a coffee in the morning, whatever. That's it.'

'What about a phone number?'

Heather reached for her phone and began scrolling. 'Yeah, I've got one ...'

'I didn't know you were that close,' Caroline said.

'Well, we were friendly enough, so we swapped numbers. Here you go ...'

She handed the phone across. Thorne dialled, then shook his head. 'Not in service.'

Tanner did not look particularly surprised.

'Oh,' Heather said. 'I only called her the other day.'

Caroline nodded towards David and Savita. 'I mean, *we've* got each other's numbers, but that's because we're involved with various school committees. Our kids play together.'

'Sarah never really wanted to join in,' Savita said.

'True,' David said.

'She always kept her distance. I mean, it's pretty obvious why now, isn't it?'

'She had a boyfriend,' Savita said suddenly. 'They'd just moved in together, I think. I don't know if that's any help, but . . .'

'Ah, yes of course, the wonderful *boyfriend*.' Caroline nodded knowingly at Thorne and Tanner. 'Very smitten, she was. Wouldn't stop banging on about him.'

'Do you have a name?' Thorne asked.

'Conrad . . . something.' Caroline looked to her friends for help, but none of them appeared to know any more than she did. 'We were all there when she met him in the coffee shop, as a matter of fact.' She turned to Heather. 'Remember? The bloke I thought was a friend of yours?'

'Was he?' Thorne asked Heather.

'No.' Heather sounded a little irritated at the suggestion. 'I'd never seen him before.' She glanced at Caroline. 'I told you.'

A look of horror spread across Caroline's face as she stared at Thorne. 'You don't think he's got anything to do with . . . *this*, do you?'

'This being . . . ?'

'The murder. One of the teachers.' Seeing that she wasn't going to get an answer, Caroline turned to Savita and David. 'I didn't much like the look of him if I'm honest. And like I said, I always thought there was something very peculiar about *her*.'

Thorne looked at Tanner, who was scribbling in her notebook. He mouthed, 'Fuck's sake . . . '

When he turned back to the parents, Heather was saying something to Caroline about 'serious emotional problems' and David had begun talking to Savita. As though influenced by her surroundings, Tanner had raised her arm, and was waving a hand in an effort to get everyone's attention again when her phone rang.

She looked at Thorne. 'I need to take this . . . '

When Tanner had stepped out of the room, Thorne asked for everyone's details. As soon as he'd finished taking down numbers and email addresses, he said, 'We might ask a couple of you to come in to help us put an e-fit together. Whichever of you knew Sarah best, or has a good memory for faces. Same thing for this boyfriend of hers.'

'I'm happy to do it,' Caroline said.

Thorne was not surprised that the woman had been the first to volunteer. Anything for a half-decent story at her next dinner party, he guessed. He said, 'Thanks.'

'Actually, I might even have a photo of her somewhere.' David took out his phone and began to stab and scroll. 'I think I took a picture of everyone in the coffee shop.'

'I remember that,' Heather said.

Thorne waited.

'Sorry, I can't find it . . .'

'Well, if you do, we'd be grateful if you could send it to us.' The door opened and Thorne looked up to see Tanner in the doorway. Her expression made it clear that she needed to talk to him urgently, that there was no time for a lengthy winding up. He moved quickly to join her, confident that the parents would stay put for a while, with plenty to talk about among themselves.

When Thorne came out, Tanner closed the classroom door.

'They managed to extract DNA from the skin Phil took from under Gemma Maxwell's fingernails,' she said. 'And we've got a match.'

Tanner looked rather more bewildered, shocked even, than Thorne would have expected, given such good news. 'What?'

'It matches the suspect in the Margate killing.' Now she *sounded* bewildered. 'The same suspect whose DNA was all over Philippa Goodwin's flat. Your con-artist again.'

Thorne stared at her.

'Looks like he's getting a taste for this kind of thing.'

He said, 'That's . . . mental.'

Tanner began to say something about what a ridiculous coincidence it would be if this woman they'd just been talking about wasn't somehow connected to Gemma Maxwell's murder.

How she may well be involved in some way with whoever had killed Gemma and how, if that *was* the same person who'd killed Kevin Deane . . .

Thorne's hand was already busy at the back of his head, fingers moving through the fine hairs at the nape of his neck; the prickle that had begun to spread.

Tanner didn't need to say it.

'Looks like we've found your mystery woman.'

THIRTY-FIVE

In the garage, she took a joint from the tin, carried it across to the deckchair and lit up. She had decided that it didn't much matter if Conrad were to catch her. It wasn't like she was on heroin or a secret alcoholic or anything, and hadn't she been the one insisting that there should be no secrets?

Besides which, she needed it.

After they'd eaten, he had suddenly announced that he was tired and fancied an early night, which was certainly not something that had ever happened before. She couldn't remember a single night when they hadn't gone to bed at the same time, when they hadn't made love. She had chosen not to say anything, deciding that things might have been tricky after their conversation earlier – that horrible business about what he'd seen in the paper – so instead she'd just smiled and watched Conrad trudge upstairs, thinking that he *did* look worn out suddenly.

Thinking that a smoke might stop her wondering what he had been doing to exhaust himself quite so much.

I've been calling you.

I had my phone turned off.

She drew hard on the joint and sucked in fast. It tasted harsher than she was used to and she had to stop coughing before she could take another hit. A different batch of weed, maybe and hadn't she read somewhere that stuff got added sometimes?

She sat back and waited for the lovely, slow *shush* of it.

She needed to relax, she knew that, to think about how lucky she was and to enjoy it. More than anything she wanted to let herself sink and go back just a little, to those first few days together, when this new relationship had pushed everything out of her head and heart . . . God, even Jamie, if she was being honest with herself. She needed to remember what Conrad had smelled like that first time, the taste of him.

What he did to her . . .

She brought the joint to her lips again and closed her eyes.

The memories gathered speed quickly, though, and began to blur, refusing to slow for more than few moments at anywhere like the recent past, taking her a long way further back than she would have liked, until finally they juddered to a halt in the usual place.

That small garden.

When Sarah was exactly ten years old and it was just the two of them . . .

Those handlebars, poking up from their scrubby lawn. The rest of her bike underground, unreachable . . .

She walks slowly across the garden and for a second or two she wonders if she's actually woken up yet. It can't be real, surely. How much work must that have been?

All night, probably, for him to dig a hole deep enough, to arrange it exactly like this.

So she can see it, but she can never have it.

There's a brief moment of hope, when she thinks that maybe her bike will be much easier to pull up than she thinks, that's it all just a daft joke, but as soon as she makes the effort, she knows it will be impossible.

'Some things you have to work for,' her father says.

She settles down in the dirt, still in her pyjamas, kneeling over the spot where she guesses the saddle must be. She wraps her hands around the handlebars, the black rubber grips with yellow streamers attached that she'd pointed out to her father in the shop.

She pulls and pulls and pulls.

'You don't deserve it if you don't try,' her father says.

The handlebars don't budge, not even an inch, because there's just too much weight, too much earth to move and her arms aren't strong enough. Still, she stays there until it gets dark, pulling and crying, and there are blisters on her hands by the time her father says, 'Enough,' and she walks back into the house. Her father shakes his head and puts an arm around her shoulders, and says, 'Look at the state of you . . . '

He stands her in the bath and washes the mud off her, slowly.

She knows how fierce her father is because her friends are all scared of him, she's always known. His anger at . . . something; at her because she's the cause of it, or because she's simply the nearest thing. Angry enough to carry her new bike out into the garden and dig through the night. She knows, but even so, her own anger doesn't last, it never does. All the hatred that has built until it's like something drumming fast inside her starts to fade, then run away with the mud that streaks down her chest and legs until the bathwater is black with it.

Because she can feel how fierce his love is, too.

She can feel it in his hands on her, and she will carry on feeling it, the terrifying heat of it, as she spends days looking out at the garden through a curtain of rain and watches the handlebars of her bike begin to rust.

His hands on her.

The hands of men who would use her then push her away.

185

Conrad's hands . . .

Sarah opened her eyes and stood up. She brushed the ash from her shirt and threw the butt into a bucket, let a minute or two pass until she was breathing normally again.

Then she walked back into the house to wake him.

THIRTY-SIX

Dr Melita Perera handed the picture back across the table to Thorne. A printout of the photo taken in the Enfield coffee shop, which David Herbert had eventually managed to locate on his phone and sent across three days earlier.

'She looks perfectly ordinary, of course,' Perera said. 'Well, what you can see of her. Because they almost always do.'

Thorne looked at the photograph again. Heather Turnbull, Savita Kohli and Caroline Wood-Wilson. The woman with them – whom they and the police still knew only as 'Sarah' – sitting at the end of the table, her face half hidden by a carefully positioned menu.

Coffee and cake.

Just one of the mums.

'I didn't think it would tell you anything very much.' Thorne folded the printout and put it back in his pocket. 'I just thought you might be interested in seeing it, that was all.' He had immediately sent the photo, such as it was, to Colin Hatter, with the presumption that it would be widely circulated around Margate, but for all he knew the DI from Kent had pinned it up above his desk and done bugger all else. He might just as well have done. As far as the Gemma Maxwell investigation went, the picture had been shown on *BBC London* and printed as part of a major follow-up story in the *Standard*, but, despite a number of reported sightings, it had thrown up no major leads.

'What about the man you mentioned on the phone?' Perera lifted her glass of sparkling water from the table and sat back. 'No photos of him, I suppose?'

Thorne shook his head. 'An e-fit, but I don't think it'll do us a fat lot of good.' Having seen him in the coffee shop, Heather Turnbull and the others had been able to provide a decent enough description of the man they'd known as Conrad and Thorne still thought of as Patrick Jennings. He was clearly someone who changed his appearance on a regular basis. Knowing what they did about the woman he was now involved with, there was every reason to believe that she had already done the same thing.

Now, Thorne and Tanner were looking for *two* ghosts, and though DNA and prints were certainly a start, false names and a pair of iffy pictures had left them with nowhere to go.

It was why he had called Melita Perera.

She was the forensic psychiatrist brought in seven months before, during an investigation which had begun with a series of cat-killings, and Thorne had consulted with her several times once that case had ... broadened out. Because it was close to her office in Lincoln's Inn Fields, they had met in this same Holborn bar several times back then. Today, the place was crowded with lunchtime drinkers, and though Thorne had been disappointed to discover that the chalkboards and exposed pipes were still there, he was pleased to see that Melita Perera had not changed either.

Willowy, in a dark business suit, long dark hair pinned up, the Sri Lankan heritage evident in her looks ...

'Easy, tiger.' What Hendricks had said on the phone the night before, when Thorne had mentioned who he would be meeting, well aware it was a woman to whom Thorne had taken something of a shine seven months previously.

'Don't be daft,' Thorne had said.

Thinking wasn't doing.

'No, course not, it's purely professional, obviously. Don't know what I was thinking . . . and you weren't like a dog with two dicks when you were talking about that photographer woman a few weeks back, either.' Hendricks had clearly found the whole thing hilarious. 'What's the matter with you, mate? You got a job lot of Viagra you need to get through?'

Not for the first time, Thorne had told himself that perhaps he confided in Phil Hendricks a little too much, but he couldn't really deny his friend had a point. This twitching of certain . . . antennae was clearly a reaction of some sort to what was happening with Helen, to being – theoretically – on the market again.

But all the same . . .

'Before I forget,' Hendricks had been unable to resist, 'you know that old tramp, the really smelly one who sits outside Kentish Town station every day? He is definitely giving you the eye.'

'What *would* be interesting is to see the two of them together,' Perera said now. 'To see how they appear as a couple.'

'Right.' Thorne stared across the table at her.

'It might tell us nothing, of course.' She leaned forward. 'But sometimes you can get a sense of a hierarchy at least. Even a picture might provide some indication of which of them is the dominant partner.'

'There's always one of them calling the shots, you mean?'

'Usually,' she said. 'Even when it's not a conventional couple, even if it's two straight men killing together. One partner is almost always submissive to the other in some way. Actually, I shouldn't even use that word because, strictly speaking, it isn't a partnership.' She sipped her water and looked at him. 'You had a case like that once, I remember you telling me.'

Thorne nodded. During the cat-killing inquiry, he had asked her about Stuart Nicklin; a serial offender who had once operated as one half of a murderous double act. There could be little doubt as to who had been the dominant force in that pairing and though Nicklin's current whereabouts remained unknown, it was a force of which Thorne remained very much aware.

'So you know what I'm talking about.'

Thorne told her that he did.

'OK, so if we're looking specifically at *couples* who kill, let's take Hindley and Brady . . . a long time ago, obviously.'

Thorne nodded again. The best example. The worst.

'Well, I was a kid,' he said.

'Luckily not one growing up in Manchester, though.'

'No.'

'They're always cited as the perfect model of a *folie à deux*, but I'm not convinced.'

Thorne waited. He just about understood the French, but was more than happy for Perera to explain.

'Literally, madness of two,' she said. 'Which suggests an equality which I'm not sure was actually the case. So, broadly speaking, we're talking about some weird chemistry between two particular people that creates delusions or exaggerates delusions that were already there. A sum that's greater than its parts, which, if you're talking about delusions that lead to murder, is a sum that can be truly horrific.'

'Not like that with Hindley and Brady, though?'

'Well, it's exactly what happened in their case, of course, but based on what I know about it, I don't think it was any kind of joint madness, which is why I don't actually believe they were equal partners. I think he was the dominant force.' Both moved their chairs a little closer to the table and Perera lowered her voice. 'So, Brady wrote a letter to the Home Office in the late nineties, explaining why he thought that Hindley should not be granted parole. He denied absolutely that theirs was a case of *folie à deux*, which he would, because he didn't like any suggestion that madness might be involved, but he did insist that what they'd done was very much a shared enterprise. That they were a unified force. He was basically denying that he was any kind of evil influence, and there was all sorts of predictable stuff about emotional affinity and the spirituality of death, with the murders as their own, twisted marriage ceremonies.'

'Christ,' Thorne said.

'He also said that Hindley was more Messalina than Lady Macbeth.'

Again, Thorne was happy to wait.

'Lady Macbeth encouraged her husband to kill, but then she was plagued with guilt. Whereas Messalina, who was the wife of the Roman emperor Claudius, was famously devious and predatory. Oh, and sexually insatiable.' Perera nodded. 'Sex has usually got a lot to do with cases like this.'

Thorne's hand moved to his jacket, to the pocket containing the photograph. 'Sarah had sex with the boy before he was killed.'

'Right.' She reached for the bottle and poured more water. 'Sex as part of the ritual of killing and almost certainly a strong part of what's binding the killers together in the first place. Now, this may or may not be helpful as far as your case is concerned ... but the truth about Hindley and Brady, as far as I see it anyway, is that he did what he did because he was insane. Simple as that. Properly insane ... voices in his head, visions, the whole lot. And she did what she did because she loved him. She worshipped him and she wanted to keep him happy. So, knowing that, you can argue all you want about which of them was worse, but to me it suggests that there was no real *partnership*. His delusions made him want to do terrible things and she went along with it because she was, quite literally, mad with love.' She paused for a few seconds and sat there watching Thorne trying to process everything she'd told him. 'One piece of good news ...'

'Please,' Thorne said.

'Well, these couples do tend to fall out in the end. Unfortunately, it didn't happen with Brady and Hindley until after they'd been caught, but usually the cracks start to show long before that. Sometimes it's why they get caught, you know? That dependence on one another can easily turn into suspicion and, once the trust goes, they're in trouble, because he or she is the only thing between them and prison. That's when they'll turn on each other.'

'Fingers crossed, then,' Thorne said.

Perera smiled and did as Thorne was suggesting. 'It happens.'

Thorne reached for the coffee he'd ordered, though right then something a lot stronger would have been more than welcome. He said, 'So, which of them do *you* think was worse?'

Perera grunted, as though this was something she had considered many times without reaching any sort of conclusion she was happy with. 'It depends on your attitude to these things, doesn't it? Hindley was arguably the more reviled of the two ... still is, probably ... but I think a lot of that is because she was a woman and their victims were children. It just seemed so ... unnatural.' She opened her mouth then closed it again, waiting for the words. 'If she *was* worse than Brady, and I can't see there's much to be gained from making it a competition, it's because there's no sort of love that can ever excuse what she did.' She shook her head and her eyes slid away from Thorne's for the first time. Her tone had changed, subtly, and she no longer appeared to be talking as a professional. 'I mean, madness is not an excuse either, but it's an ... explanation.'

Thorne's coffee cup was empty, but he picked it up again anyway and stared into it for a few seconds. 'Look, I don't want to put you on the spot, but are you suggesting that we might be looking at a similar situation here?'

Perera looked at him again. 'It's possible.'

'A similar sort of relationship, I mean. A Hindley and a Brady.'

'Like I said—'

'Yeah, it's possible, I know. I'm just looking for any kind of take on this that might help. So . . . '

'One thing you need to bear in mind, though.'

Thorne looked at her.

'Right now,' she said, 'there's no way of knowing which one is which.'

On their way out, Thorne said, 'I just wanted to ask you . . . God this sounds daft . . . I've been dreaming about my mother a lot.'

Perera was laughing as she pushed out through the door on to the pavement and began buttoning her coat. 'Do I need to put a clock on? It's a hundred and fifty pounds an hour, you know.'

'Yeah, sorry,' Thorne said. 'My mate's a doctor and he can't go anywhere without people asking him about their bad backs or some weird pain or whatever.'

'It's not really my area,' she said. 'Dreams.'

'It doesn't matter,' Thorne said. 'I probably shouldn't have asked.'

They both began walking; Perera towards her office and Thorne towards Holborn tube station. 'What kind of dreams?'

'Just normal things, you know?' Thorne shrugged. 'Just like memories of her, really. Oh, my mum's dead. I probably should have said that.'

They stopped at the turning where Perera would be heading right. 'Like I said, not really my area. Now, if you'd been dreaming about *killing* your mother . . . '

When Perera had walked away, Thorne took out his phone and attempted to give Tanner a potted version of what the psychiatrist had told him before he reached the entrance to the tube station.

'Well, we'd better hope they fall out then,' Tanner said. 'Sarah and her killer con-man.'

'There's every chance.'

'Because . . . ?'

'Because couples usually do, don't they?'

'Speak for yourself,' Tanner said.

'Yeah, I know I'm basing that on my experience rather than yours, but . . . '

'Talking of which.'

'What?'

'Alice Thomason.'

It took Thorne a second or two to place the name. 'Oh, your lovely teacher?'

'A lovely teacher who lives with her boyfriend and their new baby.'

'You called her?'

'I ran her name through the PNC.'

Thorne dodged cars as he jogged across Kingsway towards the station entrance. 'And there was I thinking romance was dead.'

THIRTY-SEVEN

Conrad sat in the car, parked two streets away from the house of a woman he had twice committed murder with. Or *for* . . . because in truth he was finding it increasingly hard to tell the difference. He stared out through the windscreen, rigid and unblinking, his breath slowing until it was shallow as a sniper's and his eyes screwed shut. Struggling to remember a life before all of this, even if now that seemed like one lived by someone else entirely.

When Conrad was a different kind of criminal, a different kind of man.

Thinking about his past, though, would mean thinking about a different woman too. A different lover, a different kind of accomplice. Her insistence that their relationship was not over was making things horribly difficult, but even so, remembering how things had been back then might still . . . dull things a little, like laying a cold flannel across a burn.

Only temporary, he knew that, but some relief all the same.

A chance to try and regain some control.

A few minutes without Sarah in his head, without rocks and hammers and blood.

It was beyond stupid, what had happened, what he'd *let* happen, because he'd always been so good at becoming someone else whenever he chose to. A new name, a new look. A potted history neatly crafted and with just enough detail to be convincing. Lonely, divorced, bereaved. Serious and reserved if that's what was needed, the life and soul if he had to be. Whatever it took to get close to some woman with more money than sense. It was a useful skill, he'd always thought so, and from the very first time the opposite sex had become interesting and interest*ed*, he'd found a way to make it pay. Slipping in and out of roles like an actor, playing several at the same time on a few occasions, when his targets overlapped and he couldn't pass up the opportunity.

Now, he was fighting to remember who he really was.

As if he'd ghosted *himself* . . .

It was hard enough to remember what he'd felt, those first few moments in that poncey coffee shop. His eyes meeting hers. Turning on the charm, ready to go to work, buzzing with it. Had it really been any different from his initial encounters with any number of other women? In supermarkets, in pubs, in queues at the post office . . .

Can I help you with that?

I wish I'd ordered what you're having.

I couldn't help overhearing . . .

Who did he think he was kidding?

It had been *totally* different, arse-about-face, because, whatever had been going through his head back then, whatever killer scheme he might have cooked up for her, there had not been a single moment from that morning on when he had been the one with the power.

How could he possibly regain control, when he had never had any?

It made no sense, because when it came to sniffing out danger, his instincts had never let him down before. Some

196

inbuilt ... warning system. He knew when a plan was going pear-shaped, when it was time to quickly cut his losses and walk away. He could vaguely recall some semblance of alarm, those first few dates with Sarah, but none of that meant anything now, because he had chosen to ignore it or had mistaken it for something else.

And from that first night in bed ...

What they'd done to each other, but so much more than that.

Suddenly the danger was everything, had become irresistible, a sucking darkness that, for whatever reason, he had been driven to lose himself in. A need to protect and to be protected, and something so ferocious in her; a love and a fury that he could not walk away from.

Even if he wanted to.

Conrad opened his eyes to see two young children peering in at him through the passenger window. Laughing and whispering. He stared hard at them until they bolted, then started the car and drove it towards Sarah's house.

Past or present, either felt empty without her in it.

He needed to feel that burn again.

He woke a few hours later to find Sarah's face close to his own.

She touched his cheek. 'You were crying.'

He stared at her.

'A bad dream, was it?' She leaned even closer and grinned. 'Or maybe you think *this* is the bad dream?'

He shook his head and closed his eyes again.

'Are you even awake yet?' She laughed and her hand crept beneath the duvet, fingers spider-walking down his belly. 'Well, *part* of you is definitely awake,' she said. 'My favourite part.'

Conrad could smell her breath, sharp and sour, in the moments before she threw her leg across his body, reared up suddenly and adjusted her position until he was inside her.

'Sarah—'

'This is how it started, remember?'

'Of course I remember . . . '

She began to move. 'With me above you, like this.' She laughed again and then the laugh became a long, low moan. 'Above and beyond, that's what we are, my love. Above and beyond everything.'

THIRTY-EIGHT

'Oh . . . right.'

Thorne leaned close to the small speaker on the entry system. Ella Fulton's voice sounded tinny, but the surprise in it was clear enough. He said, 'I left a message on your phone last night to ask if it was all right to pop round.'

The door buzzed open.

As Thorne climbed, he could see Ella waiting at the top of the stairs waving her phone. 'Sorry. I'm terrible at checking this bloody thing.'

'Not a good time?'

'It's fine.' She waited for him to reach the top, then stepped back into her flat. 'Place is a bit of a mess.'

Thorne followed. 'I thought it was always a bit of a mess.'

'OK, make that a *lot* of a mess.'

'If you're working I can come back.' Looking around, Thorne could see a good many photographs he did not remember from his last visit. Several were lined up on the floor along one wall: an elderly Asian woman whose face seemed to be collapsing in on itself; a man looking up from beneath the peak of his cap, the bottom half of his face in shadow; a child beaming through a cloud of cigarette smoke. 'It's on the way to the office though, so I thought I'd take the chance.'

Ella flopped on to one end of the chesterfield. 'I think I can take a break from touching up my burger shots. That's not a euphemism, by the way.' She saw Thorne hesitating and pointed to the pile of newspapers at the other end of the sofa. 'Oh, just put them on the floor . . . '

When Thorne had sat down, he said, 'So, Patrick Jennings.'

Ella kicked off her Crocs and lifted her feet up. 'Well, I'm guessing you'd look a bit more cheerful if you'd come round to tell me you've found him.'

'No, we haven't found him,' Thorne said. 'And I probably look like this most of the time.'

Ella smiled.

'But we *are* looking for him a lot harder.'

She shook her head. 'I reckon the slimy bastard's long gone by now. He finds someone like Auntie Pip, takes them for everything they've got, then moves on.'

'Actually, we're fairly sure he's still in London.'

'Really?'

'Or at least he was a few days ago, and these days he's calling himself Conrad.'

'*Conrad?*' Ella barked out a dry laugh. 'With the emphasis on the *con*, I suppose.'

'So, I just wanted to ask you a few more questions, see if there's anything else you can remember about him that might help us.'

'Why a lot harder?' Ella asked.

'Sorry?'

'Why are you suddenly looking for him a lot harder?'

As was so often the case in such situations, Thorne saw no good reason not to tell this woman what was happening; the headlines, at any rate. What harm could there possibly be? He

200

could think of nothing Ella Fulton might say or do with the information that would interfere with the inquiry.

But he could also feel the spectre of Nicola Tanner at his shoulder.

'It's an ongoing investigation,' he said. 'I can't really go into the details. I'm sorry.'

Ella turned to stare at him. 'He's killed someone, hasn't he?'

'Why would you say that?'

She looked pale suddenly and struggled to get her words out. 'It's ... I saw it in ... *shit* ... ' She got up and moved quickly to Thorne's end of the sofa, crouched down and began rifling through the pile of newspapers he had dropped on the floor. 'There was a picture, the other day ... I didn't really read the story, but I remember thinking there was ... *something*, but I never ... *here*.' She tugged out a copy of the *Standard* and held it up for Thorne to see.

The e-fit on the front page.

She sat down next to him and studied it. 'He didn't look *exactly* like that when he was with Pip.' She pointed. 'His hair was a bit thicker than that, I think, and he didn't have that stupid little beard. But the features are similar, I suppose, the shape of his face ... and the eyes look right. Yeah, I reckon that could be him.'

Thorne said nothing, while Ella read the story, holding her breath.

When she'd finished, she turned to him again, shaking her head. 'Patrick Jennings murdered a *teacher*? Fuck.' She reddened a little. 'Sorry ... '

'Don't worry,' Thorne said. 'That was pretty much my reaction, too.'

Ella sat back and let out a long breath. 'OK ... ' She stretched the word out, still processing the information.

'Not just a teacher.' Now she'd put it together herself, Thorne saw even less reason to keep her in the dark. 'There was another murder in Margate, a few weeks ago. A seventeen-year-old boy. Very different, but his DNA at both crime scenes.'

'Why? I mean . . . for money?'

'I don't think so,' Thorne said. 'But it's the reason I need to ask a few more questions. In case a few things about him have come back to you since your aunt's death.'

'I've tried not to think about him,' she said.

'You said that he met Pip in a pub.'

She nodded.

'Can you remember what that was called?'

'Yeah, it's right by City University.' She thought. 'The Blacksmith and something?'

'Toffeemaker.' Thorne nodded. He knew the pub. It would certainly be worth sending someone down there to show the e-fit to a few of the staff and regulars. 'No other places . . . bars, restaurants, you think he might have gone to regularly? Anywhere he might have mentioned?'

'Sorry.'

'Well, if anything comes to you later on.'

'He just used to go wherever Pip wanted, I think.' Her expression was thick with disgust. 'To show how devoted he was to her.'

It made sense. The man they were discussing was obviously someone who could easily feign such things, though now it looked as if he had finally found someone towards whom such devotion was genuine. 'We know he was pretending to be something he wasn't back then . . . but did you ever get any sense of what his real background might be? Anything about a family, any cities he might have talked about.'

Ella took a few seconds. 'It was like he was always trying to show everyone how clever he was, how brilliant this online thing of his was, to impress Pip. Trying a bit too hard. I thought that, even then, and I know Mum certainly did. I definitely remember thinking he might have been a working-class boy done good, you know? There was a bit of an accent sometimes.'

202

'What accent?'

'Midlands, I reckon. Flat vowels, whatever. *Grass, bath* ...'

'OK.'

'I'm thinking Coventry, for some reason. Might just be something he said once. A football thing, maybe?'

Something or nothing. Thorne scribbled it down anyway.

He said, 'We think he's involved with a woman ... that she's involved in these murders with him.'

'Right ... blimey.'

'Did you ever see him with a woman other than Pip?'

'They went out in a group sometimes, but I think they were all Pip's friends.'

'He never mentioned a woman called Sarah?'

Ella shook her head. She still appeared stunned by the revelation.

'Never mind,' Thorne said. It had been worth asking. Witness statements provided by the Brooklands Hill parents suggested that the man known to them as Conrad and the woman who called herself Sarah had first met in the coffee shop, several days after Philippa Goodwin's death, but there was always the possibility that their meeting had been staged for the benefit of others.

Thorne could not be sure how long this couple had actually been together.

He stood up and said, 'I'll get out of your way.'

'You're not in the way. I'm just a bit ... you know.'

'If it helps, it means there's way more chance we're going to catch him.'

'Yeah, course, I get that. Jesus, though.' She stood up too and they both took a few steps towards the door, then stopped and looked at one another a little awkwardly.

Thorne nodded towards the new photographs. 'I like those,' he said.

'Oh, cheers.' She shoved her hands deep into the pockets of

her long cardigan. 'You should go to the Photographers' Gallery in Soho; there's some fantastic stuff in there.'

'Yeah, maybe.'

'No kebabs or anything, but definitely worth a visit. I'm happy to go with you if you want.' She smiled and looked down at her socks. 'So I can tell you what's good and what's crap.'

Thorne shifted from one foot to another ... and there was Tanner again, having conveniently forgotten her own recent 'interest' in a potential witness, scowling and wagging a finger at him.

He said, 'To be honest, I don't get a lot of free time.'

THIRTY-NINE

As soon as Thorne got to Becke House, Tanner suggested that the two of them grab a few minutes to talk things through, in advance of a full team briefing. 'Get our ducks in a row before we address the troops,' she said.

As they sat down together in his office, Thorne said. 'Why does anyone need ducks to be in a row, anyway?'

'What?' Tanner seemed keen to crack on.

'Never understood it, that's all.'

'I've no idea,' Tanner said. 'So they're easier to shoot?'

Thorne shrugged and told her about the conversation he'd had with Ella Fulton.

'Right, I'll get Dipak to go down to the Blacksmith and whatever-it-is, wave our e-fit around.'

'Toffeemaker,' Thorne said. 'In Clerkenwell. It was a song by a bloke called Jake Thackray ... did comedy folk songs, sort of thing. I've been in there a couple of times.'

'Right.'

'It's decent enough, but the food's vegan, so—'

'I also think we need to revisit the house-to-house,' Tanner said. 'Step things up a bit. Widen the net and get officers working the streets near to where Gemma Maxwell lived *and* the area around Brooklands Hill.'

'That's a lot of officers,' Thorne said.

'I know it is.'

'Have you spoken to Russell?'

'It's a double murder,' she said. Matter-of-fact, like the boss of a small company which had got busy suddenly and needed to increase its stationery order. 'I got the go-ahead from Russell first thing.'

Thorne was impressed, but not altogether surprised. Tanner was good at getting what she wanted and she didn't have his chequered history with the brass. 'Why this sudden focus on house-to-house?'

'Because this pair are local,' Tanner said. 'They have to be.'

'Margate's hardly local.'

'Margate was about ... something else. Gemma Maxwell was killed because she needed to be. She'd confronted Sarah and told her she knew what was going on at the school, so they had to get rid of her. There's no way Sarah could be sure that Gemma wouldn't bring the police in and she didn't want to take that risk.'

Thorne could not deny that Tanner's theory made sense. He thought about what Melita Perera had said about Brady and Hindley, about murder as a marriage ceremony. 'So maybe killing Kevin Deane was just them making some sort of weird commitment to each other.'

'Exactly,' Tanner said.

'They picked Margate, but it probably could have been anywhere.'

'Because it didn't matter.'

'And Kevin Deane could have been anybody.'

'But Gemma Maxwell was targeted and killed at home. Gemma lived near to the school because that was where she worked, so it's reasonable to assume that Sarah, as a "parent" didn't live far away either.'

Thorne wasn't quite so sure. 'Some parents travel for miles though, if they think it's the right school.'

Tanner shook her head, convinced. 'She went to and from Brooklands Hill twice a day and we know she met up with the other parents in the local coffee shop. They live somewhere nearby . . . Enfield, Walthamstow, Southgate.'

'OK, so let's say they do live somewhere close to that school, isn't there every chance they've already upped sticks and moved?'

Tanner nodded. 'I thought about that.'

'I mean, she can't go back to Brooklands Hill, so she's probably on the lookout for another school and that could be anywhere.' Thorne found it hard to believe that a woman disturbed enough to pick up and drop off a child that did not exist would want to stop. 'Anyway, if you're right, it would make sense for them to move, now he's killed someone on their own doorstep.'

'You would think so.'

'They're all over the papers, the local news.'

'Which is why we need to talk to every lettings agency in the area. Find out if any of their tenants have left in a hurry, skipped out without giving notice, whatever. That's if they were renting somewhere. Maybe one of them owns a house, in which case we should also be talking to local estate agents and getting details of any properties that have been put on the market in the last week or so. Looking for anyone who seems a bit over-keen to sell quickly.'

Tanner was as fired up as Thorne had seen her in a while. She had certainly been busy.

'The lack of forced entry was bothering me, too,' she said.

It was why Thorne had been quick to question the where-abouts of Gemma Maxwell's boyfriend. Once he had been eliminated, only one other explanation seemed possible. 'She opens the door and Patrick or Conrad or whatever his name is just forces his way in. Then he kills her in the hall as soon as she turns her back on him.'

'Or she knew whoever was at the door,' Tanner said. 'I mean, she might not have been comfortable with it, not after she'd confronted her, but she would probably have let her in, right?'

'Let *Sarah* in?'

'I went through the CCTV again,' Tanner said. 'No cameras on Gemma Maxwell's road, no security cameras on neighbouring houses, but I checked the footage from a traffic camera on the main road and got this . . .'

She produced a photocopy from her bag and passed it across.

A couple walking away from the camera. Long coats and hoodies. The time code on the bottom read: 21.36.

'Fits in with our approximate time of death,' Tanner said. 'No, it's not the best bit of evidence I've ever come across and it probably wouldn't hold up in court, but I think it's them. Parked up somewhere nearby or maybe heading to the tube station. I've checked every other camera in the area, but that's the clearest shot I can find.'

Thorne put the picture down on his desk. 'So you think they were *both* there?'

'Why not? This Sarah rings Gemma Maxwell's bell and says, "Really sorry to bother you like this and I know it might be a bit awkward after our conversation earlier, but could my husband – or boyfriend or whatever – and I come in for a quick word?" Easier for them to do it together, don't you reckon?'

Thorne remembered one of the other teachers saying that their murdered colleague had felt sorry for the woman she was planning to confront.

Yeah, that sounds like Gemma . . .

'And I spoke to Phil . . .'

Thorne waited.

'He can't swear to anything, but he thinks it's at least possible that it could have been a woman wielding the hammer.' Tanner turned her palms up. 'I mean, we probably won't know either way until they're in custody, and we can separate them. Even then . . . ' She looked at her watch and pushed her chair away from the desk. It was time for the briefing. 'Right, I think they're more or less lined up.' She looked at him. 'The ducks.'

Thorne nodded, but said nothing; thinking about the damage that even the slightest of women could do if the weapon was deadly enough.

Thinking about the thickness of a skull.

'So, let's go and shoot the fuckers . . . '

FORTY

The first day at a new school was always nerve-racking, so she had decided to ease herself into it by starting with a pick-up. The afternoon runs were usually more straightforward than the morning drop-offs, because people were that much more likely to look twice at anyone arriving first thing without a child in tow. Even then, Sarah had a story – she'd come rushing back with something Jamie had forgotten when she'd dropped him off ten minutes earlier – but all the same, she didn't want to take any chances on their first day.

Traumatic enough for Jamie as it was.

The drive to Woodford had not been as bad as she'd feared. She knew she'd get used to it quickly enough and, having scoped out the parking set-up the first time she'd visited the school, she had no problem finding somewhere handy, a few streets away.

Not quite as full of itself as Brooklands Hill, that was obvious.

Not quite so many 4 × 4s clogging up the roads around the place.

She guessed the parents would be a bit easier to deal with . . .

Still jittery, though, on that five-minute walk back to the school gates, still desperate to make the right impression straight away, and it didn't help that she was so concerned about Conrad.

What Conrad was up to.

He'd left home just before she did and hadn't seemed particularly keen on telling her where he was going; changing the subject like she wouldn't notice, then being a little too affectionate at the door. Even though she was never likely to complain about *that*, it had felt like he was making rather too much effort, especially considering he'd had her against the dressing-table just before breakfast. Saying goodbye as if where he was going didn't matter, like it was unimportant compared to how much he'd miss her while he was away and what he would do to her when he got back.

'I'll be thinking about that all day,' he'd said. Smiling as he pulled on his jacket, then rubbing himself against her just before he opened the front door, so she knew exactly what he was talking about.

Still busy, lining up a new mark.

Still in those early, *tricky* stages, feeling the woman out, needing to be sure she was a worthwhile target, taking his time.

That was what he'd told her the night before . . .

Those first few minutes were always the worst, hovering a few feet away from a group of women who clearly all knew each other well. Not wanting to intrude. A shy smile when one of them – permed and stubby – looked her way. Then, finally – thank God – a wave which let her know it was all right to join them.

'I love your hair,' the stubby woman said.

An empty compliment before a 'hello' or even a basic introduction. Why did women *do* that? Men always seemed happy enough just to stick out a hand and say, 'I'm Terry,' or whatever. That said, she *was* very pleased with her new look. She was still getting used to being blonde, but she loved what the stylist had done. Her hair was shorter, almost a bob. Ironically, it wasn't *un*like that of the woman whose fault it was Sarah had needed to change her appearance in the first place.

Mind you, that teacher's hair had not been looking its best, last time Sarah had seen it.

She smiled and brushed at her fringe. Said, 'Oh, thanks.'

No, *that* was not a look she'd be seeing in a shampoo advert any time soon. *Matted with blood? Because I'm* worth *it . . .*

'I'm Patti.'

'Sarah.' She smiled again, nice and nervous this time, and stared expectantly through the gates towards the school entrance. 'It's my son's first day.'

'Oh.' The stubby woman turned to her friends. 'First day . . .'

There were assorted oohs and ahhs. A thumbs up and a pair of crossed fingers. One of them said something about her own child's first day, which was clearly a lot more interesting.

'What's your son's name?' Patti asked.

'Jamie.'

'Bless him.' The woman's curly mop wobbled as she nodded. 'I'm sure he'll be fine. You're probably a lot more nervous than he is.'

'I think you're right.'

The kids began to emerge and the women turned to watch. 'Just moved to the area, then?'

'Yeah, still in boxes.'

'So, where were you before?'

'South of the river,' Sarah said.

'Oh, *big* move, then.'

'My partner has a company that makes online videos for students. You know, lectures and things? The office has moved out here, so . . .'

Patti stood on tiptoe and waved to a girl who was ambling towards the gates, eyes fixed on the screen of a pink mobile phone.

'Actually, I think I'd better go in and get him,' Sarah said. 'He's a lovely boy, but bloody hell does he *dawdle*!' A couple of the other parents laughed and nodded in sympathy and by the time Patti had embraced her daughter and was shouting 'Nice to meet you', Sarah was halfway across the playground.

They seemed nice, Sarah thought, the other parents, and she'd know all their names within a day or two, because she always did. It had all gone as well as she could have wanted. She smiled at the children as they ran past her and waved to one of the teachers, confident that she'd find somewhere inside easily enough where she could skulk for ten minutes.

Now the niceties were over with, though, her feet at least partway under the table so to speak, all she could think about was Conrad.

Fuck, why was she letting him ruin her big day?

Well, because she loved him, it wasn't rocket science . . . but if he loved her as much as she thought he did, as much as he said he did, why wasn't he being open and honest with her?

Why would bloody, bastard Conrad keep anything from her? How *could* he?

They were not Conrad and Sarah, any more, not Sarah and Conrad. There was no *and* anything. They had become something else entirely, a third person to whom they both gave flesh and blood, and secrets would only make that person sick if they weren't winkled out.

Terminally.

She pushed through the door into the school and marched past a row of brightly coloured lockers to the Girls' toilets. She nipped smartly inside, cut straight into a cubicle and locked the door.

And breathed . . .

It was ridiculous, she thought, nonsensical. Hadn't everything Conrad had done before he'd met her, or had *told* her he'd done, been reliant on what an amazing liar he was? Cheating women, creating false identities and fake businesses, all of it? It was the way he'd made his living, for pity's sake. The success he'd had, the money he'd been able to make, would certainly suggest that

213

he *was* very good at lying and he definitely *thought* he was. He'd bragged about it more than once.

Sarah wasn't convinced, though.

Perhaps because she was even better at it than he was.

The stupid thing was that, having been lied to by enough men to last her a lifetime, the fact that Conrad was a *professional* liar had, in a strange way, been part of the attraction. She had known all along what she was getting. It had been a comfort, of sorts, provided of course that the lies were restricted to the women he targeted and were never about anything that really mattered, that affected *her*.

Not that it made a fat lot of difference in the end. Conrad could be the greatest liar the world had ever seen, for all the good it would do him.

Because she would know.

FORTY-ONE

The woman's eyes narrowed when she asked him if he'd been ignoring her messages.

'I've had a lot on,' Conrad said. 'I've been busy.'

The woman told him she understood, that it must be terribly hard to be apart from someone so *special*. That tearing himself away must be almost impossible.

'Don't be ridiculous—'

She leaned back on her sofa and closed her eyes in mock ecstasy, then hissed the name slowly, as if it was an incantation. 'Sarah . . .'

'It sounded urgent,' Conrad said. He was standing close to the door, keen to get this over with.

She looked confused, the picture of innocence.

'Your message.'

She nodded fast, as though she finally understood. Her *last* message. The one which had somehow managed, finally, to get his attention.

'So . . . ?'

She wanted to see him, she said. That was all. She missed him.

Conrad moved to sit down close to her. He was not totally convinced, but the words spoken softly were enough; the expression on her face which, once upon a time, had been enough to get anything she'd wanted from him. A wetness when she blinked and small teeth chewing at her bottom lip.

The words bubbled up and tumbled out.

'I did something.' As soon as he had said the words, Conrad realised how very much he had needed to, and the long breath he let out felt like poisonous air being released. '*We* did something. Sarah and me.'

She waited.

'The worst thing . . . '

He told her everything, quickly, his eyes fixed on the floor and a tremor moving through him that he could not control. The boy on the beach, the teacher . . . the things he had not been able to stop himself doing. That in the . . . heat of everything he had *wanted* to do, because of her; because they had needed to share those moments.

'It sounds stupid, but it was like someone *taking* you somewhere and there's no going back, like . . . almost making you come,' he said. 'You know? There's a point where you can't stop it, when you'd do *anything* rather than stop it.' He closed his eyes. 'Christ . . . '

When he finally looked up, he saw that she had paled a little.

Her eyes were wide and dry.

She inched towards him and laid a hand gently on his arm. Conrad made no move away, welcomed it. 'It's been all over the papers and on TV,' he said. 'I don't—'

'Shush,' she said.

'They'll have my fingerprints and my DNA.' That tremor was building again. 'There was so much blood.'

For a few seconds they said nothing, and then she began to talk quietly, her hand moving against his arm. She told him that she wanted to help. That she had *always* been there to help him.

DNA would only ever be a problem, she said, if he was caught. If he did something stupid, or if his partner did. She said she knew him well enough to know that he was usually quite careful, so the only thing he really needed to worry about was someone else supplying the police with the information they needed. Someone coming forward with an anonymous tip-off, something like that.

Now, Conrad moved away and got to his feet. 'What are you saying?'

She looked alarmed and told him that she wasn't saying anything, that she was just laying it all out for him.

Conrad felt dizzy, delirious. That day in the coffee shop . . . now he knew for certain that he should have run.

She was just talking about possibilities, she said, worst case scenarios. After all, what did *she* know?

He could hardly believe that he'd once thought this woman's smile was one of the sweetest, the sexiest, he'd ever seen. That she'd been irresistible.

What she *did* know, she told him calmly, was that he probably wouldn't be ignoring her messages from now on.

She patted the cushion next to her and told him how tired he looked.

Conrad sat down again.

FORTY-TWO

Searching for something to listen to, Thorne flicked through the box of CDs he'd carted back from Helen's. After a few minutes studying track listings, struggling to decide what mood he was in and to choose between his two favourite artists, he compromised. He put on *George Jones Sings Hank Williams*, then walked slowly from living room to bedroom before retracing his steps, unable to settle.

Three months since coming back here and the truth was, it still felt . . . strange.

What had he told Helen, a week and a half before? Sitting there like a visitor in her front room, drinking her beer while he tried to make sense of it all and making out the readjustment was really no big deal?

It's just . . . my flat.

Which it was, of course, but though he had lived here for a long time before moving down to Helen's place in Tulse Hill, the flat he had come back to had seemed very different from the one he'd left. Not simply the four walls, but the air moving within them. He had not been lying when he'd told Phil Hendricks how much he was enjoying being north of the river again, but for whatever reason, stepping back over his own threshold had not felt like coming home.

Largely, of course, it was because the place *wasn't* the same as when he'd left it. It was disconcertingly ... nice, for a kick-off. Renting out the flat – most recently to a pair of gormless-but-likeable uniforms from Kentish Town station – had meant tarting it up a good deal. A fresh coat of paint and some hard-core carpet cleaning; new crockery, cookware and linen; an assortment of stripy rugs and scatter cushions (all picked out by Helen) and several sacks of rubbish cleared from the weed-strewn arrangement of paving slabs and scrub that passed for a back garden.

Coming back here, there had been plenty that was familiar, of course, but far too much that wasn't. Too many things around him that were unmarked, that meant nothing. Thorne knew the layout with his eyes closed: the number of steps from one room to another, the shape of every shadow thrown across the walls, yet he remained happier leaving the place every morning than he was coming back to it.

His key felt like the only thing that still fit.

Thorne was hungry but wasn't sure he could be bothered to make himself anything to eat. He walked out into the hall and snatched up the paper he'd left on the table when he'd come in. He glanced through the TV listings, but there was nothing he fancied, so he drifted back into the living room, wondering if he should just get an early night.

The place felt different because he felt different, simple as that, but he still could not be sure what – aside from the obvious – had changed and how he felt about that. What he should *do* about it. Limbo was a fun thing to try if you were pissed at a party and didn't mind making an idiot of yourself, but it wasn't much fun as a place to be.

Thorne sat down on the sofa and picked up his phone.

He elbowed aside one of the cushions Helen had chosen, turned the music down and called her.

There was no reply, but this time he did not bother leaving a message. It was still too early for her to have gone to bed, so he guessed that Helen had pulled a late shift. Alfie being spoiled at Auntie Jenny's . . .

He lay back and scrolled through his contacts list, well aware that it was modest compared to some and that there were far more pizza delivery places than was healthy. He stared at several contacts he no longer recognised and tried to remember who the hell they were, thought about deleting them, then kept on scrolling.

He stopped at the Ps and, without giving himself time to think about it too much, dialled a number.

Melita Perera was already laughing when she answered her phone. 'Is this about your mother again?'

Thorne had kept her number on his phone since the cat-killing case and was pleasantly surprised to hear that she'd obviously kept his. He laughed, too. 'No. Look, I'm sorry to disturb you at home . . . that's if you *are* at home. Outside office hours, I mean.'

'Well, I *was* watching *Gogglebox*, but I'll live with it.'

'My bad,' Thorne said. Where on earth had *that* come from? He hated that expression.

'No worries, it was a repeat, anyway. As long as I've still got one hand free to hold my wine glass.'

Thorne had no idea what Melita Perera's domestic set-up was. He'd clocked the absence of a wedding ring seven months earlier but knew that didn't mean a great deal either way. She certainly didn't *sound* as if she was settled in with anyone for the night. He said, 'What you told me the other day, when you were talking about the madness of two, all that.'

'*Folie à deux.*'

'Right.' Thorne had been too embarrassed to say it in French. 'The idea that one half of these couples is usually dominant.'

'Usually.'

'You were talking about Brady and Hindley, saying how, with the couple we're looking for, I shouldn't make assumptions about which one was which.'

'Has something happened?'

Thorne told Perera what Tanner had said to him. What Phil Hendricks had said to *her*. He heard her take a drink.

'Well, remember that letter I told you about? The one Brady wrote to the Home Office? Aside from all the other stuff, he claimed that he covered up for Hindley in court and told her what to say, so that she might only get convicted of minor crimes.'

'He didn't do a very good job, then.'

'No, he didn't, and later on, when they were completely estranged, he hinted that Myra was directly involved in the killings themselves, some of them, anyway. That she'd done rather more than simply lure the victims to him.'

'What do you think?'

'I'm not sure we'll ever know,' she said. 'But I think the assumption that, in cases like this, it's always the male half of the couple that actually carries out the murders themselves, is ... naïve.'

'So, perfectly possible that Sarah killed Gemma Maxwell?'

'In the right circumstances, women are every bit as capable as men of something like that.'

Thorne knew from first-hand experience what Perera was talking about.

'Is there any possibility that she might have carried out both the murders?'

'Doesn't look like it,' Thorne said. 'We got the man's DNA from the first murder weapon.'

'It's interesting ... '

'What is?'

'That they're sharing them out.' There were a few seconds of silence, then Thorne heard her swallow. 'His turn next, then.'

'You think there'll be a next?'

'I wouldn't bet against it,' she said. 'It's what defines their relationship by the sound of things. Keeps it strong, keeps them together.'

They talked for a few minutes more, after that: shrinks who treated other shrinks; the benefits of bad TV when it came to shaking off the stresses of a busy day at work; better bars in which they could meet up again, should they need to. She sounded genuinely keen to be kept up to date with developments in the case and Thorne promised that he would do so.

'I'll try to do it when *Gogglebox* isn't on,' he said.

'That would be appreciated.'

When Thorne had put his phone down, he turned the music back up, walked into the kitchen and opened the fridge. He dug out the ingredients to knock up an omelette and a can of beer to drink with it. He felt in a much better mood, suddenly, lighter on his feet.

He cracked eggs into a bowl and sang tunelessly along as the Possum belted out 'Take These Chains From My Heart'.

It was almost certainly down to that.

FORTY-THREE

She made sure that dinner was waiting for Conrad when he got home.

Sarah had never thought of herself as much of a cook – how often had the arsehole she'd been married to confirmed it? – but she was trying to make the effort, because she knew how much Conrad loved his food. It was nothing fancy, just a pasta thing with chicken in a spicy sauce, but she thought he would appreciate it.

'This looks great,' he said.

She'd gone the extra yard in laying the table, too; napkins and candles, the lot. Wasn't that the kind of thing they always said in those magazines, about keeping a relationship alive? Treating every night as if it was a first date, something like that. Mind you, they hadn't had sex on their first date and she was certainly hoping that was on the cards.

If the food didn't work, she knew what would, the other things he liked to eat.

Conrad sat down and she brought the plates across.

'I'm starving,' he said.

She went back and fetched beer for them both.

He was already busy with the salt and pepper by the time Sarah sat down, which she thought was rude considering he hadn't even tasted it yet. She bit her tongue and said, 'Long day?'

They began to eat.

He grunted and swallowed. 'Yeah.' He immediately took another mouthful. 'This is fantastic, by the way.'

'How's it going?'

'Yeah ... it's shaping up, I reckon.'

'That's brilliant.' She raised her glass and held it towards him.

'Could be a nice little payday.' He leaned across and touched his glass to hers. 'So, I thought maybe we could treat ourselves, go away somewhere if it all comes good.'

'I'll hold you to that,' she said.

He laid his fork down. 'Listen, I wanted to say sorry for being funny with you before, when you were asking questions about the new woman I've got lined up. Getting a bit tetchy, like it was none of your business.'

'Don't be silly, I'm—'

'Because it *is* your business, right? Everything I do ... how the hell could it *not* be? The first few days can be tricky, that's all it is. I'm always a bit jumpy early on, when I'm trying to get everything in place, making sure I'm not doing anything stupid. So ... sorry.'

He smiled and she caught her breath, because whatever else he had to say, however this panned out, that crooked smile still killed her.

'It's my fault, too,' she said.

'No, it isn't.'

'I tell you you've got every right to keep that side of things to yourself, have your own life, then I try and stick my oar in.'

He waved her concerns away. 'Doesn't matter whose fault it

224

is, because now I've got things almost ready to go, I can tell you all about it.' He grinned. 'All about *her*.'

'You sure?'

'You deserve to know.'

She said, 'OK, if you want.' Like it was entirely up to him, like there was no pressure.

He picked up his beer and leaned back. 'So ... her name's Vanessa Anderson and she lives in Clapham. I met her in a bookshop, believe it or not ... just sat down and started chatting about nothing.'

Sarah laughed. 'Your signature move.'

'Right,' Conrad said. 'Anyway, she does ... *something* in the City. I still haven't worked out what, exactly, but there's plenty of money sloshing around. Her husband died a few years ago, left her loads of it.'

Sarah nodded, hanging on every word, all thoughts of the food forgotten. She had not been particularly hungry, anyway. The candles threw weird shadows across his face as he talked and she could not recall ever seeing him quite so animated, so excited.

It made something turn in her stomach.

'How old is she?'

'She's fifty-three ... no, fifty-*four*. That's right, she said she'd just had a birthday.'

'Oh, so you're a toyboy now, then?'

Conrad laughed. 'Yeah, I suppose I am. She looks pretty good on it, though, I'll give her that much. It's always a bit easier if they don't look like the back of a bus.'

'So, what have you got in mind?'

'Not sure yet,' he said.

'What about the film thing?'

He looked at her.

'You know, the screenplay and the fake letters? I think that one's my favourite.'

'Yeah ... that might not be a bad idea. She definitely likes films.' He knocked back his beer and began to eat again. 'So come on then, where do you fancy going? When she pays out.'

'I don't know.' Sarah pushed her food around the plate. 'It all depends when, doesn't it?'

'Yeah, course.'

'I'll have to organise it around school,' she said. 'Because I really don't want to disrupt Jamie when he's just started at a new place.' She looked across and saw something in his face she did not care for at all, but it was there and gone. 'Maybe we could just go away for the weekend or something.'

While they finished eating, she told him how everything had gone over in Woodford: the journey; the chit-chat at the school gates; the stubby woman with the perm who was shaping up to be her new BFF, for the foreseeable future at least. When they were done, they carried the dirty plates out to the kitchen and Sarah watched Conrad stack the dishwasher.

He seemed happy, rather too pleased with himself.

She said, 'So, what exactly does she look like? This Vanessa. Is she tall? Short ... ?'

Conrad stood up and shut the dishwasher door. 'She's ... about the same height as you, I think. Brown hair ... '

'And where does she live again?'

'I told you, Clapham.' He shook his head. 'Bit of a schlep all the way down there, but—'

'Her address, I mean, the name of the road. Does she live in a house or a flat? What's it like inside? I'm presuming you've been inside? Does she drive, and if she does, what kind of car has she got? What kind of restaurants does she like? Has she got any kids? What are their names? Are her parents still alive? What did they do?' She gave him a few seconds, then began to snap her fingers. 'Come on, these aren't difficult questions, are they? I mean, you've got her *all lined up*, you said. *Ready to go*, you said. Come on, Conrad ... '

She stared at him, watched his brain working, desperately trying to dredge up answers that she knew were not there to be found.

Finally, he opened his mouth, but she was already flying at him.

She hit him hard across the side of the head and he staggered back against the worktop. He shouted and moved to grab hold of her arm as she went for him again, so she used the other hand, balled it into a fist and began to pummel his neck, his face.

'You piece of shit . . . lying cunt . . . '

He took hold of her wrist and turned his head away, angling his body to avoid the kicks aimed at his lower legs, the knees aimed at his groin. He told her to calm down, asked her what the hell this was about, but she shouted over him, the spit flying as she ranted and struggled.

'Who do you think you fucking are? Who do you think *I* am? Have you got any idea what I can do? You think you can lie to me like I won't know . . . you fucking low-life . . . like you might get away with it? Nobody does that to me, *nobody*.'

He turned suddenly to face her, let go of her arms and pushed her back hard against the kitchen table.

His face was flushed, his eyes blazing.

He pointed at her and said, 'Go careful now, all right? I think you know exactly what *I* can do, because you're the one who made me do it.'

They stared at each other for half a minute until their breathing had almost returned to normal. He tensed, ready to fight when she moved quickly towards him, but this time her arms snaked around his neck and her face was wet against his chest as she gasped out the words between sobs.

'I'm sorry . . . oh, Christ, I'm so sorry, my love. *Please* . . . '

Sarah sank to her knees, her face sliding down his body until it was pressed into his stomach, her arms wrapped tight around his waist. 'It's only because I love you . . . you know that, don't you? That I get like this. I wouldn't get so jealous, so worked up and so *stupid*, if you weren't . . . everything. I wouldn't blame you if you walked out right now, if you ghosted me like I was just one of your dull bitches, but I swear I won't ever get jealous again and I promise I'll always believe you.'

Her high-pitched keen softened to a moan as she felt Conrad's hand settle on the top of her head, as he began to stroke her hair.

'I swear to you, my love. I swear on my son's life . . . '

FORTY-FOUR

It was not often that Thorne looked forward to a morning spent giving evidence in court, but then there weren't too many cases as frustrating as this one was proving to be: the hunt for a murderous couple who might decide at any time to spice up their relationship with another marriage 'ceremony' and about whom Thorne still knew next to nothing.

So . . . best suit and tie on. Blah blah blah in the witness box for an hour or so. Job done.

It had felt like a holiday.

They trotted down the steps of the Central Criminal Court, ignored the reporter from *London Tonight* delivering the obligatory piece to camera, and turned east towards St Paul's. It was cold but bright and, ten minutes into lunch hour, Newgate was almost as thick with pedestrians as it was with cars and buses. Normally, Tanner walked quickly enough to make keeping up with her something of an effort, but today she seemed content to take her time.

Not quite dawdling, but about as close as she ever got.

'Now, that's how things *should* be.' Like Thorne, Tanner had been giving evidence in the trial of three men charged with a series of stabbings in Tottenham towards the end of the previous year. She dropped her phone into her bag and glanced back, almost longingly, towards the bronze figure of Lady Justice perched atop the dome of the Old Bailey.

Thorne knew exactly what she meant. With the exception of the paperwork – which Thorne had eventually managed to complete – the entire case had been about as straightforward as anyone bar the accused could have wished for. Murder weapons found, plastered with enough forensic material to keep the cast of *Silent Witness* busy for an entire series. Damning expert testimony, corroborating mobile phone evidence and fake alibis that a traffic warden could have broken. They could not guarantee that the outcome would be the one they and the relatives of the murder victims wanted, but they were fairly confident.

'Going our way, you reckon?' Tanner asked.

'Be amazed if it didn't,' Thorne said.

Back at the office, DS Samir Karim who, as always, was running a book on the trial, was offering 25/1 against a 'not guilty' verdict but had yet to find any takers.

Tanner and Thorne had both been around long enough to know that not all cases went as smoothly as this one had, but the majority of investigations made progress of sorts, however tortoise-like. Most could truthfully be described as ongoing. With the Kevin Deane and Gemma Maxwell murders, the team could do little but sit around and hope the Evidence Fairy was in a good mood.

They walked past Christ Church Greyfriars and, a minute or so further on, the entrance to the Stock Exchange, its windows reflecting sunshine that was half-arsed, but doing its best.

'I called Helen last night,' Thorne said.

'And?'

'She wasn't in.'

Tanner looked at him. 'I've heard better stories.'

'Just trying to make conversation,' Thorne said. 'I mean, we don't always have to talk about work.'

'I don't.'

Now it was Thorne's turn to look.

A few yards further on, Tanner said, 'See anything good on the box last night?'

Thorne tried to remember what he had watched after the call to Melita Perera, after that omelette he'd cobbled together. 'Premiership highlights,' he said. 'Watford against Burnley.'

'Anything *good*, I said.'

'What about you?'

'Fell asleep on the sofa in front of *Newsnight*.'

'Bloody hell, we lead exciting lives,' Thorne said.

'Suits me,' Tanner said.

She glanced at him and Thorne caught enough of her expression to know exactly what she was thinking about, though she had not alluded to it directly, because she never did. It was not how he would have described the events of seven months before, though anyone witnessing it – and thank God only he and Tanner had – might have thought very differently.

It had certainly been enough excitement to last both of them several lifetimes.

Ten minutes later, waiting on a busy platform at St Paul's, Tanner talked in more detail about the expansion of the house-to-house that had begun while they were busy in court. She said that she was still hopeful. Dipak Chall had already talked to the landlord of the Blacksmith and Toffeemaker, and though the man had not recognised the e-fit of their male suspect, Chall was set to return to the pub that evening and talk to some of the regulars.

Thorne made supportive noises, but he could already hear the rattle and rumble of the tube train approaching and was thinking about the woman who had stood waiting on a different platform four weeks before.

The start of all this.

Suddenly he felt every bit as hot and headachy as he had been that morning at Highgate, wondering what had been going through Philippa Goodwin's mind as she heard that same thunder growing louder every second.

The train rushed past him; squealing, slowing.

'Looks like we'll get a seat,' Tanner said.

Thorne nodded, trying to blink the image away, but that body-bag still sagged as it was lifted.

Having changed trains at Tottenham Court Road, they emerged twenty minutes later into the open air at Hendon Central and, like everyone else in the carriage, Thorne and Tanner reached immediately for their mobiles. The alert on Thorne's phone sounded within seconds. By the time he'd listened to the message and was returning the call, he had begun to think that, just maybe, the Evidence Fairy had got out of the right side of the bed that morning.

The officer from ActionFraud explained that they had been looking through reports on unsolved cases from the last few years, checking any physical descriptions of reported fraudsters that might tally with that given by the Fultons or, failing that, with the e-fit generated by the Brooklands Hill parents.

'Got one that looks pretty close,' the officer said. 'Victim seems to think so, anyway. Thought you might want to talk to the woman concerned.'

Thorne listened, then asked the officer to text him the full contact details.

'What?' Tanner asked, when the call had ended.

He explained. 'So, fancy a trip to Glasgow?'

'That's probably going to mean an overnight.'

'Could do.'

'I'll have to get someone to feed the cat.'

Thorne stared out of the window at a scrubby verge sloping towards a spray-painted metal fence, at the brown and grey vista of crowded car parks and warehouses beyond.

'What was I saying about our exciting lives . . . ?'

FORTY-FIVE

It was a journey Conrad had little choice about making whenever he was summoned, but after what had happened the night before, it had felt good to get away. Today, it felt like a relief; to go and spend some time with a woman who, however much she had him by the short and curlies, he didn't think was capable of losing it in quite the way Sarah had done.

Jesus, talk about a rock and a hard place.

She had woken him with a blow job, like it would make up for the stinging ear and the bruise on his cheek, and he wasn't much looking forward to explaining *that* to the woman he was on his way to see. Breakfast in bed afterwards, then more tearful apologies for the shameful way she'd behaved, while she got herself dolled up for the school run.

The school run? Christ on a bike . . .

He wondered if perhaps she'd caught the look on his face when they'd been having dinner, when she'd been talking about having to arrange their getaway around school dates. He always did his best to keep a blank expression whenever she mentioned the kid, to pretend he thought that everything was perfectly normal, but maybe, for once, he hadn't quite managed it. That had certainly been his first thought when she'd gone for him the way she had, that he'd crossed some line to do with her being a mother, or whatever.

Like that was the one thing she could never forgive.

That was until she'd lost the plot and kicked off good and proper, laying into him like she'd have happily taken his eyes out and screaming about being lied to. How dare he, all that. Once he'd got over the shock and made sure she couldn't do him any more damage, that had been what really pissed him off, because up until then he'd thought he was making a pretty decent fist of it. The story he'd put together the day before, knowing he had to, because he could sense she was getting suspicious. 'Vanessa' and the rest of it. Then, suddenly, it was like a switch being flicked inside her head and she was all over him again, wailing and saying it was all because she was jealous, on account of just how much she loved him, how much he meant to her.

Pulling him down to the kitchen floor, kissing him and everything else.

I'm sorry, my love. I'm sorry, I'm sorry, I'm sorry . . .

His head had been spinning by then, and not just because of how many times she'd smacked him.

'Shit . . . ' The car in front had taken too long pulling away from lights and now Conrad had missed the chance to go through.

He slammed his hands against the steering wheel.

He kept on slamming them.

He screamed until he had no breath left, turned and smacked his fist into the window.

How the *fuck* could he have let himself get sucked into all this? He'd always called the shots, been the one controlling the situation, however much whatever woman he'd been involved with might have believed otherwise. Now, he was . . . pinned down.

How could you love someone this much and be at their mercy?

That first time, the business at the beach, it was as though he'd been drugged up or something, and he might just as well have been. He'd been high on *her*, all over the place, and picking up that rock had felt like nothing at all. By the time the comedown had hit and he was able to really think about what he'd done, it was too late. He was hers and they had become this ... thing, and there was nothing he could do about it. When she'd said they needed to pay a visit to that teacher, he'd had to go along with it, hadn't he?

Had to, *wanted* to ... he wasn't sure there was much difference any more.

He pulled slowly away from the lights and tried to calm himself, because he couldn't turn up in this state, could he?

If Sarah was done with all the bad stuff ... if they could settle, wasn't there a chance they could move past what had happened? Years from now they could be different people in a different place, another country maybe, and what they'd done on that beach and in that teacher's house would just be like scenes in some scary film they'd once watched together.

Things they would both pretend to have forgotten.

Clutching at straws was something else he didn't have a lot of choice about.

Fifteen minutes later, when Conrad rang the bell, he touched his finger to the bruise on his cheekbone and swore out loud. He was every bit as pinned down here, too. There wasn't much point in telling her he'd walked into a door or anything, because this one knew when he was lying every bit as well as Sarah did.

It didn't much matter what she thought in the end, the fun she'd have, whatever shit she'd make him eat. She'd love every minute of it and how could he honestly say she didn't deserve that much, at least?

She'd laugh and she'd call him a pussy and he'd let her.

Because he was.

*

In the end, following Conrad had not proved particularly tricky. Sarah had watched enough cop shows to know that it was best to stay a couple of vehicles behind, and even though she'd lost sight of his car once or twice – missed lights or whatever – it wasn't very hard to find him again. She'd set up the Find My iPhone thing, so with a couple of taps she could see what road he was on, even if she didn't know exactly where he was going.

She had a rough idea, of course, because she'd tracked him using the phone before.

She knew damn well it wasn't Clapham.

He was showered and dressed when she'd got back from the school run, getting ready to set off, so she'd taken the opportunity to lavish plenty more affection on him before he left. It was another chance to show him just how sorry she was. She *was* sorry, for losing control, for attacking him the way she had, but she wasn't sorry about calling him a liar because that's exactly what he was.

He was the one doing the betraying.

He was the one keeping secrets.

He was the one threatening everything they had.

By the end of the journey, she'd been close enough to watch Conrad park and walk back, had seen him ring the bell and go in. She had no idea how long he would be inside, of course, but he'd told her he'd be home by the time she got back from picking Jamie up, so she was hopeful it wouldn't be too long.

Plenty of time for him to do what he was there for, presumably.

More than once, if she hadn't worn him out the night before.

She parked her own car round a corner then walked back to a café from where she would be able to sit and watch the front door. She ordered tea and opened the magazine she'd brought with her.

Absolutely Mama: For Stylish Mums.

It wasn't as if she enjoyed spying and sneaking around. The truth was that, much as she loved him, much as she would be utterly lost without him, she actually resented Conrad a little for

237

making her behave this way. Forcing her hand like this. All she wanted was a nice quiet life, just the three of them ticking along like any other family, and now, just when they were in a position to do and be exactly that, he'd thrown a dirty big spanner in the works.

Special as he was, just another bloke who couldn't keep it in his pants.

Sarah was simply not willing to sit back and watch everything fall apart, not again, not when it was so perfect. She'd do whatever it took to save Conrad from himself, to save all of them. In spite of what he was doing, she was in no doubt that he still loved her, so she was confident that he would understand. Theirs was no ordinary relationship, not even close, so how could he not?

He would do the same thing in her position, she was certain of that.

He would thank her, by the end.

Just over two hours later, when she'd read her magazine cover to cover and drunk more tea than she should have – considering she was unable to leave her seat in the window – Sarah saw the front door open. She watched Conrad step out on to the street, though annoyingly there was no glimpse of the woman he'd been visiting.

No tender farewell, no kiss on the doorstep . . .

She paid her bill, but stayed where she was for five minutes longer, until she was certain he'd have driven away. She checked the app on her phone to be on the safe side and saw that he was heading home again.

Then she took the envelope she'd brought with her from her bag.

Walking across the road, she still could not decide what to write on the front. She was sure the woman wasn't called Vanessa, but had no idea what her name actually was. She'd toyed with putting *Conrad's whore*, but decided, in the end, to leave it blank. The woman wouldn't be able to resist picking it up and opening it, whatever it said.

She hesitated, just for a few moments, outside the front door.

She could always just ring the bell and confront the woman, make her feelings known there and then. It was probably not a risk worth taking, though, she decided.

The bitch smiling at her, stinking of him . . .

Who knew what might happen?

She slipped the envelope under the door, turned away and walked back towards her car. The note was a much better idea, anyway. A message that was short and to the point, that would make the poor woman's position abundantly clear to her.

HE WILL KILL YOU IF I ASK HIM TO.

FORTY-SIX

Carrying a mug of Earl Grey through from the kitchen to the sitting room, Tanner glanced at her bag, packed and ready by the front door. It had been sitting there for several hours already, because she'd done her packing as soon as she'd got home. She knew very well how predictable her behaviour was and how much Thorne would enjoy taking the piss, but she didn't really care. It was worth doing these things properly and in good time, so as to avoid silly mistakes. An important document forgotten, a phone charger, whatever. She had made a stupid mistake during the major investigation seven months before, and though she couldn't swear that it had led in any way to what had eventually happened – because she'd been over it in her head a thousand times and it almost certainly hadn't – it wasn't something she was keen to repeat.

She had never quite understood exactly what it was that you were supposed to learn from mistakes. That you were fallible? That maybe you were working too hard?

Tanner learned never to make them again, simple as that.

Again, because of what had happened the year before, she

knew exactly what Tom Thorne would have to say about it. The annoying face he'd pull while he was letting her know what he thought. Something snarky about how forgetting to pack a spare pair of pants was fairly unimportant, you know . . . in the scheme of things.

As soon as she sat down, Mrs Slocombe jumped up next to her and Tanner was reaching for the phone before the cat had settled. She sent a text to remind her next-door neighbour where the cat food was, to fill the water bowl and to post the keys back through the letterbox the following day.

Tanner's spare keys. Susan's keys . . .

She sat and thought how bizarre it was; how funny even, sometimes. The stupid things you missed about someone.

Their absence was there all the time, of course. A hollow, inside. It was something Tanner had become used to, an ache that had perhaps already begun to ease, but then one of those little things would pounce and start to prick when she least expected it.

When she was standing on a chair, for God's sake, because she had to.

Susan had been just those couple of inches taller than she was and had been able to reach the overnight bag in its usual place on top of the wardrobe. Sitting on the bed afterwards and watching as neatly folded clothes were arranged in the same order as always. Waiting until Tanner had finished, so that she could try to answer the inevitable question.

'Have I forgotten anything?'

Alone in the bedroom earlier, Tanner had checked her list, then asked herself the question anyway.

She called Thorne, but got the answerphone and left a message, reminding him exactly where at Euston station they had arranged to meet at nine o'clock the following morning.

She carried what was left of her tea upstairs.

Brushing her teeth, she stared at herself and considered again

241

the narrow escape she had recently been granted. Sexual procliv-ities aside, had she really thought that teacher would have been the slightest bit interested? She was relieved she had been spared the chance to find out, to make another mistake to learn from.

She said, 'Fucking idiot,' and smiled at the way it had sounded, her mouth full of toothpaste. She spat then rinsed and wiped spots from the mirror with a flannel.

Then she walked into her bedroom and left Thorne another message.

'There are two branches of Smiths,' she said. 'And we're meet-ing outside the bigger one, OK? It's the one nearest the platforms. The one that sells books. I'll be there from about quarter to nine.'

'I had a missed call from you,' Helen said.

Thorne took a few seconds, then remembered calling her a couple of nights earlier. The same night he'd called Melita Perera. 'Yeah . . .'

'Why didn't you leave a message?'

'I don't know,' Thorne said. 'Didn't seem much point. It wasn't anything urgent.'

'I had a late shift,' she said.

'That's what I thought.' Thorne lifted his legs up on to the sofa and let his head drop back. He heard Helen cough. Was it just the situation making things seem awkward, or were they really running out of things to say to each other? 'How's Alfie?'

'He's good. Could be doing a bit better at school, mind you.'

'Listen, how well do you know the other parents, d'you reckon?' Helen was nothing like any of those women Thorne had met at Brooklands Hill, but he thought it was worth asking. 'When you drop Alfie off or pick him up?'

'Well, I know some of them. The ones with kids in Alfie's class. Why?'

Thorne laid out the bare bones of the case.

'How come you always get the freaky ones?' she said.

'Didn't start off like that,' he said. 'Just going after a con-artist in my spare time and it all went mental.'

'You *are* a bit of a nutter-magnet, though.'

'So, what do you think? About *her*?'

'You reckon she's the nutter?'

'No idea,' Thorne said. 'Just thinking out loud, really.'

'I don't know ... lost a child, maybe? Lost a couple?'

'Yeah, I can see how that might lead to pretending you've got a kid when you haven't, but does it explain two murders?'

'Best I can come up with right now,' Helen said.

'Just wanted to see what you thought.' It was no more than conversation, truth be told. Too much time spent thinking about why *anyone* committed murder always left Thorne feeling that explanations were for the likes of Melita Perera. It was his job to catch them, simple as that. 'Get another take on it, you know?'

'Losing a child is always traumatic,' Helen said. 'And if there are underlying psychological problems as well ...'

There was a long silence.

'Tom ...?'

Thorne was thinking about a woman called Louise Porter who had lost a child several years before, two months into the pregnancy. *His* child. The relationship had not survived it, or, if Thorne was being honest, had not survived his own reaction to it. Emotions to which he had stupidly refused to give rein at the time; sadness and rage bottled up to his own cost and to the cost of those he would be involved with later.

Unresolved issues, was what Melita Perera would probably call them.

Louise Porter had been a copper, too.

Maybe *that* was the problem.

He said, 'Why don't you bring Alfie over here one day? We could go to the heath or something.' He waited. 'What about Sunday?'

'Sunday's not going to work,' Helen said, eventually.

'If you've got something on, I could always come down and pick him up.'

'Like I said, it's tricky on Sunday. Maybe another time, though.'

There wasn't very much to say, after that.

When the call had ended, Thorne listened to two messages from Nicola Tanner which did a little to improve his mood. There were *some* nutters he could handle ...

He leaned down for the can of lager on the floor and polished off what was left, scrolling through to the Control Centre on his phone, thinking that he should set an alarm for the morning while he remembered. He smiled, guessing that Tanner had probably set several. It was only two stops on the Tube from Kentish Town to Euston, but he decided to get up that little bit earlier than he might otherwise have done.

Give himself ten minutes to throw a few things into a bag.

FORTY-SEVEN

Denise Fry worked as an HR administrator for a large insurance company in Glasgow city centre. Thorne and Tanner had called up from reception then waited for her to come down, the woman having made it clear on the phone to Tanner the day before that she would rather not talk to them at her place of work. They stood up when she stepped, a little tentatively, from the lift and, after the briefest of introductions, followed her across the lobby towards Sauchiehall Street.

'It's not that cold out there, is it?' she asked.

Thorne was surprised at the absence of the expected accent, having presumed that the woman was Glaswegian. She was clearly no more Scottish than he was, with a voice was that was high and light, a hint of nervousness in it. He was equally taken aback when Tanner told her that the weather was actually surprisingly mild, as Thorne had frozen his nuts off on the ten-minute walk from their hotel. He'd been hoping they could escort her to the nearest café or possibly a pub.

'So, maybe we can go to the park. It's not very far.'

Overweight, in a smart black business suit, the woman looked a little older than her forty-six years, and as they walked Thorne found himself wondering if she'd looked any different three years earlier, when she'd become involved with a man calling himself Paul Jenner. His victims had all suffered financial losses, of course, but there could be little doubt that being duped so flagrantly would inflict as much damage to their confidence and self-esteem as it did to their bank accounts.

Damage that had proved ultimately fatal for Philippa Goodwin.

Denise was chatty as they walked north. She indicated a few local landmarks, asked Thorne and Tanner about their train journey, and apologised again, as she had done the previous day, for her reluctance to be seen talking to the police anywhere near her office.

'Obviously I never told anyone at work,' she said. 'About what happened.'

'Understandable,' Tanner said.

'Well, I can't imagine anyone would.'

'It's really not a problem,' Tanner said.

Thorne just nodded. It was a longer walk than he had anticipated, Denise Fry wasn't moving terribly fast, and he wasn't getting any warmer.

'It's ... embarrassing,' she said. 'I'm good at my job, you know? So I wouldn't want anyone there thinking I can be taken for a ride. *Again*, I mean.'

At the end of Sauchiehall Street they cut right up into Kelvingrove Park and found a bench at the edge of a play area. Denise sat between Thorne and Tanner. 'I come here a lot,' she said. While she eagerly pointed out the bandstand and amphitheatre to one side of them, then the Gothic towers of the Art Gallery and Museum rising beyond the bowling green on the other, Tanner was removing a folder from her plastic bag. 'It's nice to get away sometimes, you know?'

246

'Could you take a look at this?' Tanner passed her the e-fit based on descriptions given by Ella and Helen Fulton.

Denise looked at the picture. Said, 'Ah . . .'

'That's a man who called himself Patrick Jennings,' Thorne said. 'This was over a month ago.'

'Same initials,' Denise said. 'Patrick Jennings, Paul Jenner.'

Thorne nodded. He had clocked it during the conversation with the team from ActionFraud two days earlier and had asked them to keep looking through their files for suspected fraudsters with the initials PJ. 'Now, this one . . .'

Tanner passed a second e-fit across; the one compiled by several of the parents from Brooklands Hill school.

' . . . is a bit more recent. A man who's currently calling himself Conrad.'

Denise stared at it, then held both pictures up together and looked from one to the other. 'Yeah, well, it's definitely him.' She handed the printouts back to Tanner. 'That's Paul . . . or Patrick, or whatever. His hair was longer when I knew him and his face wasn't quite as thin. He had glasses, too and he didn't have a beard.' She looked at Tanner, shook her head. 'I thought he was handsome.'

'Tell us what happened.' Tanner softened her voice. 'If you wouldn't mind.'

Denise nodded. 'I'd done my best to forget it until you called. Or to not think about it quite as much, at any rate.'

'Whatever you can tell us,' Thorne said.

Fifty feet or so away, a few children were making good use of the swings and monkey bars. Slightly closer, a boy of nine or ten was practising fancy skateboard moves on the path and swearing loudly in a thick Glaswegian accent, like someone well versed in the art, whenever they failed to come off.

'I met him in a bar in town about eighteen months ago,' Denise said. 'Out with some girlfriends, you know? I wasn't on the pull or anything . . . just having a good night, and we just got talking.

It wasn't like he was pushy or trying it on . . . he seemed quite shy, actually, but he said how nice I looked, something like that. He sat there and listened to me droning on about work or whatever it was, and he bought me a drink, and . . . ' She looked at Tanner. 'I wasn't as . . . heavy as I am now.'

Tanner nodded.

The boy with the skateboard said, 'Fucking *twat*.'

'So, at the end of the night, I asked him for his number. I think I was pretty tipsy by that time.'

Thorne already knew that they were talking about someone who, before turning to murder, had been very good at what he did, but allowing his target to make the running like that marked 'Paul' out as a seriously skilled operator. He guessed that it also increased the feelings of stupidity and self-loathing that his victim would be left with once he had done his job. Thorne imagined that 'Patrick' had played things much the same way with Philippa Goodwin that night in the Blacksmith and Toffeemaker.

Stalking his prey, then letting them come to him.

'It was all pretty fast after that,' Denise said. 'We went on a few dates and he told me he was divorced, that he was renting some crappy little flat until he got himself sorted out. So I told him he could move into my place. It was like he wasn't sure about it at first, like he thought he'd be imposing, but I persuaded him.' She looked at Tanner again. 'I *persuaded* him, can you believe that?'

'He was working you,' Thorne said. 'It's what he does.'

What he *did*. Before a rock replaced a pick-up line as his weapon of choice.

Denise blinked several times and took a few fast breaths. 'Once he'd moved in, he told me all about his family . . . his ex-wife and his daughter, and for a couple of months everything was fine. I was happy. I was *really* happy.'

'What did he say he did for a living?' Tanner asked.

'He told me he was some kind of recruitment consultant. Said

248

he worked for all sorts of companies, spent a few weeks at a time with different ones, you know? We'd meet in town for lunch sometimes and he'd tell me all about whichever office he was working in ... stories about the people. He'd do impressions of them, that kind of thing. He was funny, you know?'

'Oh, for fuck's sake!' The boy shouted after the skateboard he'd lost control of as it rolled away from him. He kicked at a discarded Irn-Bru can. 'You fucking *bell*-end ...'

'Like I say, it was fine. And then one day he just broke down and told me his daughter was really sick. Told me she had this rare form of leukaemia and I swear, he was properly in bits. Just sobbing and sobbing and saying how him and his ex-wife were trying to raise the money to send her to America for treatment. He showed me a picture ... this little girl who looked terrible, but she had this big grin on her face. He showed me all the flyers for sponsored runs and all that ... things he was doing to try and raise the cash.'

'So you offered to give him the money,' Thorne said.

The woman nodded, close to tears. 'He didn't want to take it at first. He kept saying it was too much, but all the time he was telling me how great I was, how much his little girl would love me if we ever got the chance to meet. I insisted in the end ... made him give me the details of his bank and transferred the money.' She turned and looked at them both. 'Like why wouldn't I? She was Paul's daughter and we were together and I wanted to do it for him.

'I remember how he was that night, the look on his face. How he couldn't believe it. I was there when he rang his ex-wife in tears and told her that he'd got the money, that his little girl was going to be able to make the trip.' She shrugged and sniffed. 'He was gone the next day.'

The woman began rummaging in her bag for tissues, but Tanner had one ready and passed it across.

'Sorry,' Denise said.

'Did you speak to anyone afterwards?' Tanner asked. 'I don't mean the police. Did you get any help?'

Denise shook her head. 'Just wanted to pretend it had never happened. I certainly didn't want to *tell* anyone. Like when you fall over in the street and the first thing you do is look round because you're scared to death someone might have seen it, you know?'

'You weren't his only victim,' Thorne said. 'That's why we're here.'

She nodded.

'I'm really sorry we've asked you to dredge all this up again,' Tanner said. 'But I promise you it's important.'

'Is there anything else you can remember about him you think might be helpful?' Thorne asked. 'Something he might have said ...' He stopped, seeing that the woman had something to say.

'I'm pretty sure I told the police this after he vanished ... or maybe I just mentioned it to one of them, but some of the time me and Paul were together, I had this weird feeling there was another woman.' Denise managed a smile. 'I mean, I've always been a bit jealous with men ... not like there've been very many of them ... but it was a bit more than that. I never said anything because I didn't want him to think I was being clingy. I didn't want to scare him off.'

'You don't mean the ex-wife?' Tanner said.

She scoffed. 'The non-existent ex-wife? Yeah, I thought that to begin with, but not for very long. It felt like he was seeing someone else.'

'What made you think that?' Thorne asked.

'I don't know ... getting odd text messages in the evening, that kind of stuff. I mean he always told me it was a work thing and like I said, I didn't want to push him.' She clutched her bag to her stomach and stared off towards the playground. 'I remember one night, I heard a text arrive ... you know, the tone ... and I

250

checked his phone when he was in the bathroom and this message he'd got ten minutes before wasn't there. Like he must have deleted it.'

The boy's skateboard flew from beneath his feet and he stomped after it.

'Could have been anything, I suppose, but I couldn't shake the idea there was a woman he was keeping secret.'

Thorne and Tanner exchanged a look.

'I don't know if that's remotely helpful, but—'

'You stupid cunt!' the boy shouted.

'We can move if you want.' Tanner stood up and glared at the boy as she marched across to pick up the empty can. 'We're about done, anyway.'

'It's fine,' Denise said. 'I know exactly how he feels.'

FORTY-EIGHT

The woman had begun ranting at him the moment Conrad had answered the call, had spoken her name.

'She's threatened my life, for Christ's sake.'

'*What?*'

'Didn't you hear me? My fucking life.'

He listened as the woman twice read out the contents of the note that had been shoved under her front door. He said, 'OK ...'

'OK? Is that the best you can come up with?'

He moved further away from the house, his voice barely more than a whisper. 'You need to calm down—'

'What are you going to do about it?'

'How do you know the note came from her?'

'Oh, wake up, Conrad. Who the hell else is it going to be?'

He had stepped out into the garden as soon as he'd seen who was calling and now he looked back towards the house to see Sarah watching from the kitchen. He raised a hand to wave and she turned away.

'I could go to the police,' she said.

'And tell them what?'

'I could go . . . that's all I'm saying. I *should* go.'

He looked back at the kitchen, but Sarah had left the room. Instinctively he raised his eyes towards the windows at the top of the house, convinced she would be watching him from one of the bedrooms, but he saw no sign of her. 'You won't go to the police. How can you?'

'*I* haven't done anything.'

'A woman killed herself.'

'How is that my fault?'

'You're involved,' Conrad said.

'Not with this, I'm not. Not with *her* . . .'

'Look, I'll . . . deal with it, all right?'

'How?'

At that moment, Conrad did not have the faintest idea, but he knew that whatever he was going to do would need to wait until he had finished shaking with rage or fear, he could not be certain which. He began to pace around the small lawn. His car keys were on the kitchen table and, if Sarah *was* upstairs, he guessed that he could grab them and get to his car without seeing her.

A drive might calm him down a little, would give him time to think.

He said, 'I'll deal with it.'

FORTY-NINE

Tanner was sitting with a glass of wine and had already ordered by the time Thorne joined her in the bar of the Travelodge on Queen Street. Passing a menu across, she told him she'd gone for the tuna salad. Having clocked a tempting meal-deal, Thorne hailed a passing waiter and asked for chicken wings, a burger and a bottle of Stella.

'Pretty good for fifteen quid,' he said. 'Not a lot more than we paid for two coffees in that place in Enfield.'

'How's your room?' Tanner asked.

'There's a bed and a TV,' Thorne said.

'It's only one night.'

'Shocking lack of porn, though.' He began to check his phone for emails and texts. 'I mean, that's one of the perks of staying in a hotel, right?'

Tanner smiled. 'I prefer to use my imagination.'

'Mine's a bit limited,' Thorne said. The waiter arrived with his beer and Thorne took a swig.

'So . . . what about this "other woman" Denise Fry mentioned?'

Thorne set his phone down on the table. 'Yeah, I've been thinking about that.'

'You think it could have been Sarah?'

'Well, we don't want to discount anything, but I don't really see how it could be.'

'Because it doesn't make sense time-wise?'

'Right. Denise hooked up with this bloke a year and a half back, but the Brooklands Hill parents seem pretty certain that Sarah met him for the first time in the coffee shop about six weeks ago.'

'What if that was all part of it?'

Thorne took another drink and waited.

'I'm thinking out loud, really, but what if this other woman was actually an accomplice of some sort? Someone he was working with to target his victims. Easier for a woman to get close to other women, I would have thought, sound them out a bit. Easier to identify the vulnerable ones, the ones with money.'

'Sounds reasonable,' Thorne said.

'So, what if that meeting in the coffee shop was staged? Maybe they were actually going after one of the mums from school.'

Thorne shook his head. 'Doesn't make sense. For a kick off, yeah ... I reckon some of those women have probably got money to spare, but I don't *think* any of them are single. Besides which, they said Sarah made it very clear to them that Conrad was her boyfriend, that they were all loved-up and living together. How could he work a con on one of those mums when they all knew he was involved with another one? I mean, we both know Sarah wasn't actually a parent, but you see what I'm saying.'

'Yeah ... like I said, thinking out loud.'

'I don't believe Sarah had anything to do with the work Conrad was doing before, because she's a very different sort of individual. I mean, for all we know she might have been his target ... when they first met in that coffee shop, at any rate. Before he knew her.' Thorne let his beer bottle swing gently between two fingers. 'Something happened once those two got together.' He remembered Hatter casually weighing that rock in his hand on Margate beach, the look of shock and horror on the faces of Gemma Maxwell's colleagues. 'Something a damn sight nastier.'

'OK, so if the other woman wasn't Sarah, who was she?'

Thorne shrugged, then leaned back as the waiter arrived and began laying down their food. 'Maybe Denise imagined it. She said herself, she was the jealous type.'

Tanner said, 'She sounded pretty certain to me.'

Dipak Chall had called while Tanner was in her room, and as she and Thorne ate, she gave him a progress report on the expanded house-to-house enquiries; filled him in on the conversations with estate and lettings agencies local to Brooklands Hill and the house where Gemma Maxwell had been murdered.

It didn't take very long.

'We keep plugging away,' Thorne said. 'All we can do.'

'I suppose.'

'And hope that, in the meantime, nobody else gets in Conrad and Sarah's way.'

Tanner nodded and downed what was left of her wine. She was about to say something when her mobile rang. She answered the call, listened for a few seconds then mouthed to Thorne, *Denise Fry.*

Thorne put his knife and fork down and listened, but the look on Tanner's face and the platitudes she was trotting out made it clear that the woman they had spoken to earlier was not calling with crucial information of any sort. Making sympathetic noises, Tanner stood up and wandered out into the reception area.

Thorne had all but finished eating by the time she returned to the table.

'What was all that about?'

'I think she was pissed,' Tanner said, sitting down again. 'Pissed and weeping.'

Thorne grunted and went back to what was left of his burger.

'Do you think we take it for granted, sometimes?' Tanner was moving bits of wilted salad around her plate. 'What victims go through.'

Thorne looked up, chewing. 'No, but ... well, looking after the victims isn't really our job, is it? There's Family Liaison for all that, Victim Support teams.'

'I'm not saying we don't think about them, obviously we do ... too much, sometimes, but maybe we should talk to them a bit more.' Tanner pushed her plate away and leaned towards him. 'Nine times out of ten, we interview them and that's it; we don't set eyes on them again until it gets to court. *If* it gets to court.'

'It's our job to catch the people responsible, that's all. To do whatever we can to see justice done.'

'Yeah, well, that's not looking promising, is it?'

Thorne looked at her. 'Where's this going?'

She shrugged. 'I don't know. Just thinking out loud again, really.' She sat back and watched Thorne finish his meal. 'You got much on tomorrow?'

'We'll spend half the day travelling back.'

'After that.'

'Well, I've still got a stack of Court Disposal files to complete and a Protective Services questionnaire to fill out, so if you've got anything more tempting on offer ... '

Tanner told him what she had in mind. When Thorne raised no objection, she fished in her handbag and took a coin from her purse.

'I'm glad we're doing this scientifically,' Thorne said.

'You call it,' Tanner said. 'Heads, you get Margate, tails you get Walthamstow.'

Tanner tossed the coin and, once she had removed her hand, Thorne looked down and said, 'Fair enough.'

'Can't hurt, can it?'

Thorne wasn't altogether sure about that, but he wasn't

thrilled at the idea of more paperwork either. He reached forward and picked up Tanner's empty wine glass. Said, 'One more before we turn in?'

They carried their glasses across to a small table in the corner of a bar in which they were now the only customers and sat there saying nothing. It was as though they had said everything there was to say about the crimes that had brought them there – the frauds and the murders – and now, as the two of them drank and avoided eye contact, the silence that grew between them gained a little more weight with every minute that passed. Ominous, in direct proportion to the cheery, plastic jazz that spewed from a tinny speaker in the corner of the room.

'What happened last year,' Tanner said, eventually.

There it was.

This thing that had *happened* . . .

Nothing ever any more specific than that. Never a name or a place. No mention of stabbing or scissors, no blood and broken skulls.

Thorne turned to look at her and nodded, inviting it.

'It feels like you're waiting for me to say thank you.'

'I'm really not,' Thorne said.

'Every minute of every day.'

'Like I said—'

'And the truth is I can't, because I'm not actually grateful.'

Thorne stared down into his beer, then drank some of it.

'I know how ridiculous that sounds after what you did . . . what Phil did . . . but the fact remains that it was wrong and I'm still struggling to get past that.'

'What do you mean, struggling?'

'I mean that just about the only thing stopping me marching into Russell's office as soon as we get back and coming clean about what actually happened, is you.' She found Thorne's eyes for the first time, but only for a moment. 'You and Phil. I know it would mean your careers ... would mean a damn sight worse for me, probably, and that's fine, but I can't. Because even though what you did was wrong too ... wrong and seriously ... *stupid* ... I can't drag the pair of you down with me, can I?'

Thorne looked at her.

'Of course I can't.' She shook her head quickly. 'I'm just saying. I can't ever tell the truth and however ungrateful and disloyal it sounds, there's a part of me that resents you for it.'

Thorne had just begun to rub absently at the soft flesh of his right hand when Tanner reached over and grabbed his fingers. She opened his hand fully and stared down at the ragged line across his palm, the scar for which she was responsible. 'And I'm not going to apologise for that, either,' she said. 'It was your idea, remember?'

Thorne pulled his hand away. 'I'm not likely to forget, am I?'

They said nothing for half a minute or more. A pair of be-suited businessmen wandered in and stood at the bar waiting to order. The muzak had become even cheerier.

'You weren't yourself, Nic.' Thorne saw that she was about to argue and raised a hand, his left, to stop her. 'When you did it.'

'I'm myself now though, aren't I?' She glared at him. 'Waking up with it every day and knowing that I can't do the right thing.'

'You sure?'

'Sure about what?'

'That telling the truth would be the right thing. Maybe what we did was the right thing. It certainly felt like it.'

Tanner winced slightly at the laughter coming from the pair at the bar and closed her eyes for a few seconds. They were wet when she opened them again. She said, 'I'm truly sorry about what happened and that you got caught up in it. I might find it hard to say thank you, but I can certainly manage that. And I'm sorry for ... all *this*, for spouting off.' The sigh rattled in her chest. 'I don't know ...'

'Just thinking out loud again?'

'Something like that.' Suddenly, Tanner looked every bit as wrung out and haunted as one of those victims she had been talking about at dinner; as wretched as Denise Fry had looked when they'd left her in Kelvingrove Park a few hours earlier.

'It's not a problem,' Thorne said. 'It won't ever be a problem.' He leaned across and laid a hand on her arm. 'As long as I'm the only one around to hear it.'

FIFTY

Sarah was in the bathroom, so Conrad sat on the bed and waited for her.

He was certainly a little calmer than he'd been earlier, after taking that call in the garden, but was nonetheless grateful for the few extra minutes he now had to prepare himself. He still had no idea at all what he was going to say to her. Driving around, he'd rehearsed a host of different lines, and even though that was something he was well used to – the sick daughter, the greatest film script he'd ever read – nothing had come to him that he felt confident about. The first thing out of his mouth was going to be all-important, he knew that, but anything he'd thought of just felt stupidly inane or else simply . . . dangerous.

We need to talk.

Listen, I'm sure you've got a good explanation for this, but . . .

You've gone too far this time.

He could hear her tuneless singing coming from the bathroom, that stupid Hall and Oates song he'd told her about. Listening to her, clattering around in there with her creams and oils like she didn't have a care in the world, brought a rush of anger back and he fought to keep a lid on it, for both their sakes. If *he* lost it, then so would she, and the last thing he needed was a repeat of what had happened three nights before.

Or worse . . .

He found himself looking quickly around the bedroom, seeking out anything she might grab and hit him with if she lost her temper. Anything he might use to defend himself if that happened, because he wouldn't stand for being a punchbag again.

A thick glass candleholder; a stiletto shoe with a heel that could certainly do a lot of damage; the framed photograph of the two of them she kept on her bedside table. His gaze shifted to the pink stick of rock lying incongruously next to a paperback thriller and the anger flipped suddenly into terror; or a memory of it, every bit as intense, rising up from his guts like acid.

'Because it's nice to have a souvenir, isn't it?' What she'd said when he'd asked her about it. 'Margate running all the way through it, and now it runs all the way through *us* . . .'

He could always say nothing, of course.

Wouldn't that be the easiest option, the path of least resistance?

He could just get undressed, slip into bed and pretend to be asleep.

Yes, he'd told the woman on the phone that he'd sort it, but if he just pretended it had never happened, it would sort itself eventually. She would calm down, given enough time, and he would come up with some story to cover his arse. He was good at that—

Conrad heard the bathroom door open, Sarah's footsteps in the corridor outside, and suddenly she was coming through the door, wearing a towel wrapped tightly above her breasts and a grin that made his decision for him and brought him to his feet.

He said, 'What the fuck did you think you were doing?'

If her grin faltered, it was for no more than a moment. 'Well, I've just been doing something rather naughty in the bathroom, but I promise I was thinking about you.'

They looked at one another for a few seconds.

'You followed me the other day.' Conrad was breathing like he'd just done an hour at the gym.

'I wouldn't have needed to if you'd told me where you were going.'

'You *followed* me.'

'You're very angry.' She spoke as though she was paying him a compliment.

'And you delivered a note to someone.'

'To *someone*?'

Conrad stepped suddenly towards her, but she did not flinch. 'You know what you did. What you threatened her with.'

'You should have told me you were seeing her.' Sarah raised a hand and clawed fingers through her wet hair. 'No secrets, we said.'

'You don't understand.'

'So, tell me.'

'I didn't *want* to see her ...' Conrad stopped, because he understood suddenly that he was cornered, that telling her the truth would be the very worst thing he could possibly do.

'Why not?'

Conrad lowered his eyes and watched a single bead of water slide along her collarbone and when he raised them, the look on her face confirmed his worst fears. If he told her that he was being as good as blackmailed, that this woman she was now threatening knew exactly what he and Sarah had done, it would only be a matter of time before it became another problem Sarah needed solving. He had seen how she did that at the teacher's house, how efficiently she had gone about it.

He could not be part of that again. *Would* not.

'You've gone very quiet,' she said.

Did she already know?

Conrad could not immediately see how she would, but he could not be sure how long she had been watching him or the woman he had been seeing, and he had long accepted the fact that he had no idea what went on in Sarah's head.

'I'm sorry,' he said, the strength gone from his voice.

'For being angry with me? Or for something worse?'

'I shouldn't have lied.'

'No, you really shouldn't.'

'But it's not what you think.'

She nodded, pleased. 'I was only doing what I thought was best for us, you get that, surely? For you, me and Jamie.'

And suddenly, the control, the *indulgence* Conrad knew he had to summon at moments such as this was not within his reach. Or perhaps he had simply lost the desire to exercise it. '*Jamie?*'

'He needs stability—'

'What are you talking about? How can someone you've made up need *anything*? What the fuck's the matter with you?'

For ten or fifteen seconds, Sarah looked as though something had been ripped from her, as though she were fighting to stay upright. Conrad could only watch, transfixed, until her expression began to harden and set, and he found himself thinking about how quickly he might get to that candleholder or the stiletto a few feet away at the end of the bed. He tensed, waiting for it, then saw something else wash slowly across her face, as though she'd reached a decision of some sort.

She untied the towel and let it drop to the floor.

She smiled and moved a hand across her stomach.

She said his name as though hearing herself say it for the first time.

Hardening in spite of himself, Conrad was already thinking that scratches and slaps would have been so much easier to deal with, as Sarah walked slowly past him, climbed on to the bed and knelt on all fours.

'Sometimes, my love, it's good to be angry.' She clutched at the sheets, raised her backside and laid her head flat against the pillow. 'And you know I don't mind if it hurts a little bit . . .'

FIFTY-ONE

Thorne followed Andrew Ruston along the narrow hallway in which his girlfriend had been bludgeoned to death ten days before. The carpet had been removed for obvious reasons – though Thorne could not be sure if that had been done by CSIs at the crime scene or later, by Ruston himself – and there were a few gaps, revealing dust-balls and tangles of wiring, where sections of the floorboards had been taken up.

'There's a couple of nails to watch out for as well.' Ruston was soft-spoken, a trace of a northern accent. 'I keep forgetting. Come down in the morning in my bare feet, then have to go straight back upstairs and put some slippers on.'

If the young man had been remotely taken aback a minute or so before to find a detective he had not met brandishing a warrant card on his doorstep, he had not shown it. The blank expression might have been the same he wore whenever he opened the door to a Jehovah's Witness or someone selling cleaning goods. When Thorne had asked to come in, Ruston had simply nodded and turned back inside.

He was fully dressed, in jeans and a checked shirt, but he'd looked to Thorne like someone who was not yet fully awake.

He asked if Thorne wanted coffee and Thorne thanked him, though as it was late afternoon and, considering the nature of a visit that was more or less off the clock anyway, he had half thought about calling in somewhere on his way over and turning up with a few bottles in a plastic bag.

He followed Ruston into the kitchen.

'I'm not here with any news.' Thorne watched Ruston pulling mugs down from a shelf, stepped aside to let him get to the fridge. 'I should tell you that straight away.'

Ruston slid a pod into a flashy-looking coffee machine. 'Why've you come, then?'

Informing someone so recently bereaved in such terrible circumstances that visiting them had seemed a better option than paperwork, was clearly out of the question, so instead, Thorne told what seemed like a relatively small lie.

He said, 'I thought I should.'

Ruston turned to look at him, his expression unchanged, then went back to preparing the coffee.

'Are you . . . on your own?'

'Only for the last day or two,' Ruston said. 'Gemma's mum and dad were staying, then my mum and dad. They'll all be back for the funeral, whenever that is.'

'I'll see what I can do about hurrying all that up,' Thorne said. 'Getting Gemma . . . released.'

'So, yeah, on my own until then, I suppose. It's fine, though. I'm going to have to get used to it, aren't I?'

Thorne thought about Nicola Tanner, who by now was probably in Margate talking to Kevin Deane's parents, and decided that, all things considered, the coin toss had probably worked out best for both of them. This was really no more than a pastoral visit and, bearing in mind how both their partners had died, Tanner and Andrew Ruston might have had a little too much in common for her comfort. Or perhaps he was over-thinking it; underestimating his colleague's . . . professionalism.

Tanner would have handled it perfectly.

She would probably have recommended somewhere cheap to buy a new hall carpet.

They took their mugs into a sitting room that showed fewer obvious traces of any previous police presence, though it was rather more untidy – a little less cared for – than Thorne guessed it might otherwise have been.

There were a few clothes tossed into a corner, a pizza box next to the sofa and an ashtray whose contents explained the strong smell of weed that Thorne had recognised when the front door was opened. A laptop sat open on a low table, a screensaver showing a picture of Ruston and a young woman of whom Thorne had only seen post-mortem photographs but knew to be Gemma Maxwell. It looked as though it had been taken in one of those photo booths that were now so popular at parties. He wore thick, comedy glasses and had a stethoscope around his neck, while she was sporting a mortar board and flexing a cane.

They were both grinning like idiots.

Ruston closed the laptop and sat down, invited Thorne to do the same. He said, 'The hospital have been really great. Told me I can come back whenever I'm ready.'

'That's good,' Thorne said.

'God knows when that'll be. Right now, it feels like I wouldn't know a migraine from a melanoma.'

'It's important to take some time.' Thorne felt like he was quoting from some Bereavement Support Handbook For Morons. 'That's . . . important.'

'What happened to Gemma.' Ruston looked across at him. 'It's to do with that woman who was hanging about at the school, isn't it? The one pretending to have kids or something. Karl Sturridge told me you'd been asking about her.'

Thorne took a long sip of coffee, giving himself a few seconds. He had anticipated having to deal with general enquiries about the investigation, but it would have been easier to simply admit that they had made no real progress than answer a direct question such as this one, however much he wanted to. Questions like those Ella Fulton had asked, and Gemma Maxwell's friends at the school; questions that people in such situations had every right to ask, but to which Thorne was only ever supposed to give regulation responses.

Saying nothing would probably cover him both ways.

He said, 'Yeah, we think it is.'

'So, she's the one you're looking for?'

'Her and her boyfriend, yeah.'

Ruston stared.

'There were two of them here that night.'

'Oh, right. Do you know which one of them actually . . . ?'

Now Thorne had no need to lie. 'No, we don't.'

'I told her she should have talked to Rachel Peake about it or gone straight to the police.' He let out a long sigh, his hand rasping against the stubble on his cheek. 'Gemma wouldn't have it, though . . . said the woman must have problems, that she'd rather try and be nice about it.'

'She's certainly got problems,' Thorne said.

Ruston nodded, as if he didn't really want to know any more. Like that was enough to be going on with, plenty to be lying awake in the middle of the night thinking about. 'They told me about the baby,' he said. 'That it was only a week or two and Gemma probably didn't even know about it.'

Thorne swallowed. 'Right.' Fierce as the temptation had been to keep the fact of Gemma Maxwell's pregnancy from him, Ruston had a right to know any detail of the post-mortem which would later be seen as relevant in the event of a trial.

'If she did, she certainly hadn't said anything to me, and she would have because we'd been . . . trying.' He nodded again. 'I was thinking . . . it was probably a good thing she didn't have any idea. That at the end, she wouldn't have been thinking about the baby, you know?' He glanced briefly towards the corridor. 'That's something, isn't it?'

Watching Andrew Ruston's head drop and seeing, for the first time, how completely shattered the man's life was, Thorne felt himself starting to struggle. Flailing for the right words, for *any* words. The silence began to grow as uncomfortable, in its own way, as the one that had bloomed between himself and Tanner in that Glasgow hotel bar, and he had not the first idea what he should say to end it.

Everything sounded so pat, so insincere. Should he abandon any notions of support or knee-jerk consolation and just . . . keep the man company? Should he try to take his mind off what he was going through? Even as the idea occurred to him, Thorne realised how ridiculous it was.

How's your football team doing?

Seen any decent films lately?

Why couldn't he *do* this? What was he . . . lacking? He guessed that Tanner would be having no such trouble in Margate. He had seen her comforting Denise Fry on the phone the night before.

He said, 'I thought it was you. You know, initially.'

Ruston looked at him, then nodded. 'Makes sense, I suppose.'

'Right. Just statistics, you know? It's almost always the partner.'

'Yeah,' Ruston said. 'Almost always.' He stood up and walked across to gather up some of the clothes in the corner of the room. He held the bundle in his arms and turned to stare out at the street. 'So, is this some new initiative or something?'

'What?'

'Sending detectives like you out to talk to the victim's relatives. The caring face of the Met, or whatever.' He turned to look at Thorne. 'I've already been offered counselling and stuff, had a couple of uniformed coppers dropping in with pamphlets.'

'Not really,' Thorne said. 'Just thought it was something we don't really do enough of. Well, a colleague of mine thinks so. It was her idea, if I'm honest. DI Tanner?'

Ruston nodded. 'Yeah, she was nice. Like ... she clearly gave a toss, but she didn't talk to me like I had cancer, you know?'

'She's one of the good ones.'

'That explains it, though,' Ruston said.

'What?'

'Why you don't look any happier than I am.'

FIFTY-TWO

An hour and a half after leaving Walthamstow, Thorne was on home territory again; playing pool with Phil Hendricks in a dank and draughty room above the Grafton Arms that, thankfully, none but the most hardcore of regulars – including those who had reluctantly decamped to south London for a while – seemed to know about. This was ground on which he felt decidedly more comfortable than he had at Andrew Ruston's place, even if it was, literally, a fair bit stickier.

'*Get* in!' Thorne pumped his fist after sinking a long ball into a corner pocket.

'Shot,' Hendricks said, approaching the table. 'Shame it was one of mine.'

'What?'

'*I'm* stripes. You're spots.'

'Oh, for f—' Thorne was already three frames down and, with the loser of their best-of-seven match having to cough up for the evening's bar bill, things were not looking good. He stood and watched as Hendricks put a couple more of the right balls away.

He chalked his cue and said, 'Do you think it's a bit weird that I don't dream about my mum a bit more?'

Hendricks played a safety shot and watched as the white ball nestled nice and close to the cushion. He straightened up. 'God knows. I think it's a bit weird that you're asking me about it.'

'I've been dreaming about her loads lately, that's all.'

'Right . . .'

'Loads more than I normally do.'

'So, what, you're worried that you *are* dreaming about her or that you're not dreaming about her enough?'

'I don't know,' Thorne said. 'Both. I asked Melita Perera about it.'

'You did, did you?'

'Felt like a bit of an idiot asking her, to be honest, but she wasn't much help anyway.'

'I see. So, it's the hot shrink's *professional* services you're interested in, is it?' Hendricks smirked, but when Thorne refused to rise to his bait, he went back to his beer. 'Look, they're just dreams, mate. I wouldn't worry about it. The other night I dreamed I was getting noshed off by Bradley Cooper and the only thing I was worried about when I woke up was the fact that it wasn't actually happening.'

'Bradley Cooper?'

'Oh, yeah. He knew exactly what he was doing.'

The rest of the frame played out much as the first three had, though the result was to prove rather more controversial. With four of Thorne's balls still on the table, Hendricks was left with only the black to put away, and when the white went down as he attempted to pot it, Thorne claimed the frame.

'What are you talking about?'

'If you pot the white when you're trying to pot the black—'

'Yeah, when it's *only* the black left.'

'It's the way we've always done it.'

'Since when?' Hendricks waited, then shrugged and laid his cue down on the table. 'Fine, you have it, mate. You know, if cheating's the only way you can avoid a whitewash ...'

While Hendricks gathered the balls and slowly re-racked them, he told Thorne about the long weekend away in Barcelona that he and Liam were planning. Thorne, a little envious, and remembering a trip that he and Helen had taken to Bruges the year before, said, 'Sounds nice.'

'Can't bloody wait,' Hendricks said. 'Good bars, great food, all that. Bit of shopping on Las Ramblas and the odd gallery to keep Liam happy.'

'He into that, is he?'

'Sadly.'

'I've been thinking about art a bit lately,' Thorne said.

Hendricks said, 'I'm getting seriously worried about you,' and broke, hard. When two spots rolled into pockets, he began to strut around the table, singing 'Werewolves of London'.

'I know bugger all about it,' Thorne said. 'That's all. I know bugger all about loads of things, come to think of it.' He picked up his beer while Hendricks was lining up his next shot. 'Wine, politics, history.' He took a drink. 'Geography, classical music, books ...'

'I know sod all about nuclear physics,' Hendricks said. 'But it's not keeping me awake at night.'

'Sometimes you feel a bit stupid, all I'm saying.'

'For a very good reason.'

'The people that do know about that stuff can make you feel a bit stupid, even if they're not trying to.'

Hendricks missed his shot and swore loudly. 'Listen, mate, I can tell you everything you need to know about art. Or at least how you can make yourself sound like you know what you're talking about. Basically, if it's some famous dead artist, Rembrandt or one of them, you just nod a couple of times and say, "Oh, isn't it fantastic the way he's done that ... horse?" or "look how nicely he's painted that angel's tits" or whatever. And if it's *modern* art, you know, like squiggles or an "installation" or something . . . it's pants. Piece of piss.'

Thorne laughed.

'You're welcome,' Hendricks said.

'*Fuck* . . .'

'What?'

'My mum,' Thorne said. 'She used to *paint*.' He was smiling, shaking his head. 'How could I have forgotten that?'

'That's great.' Hendricks pulled a face, like Thorne was losing his marbles. 'It's your shot, by the way.'

Thorne didn't move, still a little stunned by the memory, the way it had dropped from nowhere into his head. 'I mean, I've no idea if she was any good or anything, but I remember watching her do it when I was . . . I don't know, six or seven or something. I had these paint-by-numbers kits, remember them?'

'I think I was too busy masturbating.'

'I'd do one of them and watch her while she was painting . . . whatever she was painting. She did it for ages.' He looked at Hendricks. 'What the hell happened to them all?'

'Wouldn't your dad have kept them somewhere?'

Thorne tried to think back to those days and weeks after his father had died. He remembered dealing with all the official stuff, seeking out a few of the old man's personal items for himself, but much of that period was a bit of a blur. Then he nodded. 'Auntie Eileen.'

'Auntie Eileen . . . what?'

'She offered to give me a hand after Dad died. She was the one that went through the boxes and bags in the loft.'

'There you go then,' Hendricks said. 'Maybe that's why you've been dreaming about her, maybe there's a lost Mrs Thorne masterpiece knocking about somewhere. Why don't you ask your lovely Dr Perera what she thinks about it?'

Thorne gave him the finger, then bent over his shot and smashed a stripe into the top corner.

'Four-one.' Hendricks shook his head, as though saddened to be drinking beer Thorne had paid for. 'I reckon you've lost your edge, living down there.'

Thorne reached for what he decided would be his final pint of the evening. Recalling his last conversation with Helen, it was certainly starting to look as though his time on the wrong side of the river had come to an end, and he still couldn't make his mind up how he felt about it. 'You might be right.'

'And even the *one* was iffy.'

They had come back downstairs to the bar. Despite the drubbing he had been on the receiving end of upstairs, and the fact that some sadist had put an Ed Sheeran song on the jukebox, Thorne was feeling a lot more relaxed than he had in a good few days. He and Hendricks had enjoyed a couple of hours together during which they had not once talked about work.

There had been no mention of blood and blunt-force trauma, of conmen or corpses.

And now Thorne was going to spoil it, because he had to.

He said, 'I had a long chat with Nicola Tanner last night.'

'Oh, yeah?' The change in Hendricks's expression made it clear he understood what the chat had been about.

Thorne told him exactly what Tanner had said.

'Is she a Catholic?' Hendricks asked.

'I don't think so. Why?'

'She does guilt better than anyone I know, that's all.'

'Maybe that's what makes her a good copper,' Thorne said. 'Maybe she can recognise it.'

'You think she'd ever say anything?'

'No.' Thorne shook his head, looked at his friend. 'No, I definitely don't. She just needed to get some stuff off her chest, I think.'

They drank in silence for a minute. The Ed Sheeran song gave way to something marginally less annoying.

'There's an expression, isn't there?' Hendricks said. 'Three people can keep a secret as long as two of them are dead. Something like that.'

'Seems a bit drastic,' Thorne said.

Hendricks smiled and tore into a packet of crisps with his teeth. 'Like that pair you're after.'

'What?'

'The couple . . .'

'Conrad and Sarah.'

'Right. Similar sort of situation, when you think about it. They're reliant on each other, aren't they? Same as we are. Keeping the secret, I mean. If one of them . . . weakens, they're both screwed.' Hendricks stuffed a handful of crisps into his mouth. 'So, who's the weakest in our little chain, do you reckon?'

FIFTY-THREE

The weed made Sarah think about her father again, but that was fine. She had read interviews with rock stars and writers who talked about the way smoking had opened them up creatively; freed something. Maybe this was the same sort of thing, because it certainly helped her think a little more clearly.

It helped her plan.

Yes, it was painful to recall some of the things her father had done, the way his cruelty – his *use* of her – had made her feel, but the pain was bearable, the dull ache or the sharp sting of it, because it was something she could harness.

You know I don't mind if it hurts a little bit . . .

She remembered the last time she had seen him, dribbling and unable to speak in a room that stank of urine and overcooked liver, how that disgusting smell had lifted her spirits. The happy stink of getting what you deserved. She remembered just how much she had enjoyed making it clear exactly what she thought of him, knowing he could not answer back or get away, and she would never forget the weight she had felt lifting from her as she marched out of the place, smiling at the hard-faced nurses she would never have to see again.

Thanks so much for taking care of him. Dad seems ever so happy.

That had been a day or two after Peter had cracked and come clean about his all-but-adolescent bit on the side. The fling and then the pregnancy, the mistake the poor, confused soul had been 'unable to help himself' making. Perhaps it was having to deal with Peter that had given her the strength to finally confront her father, and once that boil had been well and truly lanced, striding away from that shitty nursing home, she had made the decision that she would never allow herself to be betrayed by a man again.

The new woman she was becoming would not put up with that.

Sarah smiled and took a long drag on her joint.

None of the new women . . .

Conrad was mooching around in the house somewhere, and as she hissed out smoke she remembered the way he'd looked up at her that morning as she moved on top of him. Lost in it. The way he'd probably looked when they'd been doing it the night before, though she hadn't been able to see his face then, for obvious reasons.

Grunting and sweating, fucking his anger away.

Whatever else was going on, however scared and unsure he might be, he was still *enjoying* her.

He still loved her, she was certain of that.

Love alone would never be enough though, sadly, because she and Jamie could not live with doubt. They needed commitment, and the fact that Conrad no longer seemed willing or able to provide it tore at her heart. Whatever he had done and, more important, whatever he might yet do, still she would have given almost anything to have the man she had thought Conrad was back.

The two of them and whatever the two of them had become.

Above and beyond everything . . .

Moving on would not be easy, but Sarah had grown used to it and had steeled herself for doing whatever would prove necessary. In the end, all that mattered was keeping herself and her son safe. She dropped the remains of the joint on to the floor of the garage and ground it into the concrete good and hard as she gave herself a talking-to.

Whatever doesn't kill you, all that.

The mistake she had been unable to help herself making.

She had thought that bonds forged *in* blood would be that much stronger than those forged *by* it, but clearly she had been wrong.

Conrad perched on the edge of the sofa, flipping aimlessly through TV channels and scratching at the livid rash on his arm that had appeared overnight. It was a nervous thing, he knew that, the same rash he'd suffered with on and off as a teenager, when exams had loomed or things weren't going too well with some girl. Sarah had seemed genuinely upset at seeing it first thing that morning, having noticed it only once she'd had what she wanted from him in bed. She had fussed over him as if the rash was a symptom of something terminal, which as far as Conrad was concerned, it was; talking baby-talk and pressing a hand to his forehead. She had lowered her head to gently kiss the red welts and promised to pick some cream up on her way home from school drop-off.

She'd stared hard at him when she'd said that, watching for some reaction, testing him.

'Fuck's sake.' Conrad tossed the TV remote away and resumed scratching.

When things weren't going too well . . .

It was a wonder that the rash wasn't covering him, head to foot.

The woman Sarah had threatened had called him three times already today and he had been able to do nothing but sit and let it ring. Worse, he had held the phone out towards Sarah, so she could watch him refusing to take the call. He had told her

279

the woman's name so that now she would recognise it whenever it came up on his screen; so that she would know he was ignoring her.

It had pleased her, no question about that. Brownie points.

She had told him what a good boy he was being as she'd rubbed the cream into his arm, told him it was time they put these teething troubles behind them. She said that she'd always be there for him, because he was her best friend.

Conrad felt somewhere between a pampered pet mutt and an attack dog.

Kept, either way. Owned . . .

Fed and fucked and forced to do God only knew what, whenever she decided the time was right.

He scratched and scratched until the welts began to bleed, while he tried to forget the beach and the look on that boy's face, a dusting of sand stuck to the sweat on his cheeks. The bloody graze on his own palm. The sound of that teacher's skull shattering and the low moan before the hammer came down again.

We should celebrate. We should celebrate this . . .

When the doorbell rang, he sat and waited for Sarah to answer it, but when she failed to appear, he went to the door himself. He signed for the bulky parcel, almost certainly more toys or kids' clothes.

'Enjoy the rest of your day,' the delivery man said.

Conrad watched the man leave and thought how easy it would be to follow him. To cut and run. To grab what few things he needed, dash to his car and drive away right then, without looking back, without ever having to see her again.

What would Sarah do, if he did? What *could* she do?

She could not go running to the police and tell them about him and what he'd done without incriminating herself. The only possible reason he could think of for her doing anything so stupid would simply be to punish him for leaving, for daring to abandon her, but would she sacrifice her freedom for that?

Her own and her precious, make-believe boy's?

He watched the delivery man climbing back into his van, remembering the night Sarah had attacked him. The rage and the violence that a few lies had unleashed. His hand moved to the bruise on his face, which was starting to yellow.

She might go to the police anyway.

Like a dog sloping back to its own vomit, Conrad closed the front door and walked slowly into the kitchen. He looked at the worktop she had kissed him against, punched him against. He was shaking as he tossed the parcel as hard as he possibly could into the corner.

Thorne was grateful to finally get back to his flat, to dump the overnight bag he'd been dragging around all day. He dropped it on to the bed then immediately began digging through the assortment of CDs he'd brought back from Helen's, searching for the Patsy Cline anthology he'd been thinking about since he left the pub.

Patsy half smiling and lit blue on the cover, sultry and doomed.

Once he'd loaded the album, he tossed away the junk mail that had arrived in his absence and rinsed the dirty mug and plate he'd left in the sink two mornings earlier. He wandered back into the sitting room and stared at one of the empty, off-white walls, nodding along with the music and thinking that the weird, seemingly arbitrary way that memory worked might be something else he could talk to Melita Perera about.

These were songs his mother had loved, that he could remember her singing. 'Walking After Midnight', 'Sweet Dreams', 'Three Cigarettes in the Ashtray'. Fond memories, often recalled, while those of his mother busy at an easel had for some reason been filed away at the back of his brain, misplaced and unreachable until only an hour or so before.

He made a mental note to call Auntie Eileen when he got the chance.

It was probably not, Thorne decided in the end, *that* mysterious. Those memories which defied their natural propensity to fade were usually the ones attached in some way to music. Didn't most people talk about how a particular tune could call to mind a landscape not seen in years or the face of an old friend in perfect detail? Just a line or two sometimes, a snatch of a lyric. It was certainly true for Thorne, even if, occasionally, the associated memories were not quite so welcome. There were melodies which would, without fail, conjure images of killers or crime scenes he had hoped to have forgotten. One particular Eurythmics track, which had drifted down from an upstairs flat years before, would for ever prompt the memory of a particular spatter-pattern – vivid against pale-green anaglypta – and the peculiar arrangement of the victim's waxy limbs on the carpet below.

One of the more benign occupational hazards, Thorne supposed.

Just so long as murder never screwed up a Hank Williams song . . .

He walked back into the bedroom and began sorting through his bag. He lobbed dirty socks and pants towards the open washing basket then walked across, picked the pants up from the floor and dropped them in. He took out the cardboard file he'd taken to Glasgow, opened it and laid three printouts on the bed.

The e-fits of Conrad, the photograph of Sarah, taken in that coffee shop.

Perfectly on cue, Patsy Cline began to sing 'Crazy'. Strange how *that* shit happened to him a good deal as well.

He stared down at the couple who had done so much worse than tarnish a few memories. Who had targeted then killed the same way someone else might buy a ring or a bunch of flowers; pledging themselves to one another in murder and creating what Thorne did not doubt were a few precious memories of their own.

He could only hope Melita Perera had been right.

These couples tend to fall out in the end . . .

Thorne began to get undressed, happy to leave his clothes

where they fell and thinking about something Hendricks had said as they'd left the Grafton Arms. It was the tail-end of the conversation they had begun in the bar, the parallels Hendricks had drawn, and Thorne had quickly dismissed, between a pair of cold-blooded killers and the awkward situation Hendricks, Thorne and Tanner now found themselves in.

Thankfully, they had come back to Conrad and Sarah before last orders.

'Can't get a much more co-dependent relationship than those two,' he had said. 'I mean, they can't afford to fall out, can they? Each one of them is the other one's alibi, but one stupid row about taking the bins out and before you know it, they're a witness for the prosecution.'

FIFTY-FOUR

Sarah stopped dead, then took half a step back, the few seconds that followed stretching like a scream growing louder: from the instant she turned into the supermarket aisle and saw the woman at the far end, until the moment when the woman looked up and their eyes met; the paralysis of blind panic taking hold, Sarah's brain telling her to turn on her heels and head straight for the exit, but her legs refusing to obey one simple, urgent instruction.

Shoppers stepping around her, muttering and shaking heads.

A few seconds, during which the only thing she knew with complete certainty was that Conrad had been right. Misguided in so many ways, of course and probably thinking only about himself, but unquestionably right about this. Helpless and struggling to swallow, rooted to the spot, Sarah knew that, whatever else had been going through her head at the time, she should have listened to him.

They should have run.

Then, somewhat tentatively, the woman waved, and it was clear there was nothing that could be done to avoid the confrontation. Sarah waved back and began walking down the aisle, moving faster as the panic began to lift; her confidence, her strength, growing with every step because, even from this distance, it was patently obvious that the woman waiting for her at the far end was a damn sight more scared than she was.

'Oh, my God!' Sarah did not have to fake a smile, enjoying the look on the woman's face as she stared forlornly down at the phone in her hand, well aware that she did not have enough time to use it. 'It's so great to see you . . .'

The woman just managed a poorly manufactured smile in return then slipped the phone back into a Hermès handbag as though surrendering her grip on a life raft. She muttered, 'Yeah . . .'

Sarah shook her head in pantomime disbelief. She said, '*So great,*' then laid her basket on the floor before moving quickly across to hug Heather like a long-lost friend.

Elated and fierce, like she *needed* it.

When she finally stepped out of a decidedly one-way embrace, Sarah manoeuvred the woman's trolley to the side of the aisle, then took both Heather's hands in hers.

Heather said, 'Listen, Sarah—'

Sarah shook her head and squeezed. 'I know, you've got questions. Bloody hell, of *course* you have, and I promise to answer all of them.'

'The police . . .'

'It's fine. You've already talked to them, I suppose?'

Heather swallowed hard. 'They came to the school.'

The tremor in the woman's voice was music to Sarah's ears. Like the rest of them, Heather had always been so confident, so sure of herself. 'Yeah, obviously.'

'A teacher was killed.'

Sarah shook her head, sadly. 'I know. I saw it on the news.'

'They were asking about you.'

'Look, it's all really complicated, that stupid business with Jamie, but I will explain. It's just a bit difficult . . . *here.*' She stood aside as an old woman reached past to pick a bag of flour from the shelves, then noticed that Heather was looking anxiously around. 'What?'

'Is Conrad with you?'

'No.' Sarah laughed. 'Not the shopping type.'

'I think *he's* the one the police are interested in.' Heather nodded and swallowed. Something ticked just beneath her eye. 'Are you still . . . together?'

Sarah's face arranged itself into an expression she had come to rely on whenever she had been found out before. An awkward conversation at one set of school gates or another. Obviously, this was a little more serious than a few questions about a child nobody had ever seen, but she hoped it would do the trick.

Brave, despite everything, and determined to confide something that was all but unbearable to articulate.

This is so *difficult for me, so painful.*

Please trust me, I'm doing my best because I really *want to tell you.*

The truth is, you're the only one I can tell . . .

She said, 'Why don't we pay for this stuff, then get out of here?'

Somewhat nervously, Heather suggested that, seeing as Sarah only had a few bits and pieces in a basket, it would be easier for her to go to the designated six-items-or-less checkout, while Heather nosed her trolley into a small queue.

'It'll probably be quicker,' she said, her voice cracking a little. 'Up to you, though . . . '

From her own position near a till fifteen feet away, Sarah kept a close watch on those perfectly manicured hands wrapped tight around the handle of the shopping trolley; guessing that, each time Heather turned to look at her, smiling or shaking her head at the time those ahead of her were taking, she was almost certainly hoping that Sarah might have found herself distracted just long enough for Heather to get to her phone.

It would only take a few seconds to dial 999 and she probably wouldn't even need to take the phone out of the bag. Sarah didn't think Heather was brave enough to try, but she wasn't going to give the woman the chance to prove her wrong.

She never took her eyes off her.

She was already thinking ahead.

She simply smiled back whenever Heather glanced across, like she was still thrilled that they had run into one another. It had only ever been a matter of time, of course, until something like this happened. Conrad had known that, had tried to warn her. It was why he'd suggested that they get away while they had the chance.

In so many ways he had let her down, but he had an instinct for self-protection; she had to give him that much.

Sarah tapped her credit card on the scanner, then took her single plastic bag and walked over to wait for Heather, whose shopping was being scanned. Sarah watched as bag after bag was loaded into the trolley and saw Heather glance somewhat sheepishly at her one more time before reaching for her purse.

'Looks like you're feeding the five thousand,' Sarah said, as they walked towards the exit.

Heather grunted, eyes fixed front.

'I'd struggle to spend that much on food in a month.' The automatic doors opened, and Sarah followed Heather out into the car park. 'Someone's got expensive tastes.'

Heather said nothing, one wheel on her trolley squeaking rhythmically as she pushed it across the tarmac.

Sarah said, 'God, I hate it when you get one of those—'

Heather stopped. Sarah opened a bar of chocolate she'd just bought and bit into it, staring at her.

'You need to go to the police,' Heather said.

'I know.' Sarah chewed quickly and swallowed. 'I'm going to, obviously, but there's so much I need to tell you first. You deserve to know, because you were such a good friend when all this was happening.'

Heather pushed the trolley forward another couple of feet, then stopped again when Sarah stepped in front of it.

'Why don't we just go and grab a coffee?' Sarah said. 'Like we used to. I can give you the whole *bizarre* story, then maybe we can go to the police together. Just half an hour, OK?'

She glanced away for a few seconds, just long enough for another expression to set itself. A familiar mask. Stoic, in spite of everything, the hint of a trembling lip.

See how brave I am? You don't know the half *of it* ...

Then she bit off another chunk of chocolate, like it was the only comfort she could get.

'So, where's your car ...?'

PART THREE

Seagulls and Swans

FIFTY-FIVE

Things were moving towards a decidedly *un*-glorious conclusion for at least one glory-hunter Thorne could name.

This is turning into one of those . . .

It's what Colin Hatter had said just a few days after Kevin Deane had been murdered and Thorne had known very well what he'd meant, what he'd been afraid of, even with the investigation at such an early stage. Now, almost a month on from the murder of Gemma Maxwell, though the work ethic of the DI from Kent and Essex was suspect to say the least, Thorne was finding it hard to argue with the man's instincts.

One of those cases already being shunted backwards, as other, somewhat more straightforward murders had been committed and now demanded attention.

One of those cases which, despite a good deal of information about both guilty parties and enough forensic evidence to convict should they ever be brought into custody, had continued to frustrate the team's best efforts. That would probably frustrate those of others who might one day decide to take another look at it, long after Thorne and Tanner had handed in their warrant cards.

One of those cases which, even then, Thorne would drift off to sleep fretting about.

Thorne glanced up from his desk, from the telephone unit authorisation form he was dutifully completing with about the same enthusiasm he might have felt were he writing a cheque to the Inland Revenue or signing away a kidney. The view from his office was marginally more pleasant than it had been a few weeks before, even if that wasn't saying a great deal. February had given way to March. Thorne was happy enough to leave the scarf and gloves at home, but could not help thinking that, though the world around him was changing by the day, no such transformation was noticeable as far as his domestic situation was concerned.

Nothing had ... blossomed.

Nothing had so much as come into bud.

Spring might well have sprung outside his sodding window, Thorne thought, but his life outside the Job – Helen, Alfie, his living arrangements – continued to feel both stagnant and uncertain at the same time.

His life, his case, all of it.

Limbo had no respect for the calendar ...

And Thorne was not the only one who was growing weary of it.

'You're like a broken bloody record,' Hendricks had said a few nights before. 'You need to stop moaning about it and do something.'

'Such as?'

'*Anything*. Shit, or get off the pot.'

'Nice.'

'Seriously, mate, it's starting to do my head in. You're like somebody who goes out in the rain without an umbrella and then moans about getting wet.'

'You've lost me,' Thorne had said.

'I'm saying, it's not like you didn't have a choice, or like you don't still have one. Do you want to get back with Helen or not?'

'What's it matter?'

'Are you not listening to me?'

'She's clearly made her mind up, so—'

'Christ almighty.' Hendricks had sounded sincerely irritated. 'What do *you* want?'

Maybe, Thorne thought now – as he had then – he knew exactly what he wanted but felt it would be easier to wait around and let someone else make the decision for him. Or perhaps he still nursed hopes but kept them to himself for fear they would soon be dashed anyway. Or it might just be that he was failing to act decisively because he was genuinely undecided, in which case the best – or at any rate the *least-worst* – option was to do nothing.

He changed his mind about it a dozen times a day.

Thorne had never had much truck with mediums, any of that nonsense, but maybe Tarot cards might help? Or he could try to get a number for Mystic Meg, if she was still knocking around. He could always call Helen and see if she'd agree to settle things the same way he and Tanner had done, the night before he'd been to see Andrew Ruston.

Toss you for it . . .

He had just gone back to the authorisation form which, in strict accordance with RIPA regulations, was the first of three he would need to complete before they could access the phone records of a suspected rapist, when Tanner herself walked into his office.

Breezed in.

A sheet of paper in her hand. An expression Thorne couldn't quite read, but which made it clear he could forget about paper-work for a while.

She didn't bother sitting down.

'Missing Persons Unit in Enfield got in touch.'

'Right . . . ?' Thorne leaned back and waited.

'Woman drove to the supermarket yesterday morning and

never came back,' Tanner said. 'Husband's been trying to call her, but the phone's switched off.'

'Domestic?'

'Not according to him. Worried sick, apparently.'

'Run off with a fancy man?'

'Or woman.' Still that expression, as if Tanner was holding something back.

'What about the car?'

'Well, we know she left the supermarket in it, but that's where it gets interesting—'

'Sorry, but what's any of this got to do with us?'

'Plenty, I reckon,' Tanner said. 'Unless you believe in ridiculous coincidences. Which I don't.' She held up the sheet of paper. 'Mind you, we might not have picked up on this at all if it wasn't for one sharp-eyed DC on that Missing Persons Unit. She was doing background checks on the MisPers . . . filling in the forms, whatever, and the name of the school rang a bell.'

'The *school*?' Thorne sat forward fast as Tanner passed the sheet of paper across the desk. He looked down and saw the name of the woman who had been reported missing. 'Holy fuck.'

'Exactly. And it gets better . . . well, worse, I should say.' Tanner turned towards the door. 'Come and have a look . . .'

Thorne stood up and followed Tanner out into the incident room. He rubbed at the back of his neck – that feeling like a spider creeping slowly across it – as Tanner pulled up a chair for him, then sat down in front of a computer she was already logged in to. He waited while she called up the piece of CCTV footage that the Enfield MisPers team had acquired and sent over ten minutes earlier.

'Here we go . . .'

Thorne leaned forward and watched a woman he recognised as Heather Turnbull push a shopping trolley towards a dark Audi, open the boot and begin unloading bags. Behind her, another woman waited, her face all but hidden by long, blonde

294

hair. Then, just a glimpse as she turned for a second or two, eating something.

'*Sarah*, you reckon?'

Thorne peered at the picture. 'Maybe. A wig, or she's dyed her hair.'

'Makes sense,' Tanner said.

The footage ran on. Heather closed the boot and walked around to the driver's door. The women spoke to one another across the roof before getting into the car and, a few moments later, the Audi reversed out of its parking space and moved towards the car park exit.

'I don't get it,' Thorne said. 'What the hell's she doing? Heather Turnbull, I mean. If she knows where Sarah is, why didn't she call us?'

'Maybe she never got the chance.'

Thorne's eyes did not leave the screen. Tanner had rewound the clip, begun to run it again. 'Does she look like she's being coerced to you?'

'Nothing obvious,' Tanner said. 'But with everything we already know about Sarah, don't you think she's perfectly capable of scaring the crap out of someone without needing a weapon? Making them do what she wants?'

When the Audi left the frame again, Thorne said, 'Do we know where it went?'

'ANPR picked it up a few minutes later on a couple of neighbouring streets, but no sign of it after that. Maybe Sarah was telling her where to go, staying off the major roads to avoid the cameras.'

Thorne sat back, processing it all. 'Did she come back for her own car?'

Tanner shook her head as she closed the file down. 'No vehicles left in the supermarket car park by the end of the day. Which means she walked there or took the bus. Either way, it's like we thought.'

'She has to live locally.'

'More importantly, she's still *here*.'

Thorne stood up. He needed to gather the team together, brief them on this new development. Perhaps Hatter had been wrong after all and they could switch off the gas under that back burner. 'We need to get this clip out there as soon as,' he said. 'Focus on those few frames when we get a decent look at her. Someone must be able to put a name to the face.'

'Way ahead of you,' Tanner said, smiling. 'As always. They're running it on *London Tonight* . . . tonight.'

'Nice one,' Thorne said. 'Oh, and let me know the name of that officer in Enfield, because we owe her a serious drink.'

'DC Andrea Marcou,' Tanner said. 'I'll text you her number and she's already said, "thank you". She'd prefer something fizzy, obviously, but she'll settle for prosecco if you're strapped.'

Thorne took a few steps back towards his office, then stopped and turned; his arm outstretched, the fist clenched. 'Fuck it, things are looking up.'

It was clear from Tanner's face that she could not quite match Thorne's enthusiasm.

She said, 'I wish I thought Heather Turnbull felt the same way.'

FIFTY-SIX

'Why now, though?' Conrad raised himself up in bed and watched Sarah rushing around, making preparations. When she failed to answer, he asked the question again.

'I realised you were right,' she said. 'That's all. It just took me a while to figure it out.' She stopped what she was doing, turned to look at him. 'And to be honest, I could really do with a hand.'

'Yeah, I know, but—'

'This *was* your idea.'

He rubbed his stomach. 'I'm still not feeling great, is the truth.'

'I know.' She moved to the bed, leaned across to kiss his forehead and run a hand through his hair, which was damp with sweat. 'I'm sorry you're feeling so rough.' She moved away again, went back to work. 'You should really go to the doctor, I told you.'

'Yeah, and I told *you*.' He was starting to sound a little grumpy. Sarah put it down to the fact that he wasn't feeling well. 'You move around as much as I do, you can't really *have* a doctor. Different names, right? I'm still registered back in the Midlands, far as I know.'

Sarah nodded.

'Look, it's just a bug. Probably a twenty-four-hour thing.'

'Hope so,' she said. 'There's a lot to do.' The truth was that, much as she hated to see him in pain, it hadn't done any harm that Conrad had spent most of the day in bed. That he'd been sound asleep when the early evening news had been on. 'So, why I don't I nip and get you something to settle your stomach? Chemist's open until nine.'

'I'll be fine,' Conrad said. 'I just need to get a bit more sleep.'

She stepped back to the foot of the bed. 'Well, I suppose I can get most of it done myself, if I have to. You haven't got much, anyway.'

'Just another hour or two,' he said. 'Then I'll give you a hand.'

'OK, my love, get your head down and I'll carry on downstairs.'

Conrad slid beneath the duvet again. 'Probably easier without me getting under your feet, anyway,' he said. 'I know how much you like to be in charge.'

'*What?*'

'Just saying . . . you're better at this stuff.'

She let the bag she was carrying slip to the floor. She turned to stare at him. Said, 'You think I *want* to do this?'

'No.' He turned on to his side. 'Obviously, you don't.'

'You think I'm enjoying it? Everything I've worked for, everything I've had to do. All of it, pissed away?'

He rolled on to his back again and looked up at her. It was hardly the first time, but still he was shocked at how quickly Sarah's mood had turned ugly. 'I never said that. I never said anything like that.'

'You didn't have to. It's pretty clear that you don't give a shit about what this is doing to me, how upset I am.'

'For God's sake.' Now he sounded more tired than irritated. 'You clearly want some sort of argument, but this is hardly the time for it, not when you seem to be in such a hurry. Even if I felt well enough to argue with you . . . which I seriously don't.'

'Sleep well, Conrad.'

He was shouting something about sympathy and what a terrible nurse she'd make as she marched out of the room, his final words inaudible once she'd slammed the bedroom door behind her.

Downstairs, she sat on the sofa and tried to calm herself. She thought about stepping into the garage for a few minutes, but there was so much to do and she needed a clear head more than ever.

Sacrifice, she told herself, kept on telling herself. In the end, it was all about sacrifice and, painful as that was, what other choice was there when you'd run out of options?

It's what you did for the people you loved.

Yes, he was under the weather, but Conrad's attitude was certainly not helping – the suspicion, the lack of support – when she was doing all this for him. Doing what *he'd* wanted all along. Was she the only one who cared about keeping them all safe?

He would see that later on and of course he would apologise, but for now Sarah hadn't got the time to dwell on his shortcomings, to feel let down as she had so many times in the past.

She had a lot to do.

Thorne was at home watching *Come Dine With Me*, wondering how far he'd get with a menu that included cheese on toast and Angel Delight, when Tanner called.

'Bingo!' she said.

'Well, it's a bit late, but there's a place stays open just off the Holloway Road. Five hundred quid for a full house.'

As usual, Tanner had no time for his nonsense. 'There were a lot of calls after the piece on *London Tonight*,' she said.

Thorne sat up. Now he had no time for it, either. 'OK ...'

'Plenty we can discount, as usual. Someone who reckons the woman with the blonde hair is called Magda and works in a Polish delicatessen in Balham, someone else who's convinced she's an actress he saw in an episode of *Casualty*. We're following up on all the remotely credible ones, but there's a few that sound interesting.'

'More interesting than a woman off *Casualty*?'

'A bloke rang in who thinks she might be his ex-wife,' Tanner said.

'*Thinks?*'

'I know.'

'*Might be?*'

'It's probably the best we've got so far, but he sounded pretty convincing, apparently. Said she'd changed her hair, but otherwise . . .'

Having learned from painful experience, Thorne tried not to get too excited. Whether it was down to honest mistakes being made, lapses in memory or a simple desire for attention, public feedback following appeals such as this one was notoriously unreliable.

'Let's bring him in.'

'He's bringing himself in,' Tanner said. 'First thing tomorrow morning.'

'Better give the late-night bingo a miss, then,' Thorne said.

FIFTY-SEVEN

The visitors' interview suite at Colindale station was a little nicer than one of the more formal interview rooms at the other end of the corridor, even if the basic layout was much the same. There was still a table with two chairs either side. There were still built-in digital recording facilities – audio and video – if they were needed. It was called a *suite* only because the furnishings were soft and there was a hot-drinks machine in one corner which interviewees did not have to shell out to use. It was where those who were *actually* 'helping with enquiries' were usually taken, because there was a carpet that didn't smell too awful and nobody had carved *BASTERD FILTH FITTED ME UP* into the tabletop.

Peter Suzman was unaware that he had been upgraded but seemed reasonably comfortable with his surroundings. He asked them where they wanted him. He accepted the offer of coffee and sat down.

'Thanks so much for coming in,' Tanner said.

'Not a problem,' Suzman said.

He was fifty or thereabouts, wearing a dark blazer over a

cream shirt and expensive jeans that were rather too distressed for a man of his age. He still had a good head of elegantly greying hair, complemented by a few days' worth of white stubble and nicely set off by a suntan. A smile that might easily be described as *winning* showed a lot of perfect-looking teeth and there were fewer lines around his eyes – or anywhere else – than might have been expected.

Thorne was immediately curious about where the man had been on holiday while Tanner stared and found herself wondering if he'd had any work done.

'Before we get any details,' she said. 'Can we ask how certain you are that the woman you saw on that CCTV footage is your ex-wife?'

'Oh, it's Michelle all right.' Suzman picked up his coffee cup and leaned back. 'I said when I called that I was fairly sure, but I've watched that clip a few times since then, and ... I mean, she's gone blonde for some reason, but yeah, it's her. Either that or she's got a double, you know?' Tanner was about to ask something else, but Suzman carried on. 'I clocked it that moment when she turned towards the camera for a second, when she was eating something. That would have been chocolate, almost certainly.' He turned towards Thorne as though only a man would understand. 'Michelle *loves* chocolate.'

He and Tanner exchanged a look. If Sarah *was* Suzman's ex-wife, the information he was hopefully about to give them would be hugely important, even if the man did not know the woman he had once been married to anything like as well as he once did.

Thorne thought: *Michelle loves all sorts of things.*

Tanner opened her notebook. 'Could you start by giving us some of your ex-wife's basic details? Full name, address, date of birth ...'

'What's this all about?' Suzman sipped at his coffee, looked from Thorne to Tanner and back. 'A missing woman, that's what it said on the TV.'

'That's right,' Tanner said.

'So, is Michelle missing?'

'We need those details, Mr Suzman.'

He shrugged and reeled off the information Tanner had asked him for. 'I should certainly know the address,' he said. 'I paid for the bloody place, signed everything over after the divorce.'

Thorne was keen to talk about that, about the nature of their relationship and its break-up, but not until they had all the details they needed immediately. 'Do you have phone numbers?'

Suzman took out his phone, scrolled through the contacts and read the numbers out, landline and mobile. 'They're the last ones I've got for her, but this is going back a few years. It's not like we call each other up for cosy chats.'

Tanner looked down at what she'd written.

Michelle Sarah Suzman (née Littler). Aged 42.

An address in Enfield, home and mobile phone numbers.

She tore out the page and asked Peter Suzman to excuse her for a few moments. He turned to watch her leave the room but did not seem overly curious as to why she was in such a hurry.

'When was the last time you saw Michelle?'

Suzman turned back to Thorne, thought about it. 'Well, I've seen her more recently than she's seen me.'

Thorne waited.

'After the divorce, when I was living with my new partner, Beth ... we had a child fairly quickly and, well, Michelle wasn't exactly thrilled about it. I'm talking years ago, but a couple of times I saw her outside the house. Sitting in her car on the other side of the road, just watching. Beth was a bit freaked out, but, like I say, it was only a couple of times.'

'You never confronted her?'

'No ... I didn't think that would be a good idea.'

'What was Michelle upset about? You being with your new partner or the fact that the two of you had a child?'

Suzman looked a little uncomfortable. 'Well, yes ... I think it was all about Josh. I mean, she was extremely pissed off when I got together with Beth, and I hold my hands up ... I was unfaithful and I left her for a younger woman, so she'd every right to feel like that. To screw me for everything I'd got, or almost everything. But when she found out about Josh, it was on a completely different level. Her anger ...'

Thorne remembered something Helen had said. 'Had she lost a child?'

Suzman shook his head. 'No, but she wanted one.' A sour smile showed itself briefly. 'She *really* wanted one. We were actually talking about having all the tests and so on, and I'll admit that I wasn't very keen, because actually I didn't think we'd allowed enough time for nature to take its course. She was adamant though, got very worked up about the whole thing, but that was around the time I got together with Beth, so it didn't happen anyway. I think what most upset her when Josh came along was that it proved it wasn't me, you know?'

'That couldn't have kids ...'

'Right. That maybe it was her ... not her *fault*, but you know what I mean.'

It was clear to Thorne that Michelle Suzman's need for a child had made her reaction to the divorce and the subsequent birth of her ex-husband's son an extreme one. But that was a very long way from a teenager battered to death on a beach or a young woman murdered in her own hallway.

He said, 'Before you and Michelle separated, had she shown any kind of ... mental instability?'

Suzman stared at him. 'Has Michelle *done* something?'

Thorne stared back.

'Things were a bit ... tricky with her parents, I suppose. Her mum was already dead, but I know their relationship hadn't always been easy. Her dad died – either just before we got divorced or just afterwards, I can't remember now – and she was very ... conflicted about that. She was a bit up and down sometimes, but grief can do that, can't it?'

'Yes, it can,' Thorne said.

'My ex had her moments, put it that way.'

Thorne said, 'I understand.' He did not think it was the way Kevin Deane's parents, or Andrew Ruston, would put it.

He looked up as the door opened, exchanged a nod with Tanner and got to his feet.

'Thanks so much for coming in,' Tanner said, holding the door open.

'Is that it?' Suzman asked.

'That's it,' Thorne said.

'We'll need you to come back in later today and make a formal statement.'

They showed him to the main entrance, thanked him again. Suzman made a couple more attempts to find out why they wanted to know so much about his ex-wife but got no further than he had before. Thorne and Tanner followed him out, then cut right and moved quickly towards the car park.

Tanner had been busy.

'According to the electoral roll, Michelle Littler is still resident at that address. The DVLA have her as the owner of a white Nissan Qashqai and there's an active account in that name at the Enfield branch of HSBC. There's no social media presence to speak of ... just a few Facebook posts back when she was still married, but nothing since. The landline was disconnected a year ago and that mobile number's been out of service for quite a while, but we were assuming she uses disposable pay-as-you-go phones anyway, so—'

'I think we've got plenty.' Thorne keyed the remote and they climbed into his BMW. He swung the car round and pointed it towards the main road.

'Dipak's getting the team together,' Tanner said. 'They'll be ready for a full briefing by the time we get back to the office.'

Thorne nodded, putting his foot down as he moved into traffic. 'If Heather Turnbull's in that house, we'll need to put a surveillance operation together as fast as we can. We'll want Territorial Support units, medical back-up, the lot.'

'Course.'

'Even if she's not.'

'I already talked to Russell and he's on it.'

'We need to do this the right way.' Thorne glanced at Tanner who seemed supernaturally, *annoyingly* calm.

'Is there any other way?' she said.

FIFTY-EIGHT

Sarah closed the bathroom door behind her and, as soon as she had dropped to her knees in front of the toilet, she could see that Conrad had already been sick. He'd flushed of course, because like her he hated any kind of a mess, but there were still a few globules clinging to the porcelain, just beneath the rim. A lingering smell, too, which would probably have been enough to make her retch even if she hadn't been feeling as nauseous as she already was.

She steadied herself and heaved up her breakfast.

She coughed and spat, then reached for toilet paper to wipe away the sticky strings.

She flushed, then stood up to wash her hands and face.

'You OK?'

She grunted a 'fine' without shifting her eyes from her own reflection, the hair that she herself had cut brutally short the day before, that she would henna later on.

She switched off the tap and reached for the towel.

He shouted from the bedroom again. 'Welcome to my world . . . '

Suddenly, she was smiling back at herself like a teenager; lovesick, she thought, in every sense, because whatever else was happening, however much of a mess she was trying so hard to get them out of, his voice could still do that. Could fill her heart. It was very sweet that he was concerned about her, such a huge comfort, especially when he was still feeling so rough.

His condition had certainly not helped, though; the misery of the day before.

It was awful seeing him unwell, like a dull ache, yet weak as he was and despite the argument they'd had when he'd accused her of being controlling, he had still wanted her the previous night. Exhausted and good for little else, they had still wanted each other. After they had made love – somewhat more gently than usual – to celebrate the fact that they ... she ... had got everything done, she had held on tight to him until he was asleep and, for a while at least, it had almost been possible to forget that things had gone so terribly wrong.

That he had let her down so badly.

After a quick squirt of air-freshener, Sarah opened the door and stepped back into the bedroom.

Conrad was lying on the bed. 'You OK?'

'Yes, I said.'

'Perfect bloody timing.' He lowered the newspaper he'd been reading and rubbed his belly. 'Last thing we need right now is you coming down with this.'

'I'll be fine,' she said. 'Like you said, it's probably just a twenty-four-hour thing.'

'Let's hope so,' he said.

'In sickness and in health, right?'

He stared up at her, a fraction paler than he had been a moment before.

She said, 'Relax, my love, that's not a proposal.'

FIFTY-NINE

'I said I wanted ham or chicken.'

'All they had.'

'No crisps?'

The woman took a packet from her plastic bag and tossed it across. 'It was just a shitty little petrol station.' She opened a can of Diet Coke and took a sip. 'But the good news is they had toilets.'

'Your bladder's a liability.' The man used his teeth to tear at the wrapping around the suspiciously sweaty-looking cheese sandwich he had been handed. 'You're going to end up needing one of those plastic things old ladies use. The "She-Wee" or whatever it's called.'

The woman belched and gave him the finger.

They had been sitting in the front seats of the dirty-white VW Polo for a little over an hour and a half. Eyes where they needed to be at all times, of course, minds on the job, but still with plenty of opportunity for casual chat; for gossip and the obligatory light piss-taking between colleagues who knew one another well. With Magic FM providing a low-level soundtrack, they had talked about friends and family holidays, traded jokes told by a comedian they both thought was funny and bitched about a co-worker they both disliked intensely.

'Thinks he's God's gift.'

'Yeah, if God's started giving out bell-ends . . .'

They ate in silence for a few minutes, humming along with the music or drumming fingers on the dash, while they sat and watched the house with the white Nissan Qashqai parked on the drive.

'Anything while I was gone?'

The man chewed, shook his head. 'Place is empty, I'm telling you.'

He had just put down what was left of his sandwich and was wiping his fingers on the legs of his jeans when the radio crackled into life.

Thorne said, 'How's it looking?'

'If you ask me, it's a Donald Trump situation.'

'Come again?'

'The lights are on but there's nobody home.'

Thorne could hear a woman laughing, ignored it. 'How sure are you?'

'Well, there's no curtains drawn, so we've got a decent view, and nobody's come into the room at the front of the house or entered the upstairs front bedroom. No movement at all since we got here.'

'Is the dog still going at it?'

'Hasn't stopped.'

'Big one, you reckon?'

'Couldn't say one way or another.'

'Come on, you've been listening to the bloody thing barking for an hour and a half.' Thorne knew that the Dog Unit he'd put on standby as soon as he'd heard about the barking from inside the house would be able to handle almost any animal, but it was always a good idea to give officers as much information as possible in advance. 'Is it a deep bark or is it . . . yappy?'

There was muttering, as the surveillance officer conferred briefly with his partner. 'OK, we don't think it's a Rottweiler or anything like that, but probably not one of those stupid little ones, either. Best we can do under the circumstances.'

Something in the officer's tone suggested that he thought the *circumstances* were less than ideal, but Thorne didn't much care because they had been dictated by the urgency of the Heather Turnbull situation; the speed at which the operation had been put together in light of a potential threat to life.

The kick-bollock-scramble.

Given more time and resources, observation posts would have been established inside neighbouring properties front and rear, with cameras and perhaps even covert recording devices set up to provide the maximum coverage possible. As it was, the surveillance operation was a little more 'old school', with one team out front and a second, who, while unable to gain a direct view of the back of the property, were in position should anyone try to leave it that way.

Thorne cut the transmission and turned to Nicola Tanner. 'What do you think?'

'I don't really care what kind of dog it is.'

'Should we go *in*?'

'I'm kidding, by the way . . . '

Thorne's BMW was parked a couple of streets from the one in Enfield on which Michelle Littler's property was located. They had been sitting there almost as long as the surveillance team, with two vans containing Territorial Support officers and a team of CSIs lined up behind them, each waiting for the signal. All operational vehicles were unmarked, anonymous. The last thing anyone needed at this stage of the game was for the targets to come bowling back from an outing to the shops, spot a phalanx of police vehicles and slip quietly away.

'You think Heather's in there?' Thorne asked.

'No movement inside, they said.'

'The question still stands.'

She looked at him.

'You think there's a body in there?'

Tanner was already reaching for her seatbelt. 'There's only one way to find out.'

Thorne picked up the radio and gave the *Go* command.

He started the car, waited for the TSG vehicle to move past him, then put his foot down.

More than anything, Thorne wanted to be first inside. With a warrant burning a hole in his pocket, he would have given anything to be the one wielding the 'big key' but, as per protocol, he could do nothing but stand back and watch as the metal ram was thrust at the front door and, while a dog continued to bark frantically inside, a scrum of TSG officers in helmets and body armour poured into the house.

He could only hope that his surveillance team had got it wrong. That Michelle Littler and her partner in crime had just been rudely awakened and were now sitting up in bed, panic-ridden and struggling to cover themselves.

As scared and helpless as Kevin Deane had been.

Gemma Maxwell.

Heather Turnbull . . .

From his position, standing with Tanner at the end of the front path, he listened to the officers roaring less-than-polite announcements of their presence and then, a few seconds later, the individual voices shouting *Clear* as each room was entered and quickly surveyed.

As ever, Thorne's feelings were writ large on his face.

'Clear's good.' Tanner stepped towards him. 'It's *good*.'

'You think?'

'Heather Turnbull isn't in there.'

'Neither are they.'

'So, we go in there and see if we can find something that tells us where they've gone.'

As TSG officers began to file out of the house one by one, two more from the Dog Unit entered with gauntlets and a noose-pole. Two minutes later, a medium-sized and distinctly *un*-threatening dog was led out on a lead. Thorne and Tanner watched as it trotted happily across the road to a small van.

'When?' Thorne asked. 'When did they leave?'

The TSG team leader gave Thorne the nod. Thorne opened the boot of his car and took two bodysuits from a cardboard box.

'Best guess?' Tanner said. 'Probably when she saw herself on the TV.'

'Maybe we shouldn't have run it.'

'If we hadn't, we wouldn't know who she is. We wouldn't be here.'

'Found some other way then,' Thorne said.

While the TSG officers removed helmets, stab-vests and body-cams, Thorne and Tanner took their jackets off and slipped into blue plastic overalls, nitrile gloves and bootees. Looking around, Thorne could see that they had acquired an audience. Drawn by the noise and commotion, neighbours had quickly gathered and now stood gawking from the doorsteps of the houses opposite, swapping half-heard rumours and half-baked theories across low hedges and front lawns.

Thorne wondered how many of them were already rehearsing for their tabloid interviews; those front-page expressions of shock and disbelief as they trotted out the predictable platitudes.

They seemed like such a quiet couple.

Always kept themselves to themselves.

And perhaps most annoying of all, *I* knew *there was something off about those two . . .*

Always quicker about such things, Tanner was ready before him, and as she walked towards the front door Thorne pulled up

313

the hood of his bodysuit and hurried to catch her up. She stopped on the doorstep, waiting for him, and when he reached her she said, 'There *was* no other way, Tom. So let's just get in there and deal with what we've got. OK?'

A few paces behind Tanner, Thorne walked along the tiled hallway, glancing into the neat and tastefully decorated living rooms on either side. Thick carpets and expensive-looking furnishings. A state-of-the-art home cinema system in one room and floor-to-ceiling bookcases in the other. Framed prints, tongue and groove, Farrow & Ball . . .

Thorne briefly caught his own reflection in the large mirror above an ornate fireplace, a pale-blue ghost drifting through shot. He was still thinking about the onlookers gathering outside and found himself wondering how, when he and his team finally caught Sarah and Conrad, the tabloids would be able to spin this everyday slice of well-heeled suburbia into the requisite 'house of horrors'.

He guessed the red-tops would manage.

If they caught Sarah and Conrad . . .

Ahead of him, Tanner called out from the kitchen and he moved to join her. She nodded down to a pair of empty dog bowls on the floor. A third, larger, was dry but had clearly contained water. There was a scattering of small turds close to the back door.

'I don't think we missed them by much,' she said.

Thorne looked around. A pair of dirty mugs sat on the marble worktop, a copy of the previous day's *Evening Standard* next to a fruit bowl on the polished pine table. 'They knew we were coming.'

Tanner nodded. 'Just left enough food for one day. If the dog had been barking for much longer than that, the neighbours would have called the police.'

They spent a few minutes going through the contents of

kitchen cupboards and drawers, examining utility bills, shopping receipts, a wall calendar, before moving back out into the hallway and rifling through the pockets of the jackets and coats that were hanging up near the door. Then they turned on to the stairs. They would allow themselves half an hour or so, looking for obvious signs that Heather Turnbull had been kept in the house and anything that might prove useful in determining where the occupants might have gone. A hopeful once-over, before the SOCOs, who were changing and putting their equipment together outside, came in to begin the search for evidence that would not be visible to the naked eye.

Brushes, gel lifters and tape for prints. Luminol for blood traces.

Upstairs, Thorne and Tanner stood together in the doorway of the smallest bedroom and stared in at the posters of footballers and dinosaurs, the sets of *Harry Potter* and *Horrible Histories* on shelves above the single bed. The *Danger Mouse* duvet and a multicoloured rug with robots on.

'You reckon this is what it's all been about?' Tanner asked. 'The fantasy kid?'

Thorne shook his head. 'Not the murders, no.'

'You sound very certain.'

'I mean, what do I know, but—'

'She's clearly delusional.'

'It's different,' Thorne said. 'Wherever the whole having a child thing came from, something else was triggered when she got together with Conrad. For both of them. Some kind of . . . fire was started.' He turned away and crossed the corridor to the master bedroom. 'Christ alone knows.'

A few moments later, he was staring down at the unmade bed Sarah and Conrad had shared. The place where, if Melita Perera was to be believed, a killing spree may well have been hatched.

Fucked into existence, celebrated.

Thorne looked at the tangled sheets, the pillows that still bore

315

the shape of their heads pushed close together and, just for a moment, he thought he could actually smell it. *Them*.

'Tom . . . ?'

He turned and saw that Tanner was holding something she'd picked up from one of the bedside tables. He stepped across to get a closer look and saw what it was, saw how the livid pink colouring of the stick of Margate rock had melted against its plastic wrapping. Thorne felt something twist in his stomach and watched as Tanner placed it carefully into an evidence bag.

'Sick,' she said. 'But come on, we both know that juries really go for shit like this. Yeah, DNA and the rest of it is all well and good.' She nodded, job done. 'But *this* is what's going to put them away.'

SIXTY

Having announced when he'd woken up that he was feeling much better, Conrad had gone out and, for the first time in a while, Sarah did not much care where. The nearest pub, quite probably, to get a few drinks inside him now that he could keep them down. To take stock, bless him. To take a breath. It was too early for him to go back to work, to get in the swing of hunting again, and she was as sure as she could be that he wouldn't be driving all the way back into London to visit that woman. There certainly hadn't been any more soppy text messages or desperate late-night calls, pleading for attention. All things considered, it didn't much matter, but Sarah was fairly confident that, the sad little whore wouldn't be awfully keen on seeing Conrad these days.

Not now Sarah had put the fear of God into her.

Into both of them.

How would *she* have coped, Sarah wondered, watching Conrad puking and shitting and moaning like a baby. Would she still have wanted him as much if she'd had to deal with all that? Sarah seriously doubted it.

The thought made her smile as she stared out of the hotel

room window across the ornamental gardens. The wooden benches arranged around a lush lawn. There was a large pond that was home to a family of swans and a thick line of trees that masked the road, that made the place feel like it was in the middle of nowhere.

Her smile evaporated quickly.

Wasn't that exactly where they were, in every sense?

It was always going to be hard, she'd known that all along, but now they were actually here, now they'd got away, it was finally dawning on her just how much of a struggle it was likely to be.

Sacrifice. That's what she'd told herself; it had been her watchword, but now the scale of it was becoming apparent and she was still coming to terms with exactly what she'd done. Been forced to do.

It terrified her, and it made her furious.

Easy enough for Conrad, of course. He'd just had to pile all his crap into a bag and leg it, do much the same thing he'd done countless times before, but she'd had to leave everything behind, an entire life. The house she'd worked so hard for, the only thing she had to show for all those years putting up with that arsehole Peter. She leaned against the window, grim-faced, and wondered what would happen to it. Now that TV thing had gone out and there was every chance the police knew exactly who she was, she could hardly pop back in disguise and stick the place on the market, could she?

Yeah, happy to accept a reasonable offer. All fixtures and fittings included. Just send me a cheque when it's done . . .

A million at least up in smoke and whose fault was that? Couldn't keep it in his pants and now he was pissing it away in the pub, like he'd pissed away everything else.

Maybe he would choke on a peanut, do everyone a favour.

And all she had ever done was love him.

Horror-struck, she suddenly wondered if her ex-husband might end up getting his filthy hands on the house again, him and his vacuous wife and their precious Joshy. That would be . . . intolerable. No, that could never happen. He had no claim on her property, on anything that was in her name.

She stepped away from the window, took a few deep breaths. She needed to stop thinking about what had been abandoned and focus on everything that lay ahead. The things she had made these sacrifices *for*.

She grabbed her jacket, opened the door and headed downstairs.

She needed to get out.

The receptionist was the same girl who had checked them in two nights before, a touch vacant, but smiley enough. She looked up from a magazine as Sarah was passing the desk and, apropos of nothing, said, 'I saw your husband leaving earlier.'

That made Sarah smile again.

It's not a proposal, my love.

Conrad's face . . .

She walked out of the main entrance and round the side of the building towards the gardens at the back, enjoying the sound and the feel of her shoes crunching across the gravel. It had always felt like . . . success to her, that sound, like you'd really *arrived* somewhere. It was a little colder than it had been the last few days and she buttoned up her jacket as she walked down towards the pond she had been looking at from the room.

She watched the swans for a while and began to feel better.

She hadn't walked away with a fortune, nowhere near, but it was enough to get by on, and with what Conrad had taken out of his account they could afford to hole up at this place for a while at least, to tick over. Eventually, there might even be enough to put a deposit down on something.

Things would be OK.

No, they would be *better* than OK, because she wouldn't settle for anything else. Because she never had and why the hell should she? She had been to this part of the country once or twice before

319

and, though she would always be a city girl at heart, she reckoned she could get used to it. She knew there was a little village school not too far away, because she'd seen a sign, and maybe somewhere like that would actually be a better fit for Jamie. Certainly, it would make life easier for her, because there were bound to be far fewer Davids and Carolines buzzing around, unable to keep their perfectly straight noses out of other people's business.

She would make new friends, get a new dog, carve out a lovely new life for them both.

I just got fed up living in London, you know? It's so hectic, so tiring. I think this is a far nicer place for a child to grow up, don't you?

When she took another step closer to the water, a swan – pecking angrily at weeds near the bank – spread its wings and hissed at her. She hissed back, told it to fuck off.

She only knew two things about swans, the same stuff she supposed had been trotted out to everyone at some point. The fact that however graceful they appeared, they were paddling furiously beneath the water, and that old chestnut about a swan being able to break your leg if you threatened it, though she had never quite believed that one.

All the same, she was content to back off a little.

Sarah thought about the effort it took to look effortless and the damage that even the most harmless-looking of creatures was capable of meting out when it was necessary. Suddenly, she found herself genuinely hoping that, wherever he was, Conrad had found a little time to relax and take his mind off things. She hoped, more than anything, that he was still thinking of her fondly.

She was smiling again as she turned and walked back towards the hotel.

SIXTY-ONE

'It's all a bit "After the Lord Mayor's Show", isn't it?' Tanner said.

Thorne turned to look at her. 'A bit *what*?'

'It's just . . . an expression.' Tanner shrugged and took a slurp of coffee from the plastic travel mug she'd brought from home. She seemed a little uncomfortable suddenly at the fact that Thorne, and everyone else in the room, was staring at her. 'A bit of a let-down, you know? Something humdrum or ordinary coming straight after something exciting, you know? This . . . us.' She waved an arm, the gesture taking in their corner of the sparsely populated incident room, the empty desks, the half-dozen members of the team that were gathered, slumped in an untidy circle of chairs around her. Thorne himself.

The morning after the raid on Michelle Littler's home address.

'Because there's always someone who has to do the menial stuff, to clean up after the horses when the Lord Mayor's procession has gone past.' She raised her cup in a toast to the passing on of pointless knowledge. 'It's where the expression comes from.'

'Yeah, well clearing up shit sounds about right,' Chall said.

Thorne had not stopped staring. 'So, what was so exciting?'

321

'Sorry?'

'Nobody's suggesting that sitting round here feeling like this is any fun, but I'm still a bit confused about exactly what you think the good bit was that came before.'

It was clear from the look on Thorne's face that he was spoiling for a fight with someone, anyone, but Tanner was not about to back down. 'I'm talking about yesterday, obviously.'

'Are you serious?'

'It was a textbook operation,' Tanner said. 'Didn't you think so?' She looked around, but most of the officers close to her were studying their shoes.

'Up until we went in there, maybe. But I was hoping for a bit more than a few empty drawers and a starving dog.'

'We did everything right.'

'We got nothing.'

'That's not true,' Tanner said. 'You know it isn't.' She moved her chair a little closer to Thorne's, and without being asked the other members of the team did the same. She said, 'Let's look at what we *did* get.'

'Shouldn't take long.' Thorne looked at his watch. 'Which is handy, you know, because Heather Turnbull *is* still missing.'

Tanner ignored him. 'We got enough physical evidence and forensics to tie Michelle-slash-Sarah and her boyfriend definitively to the Kevin Deane and Gemma Maxwell murders.'

'We had forensics before.'

'Enough evidence to put them both away.'

'We already had enough,' Thorne said. 'Is there an echo in here?'

Tanner pressed on. 'Crucially, we didn't find a single thing to suggest that Heather Turnbull had ever been in that house. They're still running print and DNA tests, but there were no obvious traces of blood, no signs of a struggle, no indication at all that the house is a crime scene.' She sat back, gave it a second or two. 'How can that be nothing?'

'Fine,' Thorne said.

'Seriously.'

'Big pats on the back all round.'

'And let's not forget that there are still SOCOs working at the property, going over every inch of the place. Who knows what they might turn up?'

'Like a forwarding address, you think?' If Thorne saw the flash of genuine anger that passed across Tanner's face, he chose to ignore it. 'Now, let's think about what we *haven't* got . . . aside from *them*. Let's look at where we're at realistically, shall we?'

'Nicola's got a point, though,' Chall said.

Thorne waited.

'Yeah, we want to catch them, obviously, but our priority is the threat to Heather Turnbull's life, surely.'

'Of course.' While he could not help but admire Chall's loyalty to his former boss, Thorne was still not inclined to look on the bright side. 'But that threat exists *until* we catch them, don't you reckon?'

Chall said, 'Sir,' but could not look at him, could not look at Tanner.

'Despite this treasure trove of evidence we've got, we haven't got the first idea where our prime suspects are.' Thorne raised his arms. 'Not a clue. We can only presume they left in Conrad's vehicle, but we have no leads at all on that. We know that Michelle emptied her bank account two nights ago, and they're way too smart to use credit cards, so we have to assume that with the twelve grand she took out and whatever cash *he's* tucked away, they've got enough money to be going on with. Simple truth is they could be anywhere. They could be abroad already.'

'They could be,' Tanner said. 'But I very much doubt it. They'd have had to move pretty bloody quickly, and if they try to leave the country now, we'll have them. The All Ports alert went out last night and I can't see her having a fake passport, can you? Looked to me like they'd left in a hurry.'

323

'We should have put the alert out earlier,' Thorne said.

Once again, there was a good deal of team shoe-staring going on.

'In hindsight, possibly . . . but it was a bit hectic,' Tanner said.

'Even so—'

'Putting that raid on the suspects' address together in double quick time. Remember, that operation you were so keen to do the right way?'

'So, maybe there should have been better delegation.'

There was an audible hiss as somebody sucked their teeth.

'Now,' Tanner said, 'we *did* get some decent photos of our female suspect from the house—'

'For what they're worth.'

' . . . so obviously they're being circulated to every force in the country.'

'She'll have changed her appearance again. Different hair, a wig, dark glasses, whatever, so—'

Tanner smacked her hand down on the desk nearest to her. 'For God's sake, Tom!' She shook her head. 'You're behaving like some know-it-all newbie who's never had an operation go slightly pear-shaped, who's never had an iffy result. No, we've not had that bit of luck we need, but we're doing all the right things, so get over it. What we *don't* need is a DI coming on like a stroppy teenager who's acting up because he can't get his own way, and I'm telling you right now, not only is that bugger all use to a team of officers knocking their pipes out to get this case put to bed, but it's certainly no use to that woman who's been missing for three days.'

Thorne opened his mouth and closed it again.

Noticing suddenly where one or two of the team were looking, he turned to see Russell Brigstocke standing outside his office.

The DCI beckoned him with a tilt of his head.

Thorne stood and walked slowly across, like an errant school-boy on his way to the headmaster's office. Hard truths were all

324

very well when you were the one in charge, but when it came to debriefing *his* boss on the previous day's shit-show he would need to find some kind of positive spin on things. He would need to be a bit more like the woman who'd just bollocked him in front of half the squad room.

When Brigstocke had closed his office door, he said, 'That psychiatrist of yours . . . she reckoned our best bet would be some kind of falling-out, didn't she?'

Thorne dropped into a seat, mentally ran through a few lines. 'Yeah.'

'Right. But I think she meant a falling-out between the suspects as opposed to two of my detectives.'

Thorne nodded. 'Just a difference in attitude, that's all.'

'Well, for what it's worth, it was bang on.'

'Cheers.' Thorne sat back. 'I just thought they needed a bit of a reality check, that's all.'

Brigstocke looked at him. 'I was talking about what Nicola said.'

SIXTY-TWO

The car that loomed in his rear-view was white suddenly, gleaming, so he shook his head, blinked and looked again, because a few seconds before it had been dirty-blue. He would swear it had. Getting closer to him one moment . . . right up his arse . . . then a hundred feet back the next.

Or not there at all.

So many cars flashing past in the other direction, and all those signs he peered at, searching for the right one, the colours and the noise churning in his stomach. More than once already it had been as if, for a few terrible seconds, he had suddenly woken with no idea what he was doing in the car or where he was going, and then he'd remembered. Had been momentarily relieved and then terrified.

Conrad put his foot down and glanced at the dash, but the dials on the instrument panel swam in and out of focus, so he could never be sure how fast he was going.

It didn't matter, though.

The faster the better.

He wiped away the sweat from his eyes and the drool that

was growing sticky around his collar before he veered out to power past a lorry, only just managing to move back into the right lane before the vehicle coming in the other direction was on him. His heart was dancing and he could feel the throb of the pulse in his throat. The other driver waved angrily and Conrad tried to shout, but it only made the pain in his abdomen worse; unbearable.

Fuck. *FUCK*. He knew what she'd done . . .

Another look in the mirror and now it was only the lorry receding behind him, but he held his own gaze for a few seconds longer than he needed, than was safe. The colour of him, for Christ's sake . . .

The tips of his fingers like he'd trapped them in a door. The whites of his eyes . . . the *whites* . . . the skin around his sunken cheeks.

Like old newspaper.

He moaned out loud at another stab of pain and yanked on the wheel, knowing what was coming. He bumped up on to the grass verge and threw the door open, retched and cried out. There was vomit on his trousers, on the inside of the door as he dragged it shut again; vomit and blood, and he wasn't sure if it was sweat or tears that made his eyes sting as the tyres spun in the mud before the car lurched back on to the road and he began to accelerate again.

It's probably just a twenty-four-hour thing.

He knew *exactly* what she had done.

As the car picked up speed, he unwrapped his hands from the wheel and, for a few seconds, scrabbled quietly at nothing, reaching to pull up a duvet that wasn't there, needing its softness at his neck. Waiting for his mother to walk through the door with sweet tea or juice and words that made him feel better. That summer holiday when he'd fallen from a tree, spent days and days in bed, disorientated and delirious.

A bang on the head can do that, darling . . .

A punch from a woman he thought he loved.

A rock, coming down.

He wanted so much to sleep. He could not remember feeling so tired. He was grateful for the pain that was keeping him awake because, however much he wanted to pull in somewhere quiet and snuggle down beneath that duvet, he could not, *must* not drift away.

Above and beyond, that's what we are, my love.

Five minutes or thirty, he had no idea. Moaning and heaving, murmuring curses as the road was sucked beneath his wheels, until he saw the sign he had been watching out for. *That* was the place he'd been after, the place he needed to go.

He knew what the sign meant.

Without thinking, or remembering that he should care, Conrad turned hard and swerved across the lane of oncoming traffic. He tried to cover his ears against the noise. Several drivers were shouting out of windows and leaning on their horns, but all he could hear were the screams of seagulls.

SIXTY-THREE

The evening was relatively mild, certainly bearable if they kept their jackets on, so, while they waited for the food to arrive, they carried their beers out on to Thorne's small patio. It had been nicely maintained by the last tenants who had left behind a hanging basket and a number of plants in large terracotta pots. Something green that was now coming into leaf snaked up a trellis next to the table and chairs Thorne had bought when he'd first rented the place out and not had the chance to use before.

'We going to eat out here, too?' Hendricks asked.

'Don't see why not.'

'It's not *warm*, is it?'

'Well, if you had a decent jacket. *Is* that a jacket, or is it a blouse?'

'It's Italian suede, mate, and I look gorgeous in it.'

'Oh, right,' Thorne said.

'I hope they're quick.' Hendricks plonked his bottle down on the table and looked at his watch. 'I could eat a scabby dog on a bap . . .'

He had managed to persuade Thorne that another Indian

takeaway was probably not a good idea. Having pointed out that they'd already eaten just about everything on the menu, the pathologist had proceeded to stress that all those rich sauces weren't doing Thorne's waistline any favours either, and that he might want to think about such things.

Especially now.

Reluctantly, Thorne had agreed to compromise and they had ordered pizza instead.

They sat down and stared for half a minute at what was left of the smoggy sunset. They each took a swig of supermarket lager and Hendricks lit the single cigarette he allowed himself once a week.

'Bloody hell,' Thorne said. 'It's not going to be *that* stressful.'

'Be prepared,' Hendricks gave a two-fingered salute. 'I learned that in the Scouts.'

'I thought you were chucked out of the Scouts for touching up one of the Scoutmasters.'

'Oh yeah.' Hendricks grinned, took another drink. 'Happy days. So, come on then . . .'

The reason Hendricks had come over.

Thorne began to talk, not altogether fluently, about the situation with Helen; the most recent developments, the final reckoning. 'She called the other night,' he said. 'Both of us in tears by the end of it.'

There had been plenty to catch up on already. Four days on from the raid at Michelle Littler's house, it was the first chance Thorne had had to bring Hendricks up to speed work-wise, but after having arrived and been given the lowdown on what Thorne still believed was an unsuccessful operation, Hendricks had failed to offer much in the way of a constructive response. He had simply grunted and tugged at the piercing in his lower lip.

Said, 'So, what happened to the dog?'

He was there because of what had happened with Helen, the

decision she had come to. To keep his friend company. To offer advice and consolation, or to gently take the piss, whatever he thought Thorne needed.

'She didn't say the *dreaded*, did she?' he asked now.

'The dreaded *what*?'

'You know, the old, "It's not you, it's me" rubbish.'

'God, no.' Thorne let out a long breath. 'She was fairly clear about the fact that it was me. *My* fault. I mean, you know, Helen . . . she's not shy about saying what she thinks.'

Hendricks nodded, because he certainly did know. He and Helen had fallen out for several weeks the previous year, after a heated argument about the legalisation of drugs. Not to mention countless minor spats over everything from US politics to recipes and an ongoing debate about whether *RuPaul's Drag Race* was a better TV show than *Orange is the New Black*.

'So, your fault because . . . ?'

'Because I'm a miserable bastard and my moods make me a nightmare to live with. Because, apart from both having warrant cards, we've not got enough in common. Because, except when I'm pissed off about something, which is glaringly obvious to all and sundry, I don't show my feelings enough.' Thorne was trying to smile, to make light of this litany of shortcomings, but the necessary effort was obvious. 'Because, apparently, I keep myself . . . "walled off".' He shook his head and used his fingers to scratch quotation marks in the air. 'Parts of myself, anyway.'

'I can't really argue with any of that,' Hendricks said.

'Because sometimes I made her feel like it was a straight choice between her and the Job, and ninety-nine per cent of the time the Job won.'

Hendricks winced and downed what was left of his beer. 'Yeah, she doesn't hold back, does she?'

'One of the things I love about her.' Thorne picked up his own bottle and examined it. 'Maybe I should try getting used to saying *loved*. Past tense.'

'It wouldn't be true though, would it?'

'No,' Thorne said, after a moment or two. 'Not right now, anyway.'

'It'll get better.'

'I know.'

'Yeah, well that's the point,' Hendricks said. 'You *know* now. Look, it's a bugger, mate ... I'm not pretending it isn't and I'm really sorry, but at least you can finally stop mithering about what you want to happen and how you might or might not feel when something does happen, because it's happened.' He leaned to lay a hand on Thorne's arm. 'So, now you can just ... feel it.'

Thorne looked across the table as an overground train rattled noisily by on its way towards West Hampstead. The solemn expression on his friend's face made him uncomfortable and he could not hold eye contact for very long. He picked at the label on his beer bottle. He said, 'You're not going to give me the "plenty more fish in the sea", bit, are you?'

'I'm not daft.'

'What, then?'

Hendricks shook his head and took his hand away. He smiled. 'Just hoping they remember my extra pepperoni, that's all.'

Then Thorne's phone rang.

Friendly enough, but no-nonsense, the caller promptly identified herself as DC Jilani Azad from the Serious Crime Unit at Suffolk Constabulary. 'I'm calling from West Suffolk hospital,' she said. 'Something you might be interested in ... '

Thorne widened his eyes at Hendricks, who immediately shifted his chair to Thorne's side of the table, then leaned close so he could listen in.

'Where's this hospital?' Thorne asked.

'It's just outside Bury St Edmunds,' Azad said. 'About halfway between Cambridge and Ipswich.'

'OK. I'm hoping that's not the interesting bit.'

The officer grunted. 'They admitted a patient about four

hours ago, just after he staggered into A and E covered in sick, with what they thought was acute liver failure. White male, early forties. Looked like he'd overdosed on Quavers, the colour of him. Plus, there was . . . ' Now it sounded as though the DC was reading something she'd written. '*Cyanosis of the extremities.*'

Thorne looked at Hendricks.

'Blue fingers,' Hendricks whispered, waggling his own.

'They only called us after he started rambling about being poisoned.'

'OK . . . '

'So, I was going through this bloke's wallet, looking for ID of some kind, and I found a whole bunch of them. Driving licences, credit cards, all sorts in different names. I ran them through the system and your name popped up.'

'Which name?' Thorne asked.

'Your name.'

'*Which* name led you to *my* name?'

'Oh.' There was a short pause. 'Patrick Jennings?'

Thorne sat up a lot straighter. Hendricks raised a thumb. 'OK, listen, I'll need to talk to him as soon as possible, so—'

'OK, well good luck with that.'

'Sorry?'

'Poor bugger slipped into a coma,' Azad said. 'About half an hour after they brought him in.'

'Oh, for fuck's sake . . . '

'Sod's law, isn't it?' Azad said.

Hendricks raised his thumb a second time, then slowly turned it anticlockwise, grimacing.

'I'll be there as quickly as I can,' Thorne said. Azad began trying to explain that she might have gone off shift by then, but Thorne wasn't really interested in much beyond ending the call and getting on the road. By the time he was off the phone he was back inside the flat, locking the back door, gathering up papers and car keys. 'What do you reckon? Hour and a half, this time of night?'

'Yeah, probably.' Hendricks dropped the two empty bottles into the recycling bin. 'Something like that.'

'Should be there by half-nine with a bit of luck, presuming we don't hit traffic.'

Hendricks turned and stared at him. 'We? No chance, mate, I've—'

'It's a hospital,' Thorne said. 'Medical stuff. You might actually be some help for a change.'

'What about the pizza?'

Thorne had the front door open. 'They'll probably just leave it on the doorstep,' he said. 'It's better warmed up, anyway.'

SIXTY-FOUR

They drove into the hospital car park just before nine forty-five and Thorne was surprised to find Tanner, who he had called as soon as he had left home, waiting for him in reception.

'How the hell . . . ?'

'No need for the M25 from where I am,' Tanner said. 'Plus, I put my bloody foot down. Didn't you?' Before Thorne could answer, she had turned her attention to Hendricks, who did not look a good deal happier than he had been when they'd left London almost two hours earlier. 'Another favour he owes you, Phil.'

'Damn right, he does. I gave up pizza for this.'

'Greater love hath no man—'

'Are you two finished?' Thorne looked at Tanner.

'Come on then.' She rolled her eyes at Hendricks and led them across to the lifts. 'I've already sussed out where the ICU is . . . '

Having identified themselves at the nurses' station, they followed directions to a room at the far end of the unit and discovered DC Jilani Azad on a chair outside the door. She looked up from the paperback thriller she was reading, then got smartly to her feet. Thorne was impressed that she'd stayed on to wait for them and told her so.

'Bugger all else on.' She nodded towards the door. 'So, what's the story with him in there, then?'

They certainly did not need an over-keen DC under their feet, but Thorne saw no reason to be an arsehole about it and send her away ignorant, not after all she'd done this far. 'I've every reason to believe that the man you called me about is one of our prime suspects in a major murder investigation.'

'Bloody hell,' she said. 'Nice one.'

'Thanks for the good work tonight, Jilani,' Tanner said. 'You can get on your way now, but we'll let you know how it pans out.'

If she was even a little disappointed at being surplus to requirements, the Suffolk DC didn't show it, and Thorne enjoyed watching the woman walk away down the corridor with something like a spring in her step.

'Shall we?' Tanner pushed the door open and she, Hendricks and Thorne walked into the room.

They could hear the patient, or at least the wheeze and bleep of the machines he was wired up to, before they rounded a portable curtain and took their first look at the man in the bed. A breathing tube, thick as a vacuum hose, had been strapped across his face and a thin wire snaked up from his skull to some kind of wall-mounted monitor with a bag attached. A tangle of cables connected to various pumps and monitors criss-crossed his chest. With little or no idea what any of the equipment was actually doing, Thorne found himself staring instead at the IV stand; the steady drip-drip of the glucose-saline being fed through a cannula in the patient's right hand.

'Somebody's having a bad day,' Hendricks said.

Tanner leaned close to one of the monitors. 'You can say that again.'

Thorne felt a twinge of something like sympathy, because it was hard to look at anyone in such a helpless state, but it was gone the instant he reminded himself what the man in the bed had done. 'He's been responsible for plenty of other people's bad days. Their *worst* days.'

He took a step closer to the head of the bed and looked down at the patient's face. What he could see of it beneath the plasters and the plastic. A man who carried ID documents in the names of Patrick Jennings, Paul Jenner and others, but who Thorne knew only as Conrad.

Who Thorne ... *knew.*

There was something oddly familiar about the man, but Thorne had no idea what, or why it should be disturbing him so much. Something around the eyes, was it? The shape of the face? He was as certain as he could be that he had never met this man, and yet ...

There was a sharp knock at the door and the three of them turned as a woman stepped in. Fifty or thereabouts, with a shock of red hair and dressed as though she'd been called away from a posh evening out. She walked straight across to the bed and, without looking at the visitors, introduced herself as Maggie Drummond. 'I'm the consultant in charge of looking after ... well, as I understand it, we still don't have a name.'

'Actually, we've got quite a few,' Thorne said.

The woman turned and asked to see ID again, which Thorne thought was a little over the top and said as much. As he and Tanner dug into pockets for warrant cards, Hendricks stepped forward.

'I gather you thought it was liver failure,' he said.

'Well, it *was*—' She stopped and looked at him.

'He's a doctor too,' Thorne said. 'Hard to believe, I know.'

'I normally work with stiffs. But, you know ...' Hendricks jerked a thumb towards the bed, 'seeing as this one's more or less there already ...'

Drummond nodded. 'It's what *caused* the liver to fail that was stumping us. Until he started babbling about poison.'

Thorne listened as the pair of them began to discuss the man's symptoms and the treatment, or at least the care, he was currently receiving. The conversation showed little regard for the two police officers standing around like lemons, at least one of whom could barely understand one word in ten. They talked about fulminant hepatic necrosis, coagulopathy and elevated pro-thrombin time, computed tomography and oesophageal varices.

'Is there any chance of talking English?' Thorne said. 'Just for five minutes?'

Drummond looked across at him as though she'd all but for-gotten the police presence in the room and that this was anything but a run-of-the-mill case conference. 'So ... yes, all the classic signs of liver failure, jaundice and so on and it became obvious fairly quickly that the kidneys were shutting down too. That everything was starting to shut down.'

'What did he say? You said he was babbling.'

'That's right. Confusion and disorientation are common symptoms.' She glanced at Hendricks, who nodded. 'But there were moments when he was lucid enough. Thirty seconds here and there, when we could ask some questions. He managed to tell us that he'd started feeling ill four or five days ago ... vomiting, diarrhoea and so on ... that he thought it was just a stomach bug. Twenty-four hours later he was right as rain again, until yesterday morning, when he began to go downhill very fast and eventually drove himself to hospital. A little too late, as it turned out. A case like this that's caught early, there's the possibility of a transplant, but he was way too far gone for that.'

'So, when he mentioned poison,' Tanner said, 'what did he say, exactly?'

'Well, it was all a bit hectic.' Another knowing glance at Hendricks, a small shake of the head. 'You know, because we were trying to save his life, so there wasn't a lot of time to write anything down.' She shrugged. 'He said he'd been poisoned, basically. He said that he knew what she'd done, what *that bitch has done*. I can certainly remember that, because he kept on saying it. It was probably the last thing he said before we lost him.'

'Did he mention a name?' Thorne asked.

The doctor nodded. 'Sarah. "Sarah did this to me" . . . something like that.'

Thorne looked across at Tanner. Neither had been in much doubt as to the poisoner's identity, but it was good to have it confirmed nevertheless. 'So, what poison are we looking at?' he asked.

'We're still running tests.' Drummond turned to Hendricks. 'Based on the symptoms he presented with and the story he told us, we can be fairly sure it's nothing very common. It's certainly not arsenic or strychnine . . . nothing too Agatha Christie . . . and I doubt very much that it's antipsychotics or any kind of pesticide. Obviously we'll be able to find out exactly what it was . . .' She looked across at her patient. 'Afterwards.'

'What about mushrooms?' Hendricks said. 'Death Caps, maybe, or Destroying Angels?'

Drummond thought for a few seconds. 'Actually . . . that . . . might be a very good shout.'

'I've never seen it, but I've read case studies. There's definitely something about a honeymoon period. You feel fine after a while, think you're fit as a flea again, but all the time the poison's attacking your liver, your kidneys, your cardiac muscles.'

Drummond was nodding.

'Where the hell did she get poisonous mushrooms in *March*?' Tanner looked at Hendricks and Drummond, as though the hole in their new-found theory was obvious. 'Late summer, early autumn, I would have thought.'

'Oh, right,' Drummond said. 'That's . . . problematic.'

They all looked at one another.

'So, what do we do now?' Tanner asked.

Thorne had no quick answer.

'I mean . . .' Tanner pointed to the man in the coma. '*He's* not appearing in court any time soon, is he?'

'Make that never,' Hendricks said.

'So . . . ?'

'Where are his things?' Thorne took a step towards Drummond. 'Clothes, personal belongings . . .'

Drummond peered around the room and finally pointed to a black bin-bag in the corner. Thorne moved to pick it up, then sat down and began quickly going through its contents, until he found what he was looking for.

He pulled out a mobile phone.

He stabbed at a button, cursed when confronted with a pass-code, then stopped, his finger poised above the screen. He looked up at Tanner, then quickly across to Maggie Drummond. He said, 'I think we'll be fine on our own for a bit.'

'OK, if you're sure.' The doctor moved towards the door. 'Well, I hope you get . . . actually I don't really know what it is you're after, but . . . whatever.'

The moment the door was closed, Thorne was on his feet and moving across to the bed. He was still holding the mobile phone as he lifted Conrad's hand from the mattress.

'What are you doing?' Tanner asked.

'Shortcut,' Thorne said. He held her stare for a moment or two, when it became clear that she understood. There was a time he would never have asked her to be party to anything that might be seen as professionally unacceptable, perhaps even illegal, further down the line.

Those days were long gone.

'Touch ID, right?' Hendricks was grinning. 'That is sly, mate. Seriously fucking sly.' The grin got wider. 'Clever though.'

Thorne held the mobile in one hand and used the other to grasp Conrad's thumb and press it to the home button. As soon as the app screen appeared, he took the phone back to his chair and began scrolling through contacts.

'I didn't see you do that,' Tanner said.

Thorne did not look up. 'Yeah, you did,' he said.

He scrolled quickly towards the names beginning with S, only stopping once; just for a second or two to catch his breath, having spotted a name he had not expected to see, earlier in the alphabet.

When he found SARAH MOB, he began to type out a text message.

Hendricks walked across to try and sneak a look at what Thorne was typing. 'You going to ask her if she fancies handing herself in?'

'Something like that,' Thorne said. When he'd finished, he quickly examined a few previous texts to make sure the style was right and to see how Conrad would normally sign off. Obviously, on this occasion, a kiss at the end would only have been suspicious. He scrolled through his message to check it.

I know what you did. I'm at W. Suffolk hospital and if you don't come I'm telling the police everything. C

Thorne looked up, said, 'Nothing to lose, have we?' and pressed SEND.

SIXTY-FIVE

Sarah was just drifting off to sleep when the text arrived.

She was imagining Jamie – nervous but excited – on his first day at the village school. *What if nobody likes me, Mum?* The smiling teachers clucking around the new lad, making sure of a warm welcome from his classmates. Kids with ordinary names and without sharp elbows; boys and girls who had not grown up quite so fast as some of those at the schools they'd left behind in London. Hothouse flowers . . . hothouse *weeds*. Mini-bitches and cocky little bastards, ruthless and fame-hungry, already welded to their top-of-the-range phones and tablets.

All so very sure of themselves and the comfortable place in the world that was waiting, that had been reserved for them before they could walk.

Not *loved*, not properly.

She sat up, reached for her phone and read the message. It was a shock, certainly, alarming even, for that first half a minute or so, because she hadn't been expecting to hear from Conrad again. He was out of her life now and, painful as it was, she had no choice but to get used to it. She already missed him very badly, ached for his touch, his smell, even more than she'd thought she would. She had begun to think back through those wild and wonderful early days and to compose an ... ending that such a special relationship deserved. Something she would be able to tell Jamie about one day, a story that was suitably romantic. Passionate, doomed ...

We loved each other so much that it was tearing us apart.

It was easier for him to walk away in the end.

There was this man who meant more to me than anything in the world, but one day he became very, very poorly ...

She turned her phone off and got out of bed.

She was talking to herself as she got dressed, walking from one corner of the room to another, spitting curses or whispering soft declarations. Those words she would have said to Conrad if she'd been able, the things she and Jamie would say to each other before he walked into that little playground on his first day.

The two people she loved above everything, above everyone else.

What were the lyrics to that song you found for me? Something about 'you and me for ever'? I thought that's what it would be, my love. I feel like an idiot now, obviously, but I really believed that—

You'll be fine, darling and I'll be right here when you come out.

Did your *Mummy take* you *to school?*

No, darling.

Did your Daddy take you?

She moved across to the window, wondering how old Jamie would need to be before she could tell him about his grandfather. A few years yet, almost certainly.

Sarah looked out into the blackness and could just make out the tops of the trees moving back and forth in the wind. She thought about the swans, gliding across the dark water some-where beneath her; the invisible effort and the danger in one of those beautiful, white wings.

A few minutes later, when she was ready, she used the phone to call down to reception and ordered a taxi.

SIXTY-SIX

'Hospital food's a damn sight better than it used to be.' Hendricks carried his tray across and left it on a trolley by the door, having put away the steak and kidney pie, chips and beans which had been heated up and brought to the room by one of the auxiliary staff. He finished his tea and walked back across to his chair by the window. Thorne, waiting close to the bank of monitors, had barely managed half a ham sandwich, while Tanner, who was sitting on the opposite side of the bed, had eaten nothing.

It had been an hour since Thorne had sent the text message.

A quarter of that, since they'd finally been ready.

The speed at which the ad-hoc operation had been put together made the raid on the house in Enfield seem laborious, but there had been no other option. The fact that Conrad had driven himself here suggested that he and his partner had not been staying too far away. If Sarah was nearby when she received the text, she could easily have got to them in a matter of minutes.

Using DC Jilani Azad as a conduit, Thorne had quickly managed to recruit a sufficient number of locally based officers, who he had directed to take up positions in and around the hospital.

His 'direction' had been terse to say the least, the urgency leaving no room for niceties. There could be no uniforms anywhere in sight, no marked cars, no mistakes. If the woman they were waiting for *did* respond to the text, the officers on site – together with as many members of staff as they had been able to brief – would ensure that, once inside the hospital, she was unable to leave, but Thorne was adamant that she be allowed uninterrupted passage to the ICU and the room he was now sitting in.

If Sarah showed up, he wanted to be the one to take her.

The *if* was more significant than it might normally have been, because Thorne knew that he'd messed up. Sending the text had seemed like a bold idea, but within a few minutes, he'd realised that it had been a very stupid one. As soon as he'd found the suspect's mobile number, he should have passed it straight on to the Forensic Telephone Unit. They might have been able to use cell sites to pinpoint the phone's whereabouts and save an awful lot of pissing about, but by the time Thorne had thought about that and made the necessary call, the phone in question had been turned off.

Of course, it might *already* have been turned off, in which case Sarah would not have received the text at all. Or she might have seen the message, worked out exactly what was going on and *then* turned it off.

All Thorne knew for sure was that he'd screwed up royally and that it was not the kind of basic mistake Nicola Tanner would have made.

At least she had the good grace not to say as much.

Hendricks said, 'Quick game of I-Spy?'

The look on Tanner's face when she glanced up was all the answer Hendricks needed. 'Blimey, I'm just trying to—'

Thorne snatched at his mobile and answered before the first ring had died away. He listened and muttered, 'Right, thanks.' He hung up, looked at Tanner and shook his head. Just shy of midnight, there were still plenty of people coming and going downstairs, especially through A&E, but nobody matching the description of the woman they were after.

Any of her descriptions.

'You need to calm down, mate,' Hendricks said. 'You'll give yourself a stroke. Yeah, I know you're in the right place, but even so.' He waited for a response that wasn't forthcoming. 'Listen, if she's going to come, she's going to come, right?'

Thorne nodded without looking up. Stating the obvious wasn't helping, any more than his friend's strained attempts at jollity.

He was still thinking about the mistake he'd made, how costly it could prove, but he was thinking rather more about that other name he'd seen on Conrad's contacts list. There *was* a simple explanation for its presence, of course, but still. It would all depend on how long Conrad had owned that particular phone, how careful he'd been about such things.

Erasing his past . . .

Thorne would find out first chance he had, but he could not shake the feeling that the name he had recognised was there for reasons he did not want to think about.

'It was going to be V, by the way,' Hendricks said. 'I-Spy.' He pointed to the monitor and bag above Conrad's bed. 'V for ventricular drain . . . you'd never have got it.'

They waited.

The mood in the room, largely dictated by Thorne's own, had darkened significantly by the time he stood up, just after one o'clock, and said, 'Right, let's call it a night.'

'You sure?' Tanner asked.

Thorne was already on his way to the door.

'Fair enough.' Hendricks heaved himself upright and stretched. 'Gave it a good crack, mate.'

'Fucking stupid,' Thorne said.

Tanner walked across and lifted her coat and bag from a stand in the corner. 'Don't beat yourself up, Tom. It wasn't your fault.'

'Well, it certainly wasn't anybody else's.'

'It was worth a try.'

'It was the wrong thing to do.' Thorne opened the door. 'You know it was.'

'Yeah, well we've all done the wrong thing,' Tanner said. 'At some time or other.' She looked from Thorne to Hendricks, just a moment of eye contact, before the three of them walked quickly out of the room without a backward glance at the man in the bed.

Thorne called Jilani Azad on his way out of ICU and told her to stand her colleagues down, but he was not surprised to see her waiting for him a few minutes later, when he, Tanner and Hendricks stepped out of the lift into reception. He began to thank her, impatient to leave, but she raised a hand to shut him up.

'I was just on my way up.' Her tone was somewhere between excitement and panic. 'I just thought it would be a good idea to double-check, you know? So I went over to talk to the bloke on reception.'

'What are you on about?'

'Somebody came in about half an hour ago. Left something for matey-boy upstairs, in the coma.'

Thorne stared at her. 'Half an hour ago?'

'Who?' Tanner asked.

'Not the woman,' Azad said. She nodded towards the reception desk, the middle-aged man standing behind it looking somewhat confused at the sudden commotion. 'He said it was just a kid—' The DC stood smartly aside as Thorne marched past her towards the reception desk, then ran to catch him up. 'It wasn't his fault,' Azad said. 'He's not long come on shift, so he had no idea what was going on.'

Thorne's precise words were lost beneath the noise of a trolley crashing out of the lift behind them, but the blood had already begun to drain from the receptionist's face as he reached beneath the counter, as though feeling for the security button.

Now, Tanner and Hendricks moved towards the desk and, as they seemed a good deal calmer and more reasonable than Thorne at that moment, Azad turned her attention to them. 'There's just a first name on the front, so the poor bugger on reception had no idea what to do with it.'

'It's OK,' Tanner said.

'Give it to me.' Thorne held a hand out and the man behind the desk nervously passed across a large brown envelope.

Thorne stared down at it.

The name *Conrad* in what looked like felt-tip on the front.

A heart drawn underneath.

'This kid came in,' the receptionist said. 'I hadn't got a clue, so . . .'

'We need some gloves,' Thorne said, looking around. Though the envelope itself had already been handled by the man at the desk, as well as by the kid who had delivered it, Thorne had no intention of contaminating the contents.

There had been enough mistakes made already that night.

In less than a minute, Azad had come running back from A&E with a box full of thin rubber gloves. Thorne pulled on a pair, opened the envelope and carefully took out the single sheet of paper inside. Snapping on gloves of her own, Tanner leaned in close and they read the note together.

My love,

So, what do you think about THIS?? It breaks my heart that things ended up the way they did, that the big bad world (and certain people in it) conspired against us, but I know you would have been as STUPIDLY happy about this as I am.

This wonderful thing!!

This MIRACLE.

Don't think there haven't been buckets of tears, because I know you'd have been SUCH a brilliant dad, and how awful you'll feel at what you're missing. Don't feel too bad though, because I'll never forget you (how could I??) and I'll make sure this precious little one knows JUST how much you would have loved him. Or her.

You and me forever...

Sarah xxxx

Thorne turned away and took a few steps towards the doors. They opened automatically, but he stood where he was until they closed again, while behind him, Tanner was reaching into the envelope again.

'Interesting,' Hendricks said, when he saw what Tanner had taken out.

'Tom ...?' A few seconds later, Tanner arrived at Thorne's shoulder, a pregnancy-testing stick held gingerly between two fingers. She held it towards him so that he could see the two pink lines in the small window, the positive result.

'Look, I know this could have gone better.'

'You think?'

She held it up again. 'But, for what it's worth, now we've got even more of her DNA.'

Thorne stepped towards the doors and this time, when they slid open, he kept on walking. He trudged out into the car park, thinking that without the woman they had come from, a few drops of piss on a stick were worth less than nothing.

Still thinking about that contact on Conrad's phone.

A name and number he had recognised.

SIXTY-SEVEN

It hadn't been her only testing kit of course, the one she'd left with the note for Conrad. That first time, she'd gone down to the local chemist with no more than the faintest of hopes; thinking she was probably being stupid, because her periods had never been regular anyway and there were any number of reasons why she might be throwing up. Afterwards, she'd done another test almost straight away – unable to believe it, her hands shaking so much she could barely hold the thing – and she'd bought four or five more after that, simply because she'd enjoyed watching those pink lines slowly materialise.

Sitting in that little hotel bathroom, the grin making her jaw ache, while Conrad went from bad to worse on the other side of the door.

She'd cried every time.

'I'm having a baby,' she said.

The taxi driver glanced at her in his rear-view mirror. 'Congratulations,' he said.

She folded her hands across her belly. 'Thank you.'

'First one, is it?'

She actually laughed a little, before starting to cry again. 'No, it's not.'

'You all right, love?'

'I'm fine.' She reached into her bag for tissues. 'Hormones kicking in early, that's all.'

'Oh, they can be a bugger,' the driver said. 'My wife was all over the shop with hers.'

Sarah let her head fall back, exhausted. There was a long journey ahead and she was done with the conversation for the time being. She stared out at the blur of dark hedges rising on one side, a sliver of moon over grey fields on the other. She turned her face away from the lights of a vehicle coming in the other direction and smiled, remembering the look of suspicion on the kid's face. It was funny, because hadn't it all begun with a very different look on the face of a very different kid?

Do you fancy going for a walk?

That boy in Margate had thought what he was being offered was too good to be true, and he'd been spot on. Tonight though, talking through their deal a few streets away from the hospital, the kid's doubts had evaporated the moment he'd seen what she had to offer. A large bag of weed in exchange for dropping off an envelope, what was not to like?

'*All* of it . . . for real?'

'It's no good to me any more,' she'd told him. 'I'm having a baby.'

'Cool,' the kid had said, snatching the bag and then the envelope. 'Maybe you could name him after me.'

He'd told her what he was called and she'd said that she would think about it. He'd gone away happy. The truth, though, was that, boy or girl, she had already chosen her baby's name.

'So, when's it due, then?'

She had worked it out already, of course, sitting in that hotel bathroom with a diary. They had made their baby seven weeks

351

before. That first night, the only time they had made love without using a condom.

It had felt perfect, and it had been.

'First week of November,' she said.

The driver nodded. 'You'll be big through the summer, then. Let's hope it's not as warm as last year.'

'I don't mind,' she said. 'It's not supposed to be easy, is it?'

'What do I know?' the driver said.

Harder the better, she thought. *Sacrifice.* She wanted to feel her baby inside her every precious minute of every day, however uncomfortable. To suffer if she had to, because she needed to prove that she could bear this child, bear whatever that took. That she was worthy of it.

All those years before, she had been unable to claim the gift that was rightfully hers. What had been given, then taken away. She had not been able to drag that bike out of its grave, but she was a lot stronger now.

'Well, good luck with it all, anyway.'

'I've already been lucky,' she said.

'I should try and get some sleep if I was you.' The driver turned his radio down. 'Be a good couple of hours yet ...'

Michelle Littler was smiling again as she closed her eyes. Having been forced to let the love of her life go and made to deal with more than her fair share of loss and betrayal, she decided that a little good fortune at this stage of the game was no more than she deserved.

SIXTY-EIGHT

More than anything, Thorne had hoped he was wrong, that the simple explanation was the only one, but it had taken no more than half an hour to confirm his darkest suspicions. His worst fears about that name he had seen on Conrad's phone, that phone number he'd recognised. A few emails, armed with the serial number and IMEI of the handset, and he'd been able to find out exactly where, and more importantly when, Conrad had purchased the phone.

An O2 store in Southgate. January the twenty-second. The day after Philippa Goodwin had committed suicide and almost two weeks before Kevin Deane had been murdered in Margate.

It did not come as a shock, because it made complete sense. It was the reason Thorne had been so immediately uneasy when he'd spotted that name. Why would someone whose life revolved around duplicity and subterfuge *not* change his phone number and list of contacts – real or fictitious – each time he changed his identity?

After Philippa Goodwin . . .

It was why, after a series of unanswered calls to a contact that was, sadly, all too real, Thorne was standing alongside Tanner on the pavement outside a metal door, with a warrant tucked inside his jacket and a borrowed set of keys in his hand.

'Look, there's no point standing out here freezing our tits off, is there?' Tanner said. 'We won't know anything for sure until we actually go in.'

He had told her what he had seen on Conrad's phone just before they'd travelled home from Bury St Edmunds the night before. Standing together in the hospital car park, Thorne could see at once that she was struggling as much as he had to find an innocent explanation.

'Remember what Denise Fry said?'

'Yeah.' Thorne had recalled their conversation in Glasgow almost straight away; waiting in that hospital room, the minutes crawling by, sitting next to the bed in which the man Denise Fry had known as Paul Jenner lay fighting for his life.

'This might be that other woman Denise was talking about.'

'Maybe.'

'I mean it would be seriously weird,' Tanner said. 'Bearing in mind ...'

Thorne nodded. The truth was, there was very little about this case that wasn't weird. Off-kilter, unnatural. It felt as though something misshapen had woken and begun crawling towards him into the light; had done ever since the morning at Highgate tube station, when he'd watched that bag being lifted from the tracks.

An ambulance raced past on the main road going south towards Highbury Corner as Thorne stepped forward and, having found the right key, pushed it into the lock. There was mail piled up on a shelf just inside, a bicycle chained to a pipe. The heavy door slammed loudly behind them as they turned and began climbing the metal stairs towards the top-floor flat.

'Don't worry,' Tanner said. 'If she's done a bunk, we'll find her. Same as we'll eventually find Michelle.'

354

Thorne trudged upwards, wondering if Tanner really was that optimistic, or if they had simply fallen into a pattern, wherein she needed to make positive noises, simply to counter his own ... predilections. And, just occasionally, vice versa. He said, 'Right.'

Two floors up and Thorne was as breathless as he'd been the first time he was here. He stopped in the same place, ostensibly to wait for Tanner; the landing from which he'd looked up seven weeks before and seen Ella Fulton leaning over the railing and watching him.

Used to be the local dole office ...

Half a minute later, they stopped to exchange a look outside Ella Fulton's door, before Tanner leaned forward and knocked twice. They didn't wait long before Thorne used the key provided by Ella's mother and the two of them stepped inside.

The place was empty. The huge room was every bit as crowded and messy as Thorne remembered, but there was no sign—

'Fuck ... '

Thorne turned to Tanner, then looked up.

Ella Fulton's feet were bare and bluish, the toenails painted pink. Thorne raised his eyes further still, past the comfy-looking cardigan and the washing line that had bitten into her neck ... past her face, the fat, black tongue ... to where the line had been tied off on the balcony above the spiral staircase.

It had not been a long drop, certainly not enough to make it quick.

He wondered how much time it had taken.

Tanner already had her phone in her hand. 'Looks like it's been a few days, at least.' With 'recognition of life extinct' clearly a given, she made the necessary call to the coroner's office to arrange transport to the mortuary, while Thorne wandered across to where the most recent set of framed photographs had been hung.

He stopped in front of a picture he had first noticed w. he'd come to see Ella Fulton the second time, to inform her th

Patrick Jennings the con-man was almost certainly a murderer too. It was something, Thorne now understood, that she may well have already known, or at the very least suspected. Perhaps they would never discover exactly how much Ella had known about the man she'd been involved with.

How much of what *they* knew had been passed on to him.

Thorne looked at the photo of the man staring up at the camera from beneath the peak of a cap and realised why the man in the hospital bed had seemed so familiar. Something around the eyes. There in the photograph of Ella Fulton's lover that had been on her wall all along. He leaned towards the photo and carefully lifted away the envelope that had been pinned to it.

An envelope that had his name on the front.

'What have you got?' Tanner asked.

'Hang on . . .'

Thorne carried the envelope across to the desk and opened it. He nudged several books aside to make some room, then emptied the contents out on to the desktop. Some photographs, a flash-drive.

'You were right.' Thorne used the tip of a pen to separate the photographs and lined them up. 'In Glasgow, when you were talking about an accomplice. She picked out his marks for him . . .'

The women in the pictures had clearly not been aware they were being photographed. Dining alone in a restaurant, talking into a mobile phone, stepping out of a car. Thorne immediately recognised Philippa Goodwin and Denise Fry and guessed that the other three were victims they had yet to identify. He turned the photos over and saw that there were names written on the back.

Had Ella Fulton wanted to help, right at the end, or had she simply been trying to explain?

'Have you got gloves?'

Having finished her call, Tanner pulled gloves from her pocket, put on a pair and carried another across to him. Thorne used them to pick up the flash-drive and insert it into Ella Fulton's computer. Tanner leaned across to hit a few keys, and a couple of seconds later Ella Fulton's face appeared on the dusty screen.

Clawing at her hair, she looked washed-out and jittery. As she leaned towards the camera, its harsh light showed the shadows beneath her eyes and something crusted at the corners of her mouth.

'Everything turned to shit after Auntie Pip.' Her voice was hoarse. She took a breath and cleared her throat. 'It was only ever about the money, because she had loads and I was trying to help him, same as I always did. I thought if I stopped helping I'd lose him, and . . . suddenly there was his next payday, right under my nose all the time. I never dreamed it would do that to Pip or what Pip killing herself would do to Mum.'

She closed her eyes for a few seconds. Her fingers were at her hair again.

'Maybe there's something in the genes.' She shook her head. 'All so stupid and unforgivable and all messed-up anyway, because now he's found someone else and if I don't put a stop to me then *she* probably will. She's a bit . . . scary, but you probably know that already.' She leaned away and for half a minute or more was very still, the terror and the shame etched across her haggard features. She looked like the subject of one of her own photographs. The image, unforgiving.

'Most people doing this don't leave a note, not even a fancy one on video. Someone told me that once.' There was a hint of a smile then, though her eyes remained dead and unblinking. 'Typical me, right? I could never bear to be like most people . . .'

She reached forward quickly to turn off the camera and the image froze.

Thorne turned away, walked slowly back into the main part of the room and sat down on one of the ratty old sofas, his back to Ella Fulton's body.

Tanner followed and sat down next to him.

'They're on the way,' she said.

Thorne nodded and kept his head down, hoping they'd be quick, because he could not remember wanting to leave anywhere quite as much as he wanted to be away from this flat. He hoped, too, that Tanner would be content to sit and say nothing until others arrived and that he might be spared the task of delivering the second death message that Mary Fulton would receive in less than two months.

Sister, daughter . . .

More than anything, he hoped that, before slipping away into that nice, peaceful coma, Patrick or Paul or Conrad or whatever the fuck he was actually called, had suffered.

PART FOUR

Knowledge and Ignorance

SIXTY-NINE

Phil Hendricks and his boyfriend, Liam, were both happily drunk, and their friend Grace was not very far behind. The three of them were laughing a lot, talking a little too loudly, and each time one of them reached for something they threatened to knock a glass or a candle over. It wasn't ten-thirty yet and Liam had only just brought coffees across, but Tanner was already sneaking looks at her watch.

'Don't even think about it,' Hendricks said.

'What?' Grace asked.

Tanner glared at Hendricks for ratting her out.

'Come on, Nic.' Hendricks put his arm round her. 'Fun hasn't even started yet.'

'Right.' Liam poured himself another drink. 'We're going to play some games. That one where you stick a bit of paper on your head.'

'What about dirty charades?' Hendricks said.

Tanner saw that he was serious and briefly considered feigning a heart attack.

'I'm up for that.' Grace grinned at Tanner across the table.

Despite Hendricks's entreaties, his assurance that she'd have a much better evening if she left the car at home and an offer to put her up for the night, Tanner had driven across to Camden. She was very glad, now, that she had. She never felt relaxed around drunks anyway, a hang-up she'd never managed to shake, but being stone-cold sober while her fellow diners were necking the booze like alkies was not the only reason Tanner was feeling uncomfortable and wishing she'd stayed at home.

A book or a box set and a good night's sleep.

'I'm guessing it's a bit tricky for you,' Grace said. 'Late nights or parties, whatever. Because of your job, I mean. You never know what's coming the next day, right?'

'Actually, that's one of the reasons I like it,' Tanner said.

'Yeah, but still, it must be hard to enjoy yourself.' She reached past Liam for the wine. 'Staring down at a body first thing the next morning, feeling like shit.'

'Some of us can manage it,' Hendricks said.

'All I care about is what you can manage the night before,' Liam said.

The three of them laughed and Tanner did her best to join in.

Grace was nice enough; nicer, in fact. An NHS health-care assistant – 'we're a dying breed' – who lived and worked in Islington. She was in the same ballpark as Tanner age-wise, short and slim with a lopsided smile and cropped dark hair. She was sharp and funny and sported several tattoos Hendricks would have been proud of. Tanner could see why they got on so well.

Still, it had taken her a while to click.

Early on, Grace had mentioned the names of several clubs she visited regularly, but Tanner hadn't cottoned on. It was only when she'd begun talking about a female comedian from Australia who even Tanner knew was a lesbian poster-girl that the penny had finally dropped, and she'd felt rather stupid. She'd told Thorne a few weeks earlier that her Gaydar was unreliable at best, but she hadn't realised it had stopped functioning altogether.

Now, she felt awkward about being fixed up and angry with herself for being too dim to spot it.

'There's a mate of mine coming along.' Hendricks had been the picture of innocence when he'd invited her a week or so before. 'I reckon you'll get on with her, she's a right laugh.'

Tanner wasn't laughing.

'Right, then.' Grace stood up. 'I just need ...' She walked towards the bathroom, then stopped. 'And don't start the game without me. I've got a cracking mime for *Die Hard*.'

As soon as Grace had left the room, Tanner turned to Hendricks. 'Look, I'm not really comfortable with this, Phil.'

'What?' He looked across at Liam, mock-horrified. 'It's just a bit of dinner—'

'Shut up.'

'She's gorgeous though, isn't she? Look, I just thought—'

'She's great,' Tanner said. 'I just don't think I'm ready. God knows, maybe I should be, but whenever I think about it, I feel ... slaggy.'

Hendricks leaned into her. 'Come on. You've got *needs*, haven't you?'

Tanner reached for the cafetiere. 'Right now, I need to stop myself pouring hot coffee in your lap.'

'Leave her alone,' Liam said.

'I'm a widow who lives alone with her cat,' Tanner said. 'I'm not sure your friend's that excited anyway.'

They stopped talking as soon as they heard the toilet flush and the silence continued and grew awkward once Grace had sat down again. She looked around and said, 'What the hell have I missed?' When nobody seemed terribly keen to answer, she pointed to Hendricks and leaned across the table towards Tanner. 'He's a sneaky bastard, but I'm sure you already knew that, and, for what it's worth, I'm not that much happier playing "fix up a single lesbian" than you are. So ... no sweat, all right? Maybe we could just meet for a drink, if you fancy it, have a proper natter. A coffee, maybe ...'

Tanner was still struggling to formulate a response when her phone rang.

'Saved by the bell,' Grace said, reddening.

Tanner clocked the incoming number and said, 'I need to take this.' She stood up and carried the phone to a chair in the corner. She answered, then listened.

'Hurry up,' Hendricks said. 'We are *so* still playing this game.'

Tanner ended the call, then immediately began dialling. She said, 'I need to speak to Tom.'

SEVENTY

A few weeks earlier, Thorne had finally got round to ringing his Auntie Eileen. She'd sounded thrilled to hear from him – when she'd finally worked out who was calling – which only made him feel guiltier for not having spoken to the old lady for so long.

'It's been ages, son.'

'I know. Sorry. Work.'

'It's a bugger, isn't it . . . ?'

He'd driven over to Watford the next afternoon to have tea with her, and after a couple of hours' chat about family members he couldn't remember or didn't know existed, he'd clambered up into his aunt's loft and dug his mother's paintings out of several damp cardboard boxes.

Cleaned half a dozen of them up and had them framed.

Now, Thorne stood in his hallway staring at them, music drifting from the next room as he ate cereal from a bowl and wondered why his mother had been quite so fond of ships. Liners, yachts, old-fashioned clippers. Living in north London, it wasn't as if she saw them every day, and aside from the odd holiday to the seaside . . .

Or maybe that had been the point.

Something she enjoyed, or at least, enjoyed imagining.

She'd probably just copied them from pictures in a magazine, but it didn't much matter. She'd grabbed half an hour whenever she had the chance, taken her watercolours out of the cupboard and forgotten about everything else. Now he had the pictures in front of him, Thorne could certainly remember *that*; the look on her face while she'd been doing it. A glance down at him every few minutes as he worked at his paint-by-numbers kit, gnawing on the end of the paintbrush, same as she did, while he tried his hardest not to go over the edges. She'd done a couple of landscapes, too – misty mountains in the far distance, a sun-dappled lake – some dogs and birds and even a portrait of his father, despite the young Jim Thorne not looking terribly pleased about sitting still while she'd done it.

An expression that said he had a million things to do, though he'd have been hard pressed to name more than two or three of them.

Christ's sake, Maureen, how long's this going to take?

Thorne had hung the paintings in a line along one wall, stretching from front door to kitchen. He had no idea if they were any good or not, what anyone who really knew about such things might think, but either way, he enjoyed seeing them on his way out of the door every day, and again, each time he walked back through it. They brightened the place up, aside from anything else. But that was not to say that the pleasure he took in looking at his mum's pictures was not . . . tempered, somewhat, by associations he could not shake.

However much he wanted to.

It had been just over two months since he and Tanner had walked through the door of that flat off the Holloway Road. Two months, during which rage, mental illness, money or plain stupidity had propelled far too many more murders his way; cases that had been wound up quickly and others less straightforward, which were threatening to stick around a while. Two months since a man called Conrad Simpkin had died in hospital without regaining consciousness, while the woman with whom he had been involved had vanished without trace.

Two months, and still . . .

He could not look at those paintings without thinking about Ella Fulton.

It continued to shame him, those ridiculous things he'd thought, drinking tea in her flat, talking about art and murder. Had she known what she was doing, been well aware of the impression she was giving him? Had it all been part of her game, of whatever strange relationship she and Conrad Simpkin had left? Thorne guessed that it was and yet, regardless of how much that stung and despite the fact that she had knowingly helped and protected a wanted murderer, he did not believe that she deserved to die the way she had.

The fact that she had chosen it did not change anything.

Thorne had forced himself to watch, unblinking, as the line was carefully cut and the body lowered slowly to the floor.

No rickety stepladder needed on this occasion.

He nodded along to the Sturgill Simpson track and reminded himself that no more had Kevin Deane or Gemma Maxwell deserved what had been meted out to them, and that their friends and families did not deserve to live with it either. Mary Fulton did not choose to spend those years she had left hollowed out by her loss, defined by it.

He pushed a spoonful of cereal into his mouth, turned and walked into the kitchen. It had not been a long day and he wasn't feeling particularly tired, but a few minutes later, rinsing the bowl and spoon under the tap, he decided that turning in early might well be a decent idea. He'd taken some of the holiday he was due and had arranged to pick Alfie up from Helen's first thing the following morning. They would be spending the entire day together, and of the two of them,

Thorne reckoned he was the one who was probably looking forward to it the most.

Definitely, the most.

Alfie did not need a day off from anything or have a head full of stuff he could do with forgetting for a while, and Thorne was not the one being forcibly separated from his iPad.

Thorne laid the bowl and spoon on the draining board, then walked into the living room to turn the music off. He took off his shoes and unbuttoned his shirt while he was waiting for the song to finish. He had just begun to question the wisdom of taking a five-year-old to an indoor trampoline centre when his phone began to ring.

SEVENTY-ONE

Thorne dozed fitfully for most of the hour or so it took to get to Birmingham International. When, a few minutes before his arrival, a train hurtled past in the opposite direction, he woke with a start to see the woman sitting opposite staring at him. He nodded, embarrassed. He was fairly sure that he'd made a noise of some sort as he'd been jolted awake, and as soon as the woman looked away he fingered his collar to check that he hadn't been drooling in his sleep.

He sighed and wiped his chin.

After a quick visit to the Gents, he quickly composed another text to Helen, apologising again. When he'd called late the night before to explain, she had promised to tell Alfie that Uncle Tom was not feeling very well, that the two of them would have even more fun together the following week. The indoor water-park, maybe. Helen had not tried to hide her disappointment, her own plans for the day scuppered by the change in his, but she'd said she hoped everything panned out for him and told him that, of course, she understood.

She was Job, so how could she not?

Thorne sent the text. Time and . . . distance were obviously making things easier. Job or not, he knew things would not have gone quite so smoothly had the two of them still been together.

As the train slowed, he stood and reached up for his case, and for the plastic bag containing the sweets he'd picked up at Euston. A drawing pad and a set of coloured pencils, a couple of comics he knew Alfie liked. He'd drop them round when he got back to London.

Thorne had fifteen minutes before his connection and a three-hour journey still ahead of him, so he picked up coffee and a sandwich from a kiosk on the main concourse. He skimmed through a *Metro* someone had left lying on a bench. He checked the board to be sure his train was on time, then called Tanner as he wandered towards the platform.

'I'm in Birmingham,' he said.

'Nice.'

'Well, the outskirts.'

'It's a shame you won't have time to enjoy it,' Tanner said.

'I know, I'm gutted.'

'So, the train gets in just after half-three and the local boys are going to be waiting outside the station at the other end.'

'I know.' Thorne tried to keep the exasperation from his voice.

'Just making sure you do. That's why I sent—'

'I've *got* it.' The travel itinerary, which Tanner had emailed to him first thing that morning, was carefully folded in his pocket. 'If I'd had time, I would have had it laminated in your honour.'

Tanner laughed. Thorne stepped aside to avoid a woman running towards him with a pushchair, while Tanner said something that was inaudible beneath a distorted station announcement.

'Sorry, I lost you.' Thorne stopped to check the sign on the platform, to be sure he was in the right place for the Aberystwyth train.

'How do you think it's going to go?'

'No idea,' Thorne said. 'The intel sounds solid.'

370

'Be good to put this to bed, won't it? Open a big bottle of fizz when you get back?'

Thorne said that it would.

'I used to go up there on holiday when I was a kid,' Tanner said. 'Did I tell you that?'

'No.' Thorne arrived at an open door, then stood aside to let a family board ahead of him. 'You didn't.'

'It's nice. There's a castle ... and a fort. Well, actually, it poured with rain most of the time, but still.'

'Well, I'm bound to have plenty of free time, so why don't I bring you something back as a little reminder?' Thorne stepped on to the train and looked right and left. Both carriages were crowded. 'What about some Welsh cakes? Or a nice tea towel?'

'Anything except a stick of rock,' Tanner said.

She was standing outside the school gates, talking animatedly to three other women. Her hair was red, longer than in the last picture Thorne had seen, but she wasn't difficult to spot. She turned slightly as he approached, and he could see the bump.

Her hand, rubbing it.

She glanced at him when he was a little closer, but clearly thought nothing of it, saw no reason for concern. Another parent ambling towards the school and not looking awfully thrilled about it, a stay-at-home dad. She turned back to her conversation, laughed loudly at something one of the other women said.

'Hello, Michelle.'

The shock when she turned and saw the warrant card was no more than fleeting and quickly disguised, but watching her face change, even for an instant, was something Thorne had been looking forward to for a long time. He had imagined this moment in even greater detail since the call had come through the night before, when it had begun to sound as though it might really be imminent.

Would she scream and fly at him? Would she try to run?

As it was, she simply took half a step away from her friends and cocked her head, as though a little confused. As if this police officer might merely have come to warn her there were thieves operating in the area or to tell her that she'd dropped her purse.

The other women were already whispering, watching her or looking at Thorne. One of them said, 'Everything all right, Sarah?'

Thorne did not take his eyes off her.

'We need to have a chat,' he said.

'OK.' She sounded cheery, unconcerned.

He backed away slightly, inviting her to come towards him.

She peered past Thorne as she began to walk, then turned to look back the other way. She gave a small nod as she clocked the marked cars that had begun approaching slowly from either end of the road.

HEDDLU. POLICE.

Thorne raised a hand and she stopped. He said, 'Do you want to do this here, or in the car?'

'Well . . .' She cradled her bump again. 'I think I should probably be sitting down, don't you?'

Thorne turned and led her back towards the nearest of the cars. She walked slowly, raising her face skywards or gazing around as if determined to enjoy the good weather, the neatly kept front gardens and the yellowing catkins hanging from the beech trees that lined the road.

She said, 'I'd been hoping it might take a little longer.'

'Sorry about that,' Thorne said. It had all been quite straightforward in the end. 'We always knew you wouldn't take any chances with the baby and that wherever you ended up you'd go for all the scans and blood tests. We just had to make sure there wasn't a single doctor or antenatal department in the country that didn't know who you were. Matter of time.'

The uniformed driver stepped out and opened the car doors as they approached.

As soon as Thorne had climbed into the back seat, he turned

372

to face her and said, 'Michelle Littler, I'm arresting you on suspicion of the murders of Kevin Deane and Gemma Maxwell and the abduction of Heather Turnbull. You do not have to say anything, but it may harm your defence if you do not mention, when questioned, something which you later rely on in court. Anything you do say may be given in evidence.'

'Thank you,' she said.

Thorne nodded to the driver and the car moved away.

Their first port of call would be the station in Aberystwyth, fifteen minutes' drive away. Michelle Littler would be checked to make sure she was in good health physically, then offered something to eat and drink before a brief formal interview, at which, should she so wish, a solicitor would be present. Then they would be driven to the station, from where Thorne would escort his prisoner, in handcuffs, back to London.

It was all spelled out in Tanner's itinerary.

There were some questions the woman would of course be asked once they'd got to Aberystwyth station, and a great many more when they had her back in London, but that was hours away. Twelve, possibly, if she insisted on a night's sleep after they got there. Thorne knew that the possibility of a threat-to-life gave him the authority for an 'urgent interview' to be conducted there and then. It was good to know, but even without it, he would not have been able to keep his mouth shut.

There were answers he was not willing to wait for.

'What happened to Heather?'

Michelle Littler blinked slowly but said nothing.

'Is she alive, can you at least tell me that much?'

'Well, she *was*, the last time I saw her.'

She turned to look out of the window, the traffic building up as they approached the town centre. A young boy waved at the police car from the doorway of a shop and she raised a hand to wave back. She said, 'How did things turn out for poor old Conrad, by the way?'

'*What?*'

'You've no idea how painful that all was. For both of us.'

'I think you know very well how it turned out,' Thorne said. 'Exactly the way you wanted, I presume.'

'It was the last thing I wanted,' she said. 'If you can't understand that, you can't understand anything.'

The car turned off the main road, slowed and drew up outside the station gates. The driver sounded his horn and, after a few moments, they began to swing open.

'Just out of interest, where the hell did you get Death Cap mushrooms in March?'

Now, she turned back to look at him, as though the answer were blindingly obvious. 'I had some left over.'

Thorne stared at her.

'Dried, in a cupboard in the garage.' Once again her hands moved across her belly, rubbed in small circles. 'Because here's the thing . . . if you're old, and rotting away in one of those terrible places where everyone's old and nobody really gives a toss, who's going to bat an eyelid when your liver suddenly gives out?' She laughed and held up her palms as if expecting an answer. 'There's hardly going to be an urgent post-mortem, is there? Not when you're halfway to the grave anyway and you've been a drinker all your life. Pouring the family's money down your throat and shouting the odds and torturing the people you're supposed to love. Nobody's even going to notice . . . not really, let alone care very much . . . and your next of kin certainly isn't going to cause a fuss, even if they've been the only one who ever bothered coming to see you. Muggins here, who sat there knowing she'd have to wash the stink off her clothes afterwards . . . talking to you when you could barely get a word out. Who brushed your hair and wiped away the dribble. Who brought you food in, so you wouldn't have to eat the slop they dished out . . . '

The car moved slowly through the gates into the car park, then stopped.

'I'm not exaggerating,' she said. 'The food in that place really was atrocious. And my dad *loved* mushroom soup.'

When Thorne opened the door for her, Littler held a hand out towards him for help. Thorne took it and squeezed. He pulled her – somewhat less gently than he might have done – from the car, and nodded towards her stomach.

He said, 'Shame really, about your baby.'

She straightened up and looked at him, cold.

'I mean, it's not like you're ever going to see much of it.' He put a hand in the small of the woman's back and ushered her firmly towards the station doors. 'Still, look on the bright side. By the time you get out, you'll probably be a grandmother.'

SEVENTY-TWO

Later on, Thorne would tell Phil Hendricks that meeting in the Grafton Arms had been Melita Perera's idea. That he'd called the psychiatrist just because he thought she might be interested to know that both suspects in the case they had been discussing were now accounted for. One dead and the other on remand awaiting trial. It had been a professional courtesy, no more than that . . . though *yes*, he had been happy enough when Dr Perera suggested meeting up . . . and *no*, he could not deny that it was a pleasant surprise to discover she was every bit as comfortable talking over a pint in a north London pub as she was in a swanky Holborn bar.

'Turns out she lives in Crouch End,' he would say to Hendricks. 'So it was convenient, that's all. On her way home, near as damn it.'

The pub was crowded, but, after waiting around for ten minutes, they had managed to bag two stools at one end of the bar. Perera laid down a glass that already contained significantly less beer than Thorne's. 'So, she's still saying nothing about the woman who disappeared?'

Thorne shook his head. Heather Turnbull had now been missing for ten weeks, without so much as a possible sighting and no trace of the vehicle in which she had last been seen. Michelle Littler had been content to talk in great detail about the part she had played in the murder of Kevin Deane, to confess that she, and not Conrad Simpkin, had bludgeoned Gemma Maxwell to death, but she had blankly refused to make any comment about the missing woman.

Struck dumb, suddenly, at the mention of her name.

Along with Nicola Tanner and the rest of those doing the questioning, Thorne tried not to let the woman see how much it bothered him. The gaping wound her silence left in the body of their case. Nobody truly believed that Heather Turnbull was still alive, and they remained confident that Michelle Littler would go down as long for two murders as for three, but that was not the point.

It would be no sort of justice for Heather Turnbull's husband and children, for the rest of her family and friends. Sitting there in the pub, laughter from the group on the next table, Thorne could recall every word of his most recent conversation with Brian Turnbull, the sound of the man sobbing at the other end of a phone.

The platitudes and the protocols, the easy assurances. 'We're doing everything that we can ...'

'What do I tell the kids, though?' The man had hardly been able to speak, by the end. 'They know their mum would never go away on her own and not call them. Not even for a week, never mind ...'

Thorne had struggled for the right words, just as he had with Andrew Ruston, as he usually did.

'What do I tell *myself*? I'm not an idiot and I know exactly what this woman you've arrested is capable of, so should I stop imagining that my wife's just ... gone off to find herself or that she's lost her memory or something?' He had broken off for a

377

few seconds to gather himself, to ask the questions that really mattered. 'Will you be honest with me?'

Thorne said that he would, because he had no other option.

'You think there's still hope?'

'There's always hope,' Thorne had said.

Now, he looked at Melita Perera. 'It's a power thing, right? Her refusing to tell us?'

'Probably,' Perera said. 'Or maybe she thinks that as long as there's something you still want, you'll . . . go easier on her.'

'We won't,' Thorne said.

'Power then, yes. What she thinks of as power, anyway. Same as Shipman, remember? Saying nothing, not explaining.'

Thorne tapped a nail against the edge of his glass. 'I still don't get it.'

'You've taken everything else away from her, so that's all she has left to cling on to. A single piece of information you can't get anywhere else. She enjoys tormenting you with it and she'll almost certainly carry on enjoying it, even when she's lying in a prison cell.'

'Does she care about what it's doing to Heather Turnbull's family?'

'I'm not sure *care* is the right word.' Perera raised her beer again, thought for a few seconds. 'She probably doesn't even think about them very much, at least not in the way you're talking about. It's all about her knowing and you being ignorant.' She took a drink. 'I don't think there's a lot you can do about it.'

'Yeah, I did put in a request to try waterboarding, but the Chief Superintendent's a bit squeamish.'

Perera laughed.

'It's political correctness gone mad,' Thorne said.

They said nothing for half a minute or so, looking around at fellow customers, eavesdropping on an argument between two women on a nearby table. They took turns delving into a large packet of crisps sitting between them on the bar.

378

'What about the baby?' Perera asked.

Thorne shrugged. 'The big question is whether we'll even get to court, let alone make it through the trial, before she gives birth. Could be touch and go, I reckon.'

'How soon . . . ?'

'Well, she's about twenty-nine weeks, and we need to get a jury sworn in within the next four months or so. But even after that's done, the judge could decide to extend the custody time limit, if she's ready to pop. Could be interesting, otherwise . . . her waters breaking halfway through the trial.'

Perera pulled a face.

'Much as I want to get her in court as soon as possible, I'm hoping she's already had it by then. Because I think she'd love that, you know? Standing there in the dock, as big as a house . . . all the attention, the press.'

'The baby, though,' Perera said. 'What's going to happen to it?'

'It'll be the standard process,' Thorne said. 'Whether she has it before the trial or once she's in prison. She'll apply for a Mother and Baby Unit, but there's not very many of those anyway and they don't tend to allocate places to women who are inside for murder.'

'So, then what? The child gets handed over to Social Services?'

Thorne nodded, stared down at the bar. 'Not the greatest start in life, I grant you. I can't help thinking, though, that whatever happens after that, the child's going to be better off.'

'You could always try telling her that you can get her a place,' Perera said. 'On one of those units. If she tells you about Heather Turnbull.'

'I don't think we could swing that,' Thorne said.

'I know.' Perera reached for crisps. 'But there's nothing to stop you *saying* you can.'

Thorne looked at her. 'You're very devious.'

'I work with some very devious people,' she said. 'It rubs off.'

It was a tactic Thorne had already considered, that he might well have a crack at later on, if he was out of options. 'We'll see,' he said. 'Who knows, she might get religion or something before then, decide to come clean.'

They fell silent again for a while, polished off the crisps and downed what little was left of their drinks. They had finished with shop talk for the time being.

'I was thinking about your mother,' Perera said. 'Those dreams you were having.'

'Right.' Of late, Thorne had been thinking about them a good deal himself, making connections that were almost certainly tenuous, but which were never pleasant.

Mothers and sons.

A woman whose son had never existed.

Thorne's mother, a remembrance that had been growing sketchy.

'Actually, I haven't had one in a while.' He told her about his mother's paintings, the memory coming back. He told her that they now had pride of place in his flat.

'That's nice,' she said. 'So, maybe that's all the dreams were. The flicker of a memory you couldn't quite recall.'

'Is that how it works?'

'It's an explanation.'

'Bloody hell.' Thorne looked at her. 'I had an ... *interesting* dream about me and Harry Kane the other night. I really don't think I could have forgotten *that*.'

Perera smiled. 'Back then ... you didn't say as much, but it seemed to me that you were a bit ... conflicted? Maybe about stuff that was going on outside your job. I don't want to pry or anything—'

'It's fine,' Thorne said.

'I don't know ... as if you were trying to work something out in your personal life.'

'You're pretty good at this,' Thorne said.

'Thank you.'

380

'Yeah, there was a situation ... domestically. I didn't know whether to stick or twist, put it that way. Actually, I didn't even know if I was bust already, but ... '

'Well, like I said, this isn't really my area, and this might sound a bit like something I've read inside a Christmas cracker ... but I wondered if there was another way of looking at those dreams about your mum. She was someone you trusted, right?'

'Yeah, course.'

She inched her stool a little closer to his, allowing a man who was waiting to be served room to squeeze in. 'So, perhaps she was popping up in your subconscious to tell you it was OK to move on.'

Thorne considered what the psychiatrist was suggesting, then reached for their empty glasses. He said, 'Well, in that case ... shall we have another drink?'

Copy to: Ball & Hooper Solicitors.
Michelle Littler,
info@ballhooper.co.uk
HMP Bronzefield, TW15 3JZ
January 12th

My Darling Connie,

   Happy new year, precious!!

   Here's another one for your collection. God
knows how many of these you'll have to read when
you're old enough, but I can't stop writing,
because I need you to know how VERY much you're
loved and how horrible it is for me that we can't
be together just yet. Of course, I can't be sure
that my letters are even getting to you, because
they won't let me know where you are and those
creatures in Social Services who are all DEAD
INSIDE have SAID they'll send them, but I've only
got their word for it. They bang on about your
'welfare' being the most important thing, which
of course it is, but they seem to think that in
the long term you might be better off not hearing
from me at all, which is completely ridiculous.

   Why would you not want to hear from the person
who gave birth to you? The person who loves you
more than anyone.

   Of course you do. I KNOW you do, that you
always will, whatever they say.

   Sometimes, I think they sent me to this

particular place just to torture me, because there's a special unit in here where mothers and babies can be together, at least when the babies are still very young. Now and again, I run into one of the girls who are lucky enough to be living in there, the ones who are not being punished like me. Punished more than is fair, I mean. They have a special glow which makes me very upset and they smell of milk, and once I managed to steal a blanket which I keep under my pillow. So I can have a bit of that smell too. If I'm nearby, I sometimes hear the babies crying and that's enough to finish me off for the rest of the week. Silly, I know, but I can't help it and if I didn't have your pictures to look at, I don't know what I would do.

Well, I DO, and if these letters stop, you'll know I've done it!

I know that right now you're not actually thinking about anything much apart from wanting to eat and sleep, but I hope that when the time comes, you'll spend at least some time thinking about your daddy and me. He would have loved you so much, darling girl, and it cheers me up to know how thrilled he would be that you've *sort of* got his name. Oh, and looking at that picture, I can see that you've got his eyes, too. God, I always LOVED those eyes and seeing them in your face makes me happy and sad at the same time.

I'm sorry if I've said this before (it's a mum's job to nag a bit), but you must always remember that even if I can't be there with you, you've always got your big brother. I know Jamie loves you every bit as much as I do and he will take

good care of you, so the pair of you must ALWAYS
stick together, no matter what happens and no
matter what anybody says to you about me or
your daddy.

We are a FAMILY.

I wanted so much to send you something really
nice for Christmas. There's not much choice in
here though, only chocolate really, and it would
certainly have gone mouldy by the time you're old
enough to eat it! It was not an easy time for me,
because the only thing I wanted for Christmas was
you and that's probably not going to happen very
soon. I'm still TRYING though, sweetheart, I need
you to know that, and I won't ever give up.

I hope the nasty cough they told me you had
a few weeks ago is getting better and I'm still
furious that the people you're staying with
let that happen. How could they, when they're
supposed to be taking care of you for me? It's
obvious that they don't deserve to have you at
all. Just remember that even if they seem kind
and nice and whatever they might tell you, they
are NOT your mummy and daddy and never will be.

Blood is what counts.

For ever . . .

Mummy xxxx

ACKNOWLEDGEMENTS

OK, so *I'm* the show-off with the twisted imagination, but producing a new book each year is a team effort and I remain hugely fortunate that the team at Little, Brown is the best in the business. As always, I owe a huge debt to my wonderful editor, Ed Wood, and to a great many others at LB/Sphere, notably: Catherine Burke, Charlie King, Sean Garrehy, Thalia Proctor, Tamsin Kitson, Gemma Shelley, Robert Manser, Sarah Shrubb and the publicity marvel that is Laura Sherlock. I am equally in debt to their counterparts across the pond at Grove Atlantic, US: Brenna McDuffie, Morgan Entrekin, Deb Seager and Justine Batchelor. I would also like to thank Nancy Webber for a hugely sensitive and creative copy edit and I hope she forgives me for the handbag . . .

After so many books, I should probably know a lot more about police procedure than I do (or perhaps I just keep forgetting) so I am grateful for the enormous help and forbearance of Lisa Cutts and Graham Bartlett. Thanks also to Angela Clarke for much needed info and advice about prison facilities for those with babies. Wendy Lee's input was as invaluable as always, as was that of my fab agent Sarah Lutyens and all those with whom she works at Lutyens & Rubinstein: Juliet Mahony, Francesca Davies and Hana Grisenthwaite.

I am very grateful to Dr Frank Tallis for allowing me to quote from his wonderful book, *The Incurable Romantic*, and to Elvis Costello for kind permission to use lyrics from one of his greatest songs, 'I Want You'. While I'm about it, thank you EC for an aim that's always true and for four decades of peerless entertainment and inspiration.

And thank you most of all to Claire, Katie and Jack; *this* happy author's little secret.